Reecah's Gift

Legends of the Lurker

Book 2

Reecah's Gift by Richard H. Stephens

https://www.richardhstephens.com/

© 2019 Richard H. Stephens

Cover Art & Interior Art by kjmagicaldesigns.com
Paperback ISBN: 978-1-989257-18-0

Acknowledgements

Reecah's Gift, the sequel to *Reecah's Flight,* was estimated to weigh in at around 80,000 words and was originally scheduled for a July, 2019 release. As with all things in life, nothing is ever predictable nor goes as planned. *Reecah's Gift* took on a life of its own and the initial draft ended up over 110,000 words in length.

Needless to say, I am forever grateful to the people behind the scenes, without whose involvement, *Reecah's Gift* would not have been possible.

I have a small group of beta readers who never cease to amaze me with how much they catch. Their selfless dedication to my stories is valued more than they will ever know. My sincere appreciation goes to: Joshua Stephens, Matthew Lane, Paul Stephens, and of course, Caroline Davidson who is always the first one to read it, and the last.

Thank you to my editor, Michelle Dunbar. Through her knowledgeable instruction, my writing style is forever evolving. Find her here: http://michelledunbar.co.uk/

Thank you to my cover and interior picture designer, Katie Jenkins. Another fantastic cover to compliment the series, Legends of the Lurker. You can find Katie at, KJ Magical Designs: https://kjmagicaldesigns.com

Image of Tamra Stoneheart used by permission of the artist: Sungryun Park. https://www.artstation.com/sungryunpark

Credits:

During the writing of this series, I wanted to give my readers a chance to take part in the creation of the story as a way of thanking them for sticking with me as I grow as an author. Anyone familiar with me online knows of my 'Name a Dragon' contest. For Reecah's Gift, I also ran a, 'Name the Female Warrior' contest. Your creativity and insight have made the series magical. Thank you to the following people:

Sandy Fosdick for naming the purple, female dragon: Silence.

Georgiana L. Gheorghe for naming the red, female dragon: Scarletclaws, and also for naming the sailor: Cahira

Angela Carter for naming the high king: J'kaar.

Randy Thompson for naming the elven, female warrior: Tamra Stoneheart.

Lambert Cook for naming the princess: J'kyra.

Johnnie Wheatley for naming the princess: J'kaeda.

Lori Lane Fox and **Judith Dayton** for co-naming the captain of *Serpent's Slip*: Dreyger K'tric.

Shelley Wildgrube for naming the dwarven royal blacksmith: Aramyss. (I added the last name: Chizel.)

Gerri Giesin for naming the red, male dragon: Lasair. (Gaelic for flame.)

I'm always searching for dragon names. You can connect with me on my Facebook Author Page: @RichardHughStephens

Despite everything life threw at us; the highs and lows, the triumphs and failures, the immense joys and heartbreaking grief, you have retained your wonderful outlook on life.

Michelle, you're admired and respected more than you'll ever know. Thank you for being you.

I know. Fruity.

Duchy of Zephyr

The Unknown Sea

Mt. Cinder Mt. Gloom
Cliff Face

ALTIRIUS MOUNTAINS

DRAGONFANG PASS

THE SLITHER

Fishmonger Bay

Thunderhead

REDFIRE PATH

ZEPHYR FLATS

Storms End

Castle Svelte

Madrigail Bay

WEST CASTLE RD

Carillon

RING LAKE

S. WAMP

The Forke

HILLSEDGE RD

St. Carmichael's Shrine

Millsford

CANOROUS RIVER

ALPHEUS ARCH

Diad Ocean

THE SPINE

Songsbirth

SPLENDIDO FELLS

THE MUSE

GRIFFIN HILLS

Grittian

TORPID MARSH

Ghost Island

TREACHER'S GORGE

UNDYING WALL

THE GULCH

LOWLAND GRASSLANDS

REDFIRE PATH

NORDIC WOODS

N

THE OCHRE WAY

Nordic Town

Apexreal

Amber Breath

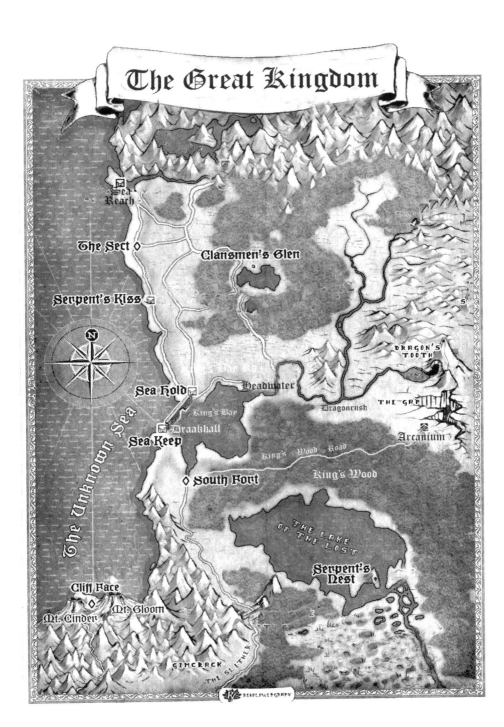

The Great Kingdom

Sea Reach

The Sect

Clansmen's Glen

Serpent's Kiss

Sea Hold

Headwater

Dragon's Tooth

THE GRP

Dragonrush

Arcanium

Sea Keep

Draakhall

King's Bay

King's Wood Road

South Fort

King's Wood

THE LAKE OF THE LOST

Serpent's Nest

Cliff Face

Mt. Cinder

Mt. Gloom

GIMCRACK

THE SLITHER

The Unknown Sea

Table of Contents

To view the full colour maps in the Soul Forge realm, please visit: www.richardhstephens.com

Reecah's Gift

Legends of the Lurker

Book 2

Reecah's Gift

End of Silence

A fortnight had passed since that horrific day in Dragonfang Pass—a day that had witnessed the annihilation of the Draakclaw Colony from Dragon Home. All except for the three dragons waiting for her to pull herself together and get on with her life.

Every passing day since Grimclaw's death filled Reecah with crushing guilt over her role in the beautiful creature's demise. She should never have left him, no matter how vehemently he insisted she save herself. Grimelda said her role was to save the dragons—not run away and allow the obliteration of the colony.

Confounding her melancholy were the faces of the two knights she had killed in the courtyard of the Dragon Temple. Visions of their blood dripping from her sword woke her in a cold sweat, night after sleepless night.

In contrast to her unease, her companion, Raver, casually pruned his feathers—his shiny raven's head pecking away at whatever irritated him. She envied him his simple pleasures—admiring the way he had moved on after such a traumatic event.

Dust motes shimmered in sunbeams shining through the solitary window in the cabin below Peril's Peak, despite the grime coating its thick glass.

Had she planned on remaining at the dragon hunt camp, she would have turned her attention to tidying up the slovenly interior. If not for her fear of the owners returning to lay claim

Reecah's Gift

to their property, Reecah fancied she might have been content to start a new life high atop the world.

Lying on a crude pallet with her hands behind her head, she grimaced. If only life were that simple.

A clamour outside the cabin's lone door made her sit up. The dragons were scuffling about, impatiently waiting for her to pull herself together and decide on their course of action.

Something about the sunshine flooding the hut melted away her languishing despair. It looked to be a glorious day. Perhaps that was the omen she had been waiting for. A reminder of her pledge—not only to Grimelda, but to dragonkind as well.

They had outstayed their welcome. The king's men had seen them escape the battle at the Dragon Temple. They would no doubt be searching the area. It wouldn't do to tarry under their noses.

Reecah shuddered. If the burning intensity on the face of the wizard she had seen at the Dragon Temple was any indication of his determination, her scaly friends were in peril anywhere near Fishmonger Bay.

It was time to put aside her guilt. A dragon war had been set into motion. Facing certain death at the Dragon Temple, she had vowed to avenge Grimclaw's death. To remain mired in self-recrimination was a grave misjustice to the noble wyrm's sacrifice. It was time to make good on her promise.

She stretched her neck one way and then the other, raising her arms overhead and taking a last deep breath of peaceful solitude. Pulling on black suede boots, she jumped to her feet to gather her gear.

Silence had risked her life returning to the forest between the Dragon Temple and Dragon Home to retrieve her discarded equipment. Thankful, Reecah slipped her quiver over her shoulder and secured her unstrung bow to her rucksack before shrugging it on.

Reecah's Gift

Pausing at the door, her gaze fell on the large table at the centre of the hut. A smirk tightened her lips at the irony. Wait until Jonas and his lackeys discovered who had sheltered at their dragon hunt camp. Reecah Draakvriend. She tilted her head, smiling a little deeper as she corrected herself. Reecah Windwalker, the hill witch, had sheltered here—along with three dragons. If only she could stick around to see the look on their faces.

The door opened with a squeal, drawing the attention of her new friends, Lurker, Swoop, and Silence—green, brown and purple dragonlings, respectively. Judging by their sheepish looks, they were up to something.

Allowing Raver to fly through the open door, she let it slam back into its frame. The raven made his way to the tiered waterfall cascading from the snow-capped peak behind the hut.

Drawing her brown cloak around her and slipping on its hood, she raised her eyebrows to stare at the green dragon. "Well, are you going to tell me, or do I have to figure it out myself?"

Lurker lowered his head, his emerald eyes alight with mischief. He glanced at his cohorts.

Reecah almost vomited when the dragons parted to reveal the remains of more than one shredded troll's carcass. She turned away from the mound of hairy gore. "Do you have to eat those here? That's disgusting."

"Sorry, Reecah. We didn't think you'd be up and about," Lurker said—his voice sounding in her head. He motioned for Swoop and Silence to get rid of it.

It was a fair assumption. She had become less and less social as the days went by. She waved a hand. "Ugh. Leave it. It's time for us to leave."

The dragons considered the carcasses, obviously not done with them yet. While Lurker and Silence ambled over to

Reecah's Gift

Reecah, Swoop snapped up a last chunk of troll flesh; noisily chewing it.

Reecah winced at the sound of bones snapping. The brown dragon swallowed, offering her a bloody-toothed grin. It was going to be an adjustment getting used to the habits of her new companions.

Lurker accompanied Reecah to the edge of the cliff fronting the field around the cabin; following her gaze over the rugged terrain to where the land abutted the glimmering ocean many leagues away. *"Where're you going?"*

The question threw Reecah. "Are you not coming with me?"

Silence and Swoop joined them—all three dragons avoiding her hazel eyes.

"What? I thought we agreed? We need to convince the high king that his mandate to eradicate dragonkind is not an acceptable solution to settling our differences." She paused, staring at each of them individually. They refused to meet her gaze.

She grasped Lurker by the chin, forcing him to look at her. "You can't be serious. I need you."

A sadness came through in his voice. *"I'm sorry, Reecah. We've struggled with this. Dragon Home is our colony. We can't abandon it in its darkest hour."*

"But...but..." Reecah searched the faces of the others. They nodded, confirming Lurker's words. "There's nothing there for you but death. Dragon Home is destroyed. Everyone is dead."

"We don't know that."

"Silence went back and scouted the area." She turned to implore the purple dragon. "You said no one was left alive."

Silence bowed her head.

Reecah returned her attention to Lurker. "If you go back, you risk being killed yourself..."

She spun to face the drop-off. "Damn it!"

4

Reecah's Gift

She had promised herself not to cry anymore. She must be strong if she wanted to face the high king. Wiping her cheeks, she turned back to her friends. "It would kill me if something happened to you."

"We feel the same way about you, pretty Reecah. Nevertheless, we cannot leave our home. Besides, our presence will likely hinder you. You won't make it anywhere near the castle with us at your side."

"Then I'm going back to Dragon Home with you."

Lurker glanced at his dragonkind, shaking his head. *"That we cannot allow. You're the last Windwalker. Grimclaw pledged Draakclaw Colony's allegiance to you. We forbid your return to the killing zone."*

Reecah didn't want to vent her frustration on her companions but she had no one else. Sounding off at Raver wouldn't be nearly the same. Lifting her chin, she straightened her shoulders and tried to cast them a stern look. "If you're supposed to obey me, then I command that you take me with you."

As soon as she said it, she hated herself. Who was she to order *anyone*, let alone three dragons who had lost everything? She, of all people, knew what that was like.

"I'm sorry. That was wrong of me. I won't order you to do anything you don't want. Please forgive me."

"You're a Windwalker. Of course we'll do as you command," Swoop said, looking at the other two, who nodded. *"But we respectfully ask you not to come. If Grimclaw's death is to mean anything, you must go to your king and plead our case before there aren't any dragons left in the world."*

The dragon faces blurred before her. Her tears flowed freely but she didn't care. Let them exhaust themselves so that she could move on. Unable to speak past the lump in her throat, she kept her eyes on the ground at her feet.

A soft breeze wafted up the mountainside, ruffling her cloak and blowing her brown hair in front of her face. A hawk's call echoed off the peak.

Reecah's Gift

Lurker nuzzled his face against her stomach, almost sending her stumbling over the brink. *"Remember what you said to Silence in Dragon Home?"*

Reecah shook her head. She couldn't think beyond the moment.

"We'll always be here for you. No matter what happens." Lurker nuzzled his snout beneath her left breast. *"As long as you feel us here, we'll always be together."*

His words gave her goosebumps. He'd remembered. Those were words spoken by Poppa a lifetime ago. Instead of pacifying her, it made her cry harder.

Shoulders shaking, she smiled and laughed through her tears, half spitting as she spoke. "Oh, great. Now look what you've done. Come here."

She wrapped her arms around Lurker's head and held him close. Eyeing Silence and Swoop on either side, she motioned for them to lean closer. Arms stretched wide, she included them in the embrace.

"I pledge to you with my last breath, today marks the end of silence. From this day forth, the Great Kingdom shall know we will no longer suffer the people's prejudice."

She sniffled loudly and squeezed their heads together. "I will never forget you."

She kissed Lurker's cheek and laid her head against the top of his nose. "Especially you, my dear friend. Thank you for allowing me into your circle of trust."

"Circle of trust! Circle of trust!" Raver landed on top of one of Lurker's horns, surprisingly gripping it the first time with his mangled toes.

Reecah looked up at the crazy bird and laughed, her heart warming despite the fact it had just broken.

Reecah's Gift

Thunderhead Thievery

If only the haters from Fishmonger Bay could see her soaring high above the Niad Ocean—her hair blowing around and a great smile on her face.

Wispy clouds moistened her skin as Lurker flew Reecah on his shoulders. The coast unfolded far below on its way to the ocean port of Thunderhead—the sprawling city, a black smear of humanity in the distance.

Boats and ships of all sizes appeared like little toys, dotting an expanse of blue water stretching to the horizon on their right. Swoop and Silence kept pace a wingbeat behind to either side.

Reecah made a mental note to ensure her hair was tightly braided if she ever had the occasion to fly a dragon again, but if it was up to her, this moment would never end. She had been mocked and picked on as a child for her fantastical notion of flying the skies, and yet, here she was, experiencing a dream of a lifetime—all her cares and worries forgotten. She savoured every moment, trying not to think of what awaited her at the end of the flight. If things went according to plan, she would have to part ways with the dragons and seek an ocean-going brig to take her to the high king's palace, far to the north.

The flight was over much too fast. Given the uprising over the summer with regard to the dragons, she refused to fly them into harm's way. She released Lurker's neck with one hand and pointed. "See that cove?"

"The second last one before the fjord?"

7

Reecah's Gift

"Yes. Land me there. I doubt the people of Thunderhead are as used to dragons as Fishmonger Bay. Your presence will frighten them. I'd rather not start off on the wrong foot. Enough people hate me."

"I pity anyone who feels that way. A truer friend they'll never find."

"Aww." She leaned into his neck and hugged him. "Thank you. The same goes for you three."

Raver squawked in the distance, barely visible above the waves.

Reecah laughed, still struggling to come to terms with the fact that the raven was able to communicate through the dragons. "Yes, of course, you mangy bird. How could I ever get by without my noisy featherbrain? You and I have been through a lot together."

Raver cawed again, barely audible above the wind in her face.

Lurker laughed. *"He says you'd better not forget it."*

Reecah's brief happiness fell away as Lurker tilted his wings and the ground rushed up to meet them. Far too soon, they were on a remote beach saying goodbye.

Reecah didn't care that she cried. There were times when tears were justified and this was one of them. Reluctantly sliding from Lurker's shoulders, she stepped back, her lower lip trembling. "I feel like I'll never see you again."

Lurker nuzzled his head against her side, his fangs clicking off her sword belt. *"Of course, you will. When you return with the king's decree."*

Reecah wrapped her arms around his head, unafraid of his deadly jaws, and rested her cheek beneath his eyes. "Be careful, okay? Don't let anything happen to you."

Swoop and Silence drifted overhead, keeping watch.

"I don't know if I can do this without you. What if I get into trouble? Grimclaw said the king had my parents killed. If he recognizes me, it might not go well." Reecah pulled her head back to stare into Lurker's eyes. "What about the black knights? If they return to the castle, they'll recognize me for sure."

"You'll have to be careful and keep away from them. They are soldiers in the king's army. I doubt they're part of his inner circle." Lurker smiled. *"Besides, you possess the journal and both Dragon Eye gems. I don't know for certain, but they must possess a significance to a Windwalker. Perhaps they have something to do with the spell Grimclaw placed in the back of your journal. To summon me in time of need."*

She forced a smile. "Great. Now all I need to do is learn how to decipher the strange runes and become a *real* witch!"

"You don't give yourself enough credit. Grimelda believed in you. So did my father. Trust me when I say that Grimclaw never trusted anyone. For him to bow down to you has got to mean something. It's up to you to figure out why."

Swoop interrupted, *"Boat coming. You better say good-bye."*

Reecah spied the brown dragon drifting above the waves to the north. Swallowing her emotions, she located Silence gliding above a hillside to the east. Waving at both of them, she held the side of Lurker's face in her hands and kissed him between the eyes.

Raver strutted about the sandy shore, absently pecking at things washed up by the tide. His head perked up and he flew to land on one of the leather vambraces Reecah wore on her forearms.

"Protect Reecah with your life, Raver. Now, off you go."

Raver bobbed his head. "Off you go! Off you go!"

Reecah covered her face, turning away from the sand storm Lurker's departure created. Blinking rapidly in a futile attempt to clear her vision, she watched until the dragons were nothing more than specks against the clouds.

Reecah's anxiety rose as she climbed the last rocky spur jutting into the Niad Ocean north of Thunderhead. Built into

9

the black stone comprising the shoreline, Thunderhead sprawled southward like a living beast, undulating on rolling hills before tracking a great fjord inland—the inlet's southern banks too sheer to inhabit.

Her breath caught. The entirety of Fishmonger Bay would fit into the cluster of buildings at the base of the hill she stood on. Wharves and jetties of varying lengths and states of disrepair extended into the surf all the way to the fjord. If she had anywhere else to go, she would have gladly surrendered to her fear of meeting new people and left the city behind.

Taking a deep breath, she glanced at Raver perched in the gnarly branches of a sickly tree. "Well, I guess this is it."

Raver blinked at her.

"Come on. Stay close."

Using her quarterstaff as a walking stick, she located a path leading down the hill between a tangle of ramshackle buildings that lined either side of a muddy road winding to the seaside.

Raver landed on a sagging rooftop where the road veered to follow the coast. Reecah feared his weight might cause the derelict building to collapse.

Chickens and geese announced their arrival, clucking and honking as they waddled out of her path. A rooster crowed from behind a dead tree, his call picked up by another across the street.

Reecah did her best not to stare at the grimy faces of malnourished children—barely dressed and sitting in the mud, or peering out from broken doorways. She forced a smile and said hello from time to time but no one returned her greeting.

Reecah wondered if the people of Fishmonger Bay had sent word ahead of her imminent arrival. She admonished herself. No one had any idea where she had gone. For all she knew, Jaxon and his father were still searching for her in Dragonfang Pass.

Reecah's Gift

Her last image of Jaxon made her smile despite her mood—his head snapping back on the end of her boot.

"You find this funny, eh?"

Reecah blinked. Someone had spoken.

A skinny woman, bent at the waist, her unkempt, black hair and young face belying an aged appearance. She glared at Reecah from the threshold of a leaning hovel.

Trying not to show her revulsion of the stench escaping the haggard woman's hut, Reecah stopped. "I'm sorry?"

"You should be. Parading about the slums in all your finery as if you're the cat's pride." The woman pointed a broken-nailed finger at her. "Get yourself back amongst yer own kind, ya trollop, and leave us simple folk alone."

"Look, lady, I have no idea what you're talking about. I came in from Fishmonger Bay." Reecah grimaced. She hadn't planned on telling people where she was from, and yet, she blabbed it to the first person she met.

The woman's brows crunched together. "Ah, I see. Fancy britches *and* a liar. A purty thing like you living up there, ha! Ain't nothing but 'ardship up that way. Yer looking much too fine to be coming from dragon country." The woman hocked and spat, her eyes narrowing. "You're one of the girls working up in the taverns if'n I have the right of it. Be gone with ya, an' leave our men alone."

Reecah swallowed, unsure how to respond, not sure what the woman insinuated. Giving herself a quick once over, she frowned. This was the first time she'd ever been accused of being in all of her 'finery'.

Hoping not to appear rude she nodded. "I will, ma'am. I mean I won't...I-I mean, good day."

Her cheeks flamed hot as she picked her way between the mud puddles.

A rabid looking dog charged at her from between two buildings, slavering and barking. Startled, Reecah side-stepped and held her quarterstaff out to intercept it, but a frayed rope prevented the crazed animal from reaching her. Judging by the condition of the rope, it wouldn't be long before the situation changed.

Forgetting her wish to keep her boots dry and her clothes from being splattered with muck, she high-stepped down the street and around the bend.

Raver took to the sky, leading her down the coastal roadway. Warehouses fronted the oceanside on her right, while rundown buildings were crammed together on her left—each building appearing to keep the next one from falling over.

Through the gaps between the warehouses, fishermen tended nets and unloaded the morning's catch. Every time a grizzled tar caught her eye, she shuddered. They reminded her of Jonas Waverunner, the head fisherman back home. The man responsible for much of the pain in her life.

Passing by a knot of bare-chested young men in breeks and ratty leather caps, she avoided eye contact but couldn't escape their lewd catcalls and whistles as she purposely hugged the far side of the street. As soon as she was by them, she picked up her pace and hazarded a glance over her shoulder. Their eyes tracked her, but thankfully they did not.

It didn't take long to second guess her decision to visit Thunderhead. Other than for the presence of the Waverunners and that weasel, Viper, who Lurker had disposed of, she felt less comfortable in Thunderhead than she had back home.

Raver cawed from farther down the street. Uneven cobblestones replaced the muddy street—a surface she had only seen depicted in Poppa's books. Raver sat on the arm of what looked like a bare, iron tree with a single branch at its top. Upon closer inspection, it turned out to be an elaborate, outdoor lantern holder. Another thing she had never seen before.

Reecah's Gift

Walking along the street lined sporadically with the lantern trees, it was like she had entered a different city from that of the hovels.

Larger warehouses lined the coast, their piers more substantial and housing boats grander than the traditional fishing skiffs she knew.

On the landward side of the street, buildings rose two stories high with straight walls and roofs appearing capable of sustaining their own weight. She stumbled several times on the uneven roadway—her concentration on everything but where she placed her feet.

Cabins and larger buildings rose up behind those lining the street, climbing the hillside as far as she could see. Plumes of smoke wafted skyward, bending inland on the ocean breeze.

The street pavers smoothed out long before the road turned sharply to the east, following the mouth of the fjord inland. People clad in all types of clothing, from elegant dresses to well-appointed men in pristine breeches that disappeared into polished, knee-high boots, filled the streets.

Reecah recalled fine clothes like these in the mercantile back home, but few people in Fishmonger Bay had the occasion to wear them, let alone the funds to purchase them. The exception being the Father Cloth and the Waverunner family.

Wondering whether an ample busted woman had forgotten to throw a tunic over her underclothes, Reecah was shocked when the blonde-haired woman spoke to her.

"Oh, look what we have here. The baron's funds must be running low for him to be hiring girly fighters to protect his city."

Reecah kept her eyes down, pretending not to hear the woman with the tightly cinched waist.

"Appears he's to be hiring rude ones at that."

A strong hand latched onto Reecah's rucksack and pulled her off-balance.

Reecah's Gift

"Hey!" Reecah tried to pull away but a large stomached man with a thin, curly mustachio and triple chin hung on tight.

"My lady's talking to you, miss. Best you be showing her the respect her station deserves."

Reecah glared at the man, but gathered herself to smile demurely at the woman who couldn't have been much older than herself. Though Reecah had never travelled beyond the mountains surrounding Fishmonger Bay, she knew enough to recognize a person of stature. Her gaze didn't miss the bejewelled hilt of the rapier protruding from beneath the man's black surcoat. "My apologies, m'lady. I mustn't have heard you."

"Let her go, Clive." The lady stepped up to her, giving her a thorough going over; her gaze resting on Reecah's filthy rucksack. "You aren't dressed like a Thunderhead militiaman. You're not from around here, are you?"

"No, m'lady."

"Then you're a mercenary, no? Hired to help rid the area of the flying beasts."

"Flying beasts?"

The woman guffawed at Reecah's ignorance.

Clive rolled his eyes. "The dragons, you twit."

Reecah scowled and adjusted her pack. "Hardly!"

Making sure Clive didn't attempt to stop her, Reecah skipped out of his reach and hurried down the street.

As she walked toward taller buildings, she couldn't help overhear Clive say, "I told you this was a dangerous part of town, princess. Good thing I accompanied you."

"Pfft, please. You think I'd be cowed by a tart like that. Break her little nose soon as she batted an eyelash. How do you expect me to enjoy life's simple pleasures cooped up in the baron's manor? With his simpleton staff? I think not."

Princess? Baron? Reecah stole a glance at the woman only to be met by a sneer.

Reecah's Gift

Looking around at other finely dressed people milling about the doorways and stumbling around the street emitting shrieks of heinous laughter, the only ones remotely dressed as well as Clive and the princess, were doormen standing at attention outside seedy-looking establishments. The plaques above their doorways promised carnal delights.

Reecah wasn't sure what went on behind their doors, but her reddening cheeks told her she knew enough. So far, Thunderhead was nothing but a lecherous town inhabited by people on opposite ends of the social classes. From the hovels in the northern section of town to the opulent woman and Clive.

Sturdier buildings lined the calmer waters of the fjord, their large jetties housing two and three-masted merchant ships bustling with bare-chested sailors and scantily clad females busy loading and off-loading crates and sacks of wares.

A large sign fronting one of the larger dockside buildings advertising, *Thunderhead Shipwright*, swung in the breeze.

Walking down an alley between the previous building and the ship maker, Reecah shrugged out of her rucksack and pulled her waterskin free, slaking her thirst as she observed the organized chaos of the shipyards.

Burly men and tough-looking women bustled around the wide dock, jumping to and from gangplanks laden with sacks and crates. Livestock clomped down a longer ramp, patiently pulled by skinny boys and girls barely old enough to be in their teens.

Further down the fjord, three black war galleons were tethered to the largest pier in view—their ominous high sides towered above the dockside.

A muscular, redheaded woman chewing on a splinter of wood with dirt smearing her pale face sneered. "Whatcha lookin' at, wench? Ain't never seen a war galley afore?"

Reecah's Gift

Reecah's head snapped back to the dock jutting into the water before her. The brown-eyed woman's stare bore into her, making Reecah afraid to say anything, especially after her last encounter with the people of Thunderhead. "Um, no, actually. I haven't."

The redhead's scowl deepened. "A wise one, eh? I oughtta chuck ya in the brine."

The woman, her thin tunic tied high up her ribcage to expose a washboard stomach, dropped her sack on the dock—brown dust wafting through the burlap—and started Reecah's way.

"Cahira! Pick that up and get to back to work or it'll be the scuppers for yer sorry hide! The ship ain't to be lading itself!" a large man shouted from the deck of the nearest ship.

"Sorry hide! Sorry hide!" Raver called from the eave hanging over the alley.

Reecah cringed. She didn't need the featherbrain to work Cahira up further.

The redhead stopped dead in her tracks, her hard shoulders tensing. Judging by her murderous look, Reecah was thankful Cahira wasn't above obeying the command of the rotund sailor standing against the bow rail of a three-masted brig—the *Serpent's Slip*. "If I so much as lays eyes on ya agin, I'll slit yer throat, ya hear me?"

Reecah offered Cahira a meek smile that only served to deepen the redness in the dockhand's face. Not wanting to risk fate, Reecah stuffed her waterskin in her rucksack and retreated down the alley.

Inquisitive stares stalked her as she strolled through the heart of Thunderhead. Judging by the expressions she received from the citizens on the street, she came to understand that a woman bearing a quarterstaff, two swords, a bow, and a quiver full of arrows wasn't the norm in the port city. She wondered how people got their food if they didn't hunt for it.

Reecah's Gift

Tables bearing pungent herbs and spices and various types of fish and bread lined the street on both sides, some beneath leaning rooftops while others sat beneath the midday sun.

Her empty stomach growled at the savoury aromas, compelling her toward a tall, scrawny youth with tight curls.

"Copper kippers here, lassie! Get your copper kippers!" The boy's attention latched onto her. "You have the uncanny appearance of a connoisseur of fine brine. Taste my deep-sea morsels and I dare you to refuse more."

Reecah lifted her chin and smiled, taking in the boy's dimpled cheeks that were framed by brown curls falling to his shoulders. The poorly put together table bore the weight of three wooden buckets, each less than half full of skinny, silver fish—herrings, mackerel, and a fish Reecah had never seen before.

She pointed to the unknown fish. "Hi. I would love to try your fish. I'm not familiar with that one."

"Oh, my pretty lady, you're in for a real treat, let me tell you. That there is a snapper."

Reecah pulled her finger back.

The boy laughed. "It's dead." Reaching into the bucket, he fished out something unsavoury looking and threw it to the ground behind him. Wiping his hand on his filthy, brown breeches, he pulled a snapper from the bucket and held it out for her inspection.

"I can eat it like this?"

The boy shrugged. "Don't see why not. They're better cooked, but they're certainly edible. Mind you, they have a strong flavour."

He produced a well-honed knife with a curved tip from behind one of the buckets and expertly filleted the fish. He handed her a darker strip.

Reecah's Gift

Reecah accepted the fish and sniffed at it, salivating. Popping it into her mouth, she tentatively bit into it. The boy wasn't kidding about the sharp flavour.

"Told you. Here. Try this piece."

Swallowing the darker strip, she bit into the rest of the fillet and grinned, sucking at her fingers and nodding. "Yes, much nicer."

The youth crossed his arms, pleased. He nodded at the other two buckets. "Care to try these?"

Reecah nodded with a big smile.

The young man pulled out a warped cutting board and sliced up chunks of fish.

Hungry as she was, Reecah couldn't resist. They would be much better over a fire, but looking around, there was little chance of preparing one in the middle of the city.

The youth urged her to eat as many as she liked. She felt rude devouring the fish in front of him, amongst the thrall of strangers pressing into the street market, but she hadn't eaten a decent meal since that first night below Peril's Peak.

As she finished the seventh small piece, the boy grinned and handed her a dirty cloth to wipe her hands. "That'll be seven coppers, ma'am."

At twenty-one years of age, Reecah wasn't sure what threw her most. Being called ma'am, or being asked to pay for the fish. "B-but I thought you said it was okay to try them?"

The boy's smile dropped. "Aye. A copper a kipper. You ate seven, so you owe me seven coppers."

Reecah swallowed, shaking her head. "Um, I don't have money. Where I come from, we trade each other for things. We don't use money unless we wish to buy a finery."

The boy's brows knit together, his voice going up in pitch. "What do you mean you don't have money? Look at you. You're a...a...a..." His gaze lingered on her gear. "*What* are you?"

Reecah's Gift

Not knowing how to explain herself, she said, "I'm just a traveller who wandered into Thunderhead looking for someone to help me."

"By giving you food?"

A couple of people stopped what they were doing to investigate the commotion.

"Well, no. Not exactly. I'm trying to find a ship to take me to the high king."

The boy's voice rose higher yet. "The high king?"

"Yes. Is that not alright?"

"You can't afford seven coppers, yet you expect passage aboard a ship?"

"I hadn't really thought about having to pay my way. I guess I'm used to people being neighbourly."

The boy turned to the spectators. "Did you hear that? She's used to people being neighbourly. Hah!"

His piercing green eyes bore into her. "Tell me, little miss, 'I don't expect to pay for anything,' where do you come from? Some backward place like Fishmonger Bay?"

"Fishmonger! Fishmonger!" Raver cawed, bobbing his head from atop a ripped awning behind the fish merchant.

Those gathered around laughed, their eyes searching out Raver.

Reecah nearly choked. "I, uh, dunno. Just someplace…"

The boy crossed his arms and nodded, reminding her of a haughty adult as he peered down his nose.

"You don't know? Just someplace, huh?" He leaned across the table. "Let me tell you something. In *this* place, we pay our way. *And*, if you don't hand over what's owing, I'll call the Watch and let them deal with you."

His creepy stare studied her physique, causing her more than a little discomfort. "Yep. They'll deal with you just fine I'm thinking." He rose up on his toes, searching the crowd.

Reecah's Gift

Reecah reached across the table, seizing an arm and pulling him down. "No, please. I don't want any trouble. I will, uh…perhaps I can trade you something."

She shrugged free of her rucksack and rummaged through it, trying to locate something of value. Nothing. Patting down her tunic, she felt the magic dragon journal and the Dragon's Eye gemstone hidden in an interior pocket of her cloak. She wasn't about to part with those.

The boy walked around the table, his eyes lingering on her swords. "I'll take one of those."

Reecah followed his gaze. "My swords? I can't let you take one of those. They're special."

He arched an eyebrow, crossing his arms and raised his voice to include the people standing around. "Ain't gonna be much use to you with only one hand, I'm thinking. That's how we deal with thieves in Thunderhead."

Reecah's eyes grew wide. Sensing tears coming on, she tried not to draw attention to the fact that Raver had landed on the centre bucket and pecked at its contents.

Some emissary for dragonkind she was turning out to be. Barely arrived in Thunderhead and already she was on the verge of emotional collapse—in the presence of a teenaged fishmonger, no less. The irony of the boy's profession wasn't lost on her.

Gritting her teeth to keep from openly sobbing, she unbuckled the sword belt hanging from her right hip and studied it with sadness. It had been her great-grandmother's. She fought to keep her voice from breaking. "I'll give you this…" The boy grabbed for it, but she pulled it back. "…To hang onto until I come back with the money. Okay?"

"Both swords."

"What? One of these is worth more than you'd make in a year. You can take one or call the Watch, I don't care." Reecah scowled, hoping she sounded tougher than she felt.

20

Reecah's Gift

Grunting, the boy snatched the weapon by the scabbard. "Fine. But don't expect seven coppers will be enough to repay your debt. I have to charge you for keeping your sword safe. And then there's interest."

Reecah's eyes narrowed. If the busybody crowd wasn't there to witness it, she might have flattened his nose. Instead, their amusement alerted the boy to what was going on behind him.

Spinning around, the boy jumped at Raver but missed. "Shoo, you thief!"

Raver landed on the awning, a large fish in his beak.

Fuming, the boy turned his vexed scowl on Reecah. "Look what you've done. Distracted me and now that stupid bird has gotten another. A shiny silver should compensate for your transgression."

Reecah struggled to keep the angered frustration from her voice, hoping the boy wouldn't figure out that Raver was with her. "Fine! If you would be so kind as to direct me to where I might find work, I'd be most grateful."

The boy cast a glance at Raver before sliding the sword free and testing its balance, nodding approvingly. The faces of the gathering also appreciated the sword's quality before they disbanded and went about their business.

Sliding the sword home, the boy considered Reecah with one hand under his chin, his eyes flicking over her body. "You wish to find employment, hmm? I might know just the place for one such as you."

Reecah's Gift

The Naughty Saucer

Carrying two buckets of fish for the fishmonger, Reecah followed the boy through the streets, back the way she had come. She was relieved the rude woman and her courtier no longer lingered around the sharp bend in the roadway. Rounding the corner, they strolled onto the uneven cobblestones until the roadway became mud.

At one point, the boy said, "I'm Tarrek, by the way."

Reecah acknowledged his comment with a scowl.

Just when she thought her burning shoulders would take no more, Tarrek stopped and put his bucket down.

"Stay here," was all he said before disappearing between two rank-smelling warehouses.

Reecah lowered the buckets and rubbed her shoulders, stretching the stiffness from her back. She wasn't used to carrying weight in that manner. Waiting for Tarrek, it crossed her mind that maybe he wasn't coming back. She thought about inspecting the darkened alleyway but before she gathered the nerve, several voices sounded from the direction of the ocean.

Tarrek led three young males into the street and stepped aside. "See, I told you. Outfitted like a ranger."

The tallest youth, a dark-haired boy younger-looking than Tarrek, stepped up to her. Without a word, he ran his gaze up and down her front and stepped behind her to do the same to her backside. "*Are* you a ranger?"

Reecah's Gift

Reecah turned to meet his inspection. "A ranger? What's that?"

Pursing his thin lips, the dark-haired boy nodded. "Ya, she'll do." He tossed Tarrek a ring of keys. "Show her a room."

The other boys raised their eyebrows, nodding in unison.

Reecah frowned. "Wait a minute. Where am I going? I thought he was taking me to a job."

The dark-haired boy glowered at Tarrek. "You didn't tell her?"

Tarrek shrugged. "Didn't want to scare her away."

"Our clients won't be impressed if she bolts halfway through, you dolt."

"Come on, Axe. She ain't going nowhere." Tarrek patted the sword hanging from his waist, raising his eyebrows twice in quick succession. "Not without this."

"Ah, that's where you got that." Axe nodded, glancing between the sword his friend carried and the one on Reecah's hip. "Nice. Well see to it she don't run, else *you know who* will be using that sword on your sorry carcass."

"Ya, ya," Tarrek said and started down the street to where it met the cobblestones. "Come on miss. Let's get you sorted."

Reecah glanced at Axe and the smirking faces of the other boys.

Axe motioned with dark eyes for her to go after Tarrek.

Happy to get away from the menacing youth who reminded her of a miniature Viper, Reecah joined Tarrek on the paving stones. "Where are we going?"

Tarrek fast stepped ahead. "You'll see soon enough."

She hurried to keep up. "So, what's my job? What am I supposed to do?"

Raver cawed as he flew overhead.

Tarrek's gaze followed the raven. "Whatever you're told, that's what," he snapped, pointing a dirty finger in her face.

Reecah's Gift

"Why so many damned questions? You want to get your sword back?"

Without waiting for an answer, he stormed toward the end of the street where it turned at the fancy buildings to head up the fjord.

"Of course, I do. I'm just curious," Reecah called after him, jogging to keep pace with his long-legged strides. "I want to make sure I do a good job."

It was hard to tell, but she was sure he said, "Do whatever they want and you'll be fine."

She slowed her pace as the words sank in, not liking the inference. The woman falling out of her undergarments came to mind. Surely, he didn't mean that.

If Tarrek knew she had stopped, he didn't let on until he approached a well-dressed doorman standing outside the fanciest building at the end of the street—its gables swooping in great arcs, adorned with intricate, gilded swirls. A shingle over the doorman's head in the shape of a fancy goblet lying atop a curved plate squeaked in the breeze.

The two exchanged words, their gaze swinging her way. The doorman smiled and nodded.

"Hurry up. Let's go!" Tarrek called.

Not knowing what else to do, Reecah approached the building. She needed to get her sword back.

Raver glided on an air current down the street, his graceful course taking him over the top of the fancy building and out of sight.

Bowing deeply, the doorman held the iron-strapped door open for her to enter a long hallway leading into the smoke-filled building. "Welcome to the *Naughty Saucer.*"

The odd name gave Reecah pause.

Tarrek motioned her inside with his head and let the door squeal shut behind him. Urging her down the hallway, he said, "Hey, I don't think you told me your name."

Reecah's Gift

Reecah met his gaze, hoping her mounting fear wasn't reflected in her eyes. She didn't dare tell him her real name in case someone from Fishmonger Bay came looking for her. "Um, Grimelda. Grimelda Grog." She winced. They were the first two names that had come to mind.

Tarrek studied her face as if he didn't believe her. Finally, he nodded. "Very well, GG it is. Follow me."

Muted music and the noise of people carrying on rose to a raucous din as they reached the end of the hallway and turned into a great room lined on the inside wall by a long, oak counter fronted with stools laden with all sorts of colourful people in varying states of dress.

Reecah grasped Tarrek by the shoulder and whispered harshly into his ear. "I'm not working here, I'll tell you that right now."

Tarrek surveyed the common room and threw his head back, laughing. "Don't you worry, GG, I have a better place in mind for you."

Reecah frowned, her nervous gaze taking in the bawdy room littered with couches and large cushioned chairs filled with lecherous men and women. The back wall of the common room, made almost entirely of glass, afforded a panoramic view of the ocean colliding with the waters of the fjord.

More than one head turned in their direction.

"What are we doing here? These people are creepy."

Tarrek laughed and strolled through the common room, his eyes taking in the sights as he passed them by. "They appear to be captivated by your appearance. Not often do people come through the *Naughty Saucer* bristling with weapons. Perhaps they think you are part of the Watch."

Reecah scrambled after him, afraid to be left alone; trying to hear what he said.

Reecah's Gift

"These, GG, are well-paying customers. But..." He spun on her, his finger in her face, making her protest catch in her throat. "Don't worry. These aren't your type of customers."

Reecah couldn't prevent her gaze wandering from a bare-chested man to a bare-chested woman to three women who were...she looked away, her cheeks flaming. Shocked, her gaze locked on Tarrek. "This is *not* what I had in mind."

She turned to leave but Tarrek's words stopped her.

"GG, come now. Do you honestly think I would lead you astray? I'm hurt. We have bigger plans for you."

We? She didn't appreciate his smirk but the thought of abandoning her sword kept her feet moving toward a wide, circular staircase ascending to a second and third floor overlooking the common room.

Tarrek bounded past the second story landing and continued to the upper floor. The red-carpeted stairwell opened onto a wide foyer, its oceanside wall fronted by several mahogany doors.

Leaning an ear against the first door he listened before knocking. Receiving no response, he tried a couple of different keys until the lock snicked open. Holding a hand up for Reecah to remain where she was, he peered inside.

Satisfied, he offered Reecah a broad grin and held the door wide, ushering her inside with a flourish of his hand.

Reecah checked her surroundings. The noise from the common room continued to fill her with unease. Swallowing her better judgement, she slipped past Tarrek into a room more decadent than anything she had ever dreamed of. Appointed with large, dark wood furniture, plush linens, and a cushioned, arched bay window that overlooked the ocean, a high bed dominated the centre of the room. Her surroundings captivated her with awe and a wariness of the darkness such a room might perpetrate.

Reecah's Gift

Fingering the dagger's hilt, her gaze darted about the room, always falling back on Tarrek who watched her with that sideways smirk of his. How she'd love to smack it from his face.

"Well, what do you think?" Tarrek asked, plopping his butt on the end of the bed and bouncing. "You won't find anything finer in all of Thunderhead, I assure you."

"I, uh…it's nice, I guess. What does it have to do with me?"

That smirk again. "This, GG, will be your base of operations."

"My what?"

"Your base of operations. This is where you'll meet your clients."

Reecah's head shook of its own accord. Her dagger slid from its sheath. She had half a mind to slit Tarrek's throat and escape with her sword. If only she had the nerve.

She pointed the dagger at him. "If you think I'm doing what I think is going on here, you're sadly mistaken."

Tarrek stood up and backed toward the window, his attention on the dagger. "Look lady, you're the one who asked for a job."

"A job! Not…not, this!"

"Hey, you're the one who said you needed to make money."

"Only because you swindled me into eating your fish!" She jabbed the dagger at him.

He held up his hands. "I asked you if you wanted to try them. I never said they were free."

She thought about their encounter in the market. "Ya? Well, the way you said it made me think they were."

"What? Free? Perhaps you should've asked, first."

She had nothing to say to that. He was right. She sheathed her dagger and grunted her frustration. How had she allowed herself to get into such a predicament? Her eyes fell on the sword hanging from Tarrek's hip. "Look. All I want is my

27

sword back. I'll do almost anything for it, but I won't do…this. I'd rather die."

Tarrek stared at her. The smirk slid from his face. "Tell you what. Let me see what I can do. The queen consort and her retinue are in town. Her courtiers are constantly seeking entertainment—"

Her dagger leapt from its sheath, interrupting him—the intensity in her glare enough to make him hold his hands up to ward off a blow.

"Whoa, GG! Let me finish before you go sticking me with that thing."

Reecah stepped back and forth on the balls of her feet, but she didn't approach.

Tarrek swallowed. "What I was going to say is these men, *and* women, seek something to do with their time while they wait on the prince's order. We provide escort services to all types of royal courtiers. Yes, some…well most, seek what you think, but not all. Let me arrange an escort that is, shall we say, not as demanding as our typical clients. Many men simply seek the accompaniment of one as beautiful as yourself. Someone they would be proud to have hanging off their arm, if only for an evening."

"You mentioned women. Why not a woman."

Tarrek's eyes widened. He sputtered, "Y-yes. Of course. If you'd rather a woman to—"

She stepped toward him, holding the dagger next to his chin.

"Hey, I'm trying to help here. I don't know what you like and what you don't."

Her stare hardened—the dagger's tip unwavering.

"Okay, okay. I get it. Just put that thing away, would you?"

She turned the dagger's edge sideways. It would be too easy. Sighing, she stepped back and lowered the blade, taking delight in the sweat beading on Tarrek's forehead.

Reecah's Gift

He appeared to consider his next words. With an obvious, fake smile, he asked, "Well, what do you say? I'll find you someone less obtrusive than our regular clientele and leave it up to you how you handle him."

"Her!"

"Yes, her. Just know where the money's at, that's all I'm saying. You'll be paid accordingly. Do well, and perhaps you can work off your debt in a few days."

"A few days?"

"Pfft. We have expenses, too. This room for example. It ain't cheap."

"I don't need a room. I'm happy sleeping under a tree."

Tarrek's face twisted in disgust. "Ya, well, that won't work here. Our clients are a little more civilized than wherever you come from. Where was it again?"

The dagger rose between them.

Hands high, he smirked. "Right. None of my business. Now, if you'll excuse me, I shall find your first, um, client." He indicated with his eyes he wished for her to lower the weapon.

She stepped aside to let him pass, her eyes never leaving his hands.

The door creaked opened and shut.

The dagger slipped from her grasp, bouncing almost noiselessly off the soft carpet; her hands visibly shaking. Hurriedly throwing the interior door bolt home, she staggered to the bay window and stared at the heavy seas. She hoped Raver had found a place to shelter.

A storm was coming.

Reecah's Gift

A Woman She Never Knew

Reecah's eyes snapped open—the sunshine cutting through the bay window forcing her to shelter them with her hand. Dark clouds formed on the horizon; ominous tendrils of what was soon to make landfall, crept across its surface, encroaching the sun. Startled by her surroundings, she gathered her bearings.

It had taken a while to calm her nerves after Tarrek left. As the well-appointed room came into focus, she sighed. The nightmare she'd woken from hadn't been far from the truth. She had dozed off, enjoying the luxurious comfort the soft bed offered—feeling as if she floated on a cloud. Her lower back ached where her sword belt dug into her skin.

Curious as to the lavish appointments, she examined the room. Her gaze lingered on three bell-pulls hanging out of the exquisitely carved headboard labelled: Water. Food. Drink. She had no idea what they did.

Reading the labels, her stomach informed her it had been a long time since pilfering Tarrek's fish but she dared not push her luck. She was under no illusion. Anything she consumed would cost money she didn't have. The more debt she acquired, the longer she would be stuck escorting people for...

Tarrek had mentioned, *we*, several times. She wondered who, *we*, were. The dark-haired boy, Axe, and his two lackeys came to mind. Surely, they couldn't afford to hold down a room such as this one by selling fish.

Reecah's Gift

She recalled their encounter. Axe had been scrutinizing her sword, but his words of warning had been directed at Tarrek. *"...see to it she don't run, else you know who will be using that sword on your sorry carcass."*

The boys answered to someone. Probably one much older. Her thoughts went to Jonas Waverunner and his slimy brother, Joram. She shuddered. Those were two people the world would be better off without.

And then there was Jaxon...

A loud rap on the door made her jump. Her terrified gaze fell on the door; relieved the deadbolt was still in place.

The door protested under someone's attempt to push it open.

Her quarterstaff and unstrung bow rested beside the bay window. Little good they were going to be.

Sliding her sword free, she gripped it with both hands. Succumbing to her rising panic, she considered escaping out the window and admonished herself. The room looked out over a pile of jumbled rock, three stories below.

A metallic scratching accompanied an audible snick. Something heavy leaned into the door. She tightened her clammy grip on her sword but the deadbolt held firm.

"GG! Open up. It's me, Tarrek."

The acute anxiety of fright washed away, leaving her reeling. She put a hand on the bed to steady herself.

The pounding sounded again.

"GG! Come on, I know you're in there!"

She stepped quietly to the door and put her ear to the wood, listening. Nothing but a squeaking floorboard.

"Who else is with you?"

"No one. Come on, open up."

Holding her sword at the ready, she wiggled the deadbolt free and stepped back. "It's open."

Reecah's Gift

The latch lifted and Tarrek shouldered his way into the room, the scowl on his face telling as he looked her over. "You haven't washed?"

She shrugged, scanning the thin, light blue fabric draped over his arm. It wasn't lost on her that he still wore her great-grandmother's sword. "Why should I?"

"Seriously?" He pushed past her into the room and spun to stare at her from the end of the bed. "We can't have you escorting our clientele looking like that!"

"Like what? What's wrong with this?"

Rolling his eyes, Tarrek held up a bodice and matching skirt. "What's that?"

"Appropriate evening attire."

Reecah had only seen clothing like this in the window of the Fishmonger Bay mercantile. "Where's the rest of it?"

"Excuse me? Oh yes." He pulled a pair of brown faux suede shoes from beneath his arm—their pointed toes half as long as the shoe itself—and threw them on the bed.

"Where's the tunic and…oh, I don't know. Surely, you don't expect me to go about wearing just that!"

Tarrek turned the garments around, examining them and gave her an innocent frown. "Uh, ya. Why not?"

"Why not?" Incredulous, Reecah stormed up to him and ripped the garments from his hands. She held them up to his face. "Because I'd rather not be seen in public wearing less than those…those…" She stewed, trying to think of an appropriate word to describe the women in the common room. "Those silly women downstairs."

Tarrek held his hands out. "Come on, GG. You have to work with me here. I'm trying to help you."

"Help me what? Catch my death of cold?" She threw the clothes into his arms and ran her hands down her sides. "Why can't I wear this?"

Reecah's Gift

"Oh yes. Real nice. I can see it now." He pretended like he was talking to someone else in the room, bowing to them. "Good evening, good sir. May I present you with your date for the evening. Meet GG, the dragon slayer."

Reecah choked on his choice of words.

"Ya." Tarrek pointed at her. "You see the difficulty, huh?"

Reecah fought to keep from saying something that might give her away. Taking a moment to compose herself, she said, "No, actually, I don't." She ran her hands along her sword belt. "Well, maybe. But!" She held a finger between his blinking eyes with one hand and snatched the bodice from his arms, dangling it in the air between them. "I'm not wearing this."

She tossed it back at him.

Tarrek shook his head. Throwing the clothes on the bed, he pushed past her—stopping at the door. Without looking back, he said, "You wear what you want, but remember," he pointed his own finger. "You only get paid a percentage of the equivalent your client feels you're worth. *If* you don't earn enough to pay for your room, you'll end up owing more than you started with. Understand?"

Reecah refused to dignify him with a response.

"Get yourself cleaned up. I'll have hot water brought to the room. Make sure you're ready by the time I return."

She spun to face the darkening window, crossing her arms beneath her breasts in defiance.

The slamming door marked his exit.

Tucking in her exposed skin as much as possible, she looked at her reflection in the dark window pane. Lightning arced across the sky, casting her with a haunting look.

After Tarrek had stormed out, curiosity had gotten the better of her. Washing away the day's grime in the peculiarly scented water an old woman had brought for her, she had squeezed into the scanty bodice—having to tuck herself into its tight confines as she laced it up.

Slipping the snug-fitting skirt on, it felt as if she weren't wearing anything below her waist as a cool draft wafted through the cracks around the window frame. She'd never worn anything but breeks her entire life.

Frowning at how ridiculous she must look, she was shocked by the vision staring back at her. A woman she never knew existed. One with tall, muscular legs, thin waist, and a bust enhanced by the constricting bodice. It took her a long while to appreciate her shapely body as she turned one way and then another. Looking over her shoulder, she was awestruck by how different the fancy clothes made her appear.

She lifted a foot, laughing at the ridiculously long-toed shoe. Emitting a shy smile, she briefly entertained wearing the outfit in public. At once, her rational brain dashed her fanciful daydream. Who was she to portray a lady of high station? Like the ladies of the king's court she had seen in Poppa's books. She wasn't cut from royal cloth. Dreading the thought of being caught in the revealing attire, she tried to undo the bodice lacing but it snagged in a knot.

A knock sounded at the door. "GG! Open up!"

Frantically tugging at the knot made it tighter. Her anxiety peaked. It was time to meet the client Tarrek had found for her, and there she stood, clad in nothing but fancy undergarments. The long drop outside her window to the break wall didn't seem that bad after all.

Sighing, she grabbed her cloak and threw it on. Pulling the deadbolt free, she expected to be met by the lecherous glare of a highborn woman, but only the fishmonger's green eyes greeted her. A temporary flush of relief washed through her. Perhaps he hadn't found her a client.

Tarrek's eyes darkened at the sight of her cloak. "I thought I told you to be ready."

Reecah's Gift

A flutter of nerves played with her voice. "I am." She started to show him that she wore the skimpy uniform beneath her cloak but shyly covered herself again.

"That's a start, I guess." He motioned for her to spin around. "At least you took off your weapons. They wouldn't have gone over well." He sniffed at her. "That's good. You no longer reek like a peasant."

Reecah steeled herself, meeting his glare with one of her own. She refused to let him intimidate her.

Tarrek shook his head. "It'll have to do." He stepped aside to let her exit.

Panic set in. She couldn't go out in public half-naked. "Turn around for a minute."

Tarrek frowned. "We have to go. Your client's waiting."

"Okay, okay, just give me a moment. Please, turn around."

Tarrek sighed, crossing his arms and facing the door.

She tugged at the knot several times to no avail. Looking for something to help, she unbuckled her dagger from her sword belt lying on the bed. She cast a glimpse at Tarrek's back. Worried he was about to turn around, she slipped the dagger in its sheath between the tight waistline of the skirt and her back—barely adjusting her cloak before Tarrek's patience wore out.

He faced her. "Are you ready?"

She was far from ready, but her time had run out. Nodding meekly, she stepped past him onto the landing.

He locked the door with a key and held it out to her. "Here. Don't lose it or it'll be another silver to replace the lock."

She placed the key in the secret pocket containing her journal and the Dragon's Eye. There was no way she was leaving them behind. Other than not knowing what she was about to get herself into, her biggest fear was returning to the room to find her clothes and the rest of her weapons gone.

Reecah's Gift

Unconsciously checking that her hair fell properly, she ran a hand behind her head, ensuring her tight braid felt as neat as Grammy used to make it. Scrambling to keep up with an impatient Tarrek, her strides inhibited by the skirt, she almost knocked him over as they descended the last stair and wove their way through the musky common room thick with smoke and human odours. The longing gazes she received from several men and women made her skin crawl—as if insinuating they knew what she and Tarrek had been up to. She pulled her cloak tight.

Welcoming the brisk, night air, she stepped onto the cobblestone street. A breeze ruffled the hem of her cloak, wafting across her bare legs, raising goosebumps. Her relief at being free of the loathsome tavern was short-lived.

A grandiose, covered carriage with spoked wheels as tall as her chest, waited on the street; drawn by a pair of shining, black mares.

A man in crisp livery and silk top hat snapped to attention at a nod from Tarrek. The coachman surveyed Reecah with obvious disdain.

Tarrek smiled for the man's benefit. "This is the lady, GG. See to it she returns here when m'lord is finished."

M'lord? Reecah shot a look at Tarrek, but before she could protest, the coachman opened the carriage door.

"Of course." The coachman doffed his top hat and bowed, casting Reecah a dark look. With a white-gloved, underhand flourish, he motioned for her to enter. "M'lady."

Reecah tried to back away but Tarrek caught her and urged her forward.

Waiting on the far side of the coach sat a pepper grey-haired gentleman clad in a frilly chested, white tunic beneath a striking, royal blue surcoat that was piped with golden filigree and fitted with padded shoulders. The man's dark eyes felt like they were boring a hole right through her, but his mysterious

Reecah's Gift

smile softened his chiseled face. Without a word, those eyes beckoned Reecah into the velvet-lined carriage.

Reecah's Gift

Lecherous Leader

Breathless, afraid of what her immediate future had in store, Reecah clumsily mounted the single step—the distance from the ground greater than the stride allowance of the restrictive skirt. Her raised foot fell short of the step and she fell into the carriage between the plush, upholstered seat and the front wall, emitting a squeak of surprise.

The gentleman reached down and grasped her by the wrist, his deep voice filling the compartment, "Easy, m'lady. We don't need to turn an ankle afore we dine, surely."

Climbing into the carriage on her knees, Reecah offered the gentleman a demure smile, gratefully accepting his assistance from the floor to a sitting position. She quickly pulled her hand from his grasp and directed her gaze to Tarrek and the coachman, well aware of how red her cheeks were.

Tarrek held a hand over his eyes, shaking his head, while the coachman's disgusted glare admonished her as he removed the step and closed the door.

Relieved to have something to brace herself on, Reecah placed her back against the door and looked shyly at the posh gentleman from beneath a lowered brow.

"You're not what I expected…" He paused, searching for her name.

"GG"

"Yes, GG. A peculiar name, that."

"Heh, ya. It's, uh, what they call me." She swallowed, feeling foolish—expecting to receive an annoyed response.

Reecah's Gift

The man surprised her by laughing. "Yes, I gathered that when you told me."

The carriage shook and wood creaked as the coachman lowered his weight onto the open bench outside. The jingle of tack preceded the order, "H'ya," and the carriage lurched forward, its iron-strapped wheels clicking on the cobblestones.

"Tell me…GG. Where are you from? Your name sounds exotic, though I'm thinking it's short for something. Am I correct?"

Reecah's mouth felt dry. Wringing her hands together she noticed how damp they were in comparison. "Um, yes. Yes, it is."

The man waited for her to explain but she offered nothing further.

His colourless lips lifted in what appeared to be an impatient smile. "What's it short for?"

She gazed out the side window. Quayside buildings passed by as the coach shook and creaked along the rough pavers. The name she gave Tarrek sounded silly but there was nothing to do about it now. She chanced a look into his eyes. Though dark and brooding, a kindness lingered there. "Grimelda Grog."

His barely perceptible nod was interrupted as the coach took an abrupt left turn and started up a steep hill, the momentum throwing the man against her.

His heady cologne was overpowered by a musky aroma of sweat. If she had the right of it, the gentleman was as intimidated by this whole affair as she was. The dagger digging into her backside gave her the confidence she needed to curb her fear of the man's closeness.

The gentleman's cheeks reddened. Separating himself, careful not to touch anything inappropriate, he shouted at the driver, "Damn you, coachman! You're going to unsettle the lady!"

Reecah's Gift

A muffled response from outside let them know the coachman had at least heard, but Reecah couldn't understand what he said.

The gentleman rolled his eyes and shook his head. "Honestly. If we were back at Draakhall, that man would lose more than his job."

Staring out the side window, the skies opened up, drenching the streets. Reecah didn't know what to say. If he was implying the coachman would be killed, she considered it harsh. No harm had been done. Thinking it better not to comment, she simply smiled and blinked at the gentleman.

"Oh, where are my manners. I know your name but I never introduced myself. My apologies...do you prefer Grimelda or GG?"

Every time she heard her aunt's name, she was reminded of the fire. "GG, please, m'lord."

Was that how she was supposed to refer to a highborn man? Avoiding his lingering stare, she peered out the window at the finely dressed people scrambling about the fronts of decadent establishments trying to find shelter in the downpour.

"GG it is." He dipped his head. "I am the Viscount of Draakhall. The caretaker of the palace if you will."

Reecah blinked at him, having no idea what that meant, but it sounded like an important title.

"You know, the steward of the high king."

Reecah smiled politely, none the wiser.

The viscount must've sensed her consternation. "Surely you've heard of Draakhall."

Poppa had told her about his time at the royal palace—an episode in his life that had taken place long before she was born. She recalled him speaking of the palace with great reverence, but the details of his stories eluded her. She nodded.

"Well, anyway, my name is Vullis Opsigter the Third."

Reecah's Gift

He watched her struggling to mouth his name and laughed. "Aye. Two others were strapped with the name before me, if you can believe that?"

She smiled shyly, her fear at what the evening had in store robbing her of her willingness to appear too friendly. Vullis came across as innocent enough but she didn't know him. Neither had she any idea where they were going—not that it would have done her any good.

The coach jerked to an abrupt stop, making them scramble to put their hands out to keep from flying off the seat and bashing off the front wall of the carriage. Vullis' strong hand gripped her bicep, bracing her.

Not waiting for the coachman to open his door, Viscount Opsigter said through clenched teeth, "Wait here."

He stormed from the carriage, slamming the door behind him, and proceeded to berate the coachman with several vulgar words Reecah had heard while shadowing the dragon hunt back home.

When the bellowing stopped, the carriage rocked slightly and the sound of the step being inserted outside her door grabbed her attention. A much-chagrined coachman, soaked to the skin in the heavy rain, opened her door and offered her a white-gloved hand to assist her onto the step. "My sincerest apologies, m'lady. Please forgive my poor manners. I have no excuse. My fate is in your hands."

Reecah squinted in the lashing rain and pulled her hood over her head. Once safely on the ground, relieved she hadn't tripped herself in the tight confines of her skirt, Reecah patted the hand seemingly unwilling to release hers. "It's quite alright, honestly. I forgive you."

The look of wonder on the coachman's face made her smile. It was like he expected a beating. Looking like a scolded dog, he bowed twice more. "Thank you m'lady. Thank you."

Reecah's Gift

Standing behind the coachman, Vullis practically pushed him aside, rescuing Reecah's hand from his grasp. "Release the lady, you imbecile, before she catches her death in this cold and rain. Fortunately for you, GG is a gentle lady. I would have you dragged to Sea Keep in fetters and thrown you to the kraken."

Reecah pulled her cloak tightly about, conscious of all the people huddling beneath the eave of the building—standing clear of a large set of double doors that fronted the grandest building on the hilltop overlooking Thunderhead. It didn't take long to spot the chainmail sleeves and plated greaves of the guards on either side of the doorway—their barbed pikes more than decoration.

Vullis held his forearm out for Reecah to grasp and rushed her through the waiting crowd—well-dressed men and women bowing their heads respectfully to the viscount.

The guards manning the doorway snapped to attention at their approach. A dignified man, whose attire closely matched Vullis, bowed low and opened both doors, exposing a sweeping oak stairway ascending to a great hall.

"What is this place?" Reecah asked in wonder, the opulence of the interior made the luxurious tavern where her possessions remained appear as a hovel.

Accepting a cloth from an interior doorman, Vullis wiped his brow and slicked-back hair to soak up the rainwater before helping Reecah ascend a short flight of flagstone steps, conscious of her limited movement. Smiling, he asked, "Have you never been here before?"

"No, m'lord."

"Please. Call me Vullis. You're my date tonight. At least pretend we've met." He raised his eyebrows, his eyes indicating the noisy throng of noblemen and stunningly apparelled women mingling about the great hall at the top of the steps. "I have an appearance to maintain."

Reecah's Gift

Reecah looked down, afraid she had insulted the viscount. "I'm sorry. I'm not used to this sort of thing."

Vullis stopped at the top of the stairs. "Really? And yet you work for *him*?"

She tried to smile for his benefit—nodding slightly, though she had no idea who Vullis referred to. She was making a mess of everything.

"Curious. I would've expected someone as beautiful as you to be in high demand at the baron's residence," he replied and led her onto the polished granite floor.

Reecah's head spun. The baron's residence? From what she understood, the baron of Thunderhead was the highest-ranking official on the entire southwestern shore of the Great Kingdom—with the exception of the Earl of Madrigail, many leagues to the south. She felt so inferior she wanted to shrink into a tiny ball and disappear. These weren't her people. She didn't belong here. She almost laughed aloud at that. She didn't belong anywhere.

The viscount's deep voice snapped her attention back to the present. "Huh?"

Vullis' dark eyes searched her face. "I asked you if you cared for a refreshment."

Embarrassed, it dawned on her that a young woman in flowing skirts stood patiently before her with a tray of fluted goblets filled with a pale, bubbling liquid.

Vullis raised his eyes questioningly, lifting his own drink to show her.

Not wanting to be rude, she smiled shyly and nodded, accepting a tall glass from the serving girl.

"To a beautiful woman on a less than beautiful night." Vullis held his glass toward her.

She frowned, seeing that he expected something, but didn't know what. Imitating him, she lifted her glass but pulled it away when he thrust his at her, fearing the glasses would smash together and break.

The viscount overextended his arm—his drink sloshing onto the floor at her feet.

"Oh!" She jumped back to avoid being hit and spilled the contents of her glass between them. Mortified, she covered her mouth, and stared at Vullis, fully expecting him to verbally abuse her like he had the coachman.

Vullis stumbled backward to avoid the splash. Catching himself, he stared open-mouthed at Reecah, his thin lips curving in a wide grin. "GG, you little prankster." He raised his free hand and snapped his fingers. "Wench! Two more drinks and a rag!"

Reecah thought his manner rude, but no sooner had he beckoned than a different young lady scurried over with a tray of the fluted goblets.

Vullis plucked a glass from the tray, drained it, and grabbed two more, giving one to Reecah. Without thanking the servant, he held out his arm and escorted her deeper into the crowd.

"I should clean that up," Reecah protested.

"Nonsense. That's *their* job. You're the baron's guest. Do not insult the man in his own house."

Reecah swallowed. Looking over her shoulder, she watched the servant girl stoop down. Catching her eye, she offered the young woman an apologetic look before being swallowed up by the crowd.

"Ah, there he is!" A loud voice bellowed from somewhere ahead.

The crowd parted to allow her and Vullis a clear path to an overweight, balding man sitting cross-legged on a plush, red velvet settee. The man handed a metal flagon to a busty servant girl standing beside the couch and attempted to pull himself out of its deep embrace.

"Baron, please. Remain seated," Vullis instructed.

Reecah's Gift

"What have we got here, Vullis?" The baron patted the sofa seat beside him. "Come, sweet girl, let's get acquainted."

Vullis must've noted the repulsive look on Reecah's face. He hugged her hand against his side, silently letting her know to remain standing.

"Not so fast, good baron. I'd be loath to lose her to your brazen charm."

The baron's face reddened more than the obvious amount of alcohol he'd ingested—his words belying his disappointment at being cheated of his sport. "Of course, viscount. Just in case you've forgotten, denying a man his wish in his own house is frowned upon in these parts. Seeing as you are His Majesty's royal vizier, I'll allow the slight to go unpunished…*this* time."

Reecah expected an argument, but Vullis grinned. "A wise decision considering I outrank you."

The baron's eyes darkened. He cleared his throat to cover his unease. "Yes, yes, of course. Now that you've *finally* arrived, perhaps we can get the royal celebration started." He craned his thick neck, searching the crowd. "Is the princess not with you?"

"She sends her regards. She's otherwise preoccupied. She may attend later at her convenience."

The baron's face turned purple. Reecah thought for sure he was in medical distress.

"Very well," the baron croaked and turned to a male servant awaiting his command. "Tell the minstrels to commence."

The servant nodded, fear evident in his haunted eyes. He started away, but the baron's next words stopped him.

"Make sure they play something uplifting to raise the dull spirit in this hall or we'll be having words."

"Yes, m'lord." The servant bolted into the crowd.

Afraid to look at the baron, Reecah unconsciously tightened her grip on the viscount's arm.

45

Reecah's Gift

"Wench! A hand," the baron ordered the servant girl.

The petite lady, younger than Reecah, strained to keep from being pulled from her feet as she helped the baron stand with one hand while expertly holding onto his flagon with her other.

As soon as his girth rested over his feet, the baron snatched the flagon from her hand and raised it into the air.

Reecah flinched, hoping not to re-enact her previous debacle.

Vullis stayed her with a shake of his head and met the baron's flagon with the rim of his glass. "To your health, good baron. May your blessings be plentiful and rife with joy."

The baron snarled, leering at Reecah. Throwing back a huge swallow, he wiped the foam from his lips with the back of his hand. "What's your wench hiding beneath that ratty cloak."

"Good baron, her name is—"

"Steward!" the baron interrupted.

A middle-aged man with greased-back brown hair, appeared from out of the crowd. "M'lord!"

"Why has no one taken this lady's cloak?" Not waiting for an answer, he shook his head and rolled his eyes, directing his words at Vullis. "Honestly. It's like I just trained them this morning."

Reecah's eyes opened wide, realizing what the baron inferred. A pair of hands touched her shoulders, grasping her cloak.

"M'lady." Without waiting for a reply, the steward pulled Reecah's cloak down her arms.

Not wishing to spill her drink, she had no choice but to allow the man to strip her from the sense of protection her cloak offered. She quickly made sure her sheathed dagger remained hidden against the small of her back. Conscious of how red her cheeks felt, it took everything she had not to cover herself with her hands.

Reecah's Gift

She couldn't be sure, but she was positive the baron did a double take as he spat a mouthful of mead back into his flagon.

"There you are, viscount!" A deep voice Reecah had heard before, interrupted.

Reecah did a double take of her own as a man dripping with water waddled up to Vullis. The same man she had encountered in the street with the buxom blonde when she'd first entered Thunderhead—the one who had given her a hard time.

"Clive! The good baron and I were wondering where the princess had gotten off to." Vullis looked over Clive's thick shoulder and frowned. "Is she not here?"

Clive dipped his head, his triple chin bulging. "No, m'lord. She's, ah…" Clive gazed at Reecah and the baron, "indisposed at the moment."

Vullis nodded. Clearing his throat, he turned to meet the baron's brooding glare. "It appears, Princess J'kyra won't be joining us this evening. She is otherwise preoccupied and sends her regrets."

The baron's jowls worked back and forth, chewing on words he appeared to be fighting to restrain. Reecah feared the man was on the verge of a stroke.

Ignoring the shaking baron, Vullis turned back to Clive. "What about the prince. Has there been any news?" The viscount pulled a neatly folded handkerchief from inside his tunic. "Here, dry yourself while you walk with me and tell me about it."

The two men slipped through the crowd and disappeared, leaving Reecah and the irate leader of Thunderhead alone together.

Reecah swallowed, trying to avoid eye contact. She wanted to follow the viscount but was afraid to push through the sea of strangers dressed the way she was. She searched for the servant who had taken her cloak, hoping to discover where he had taken it. Her journal was in its pocket.

A meaty hand grasped her wrist, jerking her attention back to the baron's lecherous, bloodshot eyes.

"Well, well. It looks like fate has shone upon us after all, eh lovey?"

Reecah involuntarily shuddered.

If the baron noticed, he made no sign. Instead, he ran his tongue over his thick lips and pulled her after him, forcing her to sit on the couch.

Fearing he might break her wrist, she had no choice but to follow his lead. Sinking into the plush upholstery, her pointed shoes lifted high off the ground. Mortified, she tried to sit up straight and adjust her knee-length skirt, aware of the dagger digging into her backside and the many eyes watching her.

The baron leaned in, grasping her other wrist and pulled her close—his rancid breath reeking of stale ale.

She turned her head and breathed through her mouth to keep from retching.

"If I know Vullis, he won't be back anytime soon."

Reecah's eyes grew wide. The thick press of bodies around the settee didn't appear concerned one way or another about what was taking place in front of them. It was as if they were used to such behaviour from the baron.

"In fact, Vullis has probably gone in search of Princess J'kyra, fearing for her safety. If that's true, we shan't see him again tonight." Heaving a contented sigh, a large grin transformed his anger into a vision of longing. He raised his thick eyebrows. "Alas, such is the life of a royal courtesan."

Shocked, Reecah looked into his glassy eyes, not liking what stared back at her.

He nodded, releasing one of her wrists. Using a thick finger, he traced her exposed collarbone—starting at her shoulder and running it into the centre of her cleavage and circling. "I'm

Reecah's Gift

growing tired of this crowd. Perhaps a little privacy is in order, eh, GG?"

Reecah's Gift

Just Reward

Cold tingled Reecah's skin. How did the baron know the name Tarrek had labelled her with? The viscount hadn't mentioned it.

If not for the curious onlookers watching their every move, Reecah would have flattened the baron's purple-veined nose against his face. As it was, she was afraid to do anything lest she invoke the man's wrath. Who knew what he was capable of?

"Wench!" the baron bellowed, holding out a hand to be assisted to his feet. Not attempting to hide his intentions, he spoke loudly to the serving girl. "See to it that the fire burns well in my chamber and then be off. I'll not be requiring your services tonight."

Reecah fought to keep her jaw from dropping.

The servant curtsied, bowing her head. "Yes, m'lord." She cast Reecah a commiserating glance as she scurried away.

Reecah watched her disappear through a panel in the wall, the hidden doorway guarded by a burly male servant.

"Come, GG." The baron held out his hands. "I'm sure you'd rather be rid of this tiresome crowd."

Before she had a chance to protest, he grasped her hands in a crushing grip and pulled her off the couch like a wee child, practically dragging her across the floor. She struggled to keep from tripping in her tight skirt.

Reecah's Gift

Reaching the hidden panel, she braced her feet and tried to extricate herself from his painful grip. "Wait. What about Vullis? He'll be looking for me."

"Pfft, that old prude." The baron nodded to the man responsible for triggering the panel's latch. "I'd be surprised if he comes back at all. A head too big for his britches, that one."

With a sudden jerk, the baron nearly yanked her from her feet. He dragged her through the doorway into a musky corridor beyond, its dark-panelled walls aglow in the scant light of wrought-iron sconces set into the wall.

Wanting the pain to stop, Reecah scrambled to keep pace, her eyes darting everywhere, looking for a distraction. All of those long, lonely nights back in her cabin above Fishmonger Bay, filled with nightmares of being caught alone with Joram Waverunner, came rushing back to her. This time, it was real. She flailed her hands to grab at a sconce—anything to slow their progress—but missed.

The hallway ended at a heavy wooden door. The baron turned the handle down, his other hand painfully twisting Reecah's arm behind her back.

Pushing into the softly lit room beyond, the baron chucked Reecah ahead of him and slammed the door.

Reecah caught hold of a dark wood column rising up from the foot of a four-post bed.

A yelp of fright came from beside an open hearth—the young girl from the ballroom jumped to her feet holding a bellows in soot-smeared hands.

"What're you still doing in here?" The baron roared, taking a step toward her.

Reecah took advantage of his distraction and started for the door, but the baron's glare stopped her. "Where do you think you're going?"

Reecah's eyes met the girl's terrified gaze. She shook her head at Reecah—as if warning her not to anger the man further.

Reecah's Gift

Reecah's short temper surfaced. "I'm not what you think I am."

The baron stepped sideways, barring the door. "Oh, you're not, are you?"

"No, sir."

"Are you not the girl who asked Tarrek for a job?"

Reecah's mind reeled. How did he know that?

"Stole his fish in the market, is what I heard."

"I didn't steal anything! He tricked me."

"You took what wasn't yours. Those fish belonged to me."

"You?"

"Caught by my fishing fleet. Who do you think pays their salary? And yours, hmm? I dare say, if you wish to earn it, you'd best start cooperating or you may find yourself worse off than when you agreed to work for Tarrek. In fact, I believe it's time I collected my just reward."

The knowledge of who the baron was took the breath from Reecah's lungs. He was the man Axe had referred to when he had informed Tarrek in no uncertain terms, *"...see to it she don't run, else you know who will be using that sword on your sorry carcass."*

The baron was in charge of the brothel district. At least the inn Tarrek had put her up in. Everything began to make sense. The baron was the leader of Thunderhead. If he was anything like Jonas Waverunner, Reecah imagined most of the city answered to him in one fashion or another.

Quivering against the wall, deathly afraid of what the evening had in store, she had to extricate herself from the baron's company. At the cost of her great-grandmother's sword, she needed to thaw the icy grip of fear immobilizing her. Judging by the servant girl's cowed expression, Reecah wouldn't find any help there.

"I-I'm s-sorry good baron." Reecah didn't have to feign her terror to throw him off guard. It came naturally. "I, uh, d-didn't realize it was you that was paying me. Forgive me."

Reecah's Gift

The baron's dark glare pinned her to the wall. Without taking his eyes from her, he snarled at the servant. "I thought I told you to leave us."

"Y-yes, m'lord. I just got here." The young woman said with a meek voice, her hands clenching the fabric of her skirts. "I, um, can't leave with you blocking the door, m'lord."

Empathy for the frightened servant fueled Reecah's rage.

The baron growled and threw the door open wide. He grabbed the girl by the arm and threw her headfirst into the doorjamb.

The servant thrust her hands out to catch herself but the strength of the baron's toss smashed her face into the hardwood frame. Her head bounced back and she collapsed to the floor—her quivering body preventing the door from closing.

Seething, the baron tried to slam the heavy door shut but one of the servant's lower legs lay in the way. "Damn it, wench. I'll have your hide!"

The girl cried out as he leaned into the door.

Pulling the door open, he stomped on her ankle. "Move!"

The woman's ankle shattered beneath his heel with a sickening crack.

Reecah cringed.

The baron bent down to grab at the screaming girl, but a sudden gasp escaped his throat. His shoulders arched backward. "Hey!"

Reecah's fingers wrapped in the pudgy flesh of his neck, giving her the leverage needed to plunge her dagger into his fleshy shoulder. Though she had killed her first person outside of the Dragon Temple a few weeks ago—the memory never far from her thoughts—feeling the blade cut through the baron's sinews and fat, scraping against his collar bone, mortified her. She wasn't a killer.

Reecah's Gift

She yanked the dagger free and stumbled backward, catching herself on the edge of the canopied bed, her dagger staining the cream-coloured duvet with his blood.

Howling in pain, the baron's bloody fingers grabbed hold of the doorjamb and he pulled himself upright. The servant crying at his feet forgotten, he spun on Reecah, his face twisted in rage. He staggered toward her, one arm hanging useless at his side. "You little bitch."

Reecah pushed away from the bed, holding her dagger between them as they circled each other.

The baron feigned a sudden move toward her.

Reecah lunged to meet him but the baron aborted his attack. He swept his good hand out wide, whacking Reecah's forearm so hard the dagger flew from her grasp. Digging his thick fingers into her wrist he twisted out and down, a malicious smile distorting his purple face.

Rolling with the baron's advance, Reecah's instincts took over. She had never forgotten her mistake with Jonas at the dragon hunt camp. Dipping low to pull the large man off balance, she drove the open palm of her free hand into the baron's ear, knocking him to the ground. Spinning her hips, she stomped on his face with every bit of strength she possessed. "I'll give you a just reward!"

The baron's head cracked off the flagstone floor and his body went limp.

Reecah's pointed shoe slipped off his face, hitting the ground hard. Losing her balance, she dropped a bare knee against his bleeding shoulder—a loud tearing noise informing her that her skirt had ripped up the back.

Scrambling on her hands and knees to get free of the loathsome man, she snatched her dagger from the floor and ran to the servant girl.

"My leg. It's broken," the girl sobbed.

Reecah's Gift

Reecah tried lifting her. "Come on, we have to get you out of here."

The girl screamed in pain. "Leave me!" Her crazed eyes fell on the baron. "Is he...is he dead?"

Reecah followed her gaze. Shrugging, she eased the servant into a sitting position against the wall. "I'm not sure."

The ramifications of what she had done began to sink in. If the baron's men or the Watch caught her now, her life would be forfeited. She had to escape but didn't relish leaving the poor girl to face the baron's wrath if he lived.

"What's going on in here?" a deep voice called out from the end of the hallway. "Is everything okay, baron?"

Reecah's nerves leapt.

The burly doorman ran toward them. The ring of his short sword pulling free of its scabbard filled her with dread.

Dagger by her side, Reecah thought quickly. "Help. The baron's taken a fall. He hit his head off the floor and I can't wake him."

The doorman frowned, his gaze taking in the servant girl on the ground. He lowered his sword and pushed by Reecah into the room.

"Baron!" The doorman dropped to a knee to examine him. Inspecting the baron's shoulder, he pulled his hand away, stained with blood. "What the...?" was all he had time to say before Reecah brought the hilt of her dagger smashing into the back of his head, laying him out flat.

"M'lady, you need to get out of here. They'll kill you," the servant girl cried.

"I'm no lady," Reecah bristled at the inference. Pulling the pointed shoes from her feet, she considered the girl. There was nothing to be done. Reecah wasn't strong enough to carry her, nor had she any idea where to take her. "I'm sorry. I want to help you but—"

Reecah's Gift

"Go, before it's too late. It won't take them long to realize the doorman is missing."

Bursting through the panel in the wall, Reecah was met by two men clad in chainmail and leather armour. She held the panel wide. "Quickly, the baron needs you."

Swords leapt into the men's hands as they scrambled down the hallway.

Closing the panel, Reecah started through the crowd, aware of the eyes on her. Suddenly conscious of how little she wore, she remembered her cloak. She grabbed the arm of the nearest servant, the girl's arms laden with a large tray bearing drinks. "Where can I find my cloak?"

The girl fought to keep from spilling the tray, glaring at Reecah as if she were mad. Her eyes flicked to a doorway beside the steps at the front of the ballroom. "In the cloakroom?"

"Take me to it!" Reecah ordered and yanked on her arm.

"Hey!" The tray tumbled from the servant's upturned palm.

Guests jumped back to avoid the fluted glassware shattering on the ground.

The servant pulled free of Reecah's grasp. "Look what you've done!"

Reecah paused but for a moment. She didn't need the girl. Conscious of every eye in the ballroom following her across the floor in a ripped skirt, a bloody dagger in hand, and blood smeared on her knees and bare feet—she mused at what a sight she must be.

She spotted her cloak as soon as she entered the long cloakroom. Checking its pockets, she was relieved to feel the journal, the Dragon's Eye, and the key to her room at the *Naughty Saucer*. Slipping into her cloak, she started to lace it up but a commotion from the ballroom forced her attention to the doorway.

Reecah's Gift

The panel on the back wall stood open. The minstrels stopped playing as an angry shout reached her above the noise of the crowd. "There she is! Stop her!"

Reecah started toward the exit.

A taller gentleman clad in royal finery made an attempt to intercept her.

She brandished her bloody dagger. "Uh, uh."

The man stepped back.

Taking the front entrance stairs in a single bound, she pushed through the bodies milling about the open double doors and burst onto the rain-soaked street to the surprise of the guardsmen stationed there.

The carriage she had arrived in was nowhere in sight.

Not heeding a guard's plea to stop, she sprinted down the steep cobblestoned hill, thankful for the revealing rip in the back of her skirt. Her cloak billowed wildly behind her.

Whistles and bells sounded the alarm but by the time she rounded the corner at the bottom of the steep hill she had outpaced the guards in their cumbersome armour. If only she could get into the *Naughty Saucer*, grab her stuff and be gone before they realized who she worked for.

Booted footsteps clattered down the hill and paused at the intersection—a familiar voice sounding from the opposite direction.

"This way! This way!"

Reecah stumbled as she looked over her shoulder, barely able to see anyone through the darkness and rain—a great smile lifting her cheeks. Where Raver perched, was a mystery.

"I saw her go this way!" one of the guards declared pointing in Reecah's direction but he clearly doubted himself. "I think."

"This way! This way!" Raver called out from somewhere on the far side of the intersection.

"Split up!" another man declared.

Reecah's Gift

Reecah picked up her pace. She ran through the deserted marketplace and past the large Thunderhead Shipwright building. The sound of pursuit drifted further behind, but more whistles and bells were sounding throughout the city. It wouldn't be long before everyone in Thunderhead was looking for her.

Reaching the *Naughty Saucer*, a different doorman made to stop her, but one look at her dishevelled outfit exposed beneath her sodden cloak stopped him. She cast him a dangerous look, not missing the fact that his gaze lingered on the dagger clutched firmly in her hand. Before he said anything, she growled, "I live here."

Equally wet, the doorman opened the door and jumped out of her way. "Ma'am."

Ma'am? Reecah fumed, striding down the hallway. She hated being called a lady, and she most certainly wasn't a ma'am.

Her appearance in the bawdy common room caused the patrons to become strangely quiet. Feeling their curious glances following her, she stopped at the base of the stairs and faced the room. Still under the effects of her raging adrenaline, she ripped open her cloak and glared at the stunned faces. Waggling her dagger at them, she shouted, "You want a piece of this?"

No one moved.

Taking two steps at a time, she fished the key from her pocket and let herself into the room. It wasn't until she stopped at the end of the bed that relief washed over her. Her belongings remained untouched.

Lightning flashed through the bay window drawing her attention to the reflection of a bedraggled, scared, young woman gazing back—wet hair flat against her head.

Another flash of lightning startled her, the sudden light illuminating Raver on the windowsill.

Reecah's Gift

A brief smile eased her panic. Opening the window, the dripping raven stared at her; rain driven on the wind lashing through the opening.

"Get in here!" She ushered him into the room.

He flapped twice, spraying her with water, and landed on the bed.

"Ugh! You dirty thing!" Reecah wiped her face with her hands, grateful he was safe.

Taking a moment to collect her thoughts, she envisioned grasping Tarrek by the neck with both hands and throttling the impertinent fishmonger. It was his fault she had gone through this.

Removing the sheath from the small of her back, she slid the dagger home and tossed it on the bed, a faint smile curving the corner of her mouth. Wait until they found out who had murdered the baron.

The baron! Her immediate danger slammed into her. It wouldn't be long before the baron's men and the Watch traced her to the *Naughty Saucer.*

Grasping the ends of the thong securing the bodice, she tugged, grunting her frustration, remembering it had knotted. Shrugging free of her dripping cloak, she retrieved her dagger and sliced through the thong—something she should have done in the first place. She slipped from her skirt and stopped to gape at the size of the rip.

It felt good to be free of the restrictive clothing—her bare skin riddled with goosebumps. She grabbed a towel the old woman had left on the bed and hurriedly dried herself before donning the welcome comfort of her own clothes.

Wasting no time, she buckled her leather cummerbund sword belt around her abdomen. Fitting her vambraces on her forearms, she strung her bow and shrugged it over her shoulder along with her quiver, and snatched up her quarterstaff. She couldn't help thinking that her speed would be compromised burdened with her gear, but there was no way she was leaving it behind. She considered her old boots. She could run faster in bare feet, but it would be foolish to leave them behind. She required their protection once she was free of the city.

If she had time, she planned on finding Tarrek and taking her sword back—by force if necessary. The boy deserved to pay for what he had put her through. As far as she was concerned, they were even.

"Come on, little chum." She tried to grab Raver but he skittered to the far side of the bed. Rolling her eyes, she walked around the large piece of furniture but when she got there, Raver waddled away from her.

"Really?" She glared at the bird who watched her with beady, black eyes—blinking twice.

She opened the bay window, careful not to get wet. "Raver, to me. We have to go. Meet me in the street."

The obstinate bird tilted his head but didn't move.

Groaning, Reecah ran around the bed, flapping her arms. "Come on. Out. Shoo."

Raver scurried across the thick bedding toward the window.

Reecah dove headfirst at him, prompting him into the air. He landed on the windowsill and stared at her.

"Go on, you crazy bird. We gotta go."

Raver cawed at her, took two steps and disappeared into the storm.

Reecah stared at the window sill, shaking her head. At least he was out.

Tying the flap of her rucksack shut, she threw it over her other shoulder and left the room, not bothering to close the door.

Descending the stairs between the upper floors, it dawned on her that the music in the common room was suspiciously absent. She reached the head of the stairway leading to the

Reecah's Gift

main floor; immediately aware of loud voices. Voices that didn't speak to the pleasures of the flesh. Angered tones—accompanied by the chinking of chainmail and creaking of leather armour.

Men clad in the baron's colours scoured the common room looking for her.

Reecah's Gift

Better off Dead

Lying on a pallet on the edge of death seemed a better fate to Junior than being under the scrutiny of that damned blue-eyed stare of his father. The pain of his broken nose paled in comparison to the burning ache beside his right shoulder blade. According to the Father Cloth's wife, if the arrow had taken him anywhere other than where it did, he would never have survived the tortuous trip out of Dragonfang Pass.

As it was, the stooped woman couldn't assure him that full mobility would ever return to his sword arm. Only time could speak to that. Knowing his father, Jonas Junior didn't think he had much time left to him. Not if Jonas Senior had anything to say about it.

Junior lay under a thin blanket—his lower back aching as much as the injury suffered at the Dragon Temple. Many good men had died that day, but the king's objective had been carried out. Led by High King J'kaar's second son, Prince J'kwaad, the campaign to eradicate the Draakclaw Colony had gone off better than the dark heir had anticipated.

Junior might have welcomed that information if not for the fact that the prince gave most of the credit to Jaxon Waverunner—Junior's younger brother.

He winced. Of all the people he would like to see honoured by the royal house of the Great Kingdom, his brother would be the last one he would choose. There was no denying he harboured more than a little resentment, and certainly a spark of jealousy, toward his brother. His only consolation was

Reecah's Gift

hearing the news that Reecah Draakvriend had broken Jaxon's nose, and by doing so, had escaped. He wished he could have seen the look on his brother's face when she smashed it.

A warm feeling washed over him. Reecah Draakvriend. The hill witch. If he never rose from this pallet, he would still be thankful for that twilit evening at the base of the waterfall. The image of her pale skin contrasting with the backdrop of the rough stone wall rising behind the cascade had etched itself forever in his mind. If only they had been able to meet under different circumstances.

Being a Waverunner had doomed any chance of him entertaining a meaningful relationship with the enchanting girl. His family had done the Draakvriend's so much harm he was ashamed to call himself a Waverunner.

Her condemnation of him at the Dragon Temple couldn't have hurt more if she had driven her sword through his heart. The horrific scene played out in his mind as if it happened in the room before him.

He had caught up to his brother and the prince's elite guard outside of the Dragon Temple. The black knights were engaged in what first appeared as a futile battle against an enraged dragon of immense size, but it soon became apparent that the dark heir was an adept practitioner of the arcane arts.

Junior had spotted Reecah in the throat of the marble dragon and foolishly tried to warn her—drawing the attention of the prince. As soon as the black dragon had succumbed to the horrific punishment inflicted on it, the prince's men turned their attention on him. Before he had a chance to run, three men pummeled him into unconsciousness. He had no idea how long he had lain beneath the stone archway, but the chinking of chainmail had awakened him.

He had spotted Reecah weeping beside the dragon's lifeless head. He wanted to go to her but a squad of king's men had entered the outer courtyard and marched toward him.

Reecah's Gift

Flooding through the ivy-covered wall, they were about to stumble upon Reecah. In a panic, he entertained fighting them, but there had been too many.

Stepping from the shadows of the archway, he tried to warn her of her peril. Her subsequent reaction haunted his thoughts ever since. The image of the beautiful woman casting hateful eyes his way crushed him. There hadn't been time to explain.

Her words gutted him as she ran at him with her sword in hand. *"You traitorous bastard! Look what you've done! You've stolen the beauty from the world!"*

Her reaction had taken the beauty from *his* world.

Lying on the pallet, Junior didn't think he'd ever smile again. His father wanted to disown him, his brother hated him, and the rest of his family wondered what was wrong with him. How come he couldn't be like Jonas and Jaxon? He half-heartedly wished they'd left him in the pass to die. If only he could lay his eyes on Reecah one more time.

Propping himself on his elbows, he searched the room. A dozen makeshift pallets had been set up to house those seriously injured at Dragon Home. Besides himself, only three pallets contained a warm body. Over the last several days, four men had received their last rites. Late last night, four of the king's men were assisted from the room and hadn't returned.

A deep voice resonated from somewhere outside of the Fishmonger Bay temple.

Junior cringed. His father. The last time Jonas had checked in, Junior had pretended to be out of it—wanting nothing to do with the man. He sighed. Listening to the old woman's glowing report of his return to health, there would be no putting him off this time.

The door banged open, marking Jonas' entrance. True to form, the hulk of a grizzled man sauntered to where he lay—his father's great, blonde-bearded face creased in a perpetual scowl.

Reecah's Gift

The hunchbacked woman shuffled in behind him and tended a bed on the opposite side of the room.

Junior returned his scowl. What more could the brute do to him?

"Ach. There you are. Lazing about like a pampered maiden." Jonas surveyed him, not a hint of relief or happiness in his blue eyes. "Shoulda left ya up the pass to fend for yourself to see if you possess the fortitude befitting a Waverunner."

Though he wasn't concerned about what his father would do in the presence of the Father Cloth's wife, Junior knew better than to speak his mind.

"With your brother gone, I'm needing you out of here. There's much work left undone with half me crew dead thanks to those nasty beasts."

"Gone? What happened to him?" He almost dared to hope.

"Bah! That damned prince took a shine to him. Said he could use a good man like Jaxon." Jonas puffed out his chest. "Seems the royal heir can't do without a Waverunner in his service."

Junior frowned, trying to understand what that implied.

Jonas must have noted his consternation. "Prince J'kwaad asked for Jaxon's assistance with his dragon campaign. They sailed off at sunrise. Imagine that. Jaxon on his way to Draakhall to meet the high king. Finally, a son to do his family proud."

Junior winced.

"It's a shame Janor wasn't around to keep the business viable."

Junior couldn't keep the hurt from his eyes. Janor was his younger brother who had been carried away by a dragon years ago.

"I hope you've moved beyond your tough patch. Perhaps that arrow in the back was the best thing to happen to you. Maybe now you see the folly of your ways. That hill witch is nothing but trouble. Had I known she'd be the nettlesome little whore she turned out to be, I'd have taken care of her long ago. Mark my words, she'll rue the day she crossed me. Imagine, escaping on the back of a dragon!"

That was the best news Junior had heard. It confirmed what he had overheard the prince's men saying. Reecah had jumped on a dragonling's shoulders and disappeared into the night sky. He couldn't fathom how she had pulled it off.

Jonas grabbed Junior's broken nose and squeezed.

"Ow!" Junior pulled his head away.

"Your face looks better like that. Gives you a bit of character. Who knows? There may be hope for you yet."

Junior glared, not daring to speak what was on his mind.

Jonas hocked and spat on the floorboards.

The old woman looked up, shaking her head, but didn't say anything.

"I'll let you be to recover but I expect you back in the boats afore long, else I'll be forced to replace you with someone worth their salt." Jonas turned and stomped away.

Junior watched him go, loathing every moment his father's back remained visible.

His nose felt like it was on fire, he couldn't move his right shoulder without screaming, and his lower back pained him so much he didn't think he'd ever walk straight again.

Tears welled in his eyes. He'd never be the man his father wanted him to be. With the prospect of returning to the merciless rule of his father, he truly felt he'd be better off dead.

Reecah's Gift

Scoundrels

Trapped! Reecah backed away from the head of the stairs and ducked low, edging her way along the railing overlooking the common room.

Half a dozen armed men milled about the main floor, speaking with patrons who were hastily covering themselves with whatever was close at hand.

A thin woman clutched a tunic to her chest and pointed up the stairs. "She went that way! She threatened to fight us all!"

Heavy footfalls pounded the steps, shaking the floor beneath Reecah's feet. She dropped to her hands and knees and scooted to the farthest end of the landing, her eyes rivetted upon the opening at the top of the stairs.

A man in livery matching the baron's guards rushed onto the landing followed by another and then another, each one running toward a room door. Three more charged past and started up the next set of stairs, but stopped as the first man caught sight of Reecah. "There she is!"

Reecah sprang to her feet, grabbed the top of the rail and threw herself feet first over the barrier, pushing off the railing to clear the barstools below and aiming for a plush couch. The bottom of her bow caught on the railing before lifting off her back and sliding over—the subtle resistance throwing her trajectory off.

The couch's occupants cried out in alarm and threw themselves off its front.

Reecah's Gift

Reecah landed heavily behind the couch and dropped into a side roll—the act complicated by her quarterstaff and sword as she attempted to hang onto her bow.

Boots thundered down the staircase. "Stop her!"

She rose to her feet, not bothering to inspect her pained ankle. She didn't have time. Her intense gaze took in everyone at once, her wild look deterring anyone who might have thought of intercepting a bizarre woman bristling with weapons—one crazy enough to leap from the second story landing.

Sprinting down the hallway to the exit, Reecah extended her quarterstaff to meet the doorman blocking the inside of the door. "Out of the way!"

She wasn't sure who the doorman thought he was trying to prevent from leaving, but as she barreled headlong at him, shock registered on his face.

He threw himself flat against the wall, his hands shaking in the air to fend off Reecah's quarterstaff.

Ignoring the man, she lowered her staff and pushed through the heavy door, her attention on the first armed man entering the far end of the hallway. Hastily laying her quarterstaff in the street, she shrugged her bow free, notched an arrow and let it fly—purposely missing.

The armoured man stopped and tried to retreat but was impeded by another guard rounding the corner. "Get down!"

Both men dropped to the floor.

Reecah slammed the door and squinted through the relentless downpour, wondering which way to go. Along the oceanside, back the way she had entered Thunderhead, made the most sense. If she made it to the slums, she might be able to lose herself north of the city.

Whistling for Raver's benefit, she retrieved her quarterstaff; struggling momentarily to secure it to the side of her quiver. It wasn't until her boots splashed off the end of the uneven

Reecah's Gift

cobblestones and onto the muddy road beyond before the first sound of pursuit clattered onto the street behind her.

Several people draped in heavy cloaks stood in the street ahead, scanning the flickering lights of Thunderhead's ritzier district atop the hill, their demeanour one of curiosity as to what had set off the alarms.

Reecah skirted to the far side of the street to avoid them, but as she drew closer, the tallest man drew her attention. Tarrek's tight curls protruded beneath a floppy brimmed, leather cap.

Tarrek noticed her at the same time. Stepping free of the others he stared. "GG?"

Reecah slowed to a walk, limping and breathing hard. Her intense gaze took in the scoundrels responsible for her recent misfortunes. She didn't trust herself to answer Tarrek—knowing her bitter words were better left unspoken.

"Where do you think you're going?" He peered closer. "Where's your outfit?"

Axe and two male youths came up behind him.

Reecah shrugged free of her bow and nocked an arrow, pointing it at a large, muddy puddle between them. "I want my sword back."

"Did the viscount pay you?"

"No. He disappeared and left me with the baron."

Axe exchanged looks with the two young men Reecah remembered from earlier in the day. Each of them produced long blades from the folds of their cloaks.

Tarrek's sword hand rested on the sword hilt at his waist while his other hand doffed his cap and wiped at the water on his brow. Skirting around the edge of the puddle, his hair appeared unaffected by the rain. "*Or*, he paid you and now you are trying to flee the city with his money."

Reecah raised the bow, the arrowhead aimed at his chest. Drawing back on the string, her eyes narrowed.

Reecah's Gift

Tarrek held his hands up, his wet cap dangling between them. "Whoa, GG. What're you doing? There's four of us. By the time you get one arrow off the rest of us will cut you to shreds. Look at you. You can barely walk." He gazed at the dark warehouse behind him. "Let's get out of the rain and discuss this."

Booted feet charged down the uneven cobbles. A voice rang out, "There she is! Hey! You there! Hold her!"

The look of surprise on Tarrek's face transformed into one of comprehension, his gaze taking in the city as a whole. "What did you do?"

Ignoring him, Reecah said with menace in her voice, "My sword. Now."

Tarrek took one more step.

Reecah drew the bowstring taut, and let fly. The arrow snatched the leather cap from his fingers.

Before anyone had a chance to react, she had a second arrow nocked. "The next one finds your heart."

Her angered response sounded distant to her, as if someone else spoke.

Axe and his henchmen lifted their hands in mock surrender, their concentration flicking between Reecah and the armed men running toward them.

"Now!" Reecah ordered, pulling the bowstring tighter.

"Okay, okay." Tarrek fumbled with the buckle.

Reecah fumed. Tarrek wasn't moving fast enough. The armed men were closing on her. Her bowstring creaked as it stretched to full pull—the action prompting Tarrek into action. The belt slid through the buckle.

She eased off on the bow and lowered her aim. "Toss it to me."

Tarrek's eyes flicked to the approaching men.

"Now!" She pulled the bowstring taut again.

Tarrek threw the sword at her.

70

Reecah's Gift

Reecah let go of the bow with one hand and caught the scabbard in her arms, the arrow falling to the mud.

The Watch splashed through the mire, weapons in hand—one warehouse away. "Seize her!"

Axe and the two silent youths rushed around the far side of the puddle while Tarrek charged at her from the opposite end.

Snatching the arrow from the muck, Reecah sprung halfway across the puddle, landing with a splash and sprinted toward the alley between the warehouses.

Axe grabbed at her, but pulled up short, barely avoiding the arrow tip she jabbed at him.

Slipping down the dark alley, trying hard to keep all of her gear in order, she paused briefly at the far end, her boots sinking into soft sand. A campfire crackled and sputtered in the downpour on the beach to her right. Several miserable faces glanced up—none of them friendly.

"Grab her!" Axe's voice called out.

The unhappy people rose to their feet, their hands going to their waists and withdrawing blades of varying lengths.

Reecah swallowed. She had no choice. She had to run back toward the *Naughty Saucer*.

Jumping crates and skirting around beached skiffs in various states of disrepair, Reecah ran up the thin strip of sand, doing her best to avoid the waves lapping the shoreline.

Passing the next alleyway, a shout went up. Two guardsmen burst from the dark lane but she was already beyond them. As hard as the sand was for her to run in, it quickly became apparent that it was even tougher for the heavily armoured men chasing her.

She was forced to jump up onto and over wooden walkways extending from the back of the warehouses; the wooden spans bridging the gap between the buildings and ramshackle jetties undulating in the stormy surf. Her thigh muscles screamed at her as she vaulted the countless walkways. She needed to get back to the street.

Turning into the next alley, she stopped to catch her breath, taking time to secure the second sword belt around her waist, before looking back the way she had come. Though her pursuers could be heard clomping over the walkways, nobody was visible in the persistent drizzle.

Scampering up the alley, she paused at its far end. Uneven cobblestones greeted her and the occasional lantern tree flickered uselessly in the gloom.

Taking a deep breath, she stepped onto the street, hugging the warehouse facades as best as she could while dodging piles of debris stacked in front of the buildings.

The cobblestone pavers levelled out as the *Naughty Saucer* came into view. She stopped. A throng of men and women were gathered outside the brothel, listening to the tale of the doorman.

Backtracking to the last alleyway she had passed, Reecah made her way to the shoreline. A quick glance told her those following were getting closer. Not caring whether they spotted her or not, she sprinted up over the rock-littered sand, distancing herself from those intent on capturing her. At one point, she heard Raver call out but couldn't locate him.

The sand gave way to jumbled rock as she approached the spot where the fjord met the sea—the footings of the *Naughty Saucer* mired amongst the beginning of the break wall jutting into the fjord. Scrambling over the rocks, some bigger than her small cabin back home, she made her way up the fjord—thankful to reach the wooden platforms extending over the shoreline from the rear of the more affluent warehouses and shipyards.

The clanking of metal on rock reached her from the break wall. The pursuit was relentless.

Reecah's Gift

She picked up her pace but a commotion ahead made her crouch behind a tangle of smelly fishnets piled atop broken crates and open barrels. Shivering in the rain, Reecah crept around the debris until she spotted three bearded men in chainmail surrounding a muscular, redheaded woman—the biggest man pinning the woman against a wall.

Reecah recalled the gruff redhead from yesterday. A sailor had called her Cahira. The way Cahira had been with Reecah, it didn't surprise her that the rude woman had run afoul of the Watch.

Careful not to draw the men's attention, Reecah soft-stepped through the shadows and ducked into the alley separating her from the building they held the dockhand against. Relieved not to be noticed, Reecah paused to catch her breath. It wouldn't be long before those chasing her alerted everyone along the dockside of her whereabouts. She needed a place to hide.

Adjusting the sword belt she had gotten back from Tarrek, she couldn't help overhearing Cahira.

"Unhand me, you fool, or I'll gut you. You got the wrong person!"

The wet smack of a loud slap made Reecah cringe.

"I ought to run you through right here," a deep voice growled. "Threaten me again and I'll forget you're a lady."

"Pfft," another voice chimed in. "You call that a lady. I'd as soon bed your wife as this seadog."

A third voice started to laugh but the original speaker interrupted.

Reecah dared to peek around the corner.

"Watch your mouth, or I'll run you through next," the man pinning Cahira snarled.

Cahira, her stomach bared beneath her tied off tunic, wriggled in the man's grasp until he pulled her away from the wall and slammed her back into it, bouncing her head off the wood. "Were you, or were you not, with the baron tonight?"

73

Reecah's Gift

Instead of answering, Cahira spat in the man's face and received a punch in the stomach for her troubles.

"Come on, she don't match the description of the one we're after," the smallest man said. "For all we know, they've already caught her."

"She's scantily dressed," the man pinning Cahira replied as if that were justification to beat her.

"She's a dock rat. They never wear much."

Reecah's eyes widened. Cahira hadn't done anything wrong. She was getting worked over because the guardsmen were searching for her.

The man holding Cahira pulled a dagger from his belt and held it under her chin. "Ya, well, she's gonna answer for spitting in me face." He nodded his large head, his crazed eyes locking on Cahira's. "They'll be fishing what's left of you off the rocks come morning."

Reecah loaded her bow and stepped free of the alley. "I'm the one you're looking for."

All heads turned—all except Cahira's. The redhead took the opportunity to smash her forehead into the side of her captor's face.

In pain, the man released her in time to receive a hard-swung knee to the groin that doubled him over.

The smallest man unsheathed a short sword but his blade clattered off the wooden decking as Reecah's arrow took him above the heart. He collapsed with a groan.

The largest man fell on top of him, bleeding profusely from a large gash in his neck.

Reecah's eyes met Cahira's wild stare—a curved, filleting knife in the redhead's grasp. Together they turned their attention on the last guard.

The man raised empty hands in the air.

Reecah's Gift

Before Reecah had another arrow nocked, Cahira attacked, stabbing and kicking the guard until he tumbled lifeless into the water.

Reecah brought her arrow to bear on Cahira's heaving chest, afraid to become the enraged woman's next target.

Cahira pointed her knife. "You! You're the one they're after?"

Reecah didn't know what to say. She didn't want to admit it to a stranger but in her heart, she couldn't deny the accusation. Even so, she didn't feel guilty—not for the way she had dealt with the baron. The lecherous boor deserved everything he had received.

She did, however, feel responsible for Cahira's torment. Judging by the bruise below her ribs and the blood smear on the side of her face, the men had roughed Cahira up pretty good before she had intervened.

Cahira kicked the large man in the ribs. "Look at the mess I'm in! I had nothing to do with whatever you did to the baron, but I'm in for it now. These are his personal guards."

Reecah lowered her bow. "I'm sorry. The baron attacked me. He wanted me to...to..." She couldn't say it.

Looking around with dread, she knew if she remained there much longer, she would be caught. "Anyway, I gotta go before they catch me."

Cahira's intense stare bore into her. Still waggling the knife with the nasty curve, she said with a gruff voice, "Come with me."

Reecah frowned, peering down the alley and searching the way she had come. If she continued running into Thunderhead, it would only be a matter of time before she was surrounded. She was running out of options.

"Look, bitch, if you want to live, I'm your only hope."

Reecah swallowed at the strange offer of assistance.

Reecah's Gift

Cahira scrunched up her face, not too concerned about the blood washing off her face in the rain. "Whatever. Let them catch you."

Cahira wrapped her hands around the larger man's ankles and dragged him off the smaller guard—the muscles in her arms bulging.

Reecah was impressed how easily Cahira manhandled the large guard—rolling him to the edge of the dock and pushing him over the edge. His waist and legs splashed in the water, but his head and shoulders fell short—smacking off the sharp rock along the shore.

Reecah winced, hoping he was already dead. His lower body pulled his upper torso into the water—quickly sinking out of sight.

The smaller man lay on his back; lifeless eyes open to the rain. Cahira dragged him to the edge and prepared to drop him after his mates.

"Wait!" Reecah ran over. "My arrow."

Cahira glanced at her. Without a word, the redhead put a boot on the man's chest and tugged at the arrow—its head catching in the tear it had made in the guard's chainmail. Wiggling it free, she inspected it. "Hmph," was all she said as she handed it, fletches first, to Reecah—not caring that she handled the bloody end.

Reecah stopped to wipe the arrow on the man's breeches, straightening up as Cahira drove a boot into his groin and urged him over the edge. Before he hit the water, Cahira walked away.

Reecah replaced the arrow in her quiver and searched through the darkness for somewhere to flee. She had never felt as alone as she did at that moment, except perhaps that night sitting against the village temple, witnessing *Grimelda's Clutch* burn.

Reecah's Gift

Should the baron's guard or the city Watch catch her, she would be lucky if they killed her on the spot. If the baron survived, she dreaded the punishment he would exact on her. She'd be better off dead. She gritted her teeth. All because of Tarrek and his scoundrels.

She thought of Lurker and the other dragons. They faced a more serious life and death struggle. One of extinction. If her great-aunt was to be believed, the dragons' fate was in her hands. She shook her head. She didn't have time to die.

Cahira's broad shoulders swaggered, disappearing into the gloomy night.

Jumping into a run, Reecah whistled for Raver and called out in a harsh whisper, "Cahira. Wait."

It was hard to believe that her life lay in the hands of the gruff, redheaded woman. The same woman who had only yesterday threatened to kill Reecah if they ever crossed paths again.

Reecah's Gift

Serpent's Slip

J'kaar's black galleon rode the waves like a dolphin, her golden kraken bowsprit barely dipping in the calm waters off the Great Kingdom's western coast.

Those aboard the *Serpent's Slip,* the ones who weren't on duty, lined the port rail, waving as the high king's flagship, *Reef Raider,* sailed past.

Reecah fretted she had missed the king by a day. His ship sailed south while she sailed north. She briefly thought about jumping into the ocean and swimming to shore. Had she been a strong swimmer, she reckoned she would have. As it was, she'd have to endure the voyage north and wait for the king's return. Not wanting to attract undue attention, she waved along with everyone else, trying to figure out why the colours of the king's ship bothered her.

According to the sun's position, hidden behind a layer of breaking cloud cover, it was shortly before midday. Looking to the rigging, she spied Raver perched high on the moonsail yard arm—the topmost, square sail on the central mast.

After her encounter last night with Cahira, the dockhand had led her to the *Serpent's Slip* and snuck her on board—hiding Reecah in her cabin until dawn.

Daybreak had come much too quickly for Reecah's liking. It had felt as if she had just fallen asleep, cramped and shivering on the floor beside Cahira's cot, when the redhead's gruff voice startled her awake.

Reecah's Gift

Together, they had paid a visit to Captain Dreyger K'tric's cabin before he came on deck to supervise casting off. Captain Dreyger was the same rotund man on the ship's railing Reecah remembered from the day before. Though Reecah hadn't seen many real ship captains in her life—Fishmonger Bay didn't have the capacity to properly accommodate a large boat—Dreyger's slovenly appearance didn't strike her as what a true captain would look like. He didn't have the appearance of a leader. Jonas Waverunner wasn't the best kept man either, but his mean demeanour had more than made up for his lack of professionalism.

Captain Dreyger, at first glance, with unkempt wisps of black hair poorly attempting to cover the wide expanse of baldness upon his spherical head, gave Reecah the impression of a bumbling alcoholic. In a roundabout way, he reminded her of the baron—his purple-veined nose and ample girth had given Reecah the shivers as a result, but that was thankfully where the comparison ended.

His face had turned a darker shade of red when Cahira first introduced Reecah. He had jumped to his feet and vehemently demanded she leave his ship at once, spitting and sputtering his displeasure at housing a fugitive from Thunderhead. The last thing he needed was to be found out offering refuge to someone wanted by the baron himself.

Reecah explained why she had been forced to do the things she had, but Dreyger would have none of it until Cahira explained how Reecah had stepped in on her behalf to save her from the baron's men.

Captain Dreyger's dour expression had gone through a remarkable transition; from one of utter contempt to one of gratitude.

Flabbergasted, Reecah was not only welcome aboard the *Serpent's Slip*, but the captain had treated her as an honoured guest.

Reecah's Gift

Sighing at how things had turned out, Reecah returned her attention to the king's galleon. The sleek ship cut through the ocean swells as if they weren't there, leaving a widening wake as it sailed toward the southern horizon.

Reecah stepped away from the rail, the roll of the *Serpent's Slip* causing her to support herself with a wide stance, riding out the pitched deck until the brig righted itself in the next trough.

The deckhands around her carried on as if they walked on dry land, going about their business now that the commotion of the king's ship had passed.

"Fishmonger Bay, ho!" A sailor stationed in the foremast crow's nest announced.

Reecah hurried to the far side of the ship—bracing herself against the polished rail. Sure enough, the rickety, old jetty protruding from the front of the Waverunner warehouse was visible off the starboard bow. No one on the *Serpent's Slip* seemed to care.

Watching the familiar shoreline pass by, she experienced a twinge of homesickness—the slopes behind the village a tapestry of spectacular colour in the autumn sunshine. It wouldn't be long before the lower forest dropped its leaves.

She stared hard at the steep bluff on the northern edge of the village, trying to see her cabin but couldn't. Had they sailed a fortnight later, it would have been visible beyond the bare branches.

Goosebumps washed across her cheeks—partially due to the cool wind generated by the *Serpent's Slip's* passing, but more to the fact that up until a few weeks ago, Reecah's entire existence had taken place on the slopes drifting by.

The dark rock promontory jutting high above the sea passed directly before her. The Summoning Stone. Her childhood haunt. A place she had loved visiting with Poppa.

Reecah's Gift

Standing by herself, alone amongst a ship full of strangers, Reecah fought to keep her tears hidden. Fishmonger Bay instilled her with so many bad memories. She wiped her eyes with the back of her hand, hoping nobody noticed.

There were good memories too, but the days she had spent with Poppa had blurred into nothing more than a fleeting happiness. A day on a hillside, and the day he had given her the crimson gemstone that had fused itself into her diary were the only ones she could recall anymore.

She grunted. Some gift the diary had turned out to be. The pages wouldn't accept ink or lead—the magic in the parchment somehow attuned to the dragons themselves. It was little use to her now that her dragon friends had accepted her into their circle of trust.

Nevertheless, her distant gaze lingered on the horizon where she had last seen the Summoning Stone, long after it disappeared from view. How many times had she secretly ventured up there, afraid Grammy would find out? She stifled an ironic laugh. According to Grammy on her death bed, the old woman had known all along. Reecah shook her head. To this day she had no idea where the bizarre rock formation had gotten its name.

"Somethin' special about that pig's wallow?"

Cahira's gruff voice snapped Reecah's mind back to the deck of the *Serpent's Slip* as it plied through the waves on a northeast tack around the rugged shores of the duchy of Svelte.

Cahira sat with her back against a large, net covered crate along the rail, chewing on a piece of wood.

Reecah knew at once that Cahira had spotted her poor attempt at masking her tears. She shrugged and looked away. "Not really."

Out of the corner of her eye, Reecah watched the muscular woman get to her feet and walk toward her. She stiffened. As much as she was grateful for Cahira securing her passage on a

Reecah's Gift

ship bound for the port city of Sea Keep—the capital of the Great Kingdom—she wasn't in the mood for her brooding company.

Cahira settled against the rail, her coarse, red hair blowing against Reecah's cheek. "What's with the tears. Ye be missing Thunderhead?"

Cahira's words startled her. She flashed a shocked look at the tough woman.

Cahira gave her a sarcastic smirk.

"Ah. Ha-ha. Uh, no. If I never go back there it'll be too soon, thanks."

"Then what? Come on, GG. Ya owe me. It's the least ya can do seein' I saved yer hide."

The woman's sudden interest unsettled Reecah. "Really, it's nothing. Just been a long couple of days."

She could tell by how Cahira looked at her that she didn't believe her, but thankfully Cahira let it be.

They stood shoulder to shoulder, lost in their own thoughts as the mountainous coastline passed by—occasionally feeling the mist whenever the bow dug deep into a wave.

Reecah realized she was grateful for the woman's quiet company. Cahira's presence made her feel welcome even though she sensed the crew weren't sold on her being onboard. Not taking her eyes from the coastline, she muttered, "I'm thinking it was *me* who saved your sorry hide first."

Reecah sensed rather than saw Cahira turn a thoughtful look her way. She waited, expecting a scathing retort, but one wasn't forthcoming. She met Cahira's gaze.

"Aye." Cahira nodded, a slight smile turning up her thin lips. "But had ye not gone and skewered the baron, I'm thinking yer intervention wouldn't have been required."

Reecah spit out a nervous laugh.

"Ye got pluck, I'll give ya that."

Reecah's Gift

Reecah gave Cahira a tight-lipped smile and looked back at the passing waves. What an odd word—pluck. Grammy had once said the same thing, long ago; that she had her mother's pluck. Come to think on it, so had Grimclaw.

"So, what do you think of the prince?" Cahira asked.

"The prince?"

"Aye, he'll be on that black galleon we passed a while back."

"Ah. With the king."

Cahira turned her whole body to face Reecah, leaning a casual elbow on the rail and staring at her with a bewildered look.

Reecah swallowed. "What? That was the king's ship, wasn't it?"

"You're serious?"

Reecah nodded, confused.

"Ye just get into the city yesterday, or what?"

Reecah nodded again.

"Really? Ye mean ya never knew the prince sailed down here weeks ago with an army of dragon slayers? It's all anyone's been on about forever. The king ain't to be dirtying his hands with the plight of the dragons. That's what 'is army's for."

Revelation washed through Reecah. If that were true, there was a good chance she would see the king soon after all. To answer Cahira's question, she shrugged. "I've been busy."

Cahira glared at her like she expected a better response than that. "With...?"

Cahira expected an answer she wasn't about to give. She didn't dare tell the redhead she had actively fought the king's men. If the prince was sailing to Thunderhead, the last thing she needed was for him to get wind of her involvement with the baron's misfortune. Thinking further on it, the king's men already knew about her. She'd fought them...

Her eyes grew wide. Glaring at Cahira, cold prickles tickled her skin. "You mean the prince was already here?"

Reecah's Gift

"Well, ya. Who else but the dark heir would be crazy enough to attack a colony of dragons? From what I hear, he and 'is Majesty's elite guard have put a proper end to the Fishmonger Bay colony. Prince J'kwaad is likely returning to Thunderhead to gather the rest of the royal fleet and pick up his sister and the royal vizier."

Reecah gripped the railing hard, the only way to keep her rubbery legs from failing her. She stared at Cahira, blinking several times and mouthed the words, "Vullis Opsigter."

Cahira nodded. "Aye. The steward of Draakhall. Ye know him?"

Reecah nodded, her mind reeling with the implications of the prince's role in Dragon Home's destruction. She wondered if she had seen him during the battle outside of the Dragon Temple.

Cahira grabbed her by the elbow. "Are ya okay? Ye ain't lookin' good." She forced Reecah to face the rail. "Ain't nothing to be ashamed of. Ye'll get yer sea legs in time. If ya gotta hurl, ye best be doing it over the rail. Us deckhands ain't to be taking kindly to swabbing vomit."

Reecah was happy to let Cahira think she suffered from seasickness. Anything to stop her questions.

Leaning over the rail and staring at the churning surf splashing off the side of the ship, she actually experienced a bit of queasiness. Thinking about Cahira's explanation, she recalled the black galleons anchored in Thunderhead.

"I'll give ye a hand to me berth if'n yer needing to have a wee lie down."

Reecah shook her head. "I'll be fine. Like you said, I need time to get my sea legs."

"Well, I'll be leaving ya to it then. I gots me duties to perform. If ya need me, I'll be in the foresail riggin' for the next while. The cap'n expects all available hands to be on the lookout across the northern coast of the duchy of Svelte." Cahira turned to go.

"Wait." Reecah grabbed her by the forearm.

Cahira regarded Reecah's hand, her eyes narrowing.

"Sorry." Reecah let go. "Sorry. I was just wondering…what does the prince look like?"

"J'kwaad? Ye claim to know the viscount but ye don't know what the prince looks like? You really *are* a strange one." Cahira said, studying Reecah. She appeared poised to say something else but didn't. Instead, she nodded with an approving look on her face. "How does the prince look? Pretty good, actually. Tall. Fit. Dark. Chiselled face and sporting a well-kept goatee."

Putting her hands on her hips and raising her eyebrows, Cahira warned, "Don't ye be getting' yer hopes up, GG. J'kwaad's station is out of reach to someone from…Where did you say you're from?"

"I didn't," Reecah said absently, searching her memory of all the people she remembered seeing at the Dragon Temple. Other than Grog, Junior and Jaxon, and the two men she had killed, only one man's face stood out. A sense of doom overcame her. "Does the prince have an angular nose?"

Cahira put a finger to her chin in thought. "Aye. Now that I think on it, he does at that. Even so, he is very handsome in me books. I wouldn't be throwing his boots out from under me bed if ya get me meaning." She strode away. Looking over her shoulder, she winked. "He's certainly magical, if that's what yer implying."

Reecah clutched the railing again. The wizard! Prince J'kwaad was the knight in the black armour with gold piping. She remembered their eyes meeting across the courtyard. If she wished to confront the king, she was going to have to do it before the prince's armada returned to Draakhall. She had a sinking feeling that bumping into the dark heir before she had a chance to explain herself to the high king would not go well for her.

Another bad feeling seeped into her thoughts. If the prince had left Dragon Home, did that mean *all* the dragons were dead? She tried to convince herself she was being paranoid, but couldn't help worrying that *all* dragons included Lurker, Swoop and Silence.

She spied Raver perched on the highest yardarm. Imitating a cardinal's chirrup, she called him to her—hoping not to draw attention to herself. It took a couple of whistles before she got his attention.

Raver ruffled his wings and dropped from the sky, catching his flight at the last moment to land on one of her leather vambraces—the wind ruffling his feathers. She glanced around, but nobody appeared to notice.

Reecah wasn't sure she could bear parting with the only living link to her past but she had to know if her dragon friends were okay. *'Damn it!'* she thought, angry with herself for allowing her emotions to get the better of her. Again. An audience with the king wasn't going to go well; she could see it now.

Raver tilted his head, his image blurred by tears. If she let him go, she might never see him again, but what choice did she have? She had to believe her precious side-kick had the ability to speak with dragons.

Being careful that nobody looked her way, she leaned in close. "I need you to find Lurker and the others. Let them know I'm travelling to the high king's castle. Tell them the wizard who attacked us outside the Dragon Temple is High King J'kaar's son. If the prince finds me, I'll be in trouble."

Raver blinked twice, tilting his head to the other side.

Wrapping her free hand around his side, she hugged him to her cheek. "Go now. Find Lurker."

Raver bobbed his head. "Find Lurker! Find Lurker!"

Reecah's Gift

She threw her arm into the air beyond the railing, casting him to the wind.

He cawed once and winged away south—his black body blending in with the dark relief of the Spine.

"Be safe, my friend," Reecah whispered to the wind. "Thank you for being my rock while the rest of the world abandoned me. I love you."

The *Serpent's Slip* dove into a trough and cut through the next wave. A plume of water cascaded high over the deck, soaking her face, disguising the tears that rolled freely down her cheeks.

By the time she cleared the spray from her eyes, Raver was gone.

Reecah was content to spend the day clutching the landward rail watching league upon countless league of inhabitable coastline pass by—snow-capped mountains dominated the eastern horizon. She wondered if all the mountains in the world were gathered in this one stretch of land—surely there couldn't be more elsewhere.

The damp spray sporadically reached her from the bow of the ship, soaking through her cloak and dampening her clothing. She shivered uncontrollably but refused to find a place to warm up—her distant stare hoping to catch a last glimpse of Raver returning with the dragons; an outrageous thought, she knew.

Conscious of keeping the pocket that held the journal dry, she thought about her intended audience with the king. She wasn't sure how to address the man. Did she curtsy, bow, or take a knee? Did she require clothing more suitable to a king's company? If so, what *type*? Being a simple girl from Fishmonger Bay left her sadly lacking worldly knowledge.

Reecah's Gift

Her dealings with Tarrek brought home a reality she hadn't considered. How would she pay for the clothes? For that matter, how would she pay for anything? If Thunderhead were any indicator, food and lodging wouldn't be handed to her. A sinking feeling gripped her. She grimaced at her naiveté. The more she thought about it, the more she wanted to throw her hands up in defeat.

How did she expect to save the dragons if she couldn't look after herself?

Peering around a pile of net covered crates, a wiry sailor with scraggly hair covering the top of a balding head, studied the new passenger with interest. There had been quite a commotion two nights ago when the ship cast off before the morning tide—leaving Thunderhead in an unusual hurry. It was rumoured that Cahira had been the cause of their flight, but watching the newcomer, he was certain he had discovered the real reason.

According to the ship's night watch, one of the baron's ships had given chase but *Serpent's Slip* shallow draft allowed her to outdistance the pursuit, sailing through the calmer waters of the coastal shallows. When dawn had broken over The Spine, the baron's ship was nowhere to be seen.

Stranger yet, it wasn't like Cappy to allow dames on board. *Especially* when their route took them into the Unknown Sea. There definitely must be something special about this girl.

He didn't think there was a man aboard who wouldn't love to have a tumble with her, but that wasn't justification to allow her presence to endanger their voyage. That's what ports were for.

A strange coincidence accompanied the girl's appearance. Rumour had it that on the evening before their hurried departure, the baron of Thunderhead had been attacked by a

Reecah's Gift

mad woman. He shook his head in disgust. It was pretty sad a man wasn't safe in his own bedchamber.

He eyed the finely wrought hilt of the woman's sword. If not for the constant attention of that redheaded bilge rat, Cahira, he might have approached the lass and discovered what she was about.

There was too much chance surrounding her appearance and the ship's sudden departure. He ventured there was more to the lass than her shy demeanour let on. Certainly someone to keep an eye on, even if Cappy had forbidden the crew's interference in her affairs.

Searching the deck and rigging, he located the bilge rat ascending the mizzen mast. It wouldn't do to have her see him watching her charge. Taking a long look at the freeloader, he rubbed his hands together. Whatever she was up to, he meant to find out. He didn't doubt for a moment that something shady was afoot. If he was right, then someone else had a stake in the outcome.

It paid to be shrewd. Licking his lips, he grinned. Sooner or later, the woman would tip her hand. When she did, he meant to profit from it. One way or another.

Reecah's Gift

All Hands on Deck

"**Pirates** off the port bow!"

It took a moment for the words to register. The urgency in the voice from the crow's nest wasn't lost on her. She faced the bow and followed the concerned gazes of the sailors.

She could only see waves from where she stood, but the sudden change in the atmosphere aboard *Serpent's Slip* was palpable. Before she had a chance to take a closer look, the ship became a flurry of activity.

Sailors emerged from every nook and cranny, scurrying back and forth in a chaotic frenzy—each sailor apparently knowing their role.

Captain Dreyger burst through the aft quarterdeck door and shouted, "All hands on deck!"

Reecah jumped out of the way as two sailors brushed by her going in opposite directions— painfully whacking her back off the rail.

Captain Dreyger disappeared up the starboard flight of stairs to the helm's deck.

The *Serpent's Slip's* deck pitched beneath Reecah's feet, the ship veering toward the western horizon. If not for the high wall of the ship's strake, she would have slipped under the rail and into the sea.

Sailors went about their business, taking the lurching deck in their stride; adjusting their gaits and moving on. Reecah couldn't imagine how long one had to live aboard an ocean-going vessel to be able to roll with the boat as confidently as

Reecah's Gift

they did. She had lied earlier to Cahira about feeling seasick, but her stomach protested now.

A squat man with black stubble shadowing his pudgy face waddled toward her from the same door the captain had exited. A dirty kerchief wrapped around the top of his head kept his greasy locks in check—the material matching the wide apron around his girth—its material white once upon a time.

"Och, lassie. Ain't no place for a missus on deck when danger's about."

Without warning, he grasped Reecah above the elbow and forced her away from the rail.

"Hey! That hurts." Reecah tried to pull out of his grasp but the man's grip was incredible.

"Ain't to be hurting near as much as a pirate's scimitar in yer belly if ya gets me meaning," the man said, leading her toward the quarterdeck door.

"What're you doing? I'm not going in there with you." Visions of the baron came to mind. She twisted in his grasp but couldn't break his hold.

"Ye'll be going wherever Cappy says yer to be going, and that's all there is to the matter." The man pushed down on a brass door handle and shouldered the door open, shoving Reecah ahead of him "Watch yer step missy."

Despite his warning, Reecah tripped over the bulkhead. The man yanked on her arm to keep her from landing on her face.

"Ow! You're going to break my arm."

The man thrust her forward, releasing her. He stopped to close the door and indicated a side door with his chin. "In there."

Reecah glanced at the door. Having no idea where it led, she shook her head and backed away but the man was quicker than he appeared.

Reecah's Gift

He caught her forearm and threw her against the wall beside the door. "I ain't got time to be messin' with ye, lassie. Either do as yer told or I'll get rough with ya."

She thought about grabbing for her dagger but he ripped the door open and tossed her into a room cluttered with cooking utensils and countertops before she could do so.

Catching herself on a central island, she took note of a small hearth burning within a stone enclosure at the far end of the long cabin—two black cauldrons hanging suspended over the glowing coals, swaying with the ship's movements.

"Make yourself comfortable. It'll likely get worse afore it gets better." He latched the door and turned the lock.

Reecah tensed, expecting him to grab for her, but he squeezed his girth past her to inspect the hearth, mumbling to himself.

Reecah side-stepped toward the door.

Without looking up, he said, "I wouldn't do that if I were ye. If I needs to chase ya, ye'll be a sorry lass. Ain't no time to be foolin' around." He looked over his broad shoulder. "Ya get me?"

Reecah stopped. There was no way he would catch her before she made it through the door, unless the lock gave her trouble.

The ship reeled to starboard throwing her against the wall amidst a clattering of pots and pans.

The man steadied the hot cauldrons with dirty cloths draped over his hands until the ship righted itself. Standing straight, a slight smile split his thick lips. "They call me Cookie. Ye can too, if yer so inclined. I apologize if I hurt ye. I just be following Cappy's orders. I needed to make sure me pots be safe o'er the fire. Wouldn't do to have a stray coal burn the ship out from beneath us."

Reecah's gaze darted from the man to the door.

92

Reecah's Gift

He raised his eyebrows. "Suit yerself. If'n yer determined to give me trouble, I got no qualms of feedin' ya to the krakens."

Reecah swallowed. The man's thick accent was difficult to comprehend, but she understood enough to realize that he didn't take well to disobedience. Her fear of Cookie being anything like the baron was misplaced. He appeared harmless enough as long as he remained where he was. She fingered the hilt of her dagger. If he made a move toward her, she'd gut him.

Cookie eyed her movement. He cast her a crooked grin—two upper teeth and a lower, middle tooth missing. Pulling a well-used meat cleaver off a peg in the wall, he brought it crashing down into a dark stained cutting board.

Reecah swallowed, her hand moving away from her sword belt.

"Look, missy. I ain't wanting to hurt ye. Just doing me job. Cappy asked me to keep ya safe."

Reecah frowned.

"Aye. I's not to being understanding either. Seems to me that harbouring a fugitive of the baron is more dangerous than tangling with a pirate ship, but it ain't me place to be making heady decisions. I'm just the cook."

Reecah forced a smile, her eyes searching the room. She'd misjudged people before, but Cookie didn't appear threatening now that they were locked within the brig's galley.

"To be honest, I can't see why the cap'n hasn't tossed ya to the krakens. In me books, you're a liability that can sink our lady." He patted the bulkhead beside him. "Quicker 'n any pirate."

Reecah couldn't keep quiet. "Because I defended myself?"

Cookie stared at her; his expression unreadable. Finally, he crossed his arms over his ample stomach. "Because you're a woman."

"Excuse me?"

Reecah's Gift

"The sea ain't no place for women. 'specially not where the Niad meets the Unknown Sea."

"What does my sex have to do with anything?" She was tired of being considered inferior because of her gender. Sure, many men were bigger and stronger than her, but there were many who weren't. As far as she was concerned, everyone had their strengths and weaknesses. She didn't know of anyone who could match her proficiency in the mountains—including Jaxon, Viper *or* Junior.

She winced. Just the thought of the eldest Waverunner boy filled her with mixed emotions. She thought she had moved past his betrayal, but judging by the feelings that just thinking about him evoked, it was obvious she hadn't.

Cookie's voice rescued her. "It's a commonly known fact that a woman's presence aboard a ship invites a curse on those unlucky enough to sail with her."

"That's a stupid superstition. How can my presence affect a boat?"

"We're being chased by a pirate ship, are we not?" Cookie nodded as if his answer was explanation enough.

"Seriously? You think that's my fault? That's ridiculous."

Cookie raised his eyebrows. "We ain't been bothered by pirates in nigh o'er a year. How else would ye explain it."

"Coincidence?"

"Bah! Coincidence me nut."

Reecah couldn't believe she was having this conversation. Nor did she believe she would sway Cookie's bias, but she couldn't stop herself from arguing the point. "Ya? And what about Cahira?"

"Pfft. Cahira is one of us."

"How does that make any sense? She's still a woman."

That threw him.

"You see?"

Cookie shook his head. "She's different."

94

Reecah's Gift

Reecah threw her hands in the air. "How? A woman is a woman."

"Cahira was born on the waves. She's seaborn. That's the difference."

"But she's still a woman!" Reecah squeaked incredulously.

Cookie shrugged. "All I know is the crew ain't happy about yer presence. If not for Cappy's stern warning that nothing is to happen to ya, ye'd already be swimming. Even with his warning, I'd be careful if I were ye. I'd keeps the walls to me back, and me dagger close. If anyone comes to harm because of the pirates, ye can bet yer under britches me mates'll be coming for you."

Reecah pulled her dagger free and flourished it in the air between them.

Cookie held up his palms. "Ye don't need to worry about me. If Cappy says to leave ye be, I leave ye be." He placed a hand on the worn cleaver handle.

The ship pitched to starboard. Stuck in the cabin, unable to see the horizon, Reecah was certain the ship was on the verge of capsizing. She emitted a high-pitched yelp as the boat's momentum threw her into the central butcherblock.

Cookie braced himself. "They're getting closer."

Reecah didn't have to ask who. She eyed the cleaver. "Shouldn't you be up there?"

Cookie gazed at the low ceiling. "Aye, but then I couldn't keep an eye on ye."

"You don't have to worry about me. I'll stay right here."

Cookie looked like he considered what she said, but he said nothing more.

The *Serpent's Slip* climbed wave after wave, crashing vehemently into the troughs between. The little food Reecah had eaten since boarding the vessel soured in her stomach—thankful to not have eaten since daybreak.

Reecah's Gift

Hoping to settle her stomach, she lowered herself to the galley floor and stared at her worn leather boots—the thongs binding the sides together ready to give out. Her green breeks disappeared into the black boots, their material thinning about the knees. It wouldn't be long before she was in desperate straits. Without resources, the oncoming winter promised to present her with difficulty.

She grabbed the hem of her cloak and rubbed it between her fingers. It appeared okay considering everything she had put it through. Her white tunic had held up well, as had the equipment Aunt Grimelda had given her—weapons handed down from Reecah's great-grandmother if the village witch could be trusted.

She leaned her head against the rough surface of the cabinet and stared at the ceiling—the underside of the quarterdeck. The planks creaked continuously, marking the passage of men moving about the top deck.

She tensed as Cookie strode around the central island, but he stopped before he reached her and opened a cupboard door above the long cabinet. Muted light flooded the galley. She tried to ignore him, but he stared into the cupboard, nodding and grunting.

Unable to overlook his strange behaviour, she asked, "What's so interesting in there?"

He mumbled something that sounded like, "They're going to ram us."

"Huh?"

"The pirates. They got themselves a rammer."

Reecah jumped to her feet and leaned over Cookie's shoulder—the man half a head shorter than her. Seeing a grimy porthole inside the cupboard wasn't nearly as shocking as the sight of the two-masted ship bearing down on them. The angle of the pirate's approach looked as if it would impact the *Serpent's Slip* where they stood.

96

Reecah's Gift

Reecah stepped back and bumped into the island. "Get away from the window!"

If Cookie heard, he ignored her, preferring to remain put and nod his head, as if accepting his fate.

She winced at Cookie's twisted features, expecting the *Serpent's Slip* to recoil under the imminent impact but nothing happened. Through the hull, she heard a thunderous collision and the rendering of wood splintering. She grasped Cookie's shoulders and looked in time to see the pirate ship dashed against a hidden reef. It teetered, stuck on the concealed obstruction and spun in the heavy seas.

Reecah had to stretch on her tiptoes and crane her neck to one side to see the next big wave smash into the side of the floundering ship—flipping it onto its side before the progress of *Serpent's Slip* took it out of view.

"Wow! That was close." She realized her fingers were digging into Cookie's fatty shoulders. Embarrassed she let go, unconsciously wiping her hands on her cloak. Her cheeks reddened.

Cookie closed the cupboard. Without a word, he unlocked the exit door and held it open. "You may leave now, lassie."

"I don't understand. Why didn't we hit the reef?"

"Cap'n Dreyger happened."

She cast him a puzzled look.

"Cappy's done and outsmarted the rogues. You see, *Serpent's Slip* runs a shallow keel. She slips through waters other vessels dare not go. I'm not a tactical man, but if I had to guess the right of it, the pirate cap'n was fooled into thinkin' he could sail through the same waters as the *Slip*. Ain't the first time we've evaded capture along this pirate-infested coast."

Reecah's Gift

King's Bay

Cahira rested against the starboard rail, chewing a sliver of wood and pointing. "See those twin peaks smoking over there?"

The day had been uneventful compared to the previous one. Luckily, the pirate ship had been sailing solo.

Reecah leaned over the rail and nodded. "Volcanoes?"

"Aye. Mount Cinder and Mount Gloom. The Svelte duchy's northernmost city of Cliff Face is nestled in between. If yer to be thinking Thunderhead's bad, I'd be advising ya to stay well clear o' that rats' nest."

Reecah shuddered. "How can any place be worse than Thunderhead?"

"How?" Cahira's faint eyebrows came together. "Because Cliff Face is a place best left to rogues and villains."

"Isn't there a dragon colony around there?"

"Aye. Two rival clans, actually. Dragons and Wyverns. Mortal enemies. The city of Cliff Face is built in the saddle between the volcanoes. That's a place even I wouldn't go." She leaned over the rail and pointed. "If ya look close, ye can see the beasts flying about the cliffs."

Reecah tried to discern a dragon through the smoke-covered mountainsides but didn't see anything. Scanning those on deck, an uneasiness had overtaken the crew—more so than when they were scrambling to deal with the pirates. Everyone's

Reecah's Gift

gaze invariably strayed to the volcanic peaks as they went about their business.

"On a clear day in the crow's nest, ye'd be able to see Draakhall off the port bow," Cahira informed her, changing the subject as if she had bored of talking about dragons.

Reecah felt her nerves jump. "We're almost there?"

"Hah. Nae. We shan't dock 'til after nightfall."

"Is Sea Keep better than Thunderhead and…" She had forgotten what Cahira had called the rat's nest.

"Cliff Face?"

"Yes."

"Aye. A different type of wariness is required in the capital."

"What do you mean?"

"Hard to explain. Especially to someone who's never been there." Cahira's eyes narrowed, her gaze taking in Reecah's sword. "I'm beginning to think yer not from the Great Kingdom."

"Why do you say that?"

Cahira pulled the sliver from her mouth, inspecting its battered surface. Throwing it overboard, she stared Reecah in the eye. "Ye strike me as smarter than regular folk. Ya strut around with an air of confidence and possess some mighty fine weapons. And yet, ye claim to know little of the Great Kingdom. That's odd if ya ask me. Yer like a noblewoman without a kingdom. Like someone who's lost their way and ended up here. Perhaps against yer will."

Reecah fought to keep the surprise from her face. If Cahira only knew how close her accusations hit home. But a noblewoman? She blurted out a laugh.

"What's so funny?"

"You. Thinking I'm highborn. There's nothing further from the truth."

"Then tell me, GG…but first, perhaps ye can start by telling me yer real name."

Reecah's Gift

Reecah gaped, and then felt foolish—her expression confirming to Cahira that she had given up her secret.

Cahira crossed her arms below her breasts. Tilting her head to one side and raising her eyebrows, she demanded an answer.

"Well, I…um, I mean…" Reecah didn't know what to say. As rough and simple as Cahira came across, a deeper intelligence existed behind those intense brown eyes. Anything short of the truth and she might find herself without her only ally on a ship full of people who wished to throw her overboard.

Heaving a heavy breath, it was time to come clean. She searched the deck, making sure nobody overheard. "My name is Reecah…" She was about to say her last name but changed her mind—officially renaming herself. "Windwalker."

Cahira stared hard.

Perhaps she *should* have lied. She hadn't thought that 'Windwalker' might be renowned in the bigger world.

"Reecah, huh?" Cahira nodded. "Suits you."

She couldn't break Cahira's gaze if she wanted to. She swallowed her discomfort and offered the redhead a brief smile.

"Look, Reecah. I don't know what you did to earn the ire of the baron, but whatever it was, it must've been serious. Did you know one of the baron's ships set out after us? We outdistanced it before daybreak. If the prince gets wind of what went on, I pray to the kraken we reach Sea Keep before he does."

Reecah stared at the glistening sea dropping behind the *Serpent's Slip*. "You mean the prince's ships can overtake us? He was sailing the other way."

"Who knows with Cappy running the reefs to steer free of the serpents?"

"Serpents?"

100

Reecah's Gift

"Ye know? Krakens. The cooler waters of the Unknown Sea are infested with them."

Reecah shook her head. She knew of krakens from reading Poppa's books, but what that had to do with where they sailed, she had no idea. "I'm not sure what you mean."

The look Cahira gave her made her wince. Just when she thought the woman would walk away, a huge grin split Cahira's face.

Cahira punched her in the shoulder. "Yer really something, Miss Reecah, you know that?"

Reecah shook her head, massaging her shoulder "Please. Just Reecah. Trust me. I'm no one special. Nor do I come from anywhere particularly exciting."

A look of understanding transformed Cahira's expression. "Yer from Fishmonger Bay! I should've known as soon as we sailed by the pig's wallow. That explains everything."

Reecah's wide eyes searched the deck. There were a few sailors working nearby, but they didn't appear to be paying them any attention. She should have been offended by Cahira's description of her home town, but she wasn't. If only Cahira would keep her voice down.

"Why didn't ya say so? Ye don't need to be embarrassed. Not many on the *Slip* have grand roots. Probably no one other than Cappy. That's why we sail the seas. To be free of the trappings the highbrows cling to. Being from Fishmonger Bay makes you a kindred spirit."

Reecah cringed at the mention of her village again. She wasn't sure being lumped in with the rough and tumble sailors was a good thing. Casting a quick look around, she motioned with her palms for Cahira to keep her voice down.

Cahira leaned in close, touching Reecah's sword hilt. Her voice dropped to a whisper. "So, what's someone like ye doing with gear like this then, eh?"

Reecah's Gift

Reecah didn't know how to answer that. She couldn't very well tell her what Aunt Grimelda claimed. Cahira would think her daft and turn her over to the captain as a witch.

Cahira's grin grew wider. "You stole them from the baron!"

Reecah shook her head, mortified, but Cahira held a dirty hand over her mouth and chuckled.

"That's awesome, Reecah. I'm liking you more 'n more. Ye'll fit right in with the crew. Once they learn to accept ya."

"That's not what Cookie said."

"Bah! Cookie's a male. They're pig-headed."

"I thought the whole crew were males."

Cahira raised her eyebrows, conceding the point. "Details. They'll come around."

The redhead's assurances didn't make a lot of sense, nor did they provide her with the solace she sought. She pushed it aside. What did it matter? Once they reached Sea Keep, she would be rid of them anyway. She just needed to survive until then.

When the sun went down, the tension on the deck rose. Mournful wails pierced the darkness; first one, and then another from a different direction; as if in answer.

Reecah sat cross-legged with her back against the side of Cahira's cot, shivering with every unnerving cry. She leafed through her journal, attempting to read the strange runes Grimclaw had left on the last pages of the diary. Her thoughts were distracted as she marvelled at everything she had gone through recently. She almost screamed in fright when Cahira burst through the cabin door.

"There ya are," Cahira said, holding the door open. "Gather yer stuff. We'll be unweighing anchor shortly."

Reecah gulped. "We're there already?"

Cahira's face twisted. "It's what I said, ain't it?"

Reecah's Gift

"Yes, sorry. I was listening to those awful cries. I guess they unsettled me."

"Ah, kraken song. Ya, it can reduce the biggest man to a whimpering babe." Cahira reached down to give her a hand up. "Come on. We should be safe on deck now. I want you to witness Sea Keep at night."

Cahira's assurance that they *should* be safe did little to ease her nerves, but she couldn't refuse the sailor's enthusiasm. Cahira had not only been responsible for her passage to the Great Kingdom's capital, she had also kept the superstitious sailors from tossing her into the sea.

Cahira led her to where the port and starboard rails joined above the bowsprit of a topless mermaid. Reecah mused about the hypocrisy of men's traditions. They claimed a woman's presence onboard the ship brought them bad luck, and yet, the symbol they used to grant them safe passage was none other than a twenty-foot, bare-breasted female.

Several sailors were gathered along the rail. Seeing Reecah approach, their conversation dropped off. A few of them nodded to Cahira, but no one spoke. Without having to be asked, the men at the pinnacle of the bow shuffled over to allow Reecah and Cahira room on the rail.

The dirty looks they received didn't bother Cahira but Reecah checked her weapons and held her quarterstaff close. She pulled her cloak tight to ward off the cold—its hems snapping in the breeze.

Shivers racked her body, but the approaching glow on the black horizon consumed her attention. It was as if the point where the steely waves met the darker sky was ablaze.

The bow dipped into a shallow trough, cutting into the backside of the next wave—spraying everyone with water. Hawsers protested, and spars creaked. Kraken song pierced the night; their unsettling melody mingling with the slap of the sea breaking over the hull.

Reecah's Gift

Mesmerized, Reecah didn't know whether to watch the sailors scuttling through the rigging, unsnagging block and tackle, or keep her eyes on the approaching skyline.

A sailor in the crow's nest called out something Reecah couldn't make out.

A deep voice responded from the helm's deck and the *Serpent's Slip* veered to port.

Glistening walls rose out of the darkness—as if they projected from the sea itself. Massive bulwarks and rooftops materialized in the faint light of the quarter moon. A solid wall of stone and wood-lined what little of the shoreline was visible at its base.

Reecah wondered where they were going to dock. The Unknown Sea crashed into the foundations of the built-up skyline—no piers, docksides or boats visible in the haunting mist lining the shore.

A cry sounded from the crow's nest and was answered from the stern, accompanied by the annoying peal of a large cow bell.

The deck beneath Reecah's feet pitched portside as the *Serpent's Slip* veered toward a massive building looming out of the darkness—stretching northward and out of sight. She grasped Cahira's forearm, fearing they were about crash into the lattice-faced wall blocking their passage.

Cahira yanked her arm free. "Ya wanna black eye?"

Reecah shook her head, unable to speak.

The tooth-rattling squeal of massive hinges pierced the night. Water frothed along the base of the iron lattice as it parted. Enormous gates swung inward—separating faster than Reecah believed possible.

She craned her neck, waiting for the inevitable crunch of the masts as they passed beneath a thick, overhead bulwark, but the ship slipped through with plenty of room to spare.

Reecah's Gift

Voices cried out from somewhere unseen and the latticed gates reversed their motion.

"Welcome to King's Bay." Cahira grinned, scanning the shoreline crammed with buildings of all shapes and sizes. "And the twin cities. Each renowned for equal parts of wonder and misery."

Reecah took her gaze away from the fiery lights illuminating the shore on either side of the bay and glanced at Cahira. The burning fires reflected off the still waters, casting the *Serpent's Slip* in an ethereal light. She couldn't help thinking Cahira looked pretty when she smiled.

"To your right lies Sea Keep, the home of Draakhall. Unless yer highborn or desire a quick death, stay away from that side." Cahira's smile was short-lived as she turned her attention to the north shore. "Over there, is Sea Hold. The fortified city housing the king's army, their families, and everyone else required to wipe the shit from his majesty's boots."

What an odd thing to say. The sailor's closest, cast Cahira uneasy looks.

The iron gates clanged shut—the noise echoing off the tall buildings lining either side of the immense bay. The *Serpent's Slip* veered toward the north shore.

"Well, I guess this be good-bye, then, eh?" Cahira said, a sadness in her eyes. "Yer a different girl, Reecah Windwalker, I'll give ya that. I don't know what yer after but I hope ya find it."

Reecah blinked at the gruff redhead. Though she'd only known her for a couple of days, she felt a strong affinity toward the unusual woman. "I'm grateful to have met you, Cahira. I'm indebted to you for getting me here."

"Pfft. Please. Come find me next time ya happen to see this old brig and let me know how thankful ya are. Ye may wish ye'd never saved me sorry arse."

Reecah's Gift

Reecah gave her a sad smile. "I would never think that. Besides, it's my fault you got into trouble. I'd be honoured if I could call you my friend."

Cahira tilted her head and looked away. She ran the back of her hand across her face. When she looked back, she struggled to keep Reecah's gaze. "I ain't to be taking kindly to people who make me cry."

Reecah could only imagine how difficult it was for such a tough person to openly share her emotions. She sputtered a nervous laugh. "I'm sorry. I never meant to…" She couldn't say anymore without breaking down, so she held out her arms.

Cahira made to shake her hand, but Reecah hugged her. Arms hanging limp, Cahira awkwardly accepted Reecah's embrace.

"Thank you," Reecah whispered through Cahira's coarse hair—its scratchy ends tickling her cheek. "You were the light I needed to guide me free of the darkness I had fallen into. I'll never forget you, my friend."

Cahira stiffened, but her hands slipped across Reecah's back, returning the embrace—hesitantly at first, and then growing in strength until she squeezed the air from Reecah's lungs.

Reecah disengaged with the hope of breathing again. The grizzled sailors standing on the bow grumbled and shook their heads at the two women, but Reecah didn't care. She held Cahira by the hands. "How do I go about getting an audience with the king?"

Cahira's eyes bulged. "Yer kidding, right?"

Reecah shook her head, a mischievous smile turning up the corners of her plush lips. She rapped her quarterstaff off the deck and patted her sword hilt.

"I knew there was more to ye than ya let on." Cahira scanned her from head to toe. Shaking her head, she pointed to the housing running along the top of the sea gate. "Ya see the northern gate tower? If ya can sweet talk yer way past the

106

Reecah's Gift

guards, ye can walk across the Sea Gate Bridge. Once yer in Sea Keep, I'm not sure what to tell ya."

Reecah nodded. It wasn't much but it would have to do. At least she was here. A few days ago, her desire to reach the city of the king had been an impossible undertaking. All she had to do now was figure out how to get an audience with him. "You've done more than enough. Don't worry. I'll find a way to get into Draakhall."

Cahira uncharacteristically grasped Reecah's hands—her moist, brown eyes full of compassion. "See to it you figure a way to come back out."

Reecah's Gift

Chizel

Stepping off the gang plank, Reecah searched the rails for Cahira, hoping to wave good-bye, but the gruff redhead was nowhere to be seen.

She stopped to look around, not knowing where to spend the night. It would have been nice to do so aboard the *Serpent's Slip* but Cahira was adamant she go ashore the first chance she got.

There wasn't much activity on the large dock, though the night air was rife with boisterous laughter and loud voices from the direction of the streets.

She started along the wooden planks, walking between several ships moored along either side of the long pier and listening to the chatter escaping the boats. The clump of boots from behind sent a shock of apprehension through her.

A wiry man stepped from *Serpent's Slip's* gangplank. He looked her way before walking down the dock in the opposite direction.

It was too dark to make out his features, but she was sure she had seen him on deck before. More than once. She shrugged. It wouldn't be unusual to have seen him a dozen times over the last couple of days. The ship was only so big.

Stepping off the dock onto dry land, she reeled, certain the ground swayed beneath her. A smile eased her tension. She had finally gotten her sea legs and now the ship's deck felt like it remained under her feet.

Reecah's Gift

Having no idea where to spend the night, she turned left, toward the gargantuan superstructure bridging the mouth of King's Bay—its mass a dark blot in the distance.

The dockside walkway terminated at the edge of a stone building blocking her path; its foundation built into a rocky crag shooting out of the black depths of the bay. Dagger in hand, Reecah slipped into a dark alley between it and a multi-storied, wooden building.

Reaching the far end, she gazed in wonder at the well-lit, cobblestoned street. People gathered in small knots outside the many doorways lining the street on either side. From the look of them, they were sailors and dockhands—tough-looking men and women she thought best to avoid. She furtively scanned the nearest groups, hoping not to notice anyone from the *Serpent's Slip*. She no longer enjoyed the protection of Captain Dreyger or Cahira.

Absently checking her bow was strung properly, she tested its tension. Sheathing her dagger, she ensured her sword belt and cummerbund were securely buckled. Thrusting her chin high she strolled into the light, her quarterstaff clicking rhythmically off the cobblestones. Her insides twisted as she feigned having walked this road many times before.

Curious gazes followed her progress. She did her best not to look at them, but it was hard to ignore a few of the catcalls directed her way. She kept telling herself, as long as no one recognized her, she would be okay. All she had to do was reach the Sea Gate.

She strolled past bars, brothels, and assorted businesses on her right, while smithies, shipwrights, and tanneries disappeared behind her on the left. Looming in the distance, the Sea Gate bulwarks dwarfed the tall buildings lining the streets.

The uneven cobblestones caused her to stumble more than once as she craned her neck to take in elaborate shop fronts

Reecah's Gift

festooned with fancy scrollwork and guarded by gargoyles depicting fantastical creatures that were dominated by fangs, claws, and sported wings of all descriptions. A couple of intricately carved dragons captivated her to the point that she didn't see the three-and-a-half-foot, brown-bearded man, smoking a long-stemmed pipe.

She almost fell over him, her quarterstaff cracking him in the skull and knocking the pipe from his hand. Before she could catch herself, her heel came down on the pipe, grinding its fragile stem into a cobblestone.

"Oi!" the yellow-toothed man shouted, spittle shooting from his thick lips.

"Oh!" Reecah stepped backward; a look of horror crossing her face as she caught sight of the broken pipe. "I'm so sorry, mister. Please forgive me."

The dwarf shook his scruffy mane. His eyes narrowed as he inspected the contents of the flagon held firmly in his other hand. Squinting, a hearty smile transformed his hardened expression. "No harm done, lassie. Ain't spilled a drop! Oi!"

Reecah didn't know what to make of the little man as he quaffed half the tankard of foamy liquid and wiped his froth-covered beard with the back of his dirty hand. She picked up the pieces of the pipe, the bowl hot to the touch. "I'd love to repay you…" She cast sad eyes at the broken pipe in her hands. "But I haven't any money."

The man considered her with a tilted head, his shoulders as wide as he was tall. Powerful arms, the size of her thighs and corded with muscle, crossed over his large stomach. "Yer new around here or I'll be a horned owl."

"Yes sir. Just got in." She wasn't sure she should divulge too much, but it was the least she could do to be civil to a stranger she had wronged. "I've never been here before and I guess I wasn't watching where I was going."

Reecah's Gift

"Ya guess, eh?" The man's right, brown eye squinted more than his left, green one.

Reecah's cheeks flushed. "Um, yes sir. It was clumsy of me. I wish I could repay you."

The dwarf smiled, running the tip of his tongue over his bottom lip.

She recoiled, expecting the same treatment she experienced in Thunderhead, but the dwarf surprised her.

"Ye can start by taking better care, missy. Ain't safe for a purty lass to be struttin' around this area after dark. Less'n yer meaning to strut, that is." His large eyes searched her body. "I must admit, by the look o' ye, I wouldn't be keen on messin' with ya."

Reecah tilted her head, scrunching her features, trying to decipher his words. "Thank you. I just sailed in and am looking to get to Draakhall."

The dwarf lifted a thick eyebrow. "Ye are, are ye? Well yer going in the right direction. Get yerself o'er the Sea Gate Bridge an' ye'll be in company more suitin' a lady."

"What about your pipe?"

"Och, don't ye be worryin' yer purty head o'er it." The dwarf accepted the irreparable bits from her hands; gazing sadly at the remains in his massive palms. "T'was the last thing I had left of me dead Mam."

Reecah gaped, an icy wave of horror washing over her.

The dwarf's green eye looked up, a great smile creasing his pudgy face. He winked. "I'm funnin' with ya. Me Mam smoked a much bigger pipe 'n this."

Letting the bits fall to the cobbles, the dwarf crushed them beneath the heel of his black boot. "Perhaps I'll be seein' ya at Draakhall sometime, eh?"

Not waiting for a response, he waddled away—toward a group of seedy-looking individuals.

Reecah's Gift

Reecah stared after him. The tough men and women towered above the dwarf, but seeing his approach, they parted to let him pass.

She thought about his last words, *"Perhaps I'll be seein' ya at Draakhall…"* She wanted to ask him a bunch of questions but by the time she worked up the nerve, he was gone.

Turning to the Sea Gate blotting out the sky ahead, she checked her gear was secure for the countless time, scanned the shadows for signs of danger, and started up the street.

The closer she got, the more incredible the Sea Gate became. Her neck grew stiff from staring at the stone structure's lofty heights illuminated by flickering sconces set along its upper edges. Latticed iron gates, as wide as the street and several stories high, blocked her progress from funnelling between two circular towers on either side; each one rising higher than the Sea Gate Bridge itself. If she wasn't mistaken, the towers were taller than the Fang—the natural rock formation at the head of Dragonfang Pass.

"Halt!" a deep voice beckoned.

Absorbed in her observations of the massive structure, Reecah jumped.

A clean-shaven man in leather armour and chainmail sleeves stepped out from a doorway at the bottom of the bayside tower. Movement across the street from the opposite tower startled her further as another guard emerged from the shadows.

The first guard approached, his dark eyes noting her weapons. "What business do you have here?"

She wasn't sure what he meant. "Why nothing, here. I wish to get to Draakhall."

"A wise one, huh? What's your business at the castle?"

"My business?" She stalled, not thinking it was a good idea to tell him she was here to stop the dragon hunt. "I don't really have *business*."

Reecah's Gift

"Be off with you, then."

"I need to speak with the king."

"The king? You know him, do you?"

"Well…" She searched for something important to say, but nothing came. "I don't."

"Exactly. Move along or I'll have you in chains."

She searched the man's face. "Does that mean you'll drag me in front of the king?"

"Ha! Hardly. Depending on the magistrate on duty, it'll likely mean an appearance in front of the harbour kraken."

Being from Fishmonger Bay, the titles of dignitaries were foreign to her. "Do you think the harbour kraken has the ear of the king?"

The guard spit out a laugh. "I should hope not. The beast certainly has the ear of many, but not High King J'kaar."

The guard didn't make sense. "Where can I find this harbour kraken?"

The guard's eyes darted to the dark water lapping at the side of the tower. His sword slid free of his scabbard. "Alright, miss. You're either a troublemaker or have consumed too much ale. Either leave now or I'll slap you in irons."

The guard from the far tower ambled closer, sword drawn. He lifted his chin at her but spoke to the guard confronting her. "Another looney?"

The first guard nodded. He turned his attention on her. "Well? What's it going to be?"

She didn't know what to do. She wasn't sure what being slapped in irons entailed but by the way the man phrased it, the process didn't bode to be a welcome experience.

"How does someone get an audience with High King J'kaar?"

"You don't. Unless you're someone of importance. His Majesty hasn't got time for the likes of you. I would hazard to say you aren't high-born or a dignitary from another realm."

Reecah's Gift

Reecah shook her head. She wasn't a good liar.

"Then be gone. I shan't warn you again," the guard growled, his eyes never leaving her hands.

The second guard adjusted his stance—his gaze taking in something behind Reecah.

Ambling into the shadow cast by the tower, the dwarf belonging to the pipe she had stepped on, confronted the guard; another pipe in hand.

"What's goin' on?" The dwarf stopped at her side. "Ye ain't giving me friend a hard time, are ye?"

The way he framed the question, Reecah thought he was talking to her but the guard straightened his posture and lowered his sword. "Just doing my job, Master Chizel. You know this lady?"

The dwarf drew on his pipe. Exhaling a puff of smoke, he laid a huge hand on the small of her back. "Aye, we go way back, don't we...?"

"GG."

"Aye! That's it. GG and I go way back. She's on her way to Draakhall. Unless ye've gotten a reason to hold her, I expect ye to be showing the lass the royal courtesy she deserves, eh?"

The guard bowed his head. "Yes, Master Chizel. If you vouch for her, she's free to go."

The dwarf smiled and held out a hand toward the gate. "There ye go, Miss GG. Come, I'll walk with ye to the castle to make sure ya ain't detained no more."

The guards bowed their heads and returned to their respective towers.

Shortly after the first guard disappeared beyond the door at the base of the bayside tower, the massive iron gates rattled and squealed, parting wide enough to allow Reecah and Chizel access to where the street met the bulwark at the base of the Sea Gate.

114

Reecah's Gift

Chizel led her to a door in the near tower, similar to the one the guard had entered. Inside, a sparsely lit stairwell spiralled into the darkness above.

Chizel let her go first and closed the door behind them—its latching mechanism echoing hollowly. "I hope ye ain't afraid o' heights."

If Chizel only knew how high a dragon flew.

"If yer prone to swooning, it'd be kind o' ya to warn a fella afore ya fall to yer death."

"I think I'll be okay."

The tower stairs spiralled around the inside of the tower for a long time. Reecah was surprised at how much her thighs burned by the time she left the top step and stopped in front of the exit door to catch her breath. Climbing steps was different from scaling mountain heights.

She glanced down the stairwell. Chizel was nowhere to be seen, but the slow cadence of his ascent reverberated in the quiet atmosphere inside the tower. Hearing him grunting far below, she decided to push through the door and wait outside, appreciating the cool night air.

Huffing and puffing, the long-bearded dwarf staggered through the door and bent over, shaking his head. "There's got to be…a better way." He glanced at Reecah. "Must be nice…to have such…a slim body…to climb in."

Reecah chuckled at the bizarre comment. "It gets me by."

Chizel tried to laugh but coughed instead. "I'll bet it does."

She didn't know whether to be offended by that comment or not, so she let it go. Waiting for Chizel to recover, she enjoyed the open-air view. A narrow span of interlocked stone ran in a straight line south of their position, across the wide mouth of the bay—the twin towers at its far end barely visible against the night sky.

Reecah's Gift

Chizel sidled up beside her and followed her gaze over the Unknown Sea. "Scary world out there amongst the waves. Not a place I like to travel."

"Someone told me sea serpents live out there. Is that true?"

Chizel grunted. "Ye be talkin' 'bout krakens. Aye, true enough. We got one in the bay we can't be rid of. So much for them darned gates."

Reecah took her gaze from the sea and stared at the top of Chizel's wavy, brown hair—the tangled mess touching his shoulders. "You mean the gates are built to keep the sea monsters out?"

Chizel looked up at her as if she were daft. "Ain't to be keepin' dragons out."

His words left her feeling stupid. "Obviously. I assumed they were built to keep human invaders out."

"Bah! Have to be crazier than a boneless skeleton to want anything to do with this place." He spat over the low wall and started along the span. "Come on. Yer gonna catch yer death up here." He looked back and winked. "There ain't bein' much to ye."

Despite her uncertainty about Chizel's true intentions, she smiled at his comment. She couldn't decide whether he was a crude, nice person or a conniving swindler trying to lead her in the wrong direction. So far, he seemed decent enough, especially considering how they had first met, and yet, he had a way of throwing in the odd comment that left her on edge.

"The guard called you Master Chizel. What does, master, mean, exactly?"

"Exactly? I ain't to be knowin'. Just a useless title that nobles like to bandy about, far as I'm concerned." He held out an oversized hand. "Me name's Aramyss Chizel. I'm in the employ of the Royal Family."

Reecah accepted his meaty handshake, her eyes full of wonder. The implication of meeting Aramyss might be more fortuitous than she imagined. She never would have believed that bumping into a stranger in a foreign city and breaking his belongings would prove a positive experience. Yet, here she was, crossing into Sea Keep with someone who worked at the castle. A master, no less—whatever that meant.

"Speaking exactly like. Who exactly is GG? Ain't to be yer real name, now is it, lass?" Aramyss winked.

Standing alone atop the Sea Gate Bridge, the powerfully built dwarf intimidated her into blurting out, "Reecah."

Aramyss' eyes narrowed. "That bein' yer last name, then?"

Reecah swallowed, unable to break his intense stare. "My last name is Windwalker."

Aramyss nodded as if that was something he already knew.

Wanting to change the subject, Reecah asked. "Do you think you can get me an audience with the king?"

The tension eased between them. "Bah!" Aramyss laughed. "I couldn't get one meself. Less I displeased him, that is."

"Why's that?"

"Lowly blacksmiths don't fraternize with the high-born. The only time I see His Grace is when he bangs up his armour. Even then, it's usually one of his knights that pays me a visit." Aramyss' hand reached out to clasp hers as they walked.

Alarmed, she tried to pull free, but his grip held her tight.

He gave her a crooked-toothed smile. "Ain't to be wantin' a gust of wind to lift ye o'er the wall and feed ya to the harbour kraken."

Reecah craned her neck. The sea crashed relentlessly against the gate. So that was the kraken the guard had been referring to. She was glad no one could see her cheeks redden.

She returned Aramyss' grip—the wind off the ocean whipping the hems of her cloak all around. Getting over the initial shock, the dwarf's meaty grasp was reassuring.

It took them a while to reach the far end of the walkway. Though she never once felt in danger of being blown off the bridge, she could imagine how dangerous it would have been had the winds been gusting.

"At least the descent will be easier on me legs." Aramyss turned the lever of the tower door and pulled hard in the face of the wind. "Watch yer step. If ya miss one, it'll be the last thing ye do."

Reecah entered the poorly lit stairwell and contemplated the gaping abyss in the centre of the stone steps carved into the perimeter of the tower. The steps were wide enough for her boots but just barely. Placing a steadying hand against the roughly hewn stone of the curving wall, she thought absently that it wouldn't have hurt to install an inside rail.

The wiry sailor from the *Serpent's Slip* stepped out of the shadows and stared at the bulk of the River Gate Bridge dominating the skyline. The girl calling herself GG had followed a dwarf through the iron gates, but not before almost getting arrested by the River Gate guards.

There was definitely something peculiar about her. He would have to call in some favours from around Sea Hold, but perhaps a trip to Draakhall was in order. The *Slip* wouldn't be pulling out for a couple of days, so he had time to make a few inquiries at the castle.

Reecah's Gift

Bone Breaker

Draakhall loomed in the distance, its lofty spires shooting high above its crenelated walls—the massive fortress a dark stain against the night sky. The thin crescent moon shone faintly above a corner tower.

Aramyss waddled beside Reecah, pointing out different peculiarities of the capital city as they made their way along a street he referred to as King's Stagger.

"So, where ye plannin' on sleepin' tonight, Miss Reecah?"

Walking through the foreign city late at night with all the leering faces watching her from the steps and windows of boisterous taverns lining the aptly named street, she almost wished Aramyss would take her hand again. "I don't know. I've never been here before. Perhaps one of the taverns?"

As soon as she said it, she winced. Even if she had money, her brief stay at the *Naughty Saucer* had curbed any desire to frequent another such establishment. But this was the Great Kingdom's capital. Surely the people here were better behaved than those in Thunderhead.

A squeal pierced the night, making her jump.

Stumbling off the bottom step of a building on the right side of the street, a man fell to his backside, holding his hands in the air to fend off an irate woman clad in a tight corset and knee-high riding boots. His attempt to protect himself came to naught as the toe of the woman's boot caught him in the chin with an audible crack. The man fell limp to the cobblestone street amidst a round of laughter.

119

Reecah's Gift

Aramyss watched the festivities—delight lifting his cheeks. Looking back at Reecah, he blushed. "Perhaps ye may wanna stay clear of the taverns at this hour. The King's Wood would be a safer place 'n that."

Reecah grasped his callused hand.

The wild-eyed dwarf gave her a warm smile and patted the back of her hand. "Ye ain't to be worryin' long as I'm around."

"Because you're the king's blacksmith?"

"Bah!" Aramyss growled. "Because I'll drive me fist down the throat of anyone foolish enough to accost ye."

"Chizel! There you are!" A man in the king's livery of black, gold, and red hurried toward them from the direction of Draakhall. "The prince demands your attendance."

"J'kye? What's he need at this hour? Surely it can wait 'til morn."

The pasty-faced man looked stricken. He shook his head, wringing his hands together. "Nay, Master Chizel. It's Prince J'kwaad, and I dare say, he's in a nasty mood."

The wizard prince! Reecah gaped at the skinny man. How had the prince made it back to the castle so fast? If he became aware of her presence, her quest to save the dragons would come to an abrupt end.

Aramyss took the news just as badly—panic creasing his face. "The dark heir? What's he doing back so soon. I thought he was in Thunderhead attacking the Draakclaw Colony?"

The messenger fidgeted, clearly anxious to get back to the castle. "Well he's back, and he's madder than a wet cat." With that said, the messenger strutted quickly past the men and women gathered in knots along the thoroughfare, never once turning his head to respond to their jeers.

Aramyss released Reecah's hand. "Sorry, lass, I must be going. When J'kwaad beckons, a wise person makes haste. Good luck to ye." He tapped her scabbard and started away, but paused to say over his shoulder. "By the looks o' ye, yer a

120

Reecah's Gift

born fighter. Yer best bet to see the king is to enlist with the royal guard. Take the road south of Draakhall to South Fort. It's a good hike down the bay shore. Stop by its main gate when you get there. Tell the guards Aramyss Chizel sent you. I'll dispatch a pigeon to let them know you're on your way." He winked and hurried after the messenger.

Reecah watched him go. With each step he took, her anxiety went up another notch. Scanning the street, the king's messenger had not only robbed her of the solitary friendly face she had in Sea Keep, but had piqued the interest of those who didn't appear to have her best interests at heart.

Ensuring her sword slid smoothly in its scabbard, she hustled after Aramyss and the messenger. If she could get away from King's Stagger without incident, a place beneath a tree along the roadway south of Draakhall was as good a place as any to hole up for the night. She was a mountain girl. It would be just like living up by Dragonfang Pass. What harm could possibly come to her in the open wilderness?

Other than the cold, sleeping beneath the stars, off the well-travelled roadway south of Draakhall hadn't been too bad, all things considered. The small campfire she had managed to throw together kept the worst of the chill at bay. She had skirted the bayside road, avoiding knots of patrolling guardsmen, before settling on a small stand of trees, their thick boughs providing ample protection from the wind.

She nibbled at a chunk of stale bread and a slab of cheese pilfered from *Serpent's Slip* as she prepared for the next step in her journey. A tingle of excitement mixed with a pang of fear. If Aramyss kept his word, she might be given a chance to train with the king's men. A logical way of gaining entrance to the high king's castle. If nothing came of it, she would at least learn how to use her blades and quarterstaff properly. Though it wasted time, staying away from Draakhall wasn't a bad idea. She wouldn't be as vulnerable to detection from Prince J'kwaad. An occurrence she couldn't allow until she stood in front of the high king. But, being found out by the dark heir was a chance she had to take. Her friend's lives depended on it.

She lifted her chin high, pushing aside her underlying dread of ingratiating herself to the people bent on the dragons' extinction—to the people born into service of the highest seat in the land.

Blowing on her hands to warm them, she left the copse of trees behind and continued down the roadway meandering the shore along King's Bay.

It was late in the day by the time the walls of South Fort appeared in the distance. The sun sat on the western horizon, losing its grip on the land. Braving another chilly night beneath the stars, she was thankful the rain that had threatened for most of the day had held off.

Getting up before the sun, she strolled as casually as her hammering heart allowed toward the imposing stone walls—all the while envisioning Prince J'kwaad watching her approach from some hidden tower window. She chastised herself. What would the prince be doing down here, away from Draakhall?

A brisk breeze threw small waves against the shores of King's Bay as she wended her way between leaning hovels and ramshackle buildings on the outskirts of the grey fort's walls.

Leaving the town behind, a moat, wider than she could throw a stone, surrounded crenelated parapets; the yellow stone of the keep towering beyond the walls appeared daunting in the first rays of the new day—a cold and unwelcoming edifice that defied anyone to lay siege to its thick walls.

Large platforms capped many of the towers, bristling with ballistae. The same dragon slaying machines Reecah had heard

Reecah's Gift

about during the siege of Dragon Home. She swallowed her distaste for the brutal death slingers.

Trebuchets were built atop the remaining wall towers, but what they were designed for was a mystery. She wasn't versed in siege warfare tactics, but she thought catapults were a weapon employed by those attacking a castle.

She shook her head. If Prince J'kwaad wasn't stopped soon, there would be no need for the nasty fortifications. According to Lurker, the fall of Dragon Home left only two dragon colonies in the Great Kingdom. It wouldn't be long before they, too, were gone.

She stepped off the path surrounding the moat to make way for a disciplined troop of soldiers bearing halberds and marching with tall shields strapped to their backs. She shivered. They reminded her of the dragon hunt back home. Though many eyes turned her way, the formation continued past without incident.

Rounding the front of South Fort, she approached twin guard huts at the end of a lowered drawbridge.

A pair of guards confronted her, swords in hand. "State your business."

She hoped her dwarven friend had managed to get word to the fort. "Master Chizel is expecting me."

The taller guard squinted. "Ah, yes. GG, I believe." The man raised his eyebrows at his partner before returning his attention to her. "So, you're the rat who's to report to the Bone Breaker. Pity. I was hoping the dwarf had conscripted the Maiden of the Wood."

Reecah didn't know what to make of being referred to as a rat, but the name of the person she was to report to gave her pause. "The Bone Breaker?"

"You've never heard of him?"

Reecah shook her head.

A covert smile passed between the guards.

Reecah's Gift

The taller man grinned. "Then you're in for a real treat, Miss GG." He gave her a mock bow. "I'm Sir Batkin. If you would be so kind as to follow me."

Reecah followed the lanky guard across the drawbridge. They were met by several guards as they approached the raised barbican, but her escort set them at ease. "This is Miss GG. She has an appointment with the Anvil."

The guards raised their eyebrows, but no one made a move to stop their progress into the tunnel leading through the base of the outer wall.

Reecah lagged behind, her interest captured by the wonder of entering an actual castle. The sheer size of the edifice had been intimidating from the far side of the moat, but walking beneath the stone bulwark was awe-inspiring. She craned her neck to take in the myriad of peculiar slits marring the length of the tunnel's surface from knee height to above their heads—the gaps too small for windows. Realizing the guard had stopped to wait for her at the end of the passage, she picked up her pace.

The tunnel emptied into a spacious courtyard separating the outer wall from a higher, thinner wall surrounding the keep. A narrow moat lined the base of the inner rampart, its shoreline littered with cows, chickens, geese, pigs and all sorts animals—many drinking or bathing in its brackish waters. The heady smell of manure and damp earth filled the air.

Following the guard to the left, they skirted around a lengthy series of wooden stables lining the interior of the outer wall. Groomsmen and farriers went about their business, barely sparing Reecah or her escort a second glance.

"Who is this Anvil?" Reecah asked, her attention on the horses. There were more of the magnificent beasts corralled there than Fishmonger Bay had people.

"Don't you worry, Miss GG, you'll find out soon enough," the guard said after several steps. He added through what appeared as a forced smile, "A word to the wise. Never turn your back."

Reecah frowned. She wanted to know more but the guard stopped and pointed to a clearing between the end of the first bank of stables and the beginning of the next.

He turned his head one way and then another, as if looking for something. "Go on. He'll be waiting for you."

Reecah searched the large open space, not seeing anyone. "Are you not coming with me?"

"Hah. Hardly, Miss. I've done my debt."

The guard turned and walked back the way they had come, leaving Reecah standing at the end of the stable, staring at an empty, dirt pitch.

"Ye just gonna stand there, lassie, or ye need me boot up yer arse?"

Reecah jumped sideways, searching for the source of the voice. She stumbled backward as a giant of a man rose from the eave of the stable and jumped to the ground, landing more gracefully than his bulk suggested he could.

Reecah blinked at a bare-chested, bald-headed man. Though tough to see through a thick layer of black hair covering his bronzed skin, the man's powerful body showed no sign of body fat.

He grinned from between a well-groomed goatee. "Me friends call me Anvis Chizel, the Bone Breaker. Ye will call me Anvil. Ya got that, rat?"

Reecah swallowed her discomfort. His voice sounded like slabs of rock grating together. Not trusting herself to speak, she nodded, doing her best to maintain eye contact with his intense, blue-eyed glare. His heavy brow, lined with thick eyebrows, did little to soften his appearance.

"I ain't hearing ye!" Anvil roared.

"Yes sir," Reecah squeaked.

Reecah's Gift

Anvil slammed a huge fist against the thick corner post of the stable—the shelter rattling under the force. Startled workers jumped and stared.

"Sir? I ain't no blatherin' noble, you numbskull! Already ye've forgotten me first order!"

So afraid of what the crazed man might do, she shook her head, not knowing what to say to appease him.

"I said, yer to be calling me Anvil," he growled, grating his clenched fist in his cupped hand. "I promise to be yer death if ye so much as forget anything else I tell ya, ye hear?"

Reecah dipped her head, her eyes widening as Anvil's narrowed. Realizing he expected an answer, she blurted out. "Yes, Anvil!"

Towering over her, he held her gaze, as if daring her to break contact first.

How long they sized each other up, Reecah had no idea. She was vaguely aware of the stable hands watching them, but dared not avert her stare.

Anvil's growl startled her, but his thick lips angled up in a crooked-tooth sneer. "If not for me brother, I'd not waste me time on a puny rat such as ye." He turned toward the outer wall between the stables, to a thick tree stump and a bucket of water that sat in the early morning shadows.

Reecah's attention was drawn to a colossal battle-axe lying on the ground beside the rusted metal bucket.

"Follow me," Anvil muttered. "If ya survive the morning, ye'll prove me wrong."

Reecah's Gift

Flying Terror

Pain was the least of Junior's worries as he crunched across the commons of Fishmonger Bay. The Father Cloth's wife had implored him not to leave—not even to get up, but Junior knew his father. If he didn't demonstrate that he was stronger than a mere arrow to the back, Jonas might disown him for good.

He feared it was too late already, but where else could a young man with no real skills go to earn a living? All he knew had been taught to him by his father. Fishing, sword play, and the dragon hunt. Perhaps he could travel to Thunderhead and look for a job there. The port city teemed with fishermen. But where would he stay?

The unknowns scared him more than the harsh treatment he would receive from his father if he remained.

Gazing at Peril's Peak, its summit lost to low-lying clouds, he didn't relish the trek up the mountain. Walking across the gravelly common area between the village temple and the family warehouse had nearly done him in. When his mother had told him his father had taken the newest members of the hunt to the training cabin, Junior had felt a great weight lift from him. He wouldn't have to speak to Jonas today.

Given his present shape, he considered waiting until morning to begin the arduous trek up the mountain, but if Jonas found out he'd delayed joining the training sessions, it would be easier to bear the pain than the abuse. His mother had inferred the same. How she put up with the man, Junior couldn't imagine.

Reecah's Gift

Not that she was much better. She just couldn't inflict the same level of punishment his father was capable of.

Outfitted in his chainmail hauberk, the trek was going to prove that much more arduous. The weight of the knee-length armour pulled painfully on his injured shoulder.

He checked that his longsword with its simple black hilt sat properly in its sheath. Lugging his bow and quiver across his back wasn't an option so he clasped them in one hand and held his old rucksack in the other. It promised to be a long climb.

Examining himself draped with black leather belts and supports, he was reminded of the dark heir's troops. If his purple-grey surcoat were any darker, he might even pass for one of the elite guards. He laughed. As if. He couldn't even pass as a worthy member of the *Fishmonger Bay* dragon hunt.

Shuffling by the temple, his gaze wandered to the pile of charred rubble against the cliff face forming the backdrop of Fishmonger Bay. The old witch's hut. Nothing remained of the curious lavender shop but the stained-glass door lying amongst a pile of weathered debris and a couple of broken dragon statues fronting the remains.

Junior remembered the day *Grimelda's Clutch* had burned to the ground on the orders of his father. Though he never had contact with the old hag—his father had strictly forbidden it from an early age—a curious sense of sorrow filled him for the way the villagers had treated the woman. He couldn't recall a time the witch had done anything untoward, and yet, she was shunned by everyone. Everyone, except Reecah.

He gritted his teeth. Reecah was lost to him. Had always been if he really thought about it. He was such a fool. It was time to put his life back together if he wished to follow in his father's footsteps.

He shuddered at the thought, but it was time he took ownership of his life. Lifting his chin, he exhaled a determined

Reecah's Gift

breath. Wincing at the pain in his shoulder, he crunched on to join the south trail leading out of the village.

Night fell fast in the mountain canyon. Junior had planned to be well clear of the defile before darkness settled across Peril's Peak, but coupled with his debilitating injury, he had started his trek too late in the day.

Evening shadows stretched across the narrow canyon's rock scattered floor when he stopped and built a meagre fire to keep the autumn chill at bay.

Shivering beneath a thin blanket, he nibbled at a chunk of stale bread, dipping it into a thin broth he boiled from the bones of a turkey his mother had sent along.

The crescent moon drifted between patchy clouds, shortening and lengthening the shadows creeping out of the deeper crevices. A coyote howled in the distance; its call carried on a stiff breeze.

He fingered the hilt of his sword, praying he wouldn't be forced to swing it tonight. Just the thought of wielding the blade made his shoulder ache.

An owl hooted behind him. He searched the darkened walls but couldn't locate the nocturnal bird until it abruptly took flight, scaring him half to death.

He chuckled and shook his head. Who was he fooling? He wasn't cut out for this. He had never enjoyed the excursions with his father into the mountains. Bringing his gaze back to the fire, he jerked backward in terror.

A purple dragon dropped from the sky, landing on its hind legs. Flapping its wings twice to settle onto its forelegs, the campfire's flames reflected in its amethyst eyes.

Junior scrambled to pull his sword free but jumped again.

A brown dragon landed behind him.

Reecah's Gift

Spinning sideways, his chest felt tight as a green dragon landed beside the purple one. Heart hammering in his chest, Junior's breath caught in his throat.

A black raven landed beside the fire. "That's him! That's him!"

The raven! He examined the darkness around the dragons but the hill witch was nowhere to be seen. "Reecah?"

He squinted, hoping to see her on one of the dragon's backs. She wasn't.

Trembling more than the night air called for, he shouted in alarm as a rough, female voice sounded inside his head. *"Are you the one they call Junior?"*

His eyes grew wide. Clamping trembling hands over his temples, he jerked his head in every direction, searching for the source of the voice.

A diminutive female voice resonated in his mind, *"He's the one she spoke with the day my brother died."*

A male voice joined the dialogue. *"He's bigger than Reecah. I don't think I'm up to it."*

Junior's jaw dropped. Though he had no way of proving it, he was certain the dragons were projecting their voices inside his head. Quickly looking from one dragon to another, he tried to discern which one was speaking.

"Scarletclaws vouched for him. Said he tried to warn Reecah of the danger at the Dragon Temple. If what Raver says is true, Reecah will need all the help she can get."

Junior thought that had been the green dragon talking.

"Help! Help!" the raven shrieked.

Junior's nerves jumped further. He didn't think his heart could take much more.

"If we're wrong, we might be delivering someone to kill her," the male voice said.

"If we don't do anything, the prince will kill her," the original female voice responded.

130

Reecah's Gift

He pulled his sword from its sheath. "Reecah's in danger?"

As soon as the words left his mouth, the dragons closed in on him. He lowered the sword's tip to the ground, not wishing to provoke them.

Reecah's Gift

The green dragon leaned its fearsome face close, appearing at least a head taller than the last time he had seen it a fortnight ago. *"Do you love her?"*

That was an odd question. He assumed the dragon meant Reecah. He didn't really know her, and yet, he had to admit, there was something special between them—at least *he* thought so.

Staring the green dragon in the mouth robbed him of his voice. Afraid if he didn't answer, the dragon would tear his throat out, he nodded—slowly at first and then more emphatically.

"Good." The green dragon sat back. *"Because if anything happens to her, I will eat you."*

The thought shocked him to the core. How did one respond to a claim like that? "I hear your voices in my head but your lips aren't moving. How's that possible?"

"Because of your friendship with Reecah Windwalker, we have allowed you into our circle of trust," the huskier female voice said, as if that explained everything. *"For the moment, at least."*

"Reecah *Windwalker?* You mean Reecah Draakvriend. The girl who owns that bird." Junior pointed at Raver, afraid to take his eyes from the dragon.

"So, you do know her." The brown dragon leaned in. *"My name is Swoop. My purple friend is Silence. You've already met Lurker. We're here to take you to Reecah. According to Raver, she's in grave danger."*

"Grave danger! Grave danger!"

"Ow!" Junior jerked his leg away to stop Raver from pecking at his ankle. Keeping an eye on the bird, he concentrated on the dragon called Swoop.

"Why? What's happened? Where is she?"

Lurker's voice entered his head; the switching of voices, unsettling. *"She's on her way to the high king. She's become aware that Prince J'kwaad fought at the Dragon Temple. We fear he's going to kill her. According to Raver, she possesses something he seeks."*

Reecah's Gift

The implication of Swoop's words sank in. "What exactly do you mean by, *taking me* to her?"

"We're trying to work that out," Swoop chimed in.

"I'm telling you. He's too heavy. Look at him. He must weigh twice as much as Reecah."

Junior turned to Lurker. "Weigh twice as much as Reecah? What do you...?" Comprehension dawned on him. He held his palms out. "Oh no."

Swoop nodded. *"Speed is essential. Reecah doesn't have much time."*

Junior backed away. "If you think I'm climbing on one of your backs, you're crazy."

Lurker advanced on him. *"If you think we're going to let Reecah die, it is you who has lost your mind. We're prepared to drag you across the treetops dangling from our claws, if necessary."*

"But...but..." Just the thought of touching a dragon instilled him with dread. There was no way he could fly one.

Silence's amethyst eyes bore into him. *"Do you care for Reecah?"*

"Of course," Junior blurted—the first time he had openly admitted it.

He stopped backing up and puffed out his chest. Raising his chin in defiance, he couldn't believe the words escaping his lips, "I would die for her."

Silence nodded once. *"Then so shall you fly."*

Junior finished packing his rucksack and secured his bow and quiver as best he could over his healthy shoulder. Filled with a newfound conviction, he mentally prepared himself to abandon the only life he knew to join a trio of dragons on a journey to the high king's castle. He wished he could see his father's face as his unworthy son mounted a dragon and took to the skies.

Reecah's Gift

He almost stumbled; his knees wobbling as the reality sunk in. His movements slowed on purpose, drawing out the time it took to kick dirt and stones onto the campfire.

Swoop's voice startled him. *"I think you got it."*

Junior stopped scraping the ground with his boots—the canyon floor bathed in faint moonlight. The fire had gone out a while ago. It was cold without his hauberk, but Lurker insisted that if he were to fly on his back, he must remove the heavy chainmail. The armour lay at Swoop's feet. She promised to carry it.

He swallowed. If he ran really fast, he might be able to…He shook his head to quell his mounting fear. He wasn't doing this for himself. This was for Reecah.

Warmth flooded him. He imagined the surprise on her face when he dropped out of the sky to save her. If he survived the trip, it would be worth every heart-stopping moment.

"Okay. I'm ready."

Lurker touched his chest to the ground and swivelled his head Junior's way. *"I've only done this twice before. Get on and hug my neck. Let me look after the balance otherwise you'll upset us."*

Junior nodded, unable to speak. The vision of upsetting a dragon in flight left him cold. He couldn't believe he was about to fly one. He exhaled a heavy sigh, remembering he was a Waverunner. Waverunners didn't show others their weaknesses. "Let's do this."

It took him a couple of tries to sort out his feet as he mounted Lurker's neck. The texture of dragon scales beneath his fingers unnerved him. Settling his weight, he could have sworn he heard the dragon groan.

Lurker leaned back. *"Hold on tight but don't choke me like Reecah did her first time."*

Startled, Junior did what he was asked not to do.

"I need to breathe if I'm going to fly," Lurker gasped.

Reecah's Gift

Junior relaxed his grip, nearly slipping from Lurker's shoulder. "Sorry. This is going to take some getting used to."

"For you and me both. Don't be too long about it, though. I can't help you if you fall through the clouds."

Glancing at the clouds wafting past the snow-capped pinnacle of Peril's Peak wasn't one of Junior's best ideas. His shaking hands tried to find a comfortable position around Lurker's long neck.

"Are you ready?"

"No," Junior squeaked.

Lurker leaned back. *"Me neither."* Unfurling his leathery wings, he crouched and sprung into the air.

Junior screamed. The dark ground fell away. He pushed his head against Lurker's neck and held on tight.

"If you choke me to death, your own demise will soon follow."

Junior lifted his head to stare at the back of Lurker's neck. Loosening his hold, he felt his body slip to one side. He reasserted his iron grip.

"Only one of us can control the balance. If you counteract me, this will be a short flight."

"Sorry." Junior did his best to allow his body to flow with Lurker's undulations, but he struggled to release his stranglehold. Daring to look around, he was stunned. Soft moonlight refracted off the jagged summit of Peril's Peak. To the north of the snowcap, the orange glow of a campfire marked the dragon hunt camp.

Thinking he had control, he unsheathed his sword—pointing its tip at the moon and shouting in euphoria. He promptly lost his balance.

Lurker dipped to one side, almost pitching him from his back, but quickly corrected his flight and caught Junior's sideways momentum.

Junior wrapped his sword arm around Lurker's neck and squeezed hard—eyes wide with terror.

Reecah's Gift

"Do that again and I'll throw you myself."

Junior nodded into Lurker's neck, his eyes shut tight. After several steady wing beats, he opened them again to gape at the dark terrain whisking by.

"How're you doing?" Swoop asked.

Junior was about to answer but Lurker spoke. The question wasn't intended for him. Speaking with dragons was going to take some getting used to.

"Better than I thought. He's heavier than Reecah but I'm learning to move with him. It's tiring compensating for his balance. I should let you try. See if you can do it without dropping him."

Junior frowned at the back of Lurker's head. Did they know he could hear them?

"I'd like that. It'll make diving at the ground a new challenge."

Junior snapped his head around, trying to locate the brown dragon, following the chinking of his chainmail as it flapped in the wind. The last thing he wanted was to become part of a dragon experiment.

"I don't think I'd like that," Junior said as he caught sight of Swoop in the moonlight; his armour dangling from one of her back feet.

He couldn't see where Silence had gotten to. Given her purple colour, she blended in with the night sky.

Lurker swung his head sideways, the motion throwing off the newly realized smoothness of their flight. *"You may have no choice if we want to reach the capital. I'm tiring already."*

Junior's grasp on Lurker's neck increased, his attention on the mountain crags far below. Moonlight glinted off the ocean. Dozens of small lights dotted the coast, grouped together in one spot.

Catching his breath, Junior managed to croak, "Is that the village?"

Lurker's head dipped. *"Aye. We'll be glad to be rid of that place."*

Reecah's Gift

Though he commiserated with those sentiments, Junior felt a pang of regret at abandoning his family. They would worry about him.

He suddenly laughed. Who was he kidding? They would be glad to be rid of him.

"What's so funny?"

"Huh? Oh, nothing." He must have laughed out loud. Or perhaps the dragons read his mind. He smiled. He didn't care. Flying a dragon through the clouds, it was as if he were the king of the world.

Everything appeared different from the air—almost flat. He wasn't sure, but he believed a darker rock formation cutting into the ocean was the great promontory known as the Summoning Stone. Lifting his face from Lurker's neck, he enjoyed the cold wind blowing through his hair.

Ahead, a white monolith rose skyward. Dragonfang! The natural rock formation marked the beginning of Dragonfang Pass.

Bittersweet memories assailed him—mostly bitter. But a few recollections put a smile on his face. Seeing Reecah at the waterfall was unforgettable, but the memory of the day he held her in his arms in her little hut on the hill sent goosebumps all over his body. He couldn't recall a time he'd ever felt so at peace.

"Lurker, do you know where Reecah's hut is?"

"Aye."

"Take me there."

Reecah's Gift

Beaten

Anvil grabbed the bucket and drank from it, water slopping off his chin and running through the matted hair covering his chest.

Just the sight of the water on his exposed flesh made Reecah shiver. The early morning air was so cold, rain would have turned to snow. Eyeing the beast of a man, she estimated he stood a head taller than Joram Waverunner—the vile uncle of Junior and Jaxon.

Anvil dropped the bucket to the ground; water sloshing over its sides. Wiping his goatee with the back of his hand, he pointed his chin at her. "Ach, lassie, why ya still wearin' all yer truck? Ye ain't to be fightin' carrying a satchel over yer shoulder are ya?"

Reecah looked at the blotchy, rust-stained ground around the stump, not sure what Anvil expected. If he didn't come out and tell her, how was she to know? She shrugged her rucksack free and put it against the wall near the bucket.

"Don't ye be eyeing me water, either. If ya ain't got the sense to bring yer own, I'm not to be offerin' sympathy."

Reecah thought about her waterskin. She hadn't filled it since leaving the *Serpent's Slip*, but it had some water left in it. Surely, she could find a well around the castle as the day went on.

"Now, off with it."

Reecah gaped.

"Ye plan on wrestlin' in yer cloak an' yer bow an' quiver strapped to yer back?"

138

Reecah's Gift

She held his gaze for a moment. It wouldn't be wise to sass him so she propped her quarterstaff against the wall and slipped her bow and quiver free.

She met Anvil's gaze.

His intense stare indicated her sword belt. "Ya plan on wrestlin' with that cumbersome thing strapped to your waist?"

He had mentioned wrestling twice now. She thought he meant sparring, but it sounded as if he wanted to engage her in hand-to-hand combat. Even if she knew how to fight with her hands, she was no match for his sheer size and strength. Breaking the village boys' noses as a child was a poor substitute to trading blows with a brute whose arms were thicker than her thighs.

"Well?" Anvil snarled, rubbing his hands together and stepping back and forth before her. "Prepare yerself, or I'll chuck yer sorry arse over the wall."

Reecah felt her eyes growing heavy with tears. The sensation fueled a deep anger about Anvil's demeanour toward her. The same, unfair way almost everyone else had treated her.

Taking a deep breath to steady her fear, she turned away from his baleful glare and undid the dual buckles securing her sword belt and attached cummerbund—propping them against the wall with the rest of her gear.

She caught a sudden movement in the corner of her eye and jumped away from the tree stump just in time to avoid Anvil's whirling battle-axe. The curved blade sliced into the hardwood stump with such ferocity, it buried itself four fingers deep.

She stumbled against her gear and tripped, falling to her backside.

Anvil stood over her, breathing heavily. "Lesson number one, rat. Never leave your back exposed. To anyone." He spat on the ground. Grabbing the cord-wrapped handle of his axe, he wriggled the blade free. "I lose half me new recruits that way."

Reecah's Gift

Reecah lay on the ground with her weapons sprawled on top of her—her heart hammering in her chest as she tried to calm her ragged breathing. Her gaze took in the rust-coloured stains on the dirt around the stump. The drawbridge guard's warning came back to her: *"...never turn your back."*

She admonished herself. A little late to remember that now. Even so, it was a dirty trick the royal weapon master employed. Before she could stop herself, she blurted, "That's a cruel way to teach someone to fight."

The battle-axe slid free of the stump. Anvil held it across his stomach with a wide grip and hovered over her. "It'd be crueler by far to let an ill-prepared whelp go off to fight without realizing what a real fight's all about. Especially if yer responsible for someone else. Lesson two. Never drop yer weapons. I'll bet yer pretty arse, ain't no one gonna wait 'til yer good an' ready afore they let you have a go at them. Take ya in the back sooner 'n spit in yer eye, or suffer the kraken's curse."

His words confused her. "I thought you were going to teach me hand-to-hand combat?"

"Pfft. Please. I use bigger things than you to wipe me arse."

Reecah glared at the hulk, biting back the angry retort threatening to fling itself past her lips.

"Now get up afore I kick ya in the teeth." He stepped away, propped his axe against the wall, and lifted the bucket to his lips.

Something inside Reecah snapped. If she had taken a moment to think about it, she never would have thrown her gear aside and launched herself at Anvil in a blind rage. Unfortunately, she didn't enjoy the leisure of a long temper.

Leaping onto Anvil's back, she wrapped her arms around his throat and squeezed tight, snarling into his ear, "Lesson number one, *Anvil*. Never leave your back exposed. To *anyone*."

Anvil's strong hands pried at her arms but she squeezed tighter, causing him to stagger backward, gasping.

140

Reecah's Gift

"Let's see you wipe your arse now." Her arms and shoulders pained her, hanging in the air from his broad back, but she knew if she let go, she was done for.

Anvil tried to say something, but couldn't get air past her grip. Stumbling, he drove his back against the castle wall, crushing her between himself and the rough stone.

Reecah's grip loosened. Before she could adjust her hold, he leaned forward and flexed backward, slamming her into the wall. A bright light flashed in her head as her skull smacked off the unforgiving surface. She lost her grip and slid down Anvil's back to sit dazed in the dirt.

Anvil staggered forward, bent over and grasping his throat.

The fury behind his eyes frightened her. Her weapons lay on the far side of the stump. She considered trying for his axe, but there was no way she could hope to wield such a weapon.

A shadow fell over her. Certain she was about to die, she tried to summon enough wherewithal to mount a defense.

He picked her up by the armpits as if she were a small sack of grain and thumped her against the wall—her feet not touching the ground. Spittle strung between his lips. "Never has anyone caught me unaware like that. Ye live for that reason alone. We'll see if the same holds true by the end of the day. Ye best be ready when I return."

Releasing his hold, she hit the ground and her legs crumpled beneath her. She dropped to her hands and knees, drool hanging off her lips as he walked away.

She attempted to go after him, but stumbled and fell to her knees. Breathing heavily, she wiped her mouth on a dusty vambrace—the grit crunching between her teeth. There would come another time the man left himself vulnerable. When that time came, she promised to be ready.

Reecah's Gift

The sun had crested the exterior wall at Reecah's back by the time Anvil returned with a score of young men and women entering ahead of him—the newcomers outfitted in dun-coloured, cheap leather armour and carrying round, battered, wooden shields.

Though she wore no real armour of her own, her vambraces and thick sword belt protected her better than the thin chest pieces hanging a-kilter from the people eyeing her with curiosity.

Ensuring her gear hung properly and was easily accessible, she held her chin high and returned their inquisitive looks.

"Grunts," Anvil's grating voice filled the yard. "Meet the bilge rat. Just sailed in last night and thinks she's ready to whoop yer arses."

Reecah gaped, her gaze jumping from one annoyed sneer to another; shaking her head vigorously. She hadn't said anything of the sort.

The weapon master walked around the end of the semi-circle forming in front of Reecah, a few bows and a quiver full of arrows in his fists. Approaching the stump, he never once turned his back on anyone.

Stopping out of sword's reach from Reecah, he faced the newcomers. "It's come to my attention that *GG*,"—he indicated Reecah with a side nod—"stowed away aboard a merchant ship out of Thunderhead and made her way to the king's city to be with ye today. Aren't ye all blessed?"

Reecah's eyes locked on Anvil. So that was why Anvil referred to her as *rat*. How he knew so much, concerned her. She hadn't told anyone of her recent adventure. Not even Aramyss Chizel.

"While ye slobs broke fast this morning, GG and I got on quite famously." A smugness creased his angular features. "Didn't we, rat?"

Reecah's Gift

Reecah tried to keep the emotion from her face but she wasn't certain she was successful. Not trusting herself, she said nothing.

"As you can see by GG's fancy weaponry, she's likely too high above yer level of training to benefit from rubbin' elbows with you lowly scum. Ain't that right, *rat?*"

Reecah's eyes narrowed. She bit back the angry denial she wanted to spit out, realizing it would sound like a whine. Her chest heaved, but she kept her temper in check.

The weapon master broke eye contact and searched the crowd, his gaze coming to rest on a taller, broad-shouldered youth who reminded her of Junior. "Flavian Silvertongue, get yer arse over here."

The young man sporting brown hair past his shoulders, straightened up. "Aye, Anvil!" He pushed past those in front of him and stepped on the far side of Anvil, taking great pains to keep his back away from the weapon master.

"Yer by far the best ranged-weapon recruit of this pitiful group. Let's see if the bilge rat is equal to the test. Perhaps we be wasting our time with her, eh?" Anvil tossed him an unstrung bow. "Pick yer targets."

Flavian puffed out his chest. "Aye, Anvil!" He leaned his shield against the wall and stepped across the bow Anvil had thrown him, bending the length of wood around his lower thigh and slipping the string's loop knot over its notched end. He tested its pull and accepted the old quiver.

The gathering backed away several steps, following Flavian's eye.

"There." Flavian pointed to a crack in the interior castle wall about a quarter of the way up.

Reecah squinted. "That spot above the black cow by the moat?"

Flavian gave her an impatient look. "Ya, why? Don't think you can hit it?"

Reecah's Gift

Reecah frowned. "I'm not shooting at a wall. The stone will ruin my arrow."

Anvil growled, "Give the rat one of yers."

Reecah accepted the arrow without comment and examined its worn, chipped shaft, noting its fletches needed replacing.

Flavian bladed his stance, nocked his arrow, took aim and let fly. His arrow arced across the training yard, soaring over the moat and hitting the top edge of the crack. Lowering his bow, he beamed.

Anvil nodded his approval. "Nice shot." He raised a single eyebrow. "Yer turn, rat."

Reecah took a deep breath, trying hard not to rise to the bait. Like it or not, Anvil's intimidation tactics were working. Making matters worse, everyone in the clearing stared at her.

Nocking her arrow, she adjusted her stance, raised her bow and took aim. As soon as the arrow left her fingers, she knew she had misjudged the flight. The arrow ricocheted off the wall and splashed into the moat near the cow.

Several titters were heard, but no one spoke.

Anvil roared, "Hah! Yer first time shooting a bow?"

Reecah seethed but kept the acid from her tone, "The arrow weight is different than mine."

Anvil crossed his arms beneath his substantial chest. "Arrow weight, is it?" He snatched another arrow from the quiver and threw it at her. "Now ye have the weight. Try again."

Reecah inspected the arrow—its shaft anything but true.

"We're aging," Anvil muttered.

Knowing better than to react, Reecah set the arrow, adjusted her draw and angle and let fly. The errant missile struck the wall midway between the ground and the crack—its aim fairly true but its flight well short.

"At least ya didn't impale the heifer," Anvil muttered, shaking his head. He threw her another arrow. "Your turn to choose a target, rat. I'm thinking ye better make it a good one."

144

Reecah's Gift

Reecah missed catching the arrow. Bending down to retrieve it, she subconsciously checked on everyone's location. Swallowing her building anxiety, she searched the clearing for something to aim at. Other than nondescript stone walls and the stable, there was nothing *to* shoot at.

"I-I'm not sure what to pick."

"Afraid ye might miss, ya mean?"

She took a deep breath, warning herself to keep her thoughts to herself. "No, Anvil. I mean, there's nothing to shoot at."

Anvil's eyes darkened. Grabbing Flavian's shield, he searched the outer wall until he found a rusted iron hook embedded between two large blocks of stone halfway up. It took several tries, but the weapon master managed to snag the shield's loose handhold.

"Try that," Anvil said. Shooing the trainees back toward the inner moat, he used the toe of his boot to draw a line in the dirt. "Stand there."

Reecah hesitated, worrying there was another test here somewhere. "If I stand there, I put my back between the others.

"If ye make it through the day, these'll be yer mates. The hands ye'll be placing yer life into. If ya have reason to fear yer mates, ye're already dead."

Anvil spoke like that was something she should have known. He made her feel so dumb, changing his rules on the fly and contravening what he had said earlier. She wanted to point out that she had no idea when to know who was who, but bit her tongue.

Stepping behind the line, her eyes darted everywhere, but no one made a move on her. The distance to the hanging shield was shorter than that of the crack they had shot at. No breeze stirred between the walls. Sizing up her shot, she had a sinking feeling that if she missed again, it would spell the end of her training.

Reecah's Gift

The arrow felt no different than the others. Compensating for her other attempts, she took a steadying breath, drew and let fly.

She winced. Confident she had aimed true, the training arrow veered right, shattering against the wall, well off target.

Snorts of derision sounded from the people gathered behind her.

Her shoulders slumped.

Anvil studied the spot where her arrow had disintegrated for some time, his huge head nodding slightly. He turned his intense stare her way. "Ain't often I goes against the wishes of me brother, but ye ain't worth me time. Grab yer gear and leave."

Reecah fought the tears blurring her vision. She was so close to taking that first big step on the road to saving the dragons, only to be undone by inferior training arrows. Despite her better judgement she glowered at Anvil. "It's not fair."

"Hah! Not fair is it now?" Anvil leaned forward, jabbing his finger a whisper from the bridge of her nose. "Life ain't fair, bilge rat. Go, before I decide to use you as a live target for me *real* trainees!"

Anvil held his finger before her for a moment longer. Stepping aside, he pointed to the stone structure housing the barbican in the distance.

Reecah felt every eye on her back as she collected her quarterstaff near the stump. The tears dripping off her reddened cheeks humiliated her further. Humbled in front of total strangers, she started for the stables.

Not caring anymore, she stopped; her shoulders and chest heaved with built-up frustration. "Perhaps you should learn how to care for your equipment."

The astonished faces of the trainees gave her a little satisfaction, but the sight of Anvil's face turning purple should have been her cue to hurry away. Instead, she pulled an arrow

Reecah's Gift

from her quiver. "Little good your training will be if you outfit them with inferior equipment. You need to train like you would fight. I'm surprised you, of all people, don't appreciate that. I doubt *you* could hit that target."

Anvil glared death at her insubordination. Without a word, he stormed over to the stump and retrieved his battle-axe.

Reecah notched her arrow but the weapon master ignored the threat. He returned to a place near the line he had drawn on the ground. Releasing a nerve-rattling shriek, he took three quick steps and launched his battle-axe through the air.

Reecah's jaw dropped.

The mighty weapon twirled through the air with hardly an arc—the vicious blade splitting the suspended shield nearly in half, lodging itself high above the ground.

The only sounds in the training yard were the royal pennants snapping in the breeze high above the ramparts and the occasional whinny from the stables.

Reecah pulled her stunned gaze from the impaled shield.

His face twisted with rage, Anvil turned his attention her way. "Look what ye've done! I'm of a mind to haul yer carcass to the top of the wall and drop ya on me axe to get it down." He started toward her.

Reecah's mind whirled. She needed to run. By the crazed look in Anvil's eye, she didn't doubt he would follow through with his threat.

Raising her bow, she considered her options. If she was quick enough, she might pump two arrows into the weapon master before he reached her, but she feared that may not be enough to bring the giant man down.

Drawing the bowstring taut, she sighted, and released.

Anvil stopped walking and gaped.

The arrow flew true, flying between the crack in the shield and severing the visible leather thong suspending the shield from the rusted hook. The shield tumbled down the uneven

147

wall's surface, breaking in two and releasing Anvil's axe before they crashed to the ground with a clatter.

"That's what proper equipment does," Reecah said through gritted teeth. Not caring whether Anvil chased her down, she defied his number one rule and turned her back—making her way to the tunnel leading out of South Fort.

Reecah's Gift

Draakval Dilemma

Soaring high above the world on the back of a dragon was an experience Junior thought would never grow old. After stopping by the Draakvriend hut on the hill north of Fishmonger Bay, they had taken to the air at sunrise and followed the coast north. He remained respectfully quiet as they flew by the entrance to Dragonfang Pass—all eyes searching the valley beyond but nothing bigger than Raver greeted their hopeful stares.

They rested several times throughout the morning upon lofty tors Junior was certain no man had ever stood on. Swoop had offered to take a turn carrying Junior, but Lurker thankfully denied her, wisely stating that her maiden flight with a passenger should be done on a flat field or over water.

Leaping off a jag of granite, the sudden weightlessness robbed Junior of his breath as Lurker's body dropped in the sky until the wind beneath his beating wings lifted them again. The coastline's northerly tack dropped away; the vista of endless mountain peaks veered eastward as far as he could see.

"Do you know where you're going?" Junior asked, astounded by the sheer scope of the Great Kingdom. They hadn't seen a sign of civilization since leaving Fishmonger Bay.

"We have no idea."

"How do you know we're going in the right direction?"

"Raver."

Reecah's Gift

"Raver?" Junior looked around, confident enough to lift his head from Lurker's neck once they were airborne. He couldn't locate Reecah's raven.

Swoop flew close to their left, his chainmail dangling from her claws.

Silence drifted much higher, her sharp eyesight constantly scanning. Junior was amazed at how the purple dragon floated in the air without ever beating her wings.

"Has Raver been to Draakhall before?"

"Not that I'm aware of. The boat Reecah sailed followed a northerly direction. It'll have to make landfall somewhere. We just have to follow the coastline and investigate every port."

Junior nodded. He hadn't thought of it that way. Scanning the line of mountains south and east he wondered if they would ever see habitable land again. He stared at the glistening water north and west, stretching to the horizon without end, and experienced a sensation of unworthiness. Who was he, a disowned child from a backward community, to sail through the skies on the wings of a dragon, thinking he could rescue Reecah from the clutches of the dark heir?

"Silence sees something," Lurker's voice startled him from his reverie. Junior wasn't sure who his mount spoke to. He couldn't figure out whether everyone in their party heard each other all the time, or if they were able to hone in on one mind.

Swoop gained altitude to join the purple dragon, her form a mere speck in the sky above.

"Looks to be two volcanoes smoking in the distance," Lurker said.

Junior strained to sit higher on Lurker's shoulder and nearly lost his balance. If not for Lurker compensating for the sudden weight shift, he may have fallen to his death.

"You're choking me again," Lurker gasped.

Junior eased his stranglehold. "Sorry."

Lurker flapped several times to maintain a steady altitude. *"I need to land soon."*

150

Reecah's Gift

Raver called out twice, his raspy caw far below.

Junior swore the bird had repeated Lurker's last two words.

"Silence thinks we're approaching the Draakval Colony," Swoop's rough, female voice replaced Lurker's.

"How does she know that?"

"She didn't say, but she knows a lot more than you or I."

Junior pondered that. "Another dragon colony?"

Swoop's voice answered, *"Dragon Home is considered by dragons everywhere as the birthplace of dragons. I'm sure Silence will correct me if I'm wrong, but I believe our colony, the Draakclaw Colony, is the oldest one in the Great Kingdom."* She paused for a few moments; her voice subdued as she added, *"At least it was. Over the centuries, several groups of dragons left Draakclaw to form new colonies."*

Fear of flying past a dragon colony tightened Junior's grip around Lurker's neck. "That's a good thing then. Right?"

The lack of response spoke volumes.

"Why? What's wrong?"

Swoop dropped headfirst from on high like an avalanche, the wind snapping at her leather wings as she levelled off beside them.

Junior hoped he never got the chance to fly the brown dragon.

"The Draakval Colony is inhabited by rogue dragons."

The phrase, *'rogue dragons,'* echoed in Junior's mind.

Swoop craned her neck, her light green eyes on Lurker and him. *"We'd best avoid them if we can."*

Other than her many horns, Swoop's colouring wasn't much different than Lurker's. A little browner than green, but from a distance, Junior wasn't sure he'd be able to tell them apart.

"I need to land soon."

The gravity in Lurker's voice made Junior tighten his hold.

"Though, if Junior keeps squeezing, we'll be hitting the ground in short order."

Reecah's Gift

"Sorry! Sorry. I can't help myself." Junior adjusted his grip for the countless time. There had to be a better way to fly a dragon than clinging to its neck and praying you didn't fall off. He couldn't imagine how hard it would be in the rain.

"Then we should find a place to land. According to Silence, if we don't find Draakhall soon, we'll have to either fly inland or out to sea to avoid Draakval." Swoop curled her wingtips and shot high above. *"I'll tell her we're landing."*

Watching Swoop soar almost out of sight, her parting comment resonated with Junior. He searched the sky and noted that Silence had flown higher—almost out of sight. The dragons must have a limit as to how far they projected their thoughts.

A sudden loss in elevation disconcerted him. Clinging tight, he watched Swoop plummet past them with Silence descending at a more reasonable rate.

"I'm choking."

"You need to tell me when we're about to change direction. I thought I was falling."

"I'll try to remember that."

Lurker set down in a wide glen near the top of the closest mountain.

Junior slid from his back, rubbing at his aching posterior before Lurker's wings had settled. The familiar chinking of his chainmail sounded behind him as Swoop released his gear and dropped into the tall grass. A breeze swept across the mountain face, providing him little respite from the bone-chilling cold he had experienced in the air. He searched the clearing and the sky above. "Where's Silence?"

"Gone to scout ahead," Swoop answered.

Thinking to don his lined armour to garner some warmth before they set off again, he asked, "How long are we going to wait here?"

"Depends on what Silence reports."

Reecah's Gift

Shivers wracked his body, making the decision for him. He walked past Swoop, removed his surcoat, and pulled his chainmail over his head—the metal links cold on his exposed skin.

Swoop watched him struggle. *"Glad I don't have to do that every time I want to protect myself."*

Junior thought Lurker laughed.

"You're not kidding. Scales are much more convenient. That looks like trouble."

Junior popped his head through the neck hole and glanced at the dragons. Ignoring them, he pulled at the bound chinks until the knee-length hauberk hung properly. Slipping into his surcoat, he buckled his sword belt in place.

The battle at the Dragon Temple was still fresh in Junior's mind. The image of the king's men facing the dragon assault on the ridge across from Dragon Home wouldn't leave him. The senseless carnage on both sides was such a waste of life.

"Don't you think we should warn the Draakval Colony? Like them or not, Prince J'kwaad will be coming for them. If he hasn't already."

Swoop and Lurker exchanged looks.

Lurker nodded. *"That's a good point."*

Junior walked up to them—something he would have never dreamt of doing a couple of days ago. "If dragons are going to survive the high king's edict, you need to put aside your differences and join forces."

"What about Reecah?" Swoop asked. *"If she can convince the king of his folly, we won't have anything to worry about."*

Junior wanted to believe that, but Reecah had no experience in negotiating as far as he knew. As great a person as she was, he doubted that would be enough to avert the high king's decision to exterminate the dragon population. By destroying the Draakclaw Colony, the line had been drawn.

Reecah's Gift

If any other dragons had survived the slaughter besides these three, Junior didn't doubt they would harbour a deep bitterness toward the royal seat. He was surprised Lurker, Swoop, and Silence had taken the defeat so well.

"If the Draakval Colony hasn't been hit, we need to tell them about their approaching peril."

"*I agree.*" Swoop turned her gaze on Lurker. "*See? I told you we shouldn't eat him.*"

Raver called out from the branches of a nearby bush, "Eat him! Eat him!"

Lurker swung his head from Junior to the raven. "*Time will tell. If anything happens to Reecah…*"

A hair-raising screech split the mountain air. Junior jumped to his feet and withdrew his sword, cringing as the pain behind his shoulder gripped him.

Lurker and Swoop craned their necks, searching the sky.

Raver emerged from the tall grass and landed awkwardly on top of a bush, his hooked beak indicating the direction of the disturbance.

High above Junior's small campfire of smoking reeds and other refuse he had foraged, a massive, red dragon shrieked as a smaller, brown dragon blasted it with flames.

At first, Junior thought Scarletclaws had found them, but there was no way the massive red beast could be her. The red dragon deflected the fire with a wing, but the action caused it to fall from the sky. Dropping from harm's way, it spread its wings wide, swooping low over the far end of the glen.

The brown dragon dove after it.

Shocked, Junior marvelled at how the smaller brown dominated the monstrous red.

The red dragon barely missed hitting the ground before skimming the high grasses. Approaching the point where the

Reecah's Gift

mountain peak rose overhead, the red dragon climbed into the air.

The brown dragon slammed into its neck like it had been shot from a ballista—bared teeth hammering into the red's neck and driving it to the ground.

Swoop stepped back and forth. *"Should we intervene?"*

"No. We don't know what they're fighting about." Lurker searched the sky. *"Nor do we know if there are more."*

Lurker had no sooner finishing speaking than another brown dragon curled around the peak and shot into the glen, its feet driving into the red's hind legs, knocking it sideways.

Junior took a few steps toward the battle. "That dragon doesn't have front legs." He squinted, trying to follow the rapid movement of the original brown. "I don't think the other one does either."

"Those are wyverns," Lurker said as if it was common knowledge.

Junior mouthed the word, *'Wyverns.'* "What's that?"

"A dragon without front legs. According to Mother, wyverns are related to us. Because of their difference in appearance and size, they are usually shunned by what some call real *dragons."*

He pondered Lurker's answer. The more he learned about dragons, the more he realized they weren't much different than people.

"Are wyverns stronger than dragons?"

Both Swoop and Lurker cast brooding glares his way.

"Okay, okay. Geesh."

The red dragon emitted a terrible screech.

Lurker spread his wings and prepared to take to the air. *"Come on, we'd better intervene. He's outnumbered."*

Swoop jumped into the air close behind him.

Junior watched them go, not sure he should follow. Stepping between five fighting dragons bristling with dagger-sized teeth and sword-length claws didn't strike him as a wise thing to do.

Reecah's Gift

There was also the fiery breath to consider. He didn't think Lurker or Swoop possessed the ability to spew flames yet, but the first wyvern had demonstrated its capability.

He ran a hand over his hauberk. Fat lot of good shiny chain links would be against dragon fire. Shaking his head, he knew he had to do something. If Lurker and Swoop perished, he would be hard-pressed finding his way out of the mountains before succumbing to the elements or worse.

The image of a brown-haired, hazel-eyed, young woman flashed through his mind. It would break Reecah's heart if anything were to happen to Lurker or Swoop.

He approached the bush Raver sat on, unsure whether the bird would understand him. "Raver. I need you to get word to Reecah."

Raver turned his beady eyes on him.

"Yes, Reecah. You know who I'm talking about, don't you? I need you to find her."

Raver tilted his head.

"Tell her we're coming. She needs to lie low until we get there. Can you do that for me?"

Raver blinked.

The red dragon's shriek made the hair on his arms stand.

His attention on the imposing dragon, Raver startled him, cawing twice and jumping into the air, winging his way toward the distant ocean. He followed Raver's progress until the bird disappeared beyond the bulk of the mountain.

Heaving a big sigh, he hoisted his sword, ignoring the pain, and ran across the glen—shouting more to bolster his own courage than to have any effect on the combatants.

Lurker joined the fray, followed closely by a dive-bombing Swoop.

The wyverns shrieked and gnashed at them—the distraction allowing the bigger red to get its feet under it. It grabbed the

156

wyvern about to spew fire at Lurker by the wing and tossed it aside.

The wyvern wrestling with Swoop disengaged and confronted the red dragon, spurting a small bout of orange flame.

Junior slowed his run and raised his sword as all dragon eyes turned on his insignificant form. A shadow passed close by his head, dropping him to his knees.

Silence appeared between him and the closest wyvern, removing him from harm's way.

"Enough!" he shouted.

Silence craned her neck to eye him with all the others.

Six sets of dragon eyes bore into him.

He gulped the little moisture he had left in his mouth and walked around Silence. "This is senseless. We need to come together, not tear each other apart."

The red dragon appeared on the verge of blasting him.

Lurker stepped in between. *"Kill our friend and we'll leave the wyverns to finish you."*

The red dragon's crimson eyes narrowed. *"You protect a human? Have you not learned the age-old lesson? They aren't to be trusted? Why do you think the colonies are divided?"*

The new voice grated in his head, its presence distracting him for a moment. He absently wondered how he could hear it.

"This one's different," Lurker answered.

"You can't be serious. Look at him. Turn your back and he'll stick that steel tooth in it. Let me finish him and we'll continue this discussion as brethren." The red dragon's eyes narrowed further, glancing at the wyverns. *"Perhaps after we rid ourselves of the wyrms."*

Lurker shuffled his feet, turning his back on the red dragon towering over the rest of the group. *"Let's go then. Red obviously doesn't require assistance."*

The wyverns hissed, lowering their heads to the ground and edging toward the red.

Reecah's Gift

Red snapped at the closest wyvern. *"Wait!"*

Lurker stopped but didn't turn around.

"For the benefit of the wretched creature with the sword, my human name is Lasair. I shouldn't need to remind you that dragons should help each other without hesitation, not abandon one of your own to these beasts."

The original wyvern shook his head. *"You attacked my sister."*

Junior glanced from one dragon to another, trying to follow the conversation. Somehow, he was able to hear everyone speaking. Scanning the winged beasts assembled around him, as far as he was concerned, a dragon was a dragon, regardless of how many legs it had.

"She flew close to me," Lasair said with disgust, as if that was all the explanation he needed.

The male wyvern was incredulous. *"We were descending the other side of the mountain."*

"Makes no difference. Wyverns should know to stay clear of dragon territory. Anything on that mountain belongs to us."

The male wyvern didn't respond.

The dragon nodded. *"Yes. You see your folly now that it is too late. I will be sure to report your treachery to Demonic. Our elder will require retribution for your transgression."*

The male wyvern bristled. *"For what? Being attacked?"*

"As is my right."

"Not when it involves my sister."

"Wyverns have no place telling a dragon—"

"Enough!" Junior pointed his sword at the red dragon. An inner voice screamed at him about how foolish it was to brandish a sword at a creature capable of spewing fire.

"While you argue petty differences, the high king plots your destruction." He pointed the sword at the wyverns. "And yours too, if I have the right of it."

Reecah's Gift

The female wyvern's voice sounded meek, but her words were anything but, *"That is no concern to us. Let the king destroy the dragons. Flea and myself would be eternally grateful."*

The male wyvern, Flea, nodded and ambled on his back legs toward his sister, using his wingtips to steady him.

Lasair's crimson eyes tracked Flea.

Junior shook his head. "The king's men won't differentiate between wyverns and dragons. When they come, they'll kill anything bigger than a hawk."

"The human speaks truth." Lurker directed his gaze at Lasair. *"Dragon Home is no more. We need to speak with Elder Demonic and warn him that what happened to our colony will soon happen to yours."* He swung his head to Flea and his sister. *"And yours."*

Lasair appeared shaken by the news, but he said with conviction, *"Demonic will kill you on sight. Especially if you bring the vermin along."*

Before Lurker responded, Flea agreed. *"Nor will Crookedfang allow you anywhere near Mount Gloom, with or without your human."*

Lurker's proposal to visit the Draakval Colony didn't sound like a good idea to Junior. Not after hearing Lasair's assertion of their hatred for mankind. He dropped his sword tip to the ground and gaped at Lurker as the green dragon's next words sunk in.

"Nonetheless, if you wish our help, I demand you take us to Demonic. Your future depends on it."

Reecah's Gift

Gift from the Gods

Reecah wondered what had become of her little friend, Raver. The emptiness in her heart was more profound than anything she had experienced since the day Grammy died. Sitting before a small campfire, not far inside the perimeter of King's Wood, she contemplated what to do next.

Returning to Draakhall while the dark heir was present wasn't a wise choice. If he recognized her from the Dragon Temple, her quest to save the dragons would stop right there. But, by doing nothing, the result amounted to the same. She had to find a way into the castle, or, at the very least, be prepared for when the high king left Draakhall's brooding confines. Perhaps she could waylay him on the road.

The setting sun stretched deepening shadows through the woods. She examined her possessions. A black quarterstaff as tall as her shoulders was nothing more than a fancy walking stick in her hands. Her finely crafted black bow and matching quiver full of low profile, fletched arrows—ideal for greater arrow speed, but trickier to keep on target—was by far her weapon of choice. She grimaced at the loss of one of her arrows on the training ground. How she would have loved to shove it up Anvil's backside. A grin creased her otherwise dour expression, but it quickly faded.

Her arming swords sat uselessly within their plain, black and dark brown sheaths. Until she found someone to train her in their proper use, they were nothing more than an annoyance hanging from her hips.

Reecah's Gift

She went through the contents of her ratty rucksack, pulling out the last scraps of bread and cheese from the *Serpent's Slip*, and nibbled at the tasteless fare.

Her thoughts drifted to her dragon friends. With the dark heir's return, they should be safe. She doubted the dragon hunt from Fishmonger Bay would continue to bother them at Dragon Home. She grimaced at her short-sightedness. Just because Prince J'kwaad had left, that didn't mean troops hadn't remained behind.

She wanted to scream at the helplessness gripping her. She knew what needed to be done, but had no idea how to make it happen.

Scouring the darkening forest, she pulled a thin rope from the bottom of her rucksack and went about stringing it at ankle height around the trees surrounding her campfire. Anything to provide her with a sense of peace while she slept. If someone wanted to catch her unaware, she counted on them tripping on the rope first.

Reecah lay awake long before the dawn, shivering on the cold ground beneath her small blanket and scratching at insect bites all over her body. Turning her nose up at how badly she smelled, she decided to find a hidden alcove along the shoreline of King's Bay to wash, but that could wait until the sun rose high enough to warm the land.

Midmorning found her on the shoreline of King's Bay between two large rocks. Hidden by a row of thick pines, she shivered in her shift as she laid her clothes out to dry on a flat-topped boulder facing the east. Goosebumps riddled her skin but she didn't mind. She was alive. With life came the opportunity to forge the future.

Reecah's Gift

The sun reached its zenith before she immersed herself into the frigid waters. Removing her shift, she used the fine sand under her feet to wash herself and the yellowed garment.

She climbed from the water and covered herself with the wet cloth. Fairly certain there wasn't a soul around for at least a league, she wasn't leaving anything to chance. She pulled her tunic on and waited for her undergarments to dry.

Snugging her cummerbund sword belt, she donned the welcome warmth of her cloak and ascended a natural rock formation that rose from the tiny cove she had bathed in. Shielding her eyes from the sun, she searched northwest across King's Bay.

Far in the distance, the brooding hulk of Draakhall and the immense structure of Sea Gate were clearly visible. So close, and yet, so far away. Three, black brigs with furled sails sat in the middle of King's Bay. Why the king's ships were anchored in the middle was a mystery.

The sun sat like a fiery ball on top of the Sea Gate Bridge, bathing the gently rolling waters of the bay in beautiful shades of orange and yellow. Living in Fishmonger Bay, stunning sunsets were commonplace, but she had never witnessed one with the added dimension of the high king's castle and the cityscape between the keep's dark mass and the gateway in relief.

Enjoying the sun's rays on her face, she held her head high and closed her eyes, taking in the magical moment before the sun disappeared behind the manmade stone walls standing between her and the future of dragonkind.

A distant caw interrupted the bittersweet moment. A twinge of sadness replaced the euphoric serenity; a gentle reminder of what she may never experience again—the undemanding love of her best friend.

Reecah's Gift

Two caws in rapid succession snapped her eyes open—her breath catching in her throat. Not daring to believe the relevance of what the call meant, she scanned the sky and caught sight of a raven high above King's Bay. To most people, one bird's call was the same as another, but Reecah *knew* Raver's caw. Two caws usually meant someone was close by, but she instinctively understood he searched for her—trying to alert her to his presence.

She whistled, imitating a cardinal's chirrup and jumping up and down. Tears blurred her vision as the black speck grew in size. She held a trembling arm out for him to land on.

In typical Raver fashion, he tucked his wings in and dove headlong, plummeting from the sky like he was shot from a bow. He unfurled his wings at the last moment to arrest his descent but his speed was too great. His feet scratched along her vambrace as he impacted with her chest—driving her to her backside as she scrambled to hang onto him.

"Raver, you crazy bird!" she cried. Straightening his wings, she squeezed him tight. "You truly are a gift from the gods."

She grasped him with both hands and held him before her, kissing the top of his head a couple of times while avoiding his attempts to peck at her. "Where's Lurker? Did you do as I asked? Is he coming?"

He squirmed out of her grasp and hopped onto the boulder beside her, opening his beak wide. "Coming! Coming!"

A lump formed in her throat. She hadn't allowed herself to believe her friends would actually appear. "Who's coming? Lurker, Swoop and Silence?"

"Coming! Coming!"

Did he mean her dragon friends were on there way? Looking up, she frowned. If that was the case, why hadn't they accompanied Raver?

She rolled into a crouch and stared through the trees. "I don't see anyone. Are they close?"

163

Reecah's Gift

Raver blinked and tilted his head.

Communicating with her best friend used to be a simple affair. She had learned early on that she could command him to perform certain actions. He had proven an invaluable scout—able to pick out things leagues away and warn her of their presence long before they were aware of hers.

The ability to dragonspeak had taught her a lot more about Raver. The raven spoke simple ideas through her dragonling friends—not enough to carry on a conversation, but enough to communicate on a more intelligent level. Without the dragonlings, their communications were limited to Raver speaking a few words at a time; usually a cryptic response to her questions.

Still, she knew enough to take anything Raver said seriously. Anyone else would think the bird spoke gibberish, but she had come to realize that he never said anything unless he meant it. Many times, his words came across as comical.

Stringing her bow, she listened to the sounds around her. If anyone was sneaking up on her, they were good at hiding themselves. She contemplated sending Raver into the air to scout, but the thick wood lining the shoreline wasn't conducive to aerial observation. She held a forearm in front of his mangled feet and clucked.

Raver pecked at the leather sleeve a couple of times, but she held it firm. "Come on, before I pluck you."

Raver blinked twice and hopped onto her forearm. She had planned to skirt around South Fort and start up the road to Sea Keep today, but washing her belongings and drying them had taken longer than anticipated. Raver's appearance removed her sense of urgency to travel to Draakhall. Scanning the forest edge, she headed back to her little campsite.

The sun had sunk to the horizon by the time she recognized the immediate area around her campsite.

164

Reecah's Gift

Raver had ridden on one arm or another all the way back and now clung to her shoulder as they approached the edge of the King's Wood, where the roadway passed through.

Reecah's Gift

She read into Raver's attentiveness that something wasn't right in the deathly still forest.

Slipping an arrow free, she nocked it and stepped from behind a line of trees; the sun at her back. She drew the arrow tight, her sights on the back of a tall man with broad shoulders and long, brown hair, crouching to inspect her firepit.

Raver cawed and took to wing, the sudden noise making the man jump to his feet and spin around.

"Flavian? What are you doing here?"

Flavian, the young man Anvil had pitted her against in the training yard, smiled sheepishly, his face red. "Ah! There you are. I'm afraid you caught me with my back turned."

Raver cawed twice from the branches above.

Reecah released the tension from the bow. "It's a good thing the bald-headed freak isn't here to chastise you for being human."

Flavian's prominent Adam's apple moved up and down with a heavy swallow. He flashed her a nervous smile; his green eyes directing her to turn around.

A cold feeling flushed her skin.

An arm thicker than her thigh wrapped around her chest, driving her bow to the ground and dislodging her arrow.

A voice like two slabs of stone grating together sneered in her ear, her captor's breath rank with ale, "Lesson one. Never leave your back exposed. Especially when I'm around."

Reecah's Gift

The Ivory Throne

Prince J'kwaad paced the throne room, impatiently awaiting his father's audience. How dare the impetuous man summon him away from his wizard's chamber atop Draakhall's highest tower, Draakhorn. Had he not feared the king's punishment, he would have thrown the shaking messenger who had delivered the order from the spiked balcony for daring to enter his domain without being bidden. He made a point to speak with the guards at the base of Draakhorn as soon as this business was done.

The Ivory Throne, built out of polished dragon horns, refracted the flames from four large hearths lining the throne room; the light glinting off polished, black marble pillars supporting the vaulted ceiling. Ivory serpents spiralled up the height of the pillars, their great heads intermingling with swooping krakens carved into the dark granite roof.

J'kwaad detested this room. Disliked any room offering homage to the deplorable beasts. At least that was one thing he and his father had in common. They resented anything more powerful than themselves.

For J'kwaad, his loathing didn't stop at his older brother. It ended with High King J'kaar.

If J'kwaad were ever to rule the Great Kingdom as it was meant to be ruled, he would have to outlive not only his father, but his flamboyant brother, J'kye, as well. There was also the high wizard who inhabited an abandoned fortress above Headwater Castle. The wizard's sanctum sat high atop a rocky

Reecah's Gift

tor overlooking the end of the Dragon Rush—a great river tumbling out of the eastern wilderness from its origin within the lofty mountain known as Dragon's Tooth. A mountain so high, superstition claimed even dragons couldn't reach its summit.

The high wizard had been his mentor growing up—the only one who understood him for who he really was, but the old dodderer may prove a liability when the time came.

"Still no sign of the bastard?"

A female voice caught him by surprise. J'kwaad hated surprises. Especially ones at his expense. He prided himself in knowing the movements of all the major players in the noble hierarchy—his drunken sister, J'kyra, included.

Suppressing his rage, he restrained himself from unleashing a disfiguring spell. J'kye's twin sister was harmless enough in her wine sloshing, whore-mongering way. In fact, if she wasn't so fond of J'kye's claim to their father's throne, J'kwaad might even have cared for his eclectic sister. He had to admit that when they were alone together, he quite enjoyed her sarcastic, abrasive outlook on life. She provided a refreshing alternative to the highbrow snobbery rampant in the rest of the royal household and its blood-sucking courtiers.

He gave J'kyra a forced smile. "Not unless he's playing hide your hide."

J'kyra studied him for a moment, digesting his remark. She blurted out a quick laugh before her attention fell on one of the unfortunate serving staff standing demurely in the shadows. "Wench! Two goblets of the king's wine. Now!"

The serving girl nodded once and scrambled to an ornate, black marble table behind the Ivory Throne. She returned almost as quickly, curtsying and proffering both intricately etched, golden chalices to J'kyra. How she did all this without spilling a drop, J'kwaad had no idea. A useless skill, but a talent nonetheless.

Reecah's Gift

"I don't need two, you twit! You take me for a sot?" the princess berated the servant. "I'll have your head, you insolent trollop!"

J'kwaad smiled at the helplessness on the girl's stricken face. Barely old enough to breed and here she was quivering before a rabid lioness. Oh well. Such was her lot in life. He inwardly hoped the dolt would answer his sister with a yes, but the girl stared dumbly at J'kyra, afraid to move. An action that probably saved her from an unpleasant consequence.

He experienced an unusual empathy for the young lass. Not caring for the softness leeching into his psyche, he strolled over and relieved her of the second chalice. Faking a smile, he nodded for her to leave them.

The servant forgotten, his sister turned on him. "What's this all about? I've got important things to do. Hanging about this drafty rock pile isn't something I care to waste my time on."

He shrugged, not doubting her for a moment. She probably had a date with a bottomless stein somewhere along King's Stagger.

"Well, if old blowhard doesn't show his pasty face soon, I'm out of here."

J'kwaad raised his eyebrows. His sister was all talk. Not even *he* dared disobey their father. The moment the king graced them with his presence, J'kyra would be all over him, batting her eyelashes, pouting her thick lower lip and playing the poor victim. He had to admit, nobody controlled their father nearly as well as J'kyra. Not even J'kye.

The only thing that made these useless audiences bearable was the knowledge that the king's days were numbered. J'kwaad had seen to it. But that time was still a while off. There was the matter of the succession to deal with first.

He searched the many shadows in the ill-lit chamber, wondering if he had missed seeing their codpiece licking brother amongst the multiple servants.

Reecah's Gift

Inconspicuous guardsmen in black, plate armour piped with crimson—the king's personal guard—hand-picked from the best of the elite guard, stood motionless at strategic places around the throne room; armed with ranged weapons and polearms. Many courtiers had overstepped their boundary over the years, airing their grievances to the crown only to spill their lifeblood on the polished, black marble floor at the base of the Ivory Throne.

A muffled click brought everyone in the chamber to attention—all eyes on the granite wall, several paces behind the throne—to the place they knew a secret door would open.

A granite slab grated into the wall and slid to one side, exposing a sconce flickering on the dark wall within.

J'kwaad rolled his eyes at his sister as J'kye emerged from the secret passageway and stopped to bow low to their father; even though the boot licker was already in his company. There was no one J'kwaad despised more than his brother.

J'kyra returned his disgusted look, but on cue, her eyes lit up and she bustled over to grab the high king's hand, dropping to a knee and kissing the back of it.

J'kwaad swallowed the bile in his throat. The only affection J'kyra had for their father was his riches. He didn't doubt for a moment the sole reason she kissed the king's hand was to get closer to the priceless jewels twinkling from his every finger.

Unless the items were enchanted, J'kwaad had no use for baubles—though his father's wealth certainly appealed to his sensibilities. Magical artefacts were acquired for a hefty price in the Arcanium marketplace. Items that weren't easily taken by force.

When the time came for him to rule the Great Kingdom, he would put his family's riches to good use. The wizard guild would open their doors wide for his pleasure, or discover to their peril that their arcane sanctuary wasn't as well-warded as they believed.

Reecah's Gift

"Arise, J'kyra. You're slobbering drunk again," King J'kaar growled, his perpetual scowl darkening his hard features. "It's high time I found you a suitor."

J'kwaad almost laughed at the sour look twisting his sister's face.

"No, Father, please. You know my feelings when it comes to men."

The king glared. "Unfortunately, I do. So does half my kingdom. There isn't a man alive capable of satisfying your carnal desires."

J'kyra clasped her hands together, pouting, giving their father her wide-eyed, hurt look.

J'kwaad shook his head as the king's face softened. What a sap. Taking a steadying breath, more to restrain himself from voicing his disgust, he approached the high king and nodded reverently.

"Ah, J'kwaad. Just the one I've been looking for."

"Your Grace," J'kwaad inclined his head and followed his father to the magnificently carved throne. It was rumoured that the unique dragon etched on each horn was the image of the actual dragon the horn was taken from.

Seating himself, the king waited for a male servant to take an obligatory sip from his royal goblet, before handing him his wine and prostrating at his feet.

Ignoring the servant who slipped away as unobtrusively as possible, High King J'kaar's fleshy lips split his bushy, black, facial hair. "It's come to my attention that a certain miscreant arrived in Sea Hold. Stowed away aboard a merchant ship out of Thunderhead."

Just like their father. No pleasantries. No small talk. No asking how they were doing or wondering how they were getting on. Straight to whatever was on *his* mind.

The news registered in J'kwaad's mind but his focus was on the king's black hair, greying at the temples. He glanced at the twins. J'kye and J'kyra had strikingly beautiful, blonde locks and soft faces. Neither looked the least bit like their father.

From what people had told him of their mother, she also had black hair. Where his siblings came by their looks intrigued J'kwaad, but he never had the gall to ask.

Growing up, J'kye would have beaten him into a pulp if he had so much as intimated such an idea. And J'kyra…well, she never possessed the capacity to fathom such an inference.

Only little J'kaeda, their youngest sibling, had the same traits as himself and their father. He envied the cheeky little princess her youth. At eleven years old, his favourite sibling wasn't required to attend these official functions. Her exposure would commence on her next birth anniversary. He would have to watch out for that one. For some reason, the high king despised her most of all.

His father's raised voice brought him back to the throne room.

"Well?" the king demanded, looking straight at him.

"I'm sorry, Your Grace. Say that again."

The usual hatred the king reserved for him hadn't lost its venom. With obvious restraint, High King J'kaar repeated, "I said, it seems as if this miscreant received help from someone inside Draakhall. I've sent the Inquisitor to speak with the guards who were on duty a few nights ago. We'll soon know the person's true identity."

J'kwaad shuddered. The only person to instil more fear into him than his father was the royal disciplinarian, the Inquisitor. "As you wish, Your Grace."

The king frowned. "I demand you take this seriously. There is more at play here than we suspect. Of that I'm sure."

J'kwaad swallowed, shifting his weight from one foot to the other. He hated his father's self-righteous attitude. Why should he bother with some stowaway? Let the Watch deal with it. It had nothing to do with his role as royal wizard. He had better

Reecah's Gift

things to waste his time on. "Yes, Your Grace. I will see to it at once."

The king held his stare. "See to it that you do. It's believed this woman was responsible for Baron Carroch's misfortune."

Oh great. A woman. J'kwaad inwardly rolled his eyes, trying not to let his distaste for his assignment show on his face. The king had his nose out of joint over the calamity that had befallen the lecherous cretin, Carroch. Some wench had probably grown tired of the boar's brutality. It would be simpler to dispense of the baron. "Yes, Your Grace. It will be done."

A deep-rooted rage threatened to boil over. His every waking moment had been devoted to the king's campaign to eliminate the dragon threat. Learning new spells and powering his talismans took more out of him than his father realized. "What of the Draakval campaign?"

The king waved a dismissive hand. "Nothing's changed in that regard. The preparations are being handled like they were for the Draakclaw Colony. The army marches within a fortnight. You will follow with the Elite Guard three days afterward on horseback. That should place you with the army in Cliff Face shortly after the leaves have fallen."

J'kwaad nodded.

"When you return, I wish to discuss taking the dragon campaign to the next level."

That was a new development. As far as J'kwaad knew, his father wished his legacy to be known as the king who rid the realm of the dragon threat. After the Draakval Colony, there was only the colony in the far east. True, it was the biggest colony, home to the dragon queen, but he doubted she would be more trouble than Grimclaw.

"As you wish, Your Grace."

"Excellent. Once the dragon threat has been put to rest, I intend on dealing with the unsanctioned use of magic. Ridding the kingdom of upstart conjurers will go a long way to securing peace."

J'kwaad couldn't help but raise his eyebrows.

The king's scowl deepened. "Don't look so surprised. I'll rest easier when I no longer fear the magic guild rising up and razing the kingdom. Rest assured, I will always have use of my own wizard."

Typical hypocrite. What suited J'kaar wasn't necessarily what the king thought suited the kingdom. The only problem was that his father had two wizards.

"Of course, Your Grace."

"That is all. Leave us," J'kaar commanded.

"Yes, Your Grace." J'kwaad bowed and spun in a flourish of black robes hemmed with bright gold.

"You too, J'kyra," the king's voice echoed in the throne room. "Get cleaned up."

"Yes, Father."

J'kwaad awaited his sister. Together, they descended the broad steps leading from the king's podium to the audience hall below and out through a set of tall, oak doors protected by the king's personal guard—four of the biggest men J'kwaad had ever laid eyes on.

J'kyra's lingering eye wasn't lost on J'kwaad as they passed into a long, open-fronted hallway overlooking the Unknown Sea crashing upon the jagged reefs along the shoreline.

"They're not worth your time," J'kwaad mumbled.

J'kyra snapped her attention away from the guardsmen. "Huh?"

"Nothing."

He ignored the strange look she gave him—fighting to dampen the fury roiling in the pit of his stomach. Imagine that. The second in line to the Ivory Throne, searching for a fugitive out of Thunderhead. What a waste of his talents. Why not dump the task on that useless bag of bones, J'kye? He had nothing better to do than polish their father's boots with his tongue. J'kye didn't even take part in the dragon campaign for fear the golden heir might split a hair.

A mischievous grin took hold of his face at the thought of splitting J'kye's hair. Soon.

J'kyra punched him in the shoulder. "You think father's funny?"

The smile fell. If anyone else touched him like that, they would find themselves eating his fist. He glared at J'kyra but she grinned, uncaring, her perfect teeth visible—an uncommon trait amongst those born north of the Lake of the Lost.

"Hardly. I was just thinking about what Father asked me to do. That woman left Carroch close to death. I mean to find her as fast as possible so I can shake her hand."

Reecah's Gift

Muscles She Never Knew

Anvil's iron grip held Reecah's feet off the ground.

Musky sweat turned up her nostrils as she struggled to break free. His unrelenting hold prevented her from reaching her sword belt.

Raver cawed continuously from a high branch.

With Reecah in his clutches, Anvil spun to observe the raven. "Shut that damned thing up!"

Flavian unslung his bow. "Yes, Anvil."

"No!" Reecah squirmed harder. She hammered her heels into Anvil's shins repeatedly.

Anvil squeezed the breath from her.

Fearing her ribs were about to break, she clawed at his bald head, but her fingers couldn't find purchase on his sweaty skin.

Bereft of air, she was unable to warn Raver to fly away. All she could do was shake her head in terror as Flavian drew an arrow back and let fly.

Raver squawked louder and jumped into the air—the arrow whistling between him and the branch. Before Flavian notched another, Raver flew past the treetops and out of sight.

Anvil shoved Reecah away. "Damn ya, Flavian. That's the reason we came out here!"

She landed on her feet and stumbled, but kept her back away from her attackers. Indignant, she asked, "You came out here to kill Raver?"

Anvil exchanged glances with Flavian.

Reecah's Gift

Reecah realized that wasn't what Anvil meant. She eyed her bow laying behind the brute. She entertained running away but refused to leave her weapon behind. Absently fingering the hilts of her swords, her gaze wandered to the vicious battle-axe strapped across Anvil's back. Her blades would be useless against the man.

"What do we do now, Anvil?" Flavian asked in a timid voice.

Anvil glowered. "Ain't nothing to do. Ye just proved GG's skill with a bow is better than yer own. I can't think of a single archer in J'kaar's Elite guard who could've dropped me shield from the wall."

Reecah's eyebrows scrunched together, her gaze alternating between the treetops and the bare-chested weapon master. "If you're not here to kill me, why *are* you here?"

A sadistic grin illuminated Anvil's face. "To train ya to kill others."

"I don't understand. You threatened to throw me off the wall. If you think I'm going back, you're crazier than you look."

Flavian gasped, his wide eyes and shaking head imploring Reecah to refrain from speaking to Anvil that way.

Anvil's bronzed face turned a shade of purple. Restraint registered in his grating voice, "I was perhaps a little hasty in me opinion. I long to know whether ya got lucky or are really that good."

Reecah lifted her chin with pride. "Toss me my bow and find out."

Anvil's heavy brows knit together. "Ye'd like that, wouldn't ye?" He reached over his shoulder and pulled his axe free. "Come and get it."

Reecah held his stare. She hoped her legs weren't trembling as badly she thought they were. She willed her feet to take the steps necessary to retrieve her bow. As brave as she presented herself, she gave Anvil a wide berth and quickly snatched her bow from the ground.

Reecah's Gift

Flavian strung an arrow and held it slack, but at the ready.

Reecah backstepped toward the edge of the forest. After witnessing Anvil split the shield with his axe, running wasn't an option. But neither was fighting. She couldn't take them both out with one arrow. Once engaged, she wouldn't live long enough to shoot a second. She pulled an arrow from her quiver anyway. "Now what?"

Anvil didn't appear the slightest bit uneasy about her nocking the arrow. "Now ya prove yer worth me bother. Pick a target."

To Reecah's horror, Raver dropped through the canopy and landed on a high branch.

"Ah, praise the kraken. One has fallen from the sky. Flavian, yer first."

Reecah screamed, "Raver, away!"

Raver didn't obey. He stared at her, tilting his head to one side.

Flavian raised his bow and drew.

Reecah did the only thing she could think of. Drawing, sighting, and loosing all in one motion, she cringed as her arrow impacted Flavian's bow above his steadying hand.

Flavian yelped. His bow flew from his hand—the wood split by Reecah's arrow.

"For the love of the bloody kraken!" Flavian shouted, staring in disbelief at his stinging hands. "You could have killed me."

Reecah glared at him. "If you ever aim at my friend again, the next arrow will fly between your ears."

Before Flavian could protest, Reecah strung a second arrow. She debated pointing it at Anvil, but thought better of it. The weapon master stood ready—his muscles flexing. If she missed a killing shot, he wouldn't.

Anvil's booming voice startled her.

"Nicely done, GG! Ye couldn't prove yerself better than that. Against all me reservations, ye've convinced me. It's high time ye began yer training."

Reecah's Gift

Reecah accompanied Anvil and Flavian to South Fort and commenced her training with the rest of the new recruits.

Anvil paired her with a blonde-haired woman around the same age and height. Catenya, or Cat, as her friends in the group called her, was the dominant personality amongst the two dozen trainees. Her physical appearance reminded Reecah of Cahira, but the similarity ended there. Cat came across as high and mighty—looking down her nose at anyone not in her clique.

Catenya took great joy pummeling Reecah that first day with various melee weapons, but it soon became apparent to everyone in the group that Reecah was not only more proficient with her bow than anyone else, but her stamina outstripped that of even Anvil. Though her swordsmanship lacked any semblance of skill, her endurance while swinging the blade left Cat bent over and panting by the end of the first day.

At Reecah's request, Anvil remained behind as the sun fell behind the keep. The weapon master agreed to stay back to improve her swordsmanship.

Despite a cool wind blowing off the bay, sweat streamed from Anvil's face long after the last recruit had left for the common bunkhouse inside the keep's inner wall. Hands on enormous thighs, a large training sword lying at his feet, he watched Reecah sip from her waterskin. "Are ye not even winded, lass?"

"Oh yes, Anvil," she said, making sure to include his name whenever she spoke to him. "I don't think I could lift my sword tip off the ground."

Anvil shook his head, staring at the drops of sweat staining the dirt between his boots. "Me brother certainly had the right o' ye."

Reecah's Gift

Reecah studied the man's enormous frame—easily the largest man she had ever known. His words puzzled her. He had said as much the first day they met, but she had been so intimidated, their meaning never registered. "I'm confused, Anvil. Who, exactly, is your brother?"

Anvil straightened to his full height, placing his hands on the small of his back and thrusting his thick shoulders forward. "Me brother? Aramyss Chizel." He spoke as if it were common knowledge.

Reecah scratched at the spot where her thin braid pulled at her scalp above her left eye. "Sorry, Anvil, but I'm confused. I was referred to you by a dwarf. One that I, um, tripped over, a few nights ago."

Anvil's tight goatee split with laughter—a sound Reecah wouldn't soon forget. She'd never seen him smile, let alone laugh.

"That's a rich one, lassie. Tripped o'er me brother. Ha! I can't wait to rub that one in."

"But, you're not ..." She struggled to find a delicate way to phrase it. "Surely, you're not a dwarf."

Anvil bent his triangular physique side to side, his corded muscles rippling. "I surely am, Miss GG."

"B-b-but you're—"

"A giant?"

Reecah had never met a giant before. From what she had read, giants were taller still. "Well, no. Not a giant. I'm not sure what I'm trying to say. You're too big to be a dwarf."

Anvil stared into Reecah's hazel eyes as if he was looking into her soul. His throat constricted with a swallow. "There's the rub, ain't it. Me Mam was a giant, bless her soul. Taken by me father at the end of the Wizard Wars." A sadness filled his eyes. "I ain't seen her since I was a wee lad."

"So, your father was a dwarf?"

Anger replaced sadness.

180

Reecah's Gift

Reecah prepared to defend herself, but Anvil's bitter words weren't directed at her.

"Aye. And a mean one at that. He's not to return to the Great Kingdom on penalty of death."

Reecah wanted to know more, but let it drop—the subject clearly upset Anvil. Besides, it was none of her business.

"High King J'kaar holds Aramyss and meself as collateral to ensure our sire adheres to the terms of his banishment."

Empathy filled Reecah's heart. She gazed at Anvil with a newfound perspective. She had a sudden urge to wrap the hardened man in her embrace, but lacked the courage to do so.

Anvil must have noticed. "Don't be getting any thoughts, Miss GG. I ain't one to be coddled because of me past. Me and Chiz have put it behind us. If I ever hear ye speak of this to anyone, I'll crush ya. Ye hear me?"

Reecah nodded. "I won't."

"Good," Anvil said and sprung at her, a blunt training sword in hand.

Reecah jumped back and sideways with a squeak, lifting her sword and smiling, despite the fact that muscles she never knew ached like they were being doused with dragon fire. She had longed to learn how to use her weapons for years. She wasn't about to complain now that she found someone willing to teach her.

181

Reecah's Gift

Old Attitudes

Jonas Junior was thankful Lurker had agreed to fly with him in full armour. He didn't welcome the bone-chilling cold that accompanied soaring through the sky.

Their take-off had been anything but smooth, but once in the air, Lurker realized the extra weight wasn't as bad as he had anticipated.

Following Lasair around the majestic peaks of the Altirius Mountains left Junior's stomach in his mouth. As grand as the Spine had been, the lofty crags of the northern mountains made the western range pale in comparison.

The wyverns trailed Lurker and Lasair, while Swoop and Silence kept watch overhead. Junior thought about Raver, hoping he hadn't sent the bird to its death. Arms wrapped around Lurker's neck, he had to be reminded more than once not to squeeze too hard.

Left to his own thoughts, he couldn't believe how his life had changed since the time he and Jaxon had stumbled across Reecah in Dragonfang Pass—the hill witch standing over a slain dragonling.

He had gone from being Jonas Waverunner's natural successor—groomed to lead the dragon hunt one day—to falling out with his family. When word got out he had thrown his lot in with the witch, he would surely become an enemy of the crown.

Now he clung to a dragon, flying toward a colony of the fire breathing beasts—creatures who notoriously detested humans.

182

Reecah's Gift

He pondered the merits of his decision to be kind to the only girl who had ever given him a black eye.

Rising through the fog obscuring the mountains, the top of a smoking volcano towered above the surrounding mountain summits—all except the peak directly behind it; also plumed with thick wisps of smoke.

Out of the corner of his eye, the wyverns broke away—flying wide over the Unknown Sea.

"Where are they going?"

Lasair answered, *"Cowards. We approach Fire Reach. They're afraid to get anywhere near Mount Cinder. They fly out to sea to get to their own mountain."*

"Their own mountain?"

Impatience and disgust came through in Lasair's reply. *"I can't believe I'm explaining this to a human. Fire Reach is the home of the Draakvals. Lowly wyverns call Mount Gloom their home. An aptly named place for their ilk."*

Junior regarded the backside of the massive red dragon, not caring for Lasair's attitude. Just because wyverns lacked front legs didn't make them inferior. They were different, that was certain, but to detest them for that reason alone didn't make sense. The harboured prejudice wasn't going to help *either* colony should the high king's men turn their attention this way.

He thought about saying as much, but shook his head. Who was he to preach to dragonkind? He didn't know the first thing about the rival colonies. There may be an underlying reason the wyverns had invoked the angst of the Draakval Colony. All he knew was that every wing beat Lurker took brought him closer to a possible hostile confrontation with a dragon named Demonic.

He closed his eyes and shivered. Despite the numbing winds blowing his golden locks behind him, his clothing was soaked in sweat. He fought the urge to shout out in alarm as he opened his eyes to the sound of many sets of leathery wings flapping on the wind. Brown, green, yellow, blue, red, copper, black, and white dragons soared past them—coming from every direction at once. Silence and Swoop dropped in on either side of Lurker, buffering their flight path.

They followed Lasair over the lip of the smoking crater and dropped into the heart of the volcano—a blast of heat flushing Junior's face.

"Easy, Junior," Lurker gasped.

Junior loosened his stranglehold, but only a bit. "We're flying into a volcano!"

"Dragons are fire creatures," Lasair grunted. *"It keeps your kind away."*

Junior tried not to look too closely at where they were headed, but when he detected roiling lava beyond the steam far below, he couldn't keep his eyes from the approaching lake of molten death.

"Fear not," Lurker's voice sounded as a caressing whisper. *"Our scales resist fire. We aren't impervious to it."*

Lurker's words did little to appease his mounting terror. As the heat threatened to singe his fine hairs and sear his skin, Lasair opened his wings wide. Dropping his hind legs, Lasair landed on a large, flat rock projecting from the sidewall of the crater—a platform similar to the Summoning Stone back home.

Lurker settled down beside him. Swoop and Silence landed between Lasair and Lurker.

The remainder of the dragon escort settled into numerous alcoves that pock-marked the crater wall—their colourful gazes never leaving Junior and the dragonlings.

"If you'd be so kind as to get off," Lurker's strained voice implored.

Junior eased his stranglehold but made no attempt to dismount.

Reecah's Gift

Lurker dipped forward and sideways, spilling Junior onto the platform with a clatter.

"Hey!" Junior shouted, instinctively pulling his sword free, expecting to be assaulted by the Draakval dragons. He thought about jumping back on Lurker's shoulders, but the green dragon shuffled around to face him.

Lurker glared at him, but it was Swoop's angered voice that spoke. *"What do you think you're doing with that? Put it away before you get us killed."*

The silence in the volcanic crater was eerie. Other than a distant wind blowing across the open peak, and the hiss and plop of lava far below, not a sound disturbed the interior of Mount Cinder.

Junior turned one way, then another, his gaze taking in a myriad of uniquely beautiful dragon eyes. The beauty stopped there. Their stares were anything but welcoming. Swoop's warning echoed through his mind but he couldn't bring himself to sheath his sword.

Lasair shifted his bulk to face a large tunnel that lead into the side of the crater at the back of the ledge. Dropping to his chest, his action elicited a deafening chorus of dragon shrieks from those assembled along the rock face—the noise so loud, Junior dropped his sword to the ground and placed his hands over his ears, fearing the dragonsong would split his skull in two.

Lasair snarled, his words barely distinguishable amongst the cacophony, *"Show respect, you fools. Demonic approaches."*

The dragonlings from Dragon Home emulated Lasair.

A darkness, deeper than the shadow veiling the tunnel entrance, moved. Led by two white dragons bigger than Lasair, a dragon greater in size than the deceased elder, Grimclaw, scraped his way into the open air. Black wingtips and long temple horns accentuated the dark, dried blood hue of the leader of the Draakval Colony.

Reecah's Gift

The thunderous din of dragonsong abruptly ceased, its residual roar echoing into the heights of the crater.

Junior feared the ledge they stood upon would crumble beneath Demonic's pounding footsteps. He grabbed his sword to stop it from rattling toward the edge.

Silence nudged him with her snout, her diminutive voice warning, "Put it away."

Junior gulped. It wasn't easy, shaking as badly as he did, but thankfully the sword tip found the opening and the blade slid home.

Lurker, Swoop and Silence placed themselves between him and the oncoming dragons, but the dragonlings were forced to one side by the white dragons.

Left in Demonic's path, Junior unconsciously backed away.

Demonic advanced until Junior thought the dragon's next step would be on his head. Looking behind him, he saw the bright glow of the lava beyond the precipice.

His terrified stare honed in on the flames visible at the back edges of Demonic's lips as black smoke wisped from the dragon's nostrils.

Junior trembled, worried he might wet himself. Being burnt alive, eaten, or falling into a pit of lava struck him as his inevitable fate.

Rows of black teeth curved between Demonic's slightly open maw. Dipping his head to the shelf, the height of his smoking nostrils were twice that of Junior.

An overpowering sulphuric stench turned Junior's stomach as a deep voice thundered inside his head.

"You have a lot of nerve coming here, human. Tell me why I shouldn't eat you?" Demonic craned his neck toward Lasair. *"I will deal with you later."*

Lasair remained still, genuflected as only a dragon of his size could.

Reecah's Gift

Demonic swung his head back; black leather lips brushing Junior's raised hands—the heat from his breath intense.

Junior couldn't think of anything to say. Stepping backward and falling over the brink seemed like his best choice.

"We came to save you," Lurker's voice interrupted.

A puff of smoke escaped Demonic's nostrils; his blood-red eyes regarded Lurker. *"You and your unwelcome companions are the ones in need of saving."*

"Nevertheless, you must hear me out."

Demonic shifted his body to face Lurker, his bulk nearly knocking Junior off the ledge.

"I must do nothing!" Demonic roared.

Lurker stood his ground. *"Then you will die."*

Junior edged around Demonic's massive forefoot—carefully stepping over a black, outer claw. He couldn't believe how calmly Lurker confronted the Draakval leader. He thought for sure that Lurker's brazen warning would be the end of them.

Demonic leaned back on his rear legs, opening his mouth wide and spewing a blast of flame overhead. *"It is you who is about to die!"*

The angry dragon pulled his head back.

Junior gaped, but there was nothing he could do. He had seen dragons react this way—just before they released a torrent of fire. His gaze fell on Lurker nonchalantly facing death.

"Dragon Home is destroyed," Lurker's voice sounded through the chaos. *"Draakval will soon follow."*

Demonic's head shot forward, his mouth wide, but no flames came. He stopped his advance and tilted his head to one side. *"What did you say?"*

"The high king dispatched an army to Dragonfang Pass. They obliterated our home. The three of us, and one who remained behind to clean up the destruction and guard Dragon Home from treasure hunters, are all that remain of our colony. J'kaar will turn his sights on your home next."

187

Reecah's Gift

Demonic growled. He pulled his head back, his eyes flicking to Junior.

Junior stopped moving and held his palms out, hoping to demonstrate to the irate dragon that he didn't pose a threat.

Demonic's eyes narrowed. *"And yet you bring one of the parasites into our midst. What treachery is this?"*

"There is no treachery, Elder Demonic," Lurker answered, bowing his head in deference to the Draakval leader. *"We seek to save the last of the Windwalkers."*

"The Windwalkers are no more. Why else would we live in fear of humankind? Grimclaw should've listened to me years ago. Together, we could've scoured the filth from the world." Demonic's eyes found Junior once more. He swung his head low and audibly sniffed at him. Lifting his head high, he twitched his nostrils in disgust. *"You lie. I sense no magic in this one. He is no Windwalker."*

"I never claimed he was. If we are to have a chance of saving the last Windwalker, we require this human's assistance."

"You insult my intelligence. The last Windwalker died decades ago."

"She had a daughter."

Demonic lowered his head to confront Lurker, huge breaths convulsing his sides. *"Where is this daughter now? Have you sensed the magic within her?"*

"I have not."

Demonic's eyes widened in what appeared as surprise, before narrowing with a dangerous glint. He pulled his head back, flames dripping from the corners of his mouth.

Lurker raised his voice. *"Grimclaw vouched for her."*

Instead of appeasing the Draakval elder, Lurker's words incensed him further. *"Grimclaw? If what you say is true, that fool couldn't prevent his own death. You don't expect me to trust the words of a senile lizard?"*

Darkness shrouded Lurker's expression. *"With all due respect, Elder Demonic, you walk on dangerous ground. Grimclaw was my father."*

Reecah's Gift

Demonic emitted a booming laugh.

Lurker's head shook slightly. *"Despite the bitterness our colonies have for each other, I fail to see the humour in your impending demise."*

Demonic stopped laughing. He flicked his gaze between Lurker and Junior. With a barely perceptible nod, he said, *"Very well. I will see you two in my chamber."* He cast a stern look at Swoop and Silence, his voice taking on a sarcastic timbre, *"You two will remain here, as guests. An assurance against treachery, if you will."*

The platform shook as Demonic followed one of the white dragons into the tunnel. The second guardian waited until Lurker and Junior passed by before she brought up the rear.

Deep within the catacombs, the air was thankfully much cooler. Junior admired the shiny, tunnel walls. According to Demonic, the luminescent black rock was known as dragon glass—forged by dragon fire. The iridescent stone cast the voluminous passageway in a soft, amber glow.

"The main tunnels and byways are lava vents, created during previous volcanic eruptions. A major flareup hasn't occurred in over a century," Demonic informed them. *"Though, if my scholars are correct, Mount Cinder prepares herself for another blast."*

Startled, Junior looked back the way they had come. He wasn't sure how much heat a dragon could absorb, but he was well aware of his own shortcomings. He picked up his pace and scrambled after Lurker, Demonic, and the lead, white dragon. The second, ancient female, sauntered after him— likely ensuring he didn't get up to anything. The thought made him smile despite his terror. What could he possibly do to disrupt the Draakval Colony?

An expansive chamber with a black lake at its centre branched off the main tunnel. The lead dragon went in ahead and searched the cavern before summoning Demonic to enter.

Reecah's Gift

The Draakval elder's great wings brushed the vaulted entranceway on his way through.

Demonic approached the lake and dipped his head—ripples disturbing the tranquil surface as he lapped at the water.

Junior passed beneath the threshold, its arched ceiling many times his height. He scanned the softly lit cavern in awe, its lofty ceiling sparkling with priceless gemstones.

"Don't get any ideas, human." Demonic followed his gaze. *"One of those is worth a small kingdom in your world. Many fools have tried. Be assured, they're magically warded. Your first touch will be your last."*

Junior stumbled on the smooth, dragon glass floor. He couldn't imagine anyone bold enough to attempt sneaking into a dragon colony. Anyone that foolish deserved their fate.

Lurker placed himself between Demonic and Junior, *"We don't have time to waste if we want to save Reecah Windwalker."*

"Reecah, is it? Hmm," Demonic said. *"Very well. I'm not convinced that even if a Windwalker has survived, she'll be able to make a difference in the world of men. Too wide has the schism become for mankind to mend their ways. It has become a kill or be killed world."*

"That's exactly the kind of attitude that has brought us to this dangerous cusp."

Junior frowned. Listening to Lurker, he found it hard to believe the dragonling capable of such insight and eloquence at his young age. As much as dragons shared many of man's shortcomings, it was apparent there were distinct differences between the races. Maturity and rate of growth being two of them.

"What can one person, even fully blessed with the Windwalker gift, hope to achieve in a kingdom ruled by a dictator coveting our extermination. If what you say about Dragon Home is true, the line has already been drawn. I cannot sanction peace with a slayer of dragons."

"No one has asked you to," Lurker said. *"All I'm saying is you need to put aside your differences with our wyvern brethren. By presenting a*

Reecah's Gift

united front, perhaps you can survive the coming battle long enough for Reecah to convince the high king of his folly."

"Entertain a truce with the Wyrm Colony? Never!" Demonic growled.

Junior forgot how insignificant he was in the company of such goliaths. He stepped past Lurker and pointed a finger at Demonic. "Old attitudes like that that will see your colony eradicated from the Great Kingdom. Clinging to idiotic prejudices harboured and perpetuated from a different age will be the death of you. Perhaps there were just reasons for the derision between man and dragon all those years ago, but they didn't occur in my lifetime. Nor did they happen in my father or grandfather's lifetime. Why should I...we..." He walked straight up to Demonic, his outstretched hand shaking violently as the foolishness of his action dawned on him. "Yes, you *and* I, oh mighty elder. Why is this our war? To witness the deaths of our loved ones for the sake of the transgressions committed by our elders? That's insane."

Flames licked along the bottom edge of Demonic's open mouth.

The white dragons perked up.

Junior trembled but didn't relent. "No! Let me finish. Our ancestors fought and died over something so egregious at the time that they felt justified to send their mothers and fathers, brothers and sisters, sons and daughters to their death. That is fine, and we should respect that and honour their sacrifices. *But!* That was their war. Let it not be ours."

"Nicely said," Lurker whispered, his snout nudging Junior aside. *"Now be quiet and get behind me before he eats you."*

Junior swallowed, lowering his head. He had lost his grip on sanity and overstepped his boundaries.

Lurker's voice drew Demonic's scrutiny from him. *"We coerced Lasair into bringing us here. Please, do not hold him accountable for our presence. It was vital that you learn of the tragedy at Dragon*

191

Reecah's Gift

Home. How you deal with the information is up to you. You'll be stronger if you put aside your differences with the Wyrm Colony. The king's forces will be taken unaware if the wyverns assault his back lines."

"That will never happen! We don't need their help, nor do we desire it. We'll deal with the king's men."

Lurker bowed his head. *"As you wish, Elder Demonic. Don't underestimate the dark heir. He and a handful of his elite knights were all that was required to overcome Grimclaw. The wizard prince is a force not to be taken lightly."*

Demonic growled, his tail smashing the ground.

"With your leave, Elder Demonic, I will remove this human from your home so that we may see to the survival of the last Windwalker. If we're ever to coexist with humans again, she is the key."

Demonic reared to his full height, flames roiling across his tongue.

Junior feared their journey had come to an end.

Demonic teetered on the verge of lashing out, his blood-red stare boring into the depths of Junior's soul. Raising a clawed, front foot, he thundered, *"Begone! If I ever lay eyes on the vermin again, I'll strip the flesh from his bones."*

Reecah's Gift

Cat Fight

Training from sunup to sundown wore Reecah out, but she retired to the flea-ridden bunkhouse each night with a gladness swelling her heart. She was finally receiving the lessons she had desperately sought since the day Jonas had told her she wasn't fit to join the dragon hunt.

The next fortnight passed in a blur. Up before the dawn to choke back as much gruel as her stomach could handle, and then onto the training pitch to lock swords, swing her quarterstaff, chase around the yard shooting targets, and grapple with daggers and bare hands. Her fair skin had taken on a purple hue—bruises and scrapes welling up overtop of aching muscles. Cat liked to point out she had inflicted the majority of them.

At the end of the fifteenth day, after a particularly demanding session of defending against two knife-wielding attackers using only her bare hands, Anvil stomped over to where Reecah crouched by herself. Without warning, he kicked her in the shoulder, knocking her onto her side.

Cat and the rest of the trainees laughed.

Had the brute done so a couple of weeks ago, she would have lain on the ground, nursing a sore shoulder, and whined about the harsh treatment. Not anymore.

She let her momentum carry her. Rolling backward and bounding to her feet, she bladed her stance in preparation for whatever the seven-foot-five weapon master brought at her.

Reecah's Gift

Anvil didn't press the matter, but he appeared angry with her for some reason.

She half smiled. "What?"

Anvil's smoldering eyes surveyed the nervous faces of the trainees sitting against the wall around the stump. His dark gaze came back to Reecah. "What makes ye so happy? The harder we knock ya down, the bigger yer smile. It's like ye enjoy a good beating. Ye must be suffering."

Reecah's dimples lifted high. "I'm lucky to be standing, Anvil. I'm surprised if I can make it to the bunkhouse every night without assistance."

Anvil's gaze encompassed the rest, but his words were directed at her. "Never have I seen anyone enjoy having the shit kicked out of them day in and day out. Ye put the rest of these slugs to shame. Ye must be a wee bit crazed."

Reecah laughed and immediately held her lower ribs. She wasn't sure, but it felt like she had cracked one earlier in the day on the receiving end of a polearm. She coughed and winced.

Anvil shook his head. He feigned a step toward her and fell back just as fast.

Reecah's right foot shot out, trying to hook his ankle.

"See? That's what I mean." Anvil pointed at the foot she had lashed out with. "What drives ye, GG? Be nice to feed it to the others."

Reecah's smile fell. Unhappy scowls watched her interaction with the weapon master. She didn't appreciate being centred out in front of her peers—especially when her actions were used to make them feel inferior.

She shrugged. "I don't know, Anvil. I've always dreamed of training with weapons. I wanted to join the local dragon hunt in Fishmonger Bay, but they refused me. Said I wasn't good enough."

Reecah's Gift

As soon as the words left her mouth, she regretted them. If anyone put it together that she was the one who had attempted to kill the baron of Thunderhead, *and* came from Fishmonger Bay, they might figure out her real identity. Training in the city immediately south of Sea Keep was a dangerous place for someone who had recently battled the king's men.

Anvil gave her an odd look, but didn't press the matter. He grunted, "Seems I'll have to work the lot of ye harder on the morrow." He spat on the ground and walked away, mumbling to himself.

Despite his teachings, no one made a move to attack his exposed backside.

Reecah thought about it but doubted she could take three steps without collapsing. She put her back against the stone wall and slid down to her rump.

The trainees waited until Anvil disappeared beyond the inner stables before climbing to their feet and throwing their crude wooden cups toward the rusty pail of water. Grumbling amongst themselves, they cast Reecah dirty looks, not bothering to help her back to her feet as they left the training ground.

She caught the eye of a couple of the disgruntled trainees, not liking the look on their faces. She had been right to fret over Anvil calling her out. Even Flavian, the one person she had built up a friendship with, scowled at her.

Catenya was the last person to leave. From day one, she had made no qualms about how she felt about the new girl with fancy weapons. Her cup hit Reecah in the shoulder. "Way to go, witch. You best watch your back. You hear?"

Shocked at the nickname Catenya used, all Reecah could do was nod.

As Cat dropped out of sight beyond the corner of the stable, she sighed. Finally on the verge of being accepted and she had gone and messed it up.

Reecah's Gift

Her waterskin lay empty beside her, its contents drained long ago. Using her quarterstaff for leverage, she rose to her feet—her protesting muscles aching and tight. She struggled to bend over the bucket as her cup scraped its bottom to gather a small sip of dirty water.

Slipping into her cloak, she was thankful for its scant warmth as evening shadows sucked the heat from the air and cooled her sweat soaked clothing. The weight of her journal comforted her—the Dragon's Eye gem, Great-Aunt Grimelda had beseeched her to find, nestled safely beneath the diary.

Raver called from his usual resting place on the eave of the outer stable. Her only companion had learned her routine and waited for her each day as the sun sank behind the keep.

"To me."

Raver jumped into the air and dropped onto her forearm.

She regarded him through misty eyes and stroked his head. "What am I going to do? Everyone hates me...as usual."

Raver nodded. "As usual! As usual!"

She spit out a wet laugh. "Thanks, buddy. You sure know how to cheer a girl up."

He nodded again and dropped to the edge of the bucket, his weight tipping it on its side and spilling the dregs onto the sand, but not before he lapped at the rivulet.

The din of hundreds of boots stomping across the double drawbridges of the inner and outer baileys sent shivers through Reecah. She almost fainted seeing the black-bearded visage of the commander of the King's Guard—the same man who had led the royal forces into Dragonfang Pass—led a well-drilled army past the gatehouses and onto the southwest road toward the duchy of Svelte.

She had heard rumours of the high king's next offensive. A late autumn assault on another of the Great Kingdom's dragon colonies. Seeing it with her own eyes left her breathless. While she frittered away the days locking swords on a dusty training field, the plight of the dragons became more serious. If she didn't find a way to get an audience with the king soon, there might not be any dragons left to save.

By the time she made her way to the bunkhouse, the others had gone off to the common mess hall. She knew something was wrong as soon as she set foot in the dimly lit hut; the interior rank with body odour.

Littered across the middle of the floor lay the tattered scraps of a thin, woollen mattress. Her eyes followed the scraps to her lower bunk in the back of the fusty room.

The mattress was bad enough, but finding her old rucksack torn to shreds, broke her heart. Why would anyone fault her desire to train hard?

She fell to her knees and collected the pieces of her rucksack, tears appearing as dark spots on the stained material. Even if she *had* listened during Grammy's sewing lessons, there was no way to salvage the old pack.

Searching the area around her pallet she found her wooden bowl cracked in half and her thin blanket torn into strips. Sorting through the mess, she couldn't find her flint stone. Whoever had done this, must've taken it.

More disturbing than anything else was finding her rope hanging from the rafters on the far side of her cot. Tied into a noose, it bore the shoddy pillow supplied by the fort—a face childishly drawn on its white surface in what appeared to be blood.

She jumped as the door slammed against the jamb. Dagger in hand, she spun to face it, expecting to see her new *friends* coming for her, but no one else had entered the bunkhouse. She released her breath. Perhaps the wind had grabbed it.

Consciously calming her breathing, she balanced on the edge of her bunk and the one next to it, in order to unloop the rope

Reecah's Gift

from the log rafter. Coiling the rope and throwing it over her shoulder, she looked around the bunkhouse. A deep sadness settled over her. It was time to move on.

The scraps of her rucksack held her faraway gaze. She needed to find a new place to sleep, but if the others thought they could intimidate her into leaving the training sessions, they were in for a big surprise come morning. Reecah vowed to push herself harder than ever before.

She sighed and shuffled to the door. Pushing it open, her heart caught in her throat. Catenya and her little clique barred the exit.

Reecah threw her hands up and stepped back, her eyes on the curved dagger in Catenya's hand, pointed at her face.

"You ain't so tough *now*, are you, GG?"

Instinct kicked in. Reecah's left forearm shot up, catching Cat's right wrist and driving the hand holding the dagger out wide. Her hand curled over Cat's forearm, forcing it toward the ground—throwing her attacker off balance.

Cat's eyes followed the movement. Her mouth opened to shout something, but Reecah's right fist smashed her nose against her face, knocking the surprised woman into a scruffy-faced, brown-haired male from their training group. Reecah had grappled with Edo and bested him earlier in the day.

Edo reached out, halting Cat's backward momentum, which allowed Reecah to complete her move. Trapping Cat's arm, she rendered the dagger harmless.

Reecah pulled her own dagger free of its belt sheath and jabbed it under Cat's chin, the sharp point drawing a thin line of blood. Eye to eye, Reecah growled, "Care to find out *how* tough I am?"

Cat shook her head, blood streaming from her nose; fear evident in her green eyes.

Reecah shoved Cat into the wall beside the door and stood over her as she slid to the dirt floor. Brandishing her dagger,

Reecah's Gift

Reecah's intense glare took in Edo and the remaining four trainees who watched wide-eyed from outside the bunkhouse. "You made your point. I'm not welcome here. I get it, but hear me when I tell you; if I ever catch you touching my stuff again, I'll slice you wide open. You won't be the first person I've cut."

Not waiting for a response, Reecah shouldered past Edo and through the gaping bystanders. No one made a move to stop her.

She searched the immediate area of the inner courtyard wall. Shrouded in evening shadows, many barracks larger than the bunkhouse met her eye, but they were for the king's standing army. She doubted anyone would welcome her in, nor was she keen to brush elbows with someone who might recognize her.

The tell-tale clanking of the inner barbican descending for the night got her feet moving.

"Wait!" she called out and ran to the inner gatehouse.

The two guards manning the crank stopped turning the large handle long enough to allow her to duck beneath the iron-spiked edge.

"Ye just made it lassie!" one of the guards called after her.

She waved back at them but kept jogging toward the outer wall—the massive portcullis thankfully still up. As she ran past the guards, she noticed they, too, were preparing to shut out the night. She briefly considered sleeping beside the stump in the training yard, but continued across the drawbridge. She needed food. The galley that fed the troops lay inside the inner wall that was now closed off to her.

The road leading north to Sea Keep stretched away to her left. In the distance on her right, the edge of the King's Wood caught the last rays of the sun. If she hurried, she could reach the campsite she had made over a fortnight ago

She shivered, exposed to gusts blowing in from the distant sea. Her mind turned to the missing flintstone, filling her with a sinking feeling. Slump shouldered, she shuffled toward the

Reecah's Gift

forest. Holding her right hand in her left, she grimaced at the pain caused by punching Catenya's face. It promised to be a long night.

Shivers wracked Reecah's body as she sat dejectedly on the drawbridge leading into South Fort. Ignoring the quizzical looks of the four guardsmen manning the tiny huts warding the wooden causeway, she dangled her legs over the brackish water of the foul-smelling moat, waiting for the sun to lighten the eastern horizon. She had gotten little sleep lying on the cold, damp, forest floor trying to exchange body heat with Raver. Nor had she eaten. If not for a small rill trickling through the woods, she didn't know what she would have done.

The rhythmic clanking of gears operating the heavy chains employed to raise the portcullis filled her with mixed emotions. Tasteless gruel would be available in the mess hall of the barracks district, but that meant she'd have to face Catenya and her crew.

She rose to her feet, breath visible in the early morning chill, and swallowed her inhibitions. If she wished to have any chance of joining the king's army and find her way into Draakhall, she needed to keep training with Anvil. As much as she tried to convince herself that Catenya deserved what she got, guilt consumed her.

Four guards she hadn't met before stood across the threshold as the great iron-latticed gate lodged into its upper holding position. Two others swung the massive wooden doors outward—thumping them loudly against the stone wall, before locking them into place.

Reecah approached the leery watchmen.

One of the guards stepped forward, giving her a once over. "Little early to be hawking your wares."

Reecah's Gift

Reecah frowned. "Huh?"

"Ain't been seeing the likes of you around here. You fall out of favour with the..." He held his nose up high and said with an air of disgust, "...the high-born?"

"I don't know what you're talking about."

The guard rocked back and forth on his feet and winked. "I bet you don't."

One of the guards she knew on the roadway at the end of the drawbridge started toward them but stopped, his attention on a new man that appeared beneath the portcullis.

"What's going on here?" The sound of rocks grating together made all six inner gate guards jump to attention.

Anvil appeared from around the corner of the inner gatehouse, hands on his hips—his chest bare. How the cold didn't affect him, Reecah had no idea.

"Nothing to concern you, Anvil. Just turning the riffraff from the gates," the guard questioning Reecah said smugly.

Anvil stepped up to the guard. "You mean GG?"

The guard swallowed, alarm on his face. "You know her?"

Anvil's dark glare could have melted stone. "Know her? You twit! It's a good thing she didn't whip the lot of ye. She wouldn't have broken a sweat."

Motioning for Reecah to enter, Anvil shook his head. "It shan't be long before yer answerin' to her, if I have anythin' to say about it."

"Yes, Anvil. Sorry, Anvil."

Reecah waited inside the gate for the weapon master. "Thank you, Anvil."

Not sparing her a second glance, Anvil walked by her, muttering to himself.

She watched his bulk saunter past the stables toward the training ground. She entertained going after him, but her stomach cramps reminded her she needed to eat if she wished to make it through today's lessons.

Reecah's Gift

The inner gates rose as she approached—one of the guards who had stopped her on a previous occasion let her pass without incident. She knew most of them by now.

The mess hall lay beyond the regular soldiers' barracks; the dirt street leading to it, empty. Most people were just beginning to stir this early in the morning.

Rows of squat, empty tables lined either side of the ramshackle hall's interior. A lone cook stirred the steaming contents of an iron vat hanging from a set of wrought-iron hooks above an open fire.

Reecah sidled up to the fire, rubbing her hands together.

The rotund cook nodded at a leaning stack of wooden bowls. "Morning miss. It should be ready. Grab yourself a bowl."

"Oh, thank you, sir. Um…" Looking around, she grabbed a bowl and wooden spoon. "Can I have two?"

"Sorry, miss. One serving each. Got lots of mouths to feed."

"Please, sir. I haven't eaten since midday, yesterday."

The middle-aged man stared at her for a moment and looked over her shoulder.

She followed his eyes to the entrance. "I won't tell anyone. I'll eat here until someone comes, and then you can top me off."

She could tell he was contemplating her words so she gave him her best pout. The one that had always won over Poppa.

"Och, lady. Make it quick." He slopped a scoop of grey paste into her bowl.

The term, lady, made her bristle, but she dared not snap at the man who was kind enough to break the rules for her. She patted his hand. "Thank you. You're a kind soul."

"Ain't nothing, me lady." The man blushed. "I wish I could do more."

"You've done more than enough. I shan't forget this," she said around a mouthful of gruel.

Reecah's Gift

The front door squealed open as she stood by the fire, finishing her second bowl. She instinctively cringed, thinking to see Catenya and her henchmen entering. The sight of Flavian Silvertongue filled her with relief. A familiar face who, other than Anvil and a few of the guards, had been the only person she felt comfortable speaking with since coming to South Fort.

A sudden slop weighed down her hands. The cook had plopped in a healthy, third portion into her bowl. She looked at the bowl in surprise.

The cook winked. "Be off with you, before you land me in the pot."

A huge smile dimpled her cheeks. She returned his wink and smiled at Flavian.

"You're back?" Flavian retrieved a bowl and spoon and held the bowl out to the cook. Not bothering to thank him, he walked with Reecah to a pair of chairs in the back corner of the drafty building near the exit. "I was worried I wouldn't see you again after what happened last night."

Reecah seated herself. Conscious of her cheeks turning red, she asked, "Really. You were worried about me?"

Flavian sat down beside her. He blinked twice and coughed. "Um, well...Ya, kind of."

She gave him a bashful look and broke eye contact, trying hard to concentrate on her breakfast. A warm feeling flushed her insides. One she hadn't known since Junior held her in her hut. That seemed so long ago now.

"Where did you sleep last night?" Flavian interrupted her thoughts. "The city guards don't take kindly to people sleeping in the streets."

Swallowing a mouthful, she said, "I went back to the King's Wood."

"The King's Wood? Weren't you cold?"

"Freezing. It would've been nice to have a fire."

"No fire either? I wish I would've known."

She gave him a genuine smile. Flavian had come across as a cocky and arrogant young man at first, but now that she had gotten to know him, he wasn't a bad sort.

Flavian finished his bowl before Reecah. "We should tell Anvil what happened. He won't be pleased."

Reecah shook her head, fearing the weapon master's involvement would only make matters worse. "No! It's okay. Just let it go."

"What that cow did to you is unforgivable." He threw his hands up between them. "Trust me, I had nothing to do with it."

"I believe you. And no, it wasn't a nice thing to do to anyone. I wish I knew what I've done to upset her so."

"She's just jealous. Being high-born, she ain't used to a lowly commoner upstaging her..." His eyes filled with dread. "I didn't mean that the way it sounded. I, um—"

Reecah laughed and patted his forearm. "Don't worry. I know what you mean. So, the Cat is high-born, is she?"

The words no sooner left her mouth, than the thin door squealed open and in walked Catenya and her followers—deep purple circles surrounded Catenya's bleary eyes. She paused to lock her bloodshot gaze on Reecah.

Reecah tensed. She didn't relish fighting inside the mess hall. Not after the cook had been so kind to her.

Catenya's stare promised malice, but the woman threw back her shoulders with haughty arrogance and proceeded to the front of the mess hall.

Reecah turned wide eyes on Flavian.

"Be careful of that one. Her father is none other than the Viscount of Draakhall."

"Vullis Opsigter the Third?"

"The one and only. If he gets word of this, your training days are over."

Reecah's Gift

Her recollection of the viscount was one of a just and honourable man. Though, given the context of their meeting in Thunderhead, his graciousness may have been a false portrayal. The ramifications of the viscount becoming involved in her confrontation with Catenya slammed into her. Vullis Opsigter was the one person who could positively identify her as the baron's attacker.

Flavian must've noticed the look on her face. "Yes, I know," he said, not realizing the seriousness of the situation. He stood up and grabbed her hand. "Come on. Let's get you out of here."

Reecah's Gift

Stoneheart

Anvil worked them hard throughout the morning, battling with swords and staves. He gave them a brief respite at high sun, before engaging them in hand-to-hand combat in the early part of the afternoon.

Reecah dreaded being matched with any of Catenya's group, but miraculously, Anvil never paired them off. It was like he knew what had occurred last night. She didn't doubt he did.

Flavian, however, got paired up several times throughout the day with Catenya's crew. Eating breakfast with Reecah hadn't done him any favours. Contrary to previous days in which Catenya had appeared to have taken a shine to the handsome, young man—he was noticeably shunned today.

Edo, the strongest of the trainees, took great joy in pummeling Flavian with his fists during one of the sessions. If not for Anvil hauling the overzealous youth away from Flavian, Edo might have inflicted lasting damage.

"Alright, that's enough for today," Anvil announced as the sun dropped behind the keep. "Afore ye lick yer wounds, know this. I'll not be toleratin' further occurrences like what happened last night, ya hear me? We're to be trainin' as a unit to fight the enemy, not one another."

Everyone except Catenya answered right away, "Yes, Anvil."

Reecah wasn't surprised the weapon master had gotten wind of yesterday's shenanigans, but the way he stormed over to Catenya and drove a thick finger into the middle of her chest, did.

206

Reecah's Gift

"I didn't hear ye, Miss Opsigter! Don't ye be thinkin' yer too high and mighty fer me class. I couldn't care less who's yer sire. He entrusted me to whip yer highbrow arse into shape. I'll be damned if I ain't doin' it me own way, ya get me?"

Catenya scowled and mumbled something incoherent.

Anvil lowered his face to hers. "I didn't hear ye!"

Obviously irate at being centred out, Catenya said with venom, "Yes, Anvil! I heard *ye!*"

The way Catenya mocked Anvil's way of speaking drew gasps from several of the trainees but Anvil didn't react.

"Anyone late to the pitch come morning shall be dredgin' the moat. Be on with ya."

Everyone scampered away, glad to be out from underneath Anvil's scrutiny. Everyone except Reecah.

Anvil glared at her. "What do *ye* want, bilge rat? I thought I told ya to git? Yer nothing but a festering nettle in me britches."

"Yes, Anvil. Just one question."

"Ya hear me? More trouble than a tick in the straw, ye are. Off with ye."

Reecah stood her ground. "As you probably know, I no longer have a place to sleep. I was wondering if I could, um, stay here?" Her gaze fell on the stump and his rusty bucket.

"I ain't runnin' no orphanage. Ye got yerself in a tight spot, ye can damned well get yerself out." He nodded toward the outer stables and raised his eyebrows. "Now be gone. I shan't warn ya again."

Reecah tried to hold his menacing stare but backed down. Bowing her head, she made her way to the gatehouse.

Flavian startled her, stepping out from behind the far end of the stable.

Her hand went to her dagger, momentarily thinking Flavian was one of Cat's clique. "You scared me."

Reecah's Gift

"Scared you? You've a lot of gumption standing up to Anvil the way you do. I cringe every time I see that look cross your face."

"What look?" Reecah raised her eyebrows.

"Aye, you know what I'm talking about."

"Why should you care what happens to me?"

Flavian shrugged. "I don't know. Guess I'm growing fond of you."

Reecah's bravado fell away at the sincerity of Flavian's admission. She stared into his green eyes. There didn't appear to be anything but concern written there. Her heart swelled.

"That's very sweet of you, but I can take care of myself."

Flavian nodded. "So I've noticed. But you're making dangerous enemies. Cat isn't one to be trifled with. And Anvil…" Flavian shuddered. "I pity anyone who gets on his wrong side. I'd rather upset the dark heir."

Reecah almost choked. She had put Prince J'kwaad out of her mind over the last few days. Being reminded of the wizard prince unsettled her more than anything happening in South Fort. She could handle people like Catenya and Anvil, but the prince was a different story.

"Don't worry. He's preparing for another dragon assault," Flavian said, misinterpreting the fear on her face. "If the rumours are true, he'll be on the road before the week is out."

Bile formed in the back of her throat. A renewed sense of urgency to speak with the king gripped her. She grabbed Flavian's wrists. "You need to help me."

"Sure, GG. Whatever you need."

"I have to find a way to speak with the king."

Flavian frowned. "High King J'kaar? Why would you want to do that? Have you ever met him before?"

Reecah shook her head.

"Me neither. But I know of some who have. People who haven't been seen again."

Reecah's Gift

"It's important."

"Hah! I'm sure it was to those that went missing. What's so important that it's worth your life?"

Reecah let his wrists go. How could she tell him about her dragon friends? Flavian was the closest thing she had to a human friend, but if she told him about her role at the Dragon Temple and everything that had happened since, he would think she was crazy. Nor could she take the chance that he wouldn't turn her in to the authorities. She didn't know him *that* well.

"Come on. I need to get to the mess hall before they close the gates." She strolled with purpose over the inner moat bridge and beneath the raised portcullis.

Flavian had to jog to keep up. "Wait. You don't mean to spend another night in the woods, do you?"

Smoke billowed from a hole in the roof of the mess hall in the distance. Already, a crowd filtered through the building's solitary door.

Reecah scanned the throng for Catenya but saw no sign of her. "What choice do I have?"

Flavian grabbed her arm to stop her. "Wait here. I want to give you something."

He started away, but Reecah knew the gates wouldn't remain open much longer. "I'll meet you inside."

Reecah had already wolfed down her portion of stew and stale bread and was scurrying back up the roadway when Flavian found her.

He directed her between two barracks and pushed a bundle into her arms. "Here. I wish I could do more."

"What's this?"

"A blanket and a flintstone."

"Where'd you get them."

Reecah's Gift

"They're mine."

"Aw, that's sweet, but I can't take them from you, silly. You'll need them. Especially the blanket."

He shook his head. "It's warm enough inside the bunkhouse and I can't recall the last time I ever used a flint."

She didn't want to accept his charity, but already the cold night air had slipped over the stone walls and gripped the street. "Thank you, Flavian. You're a real friend."

"Ya, well see to it that you heed Anvil's words and watch your back. On my way to the bunkhouse, I passed Catenya and her gang. They looked like they were up to no good."

Reecah searched the thin crowd coming and going from the mess hall. "That's odd. They haven't been this way yet."

"I should come with you."

"To the King's Wood. Are you mad? You don't owe me anything. We barely know each other."

"Still. I don't like it. They're up to something."

"Don't worry. I can look after myself."

"Not against all of them at once."

Reecah winked. "I have friends in high places."

Flavian frowned.

She pointed with her eyes at Raver sitting atop a battlement near the inner barbican.

"Fat lot of good a bird's going to be against Catenya's crew."

"You'd be surprised." She placed a finger over his protesting lips. "Shh. I gotta go before they lower the gates." Before she considered what she was doing, she leaned in and kissed him on the cheek.

Flavian stared at her, dumbstruck.

Jogging away, she said over her shoulder, "See you at breakfast."

Stopping at the outer gates, she asked one of the friendlier guards preparing to lower the main gate, "Have you seen my friends? The viscount's daughter, and a few others?"

"Aye. As a matter of fact, we were just discussing them. Seems a strange night to be camping in the King's Wood."

Reecah gave him an innocent smile. "I know. That Cat. She's full of surprises."

The guard frowned.

"Cat. The viscount's daughter, Catenya."

"Ah, yes. Lady Catenya. I'm thinking I should send word to Draakhall to inform her father."

"No!" Reecah blurted out much louder than she wished to. "Please. Lady Catenya wants to prove herself worthy of the viscount. She would be most upset if he happened upon her unaware."

The guard mulled it over, looking to another guard standing close by. The second man shrugged.

The friendly guard said slowly, "Well, I don't know…If something were to happen to her and the viscount found out who was manning the gate, it wouldn't go well for us."

"Don't worry." Reecah thumped the end of her quarterstaff on the ground and patted her sword hilt. "I'll look after her."

Not waiting for a response, Reecah's boots clomped across the drawbridge and turned right, toward the King's Wood— her eyes continually scanning the ground for signs of Catenya's group.

Raver squawked once, high overhead. He would see them long before she did.

Reecah left the roadway and skirted the edge of the woods toward King's Bay with her bow in hand. If anyone had been watching for her, they would have seen her jogging across the open field. She thought about travelling toward Sea Keep and camping somewhere along the northern road, but decided that taking herself closer to the dark heir wasn't a great idea either.

Reecah's Gift

Reaching the edge of the grassy field separating the woods from the bay shore, she dropped to her hands and knees as Raver squawked twice in the distance. Someone was coming.

It took her a moment to find him, circling above the treetops where the roadway entered the forest. Had she taken her regular route to her campsite, she would have run into whoever Raver had spotted.

Not sure whether to enter the woods or find a different place to set up for the night, she was surprised when several people darted out from the edge of the King's Wood, running hard up the roadway toward South Fort.

It was tough to tell in the twilight, but judging by the flowing blonde hair of the stocky lead runner, she was certain Catenya led the group. Edo brought up the rear, sword drawn— occasionally looking over his shoulder as if someone was chasing them.

Reecah had half a mind to sprint after them, wanting nothing to do with whatever had spooked the group. She waited until Catenya and her followers disappeared around the corner of the outer wall before she stood up to take a better look at the forest entrance.

A muffled roar came from the woods, followed by a high-pitched scream. From where she stood, she couldn't tell if they were made by people or not. The scream sounded like it had come from an enraged female.

A second roar, different from the first, disturbed the wind-blown field abutting the woods.

Raver flew along the treeline, coming her way—squawking twice.

Holding up a forearm, she caught him; Raver's plummeting weight took her to her knees as she fought to keep him from crashing into the ground "What is it? Who's coming?"

"Lurker! Lurker!"

"Lurker? He's here?"

Reecah's Gift

Raver bobbed his head.

"Take me to him!" She launched Raver into the air and chased after him, unable to match his speed.

Raver circled over the spot where the road disappeared into the tunnel of thick trees. The closer she got, the louder the commotion became.

The high-pitched scream responded to three distinctly different shrieks—the sound dragons made.

Raver settled on a branch at the forest entrance. "Danger! Danger!"

Stepping onto the roadway, Reecah threw her staff to the ground and pulled an arrow from her quiver.

In the last rays of sunshine, three dragons surrounded the fiercest looking female Reecah had ever seen. Holding two, single-edged axes with spiked points, a rough-faced, dirty-blonde haired woman draped in ragged leather and furs, stepped sideways, turning first one way and then another, feigning to attack Lurker, Swoop and Silence.

Between them lay the bleeding body of one of Catenya's clique. Given the evident loss of blood, Reecah guessed the man was dead.

If not for where the woman's leather vest swelled over her breasts, Reecah would have sworn the bulging, muscular arms belonged to a male warrior, but the woman's long, wavy hair, shaved on the left side of her head, from her temple to behind her pointed, left ear, attested she was anything but.

The woman's light, blue eyes met Reecah's, giving her the impression of a sleek feline hunter. A long scar marred her left cheek from the corner of her plush lips to just before her left earlobe; the ear adorned with a golden loop earring.

On closer inspection, the woman's left arm, bare from the shoulder down to a crude, fingerless glove, bore dark lines drawn onto her well-defined shoulder muscle—her bicep wrapped with a thin leather thong.

213

Reecah's Gift

Her right arm was curiously clothed. Looking at the calm expression on her unamused face, one would never know she faced-off with three dragons that towered over her. The dragons had grown considerably since Reecah had parted with them.

Reecah nocked her arrow and approached the sputtering flames of a campfire. "What's going on?"

Reecah's Gift

Lurker's voice sounded in her head, but he never took his eyes off of the axe-wielding woman. If he was surprised by Reecah's arrival, his voice bore no evidence. *"I'm glad to see you're still alive. We came across your campsite and discovered this woman surrounded by a group of people."*

Movement from behind a thick tree drew Reecah's gaze. Her mouth dropping open, she trained her arrow on Junior who looked every bit the noble in his gleaming chainmail. Reecah knew better. "What's that scum doing here?"

Junior lowered his sword—his vibrant green eyes beseeching Reecah not to shoot.

"He's here to help you."

"Help *me*? He helped them slay Grimclaw." Reecah's vision blurred as tears threatened to fall—her draw arm shook with the strain of not releasing the arrow.

"No Reecah, you must listen. Let us deal with this intruder, and then we'll explain it to you."

The woman's intense stare drew Reecah's gaze from Junior, but she insisted. "Whatever he told you, he's lying! He led the prince to the Dragon Temple. He…he came at me after Grimclaw's death." Her voice trembled. "Don't listen to him!"

Silence stepped between Junior and Reecah, but it was Lurker's voice that responded, *"Not everything is as it seems."*

Reecah lowered her bow. Blinking away tears, she stepped closer. "Then who's this?"

"We know not. We have searched the bay area for several days now, looking for you. We thought you were going to Draakhall, but we couldn't find you. Junior located the Serpent's Slip at Sea Hold. Other than confirming you had made it that far, no one in the city has seen you. Swoop discovered your campsite today, quite by accident, and brought us here to find this woman attacking a group of fighters. We feared you were amongst them. When we landed, the others ran off, but this one is determined to continue the fight with us."

Reecah's Gift

"I say we kill her," Junior piped in, drawing the woman's attention. "But Lurker doesn't think it's a good idea. He thought she had information pertaining to you. But, since you're here." He raised his sword.

Reecah considered the woman. Her exotic facial features were striking. She glanced at the dead man—a glaring axe wound visible where his neck met his shoulders. "I don't know who she is, but I say we let her go. She hasn't done you harm has she?"

Junior raised his eyebrows. "Other than try to kill us?"

"Three dragons and a swordsman? Sounds like a tall order."

"Nevertheless. She won't back down."

"Does she understand us?"

Junior shrugged.

Reecah ensured she remained out of axe swinging distance—something Anvil had taught her the other day—though she was certain the woman would have no trouble throwing her heavy weapons. "What's your name, ma'am? Do you understand me?"

The woman's gaze flicked between Junior's sword and Reecah—stepping back and forth on worn, mid-calf length, black leather boots.

Just when Reecah thought the woman wasn't going to answer, she licked her lips and said in a calm, angelic voice belying her deadly appearance, "My people call me Tamra Stoneheart. Those around here know me as the Maiden of the Wood."

Maiden of the Wood? Reecah had heard that name recently. "Why do you want to hurt my friends?"

"They interrupted my business."

"What business is that?"

Tamra spat on the dead man. "I was set on by this man and his friends as I prepared my evening meal."

Reecah's Gift

Two skinned rabbit carcasses lay charred in the flames, the crudely fashioned wooden spit they had hung upon smashed and scattered on the ground.

"They were looking for someone named GG. When I said I'd never heard of her, they ordered me to move on, saying they wanted my firepit. I killed this one when he came at me. I was about to slay the lot of them when the dragons flew in with *him*." She pointed an axe at Junior—the sudden movement making everyone tense.

"They ran off, screaming. The dragons have denied me my rightful due."

"Rightful due? Of what?" Reecah asked, confused.

"Revenge."

"Because they asked you to move on? I agree they were likely rude, but killing them seems a bit harsh."

Tamra's eyes narrowed, her arm muscles rippling. "You disagree?"

Despite the fact Junior had his sword held at the ready, and three dragons separated her from Tamra, Reecah feared they might not be enough to stop the female warrior.

She attempted to mollify Tamra with one of her smiles. "I'm not saying I disagree with you. I'm not privy to what happened. Knowing them," she nodded at the dead man, "I can only imagine what they said. However, I'm not prepared to die because someone else told you to move on."

Tamra licked her lips. "I won't kill you. I sense in you something my people believe has left our world."

Reecah swallowed. The forest noises fell away—her companions forgotten. It was as if only she and Tamra existed. She shook her head to clear her mind but Tamra's gaze held her captive. The exotic woman's next words sent shivers up her spine.

"In you lies the magic of the dragon."

Reecah's Gift

Wizard's Rat

J'kwaad paced the chamber high atop Draakhorn, the tallest spire overlooking the jagged shoals abutting Draakhall's southwest corner. Stepping through a round top door onto the thin balcony encircling the spire's peak, he grasped an iron spike set into the stone rail and gazed upon the south road. The rising sun burned away the morning mist, revealing the ghostly image of South Fort, many leagues away.

Earlier in the morning, the king had demanded to know why he hadn't done anything about the woman who had stolen passage aboard the ship from Thunderhead weeks ago. The brig had been ordered to remain tied off until the king gave it clearance to leave.

J'kwaad had hoped his father's request to waste time searching for this woman was nothing more than an impulse and would soon be forgotten. Apparently, he was mistaken.

And yet, staring at the distant ramparts where the king's dragon army had recently departed on their trek south, perhaps the king had inadvertently put him on the trail of a troubling new development.

His scrying bowl had indicated a ripple in the veil of magic. The portent told him that a new source of magic had entered the bay area—one more significant than that of the Maiden of the Wood.

He ran his tongue over his upper teeth in quiet contemplation. He had wanted to track down the elusive forest maiden earlier in the year, but his father had forbidden it.

Reecah's Gift

If his intuition served him well—it wasn't often he erred on matters of the arcane—the Maiden of the Wood would also seek out this ripple. As would one other.

His white knuckles had little to do with the brisk gusts tugging at his robes and long hair. Smouldering anger at his father's short-sightedness sent his blood pressure soaring. Should this ripple represent what he feared, the dragon campaign might be in jeopardy.

He raised his eyebrows. Were the behemoths ever to come together under a united front, they would raze Draakhall to the ground, despite its added fortifications.

He released the iron spike and bashed it with a clenched fist. Damn his father and his stubbornness. If the man had listened to him, they would have already vanquished the dragons to the history books and old tavern tales by now. They should have pushed the flying lizards over the brink of extinction years ago.

His personal guard, a man who reminded him of the weapon master, called to him from the doorway. Dressed in a black surcoat and plate armour, the man's sudden appearance made J'kwaad jump.

"We have the informant from the tub anchored in Sea Hold, my prince."

J'kwaad bit back the angry retort on the tip of his tongue. He didn't appreciate being caught unaware, but it wasn't Calor's fault. The man was merely performing his duty. "Very well, drag him in."

Entering the wide chamber and closing the door behind him, J'kwaad strolled to the only chair in the room—a high-backed, cushioned chair with ornate, dark wood arms. He sat down and nodded to Calor waiting by the only other door in the room—the one at the head of a steep, circular stairwell carved into the interior perimeter wall of Draakhorn. Many people had died descending that lofty enclosure—either through careless misstep or being persuaded into the gaping hole the stone steps revolved around.

Calor pulled the door open, admitting a second guard almost equal to his seven-foot frame; muscles evident beneath his black surcoat and plate. The new guard shoved a wiry, scraggly-haired man in sailor's garb into the chamber and closed the door.

Neither of J'kwaad's men looked to be any worse for having climbed the four hundred-foot tower, but perspiration beaded on the face of their prisoner.

The scrawny sailor from the *Serpent's Slip* stumbled into the room. Catching his balance, he came to a stop in front of J'kwaad.

The prince gazed into the man's terrified eyes. "I believe it's customary for commoners to show homage to those of higher station...Or have the laws changed since the last time I descended Draakhorn?"

The man's eyes grew wide. "Oh, yes, my prince...I-I mean, no, my—" He cried out in pain as Calor's metal boot cracked the outside of his knee. An audible snap punctuated the kick and the man fell to his side, screaming.

"That's better," J'kwaad said evenly, like nothing had happened. "I'm delighted to see the Inquisitor hasn't left any lasting scars on you."

The man stared wild-eyed, struggling to keep from sobbing as he clung to his ruined leg.

"Now, as I do hate to tarry, pray tell everything you know of this miscreant from the driftwood tub you call the *Serpent's Slip*. She is causing me great angst."

The man didn't respond fast enough for J'kwaad's liking. The prince gave Calor a subtle nod.

Calor kicked the prisoner in the spine.

The man screamed, his wet eyes staring death at Calor, but he was wise enough to hold his tongue. He rolled his head to catch J'kwaad's impatient gaze and said through clenched teeth. "She is a woman, my prince. One I've never seen before. Ye know 'ow they're bad luck an' all. I weren't too 'appy about 'er being onboard, I assure you, but…" He trailed off seeing the prince nod at Calor. "No—umph!"

Calor placed the sole of his boot on the man's side and applied his considerable weight.

The prisoner forced words through his agony, "Sorry! Sorry! She's a young girl—just turned womanly if I got the right of it. Wears a brown surcoat and green pants; all kitted out with fancy weaponry. If'n I 'ad to guess the right o' 'er, I'd venture to say she be 'igh-born by the way she carried 'erself."

J'kwaad nodded and Calor removed his foot. The prince put a ruby-ringed finger to his lips. "Hmm. High-born, you say?"

The man nodded. "Yes, me prince."

"Interesting. That's all fine, but searching for a high-born woman in Sea Keep isn't going to be easy. Other than castle servants and practitioners of the night, Draakhall is overrun with them. Everything you've told me, you've already mentioned to the Inquisitor. I need something more. Something to distinguish her from the others."

The man trembled, unable to break J'kwaad's stare. When J'kwaad nodded to Calor, the man squeaked.

"No, Sire! Please! There is more."

J'kwaad raised his eyebrows and Calor stood down. "Go on."

"Her name is GG."

The prince sighed. Perhaps he was wasting his time. "Aye, so you told the Inquisitor. The same woman who embarrassed that pig-dog Carroch to within a hair of his life. Pity she didn't rid us of the scourge."

The man frowned, but said, "Yes, the same person. She 'ad 'elp to escape. A female sailor named Cahira brought GG onboard."

Reecah's Gift

J'kwaad leaned forward, his gaze darkening. "That's interesting. Why didn't you tell that to the Inquisitor?"

Without warning, Calor's toe crunched into the man's spine.

Wailing and twitching in exquisite pain, the man's reply came as a tiny squeak, "I forgot. Honest."

"Is there anything else that escaped you? Think carefully. My gracious hospitality is wearing thin."

"Um, um…" The man caught sight of Calor withdrawing his sword, and promptly wet himself. Eyes rivetted on the long blade, he nodded vigorously. "Yes! I do recall something else."

"Do tell, good man."

"A bird."

"A bird?"

The man grimaced, the sweat from his greasy hair leaving a stain on the flagstone beneath his head. "Yes, my prince." His words were forced and clipped. "She 'ad a raven with 'er. A right peculiar one at that. Missing a few toes, it was. She called to it one day at sea—not long out of Thunderhead. She spoke to it and sent it inland. I ain't seen it since."

J'kwaad considered the man's revelation. Unless the bird was a homing pigeon from the bay area, he doubted anyone had seen it around Draakhall. It didn't appear like there was anything else to be gleaned by torturing the man further.

Leaning back in his chair, J'kwaad intertwined his bejewelled fingers and folded them in his lap. "Very well. I shall bestow upon you a little royal hospitality." He switched his gaze to Calor. "If you would be so kind as to show our guest the door."

Calor nodded. Oblivious to the man's crippling pain, Calor hoisted him to his feet. The sailor's legs buckled beneath him, but Calor muscled him to the door.

The second guard opened it.

"Enjoy your trip," J'kwaad said, more to his fingernails than the squirming sailor.

Reecah's Gift

The wiry spy wriggled in Calor's grasp, but his broken leg and crushed lower disc were little use in preventing the knight from pitching him into the gaping hole between the spiral stairwell.

The man's hollow scream marked his descent. Thumping and bumping off the unforgiving edges of the circular steps, his body broke long before he hit the bottom.

The door closed, shutting out the cacophony of the man's inglorious end.

Calor joined Prince J'kwaad. "It usually isn't the fall that kills them, My Prince, it's the abrupt stop at the end."

J'kwaad smiled. Something he wasn't known to do. "What about the other?"

"Should be here anytime now."

As if on cue, a rap sounded at the cellar door. Whoever had been climbing the stairs would have witnessed the sailor's demise.

J'kwaad nodded to the guard at the door.

The door swung open and two more black-clad guards thrust an irate dwarf into the room.

The stocky man searched the room with squinted eyes—one green and the other brown. "What's the meaning of this? One would have to be crazier than a boneless skeleton to manhandle the royal blacksmith this way."

Prince J'kwaad flashed him an icy glare. The dwarf was being impertinent. Anyone familiar with the workings of the castle knew Draakhorn was the wizard prince's private tower. "Aramyss Chizel. I've been looking forward to this meeting."

"Prince J'kwaad!" Aramyss dropped to a knee and bent until his forehead touched the flagstone. "I beg yer forgiveness, me prince. Ain't had no idea it was ye who summoned me."

The door clicked into place behind Aramyss. He looked back to see three guards spread out around him. Sparing Calor a quick glance, he locked eyes with J'kwaad. "I'm thinking this ain't a social visit. I hope it ends better than it did for the last fella."

J'kwaad looked down his angular nose at the kneeling blacksmith. If the dwarf had thought to make him smile, he was sadly mistaken. The dwarf knew full well who had summoned him. "How you exit this chamber is up to you, Master Chizel. Now then, tell me about a certain woman you befriended in Sea Hold. One you escorted as far as the King's Stagger."

Aramyss swallowed, obviously shaken. "I-I don't know what yer taking about, me prince."

"Is that so?" The prince raised an eyebrow at Calor.

Aramyss dared to look away from the prince, expecting J'kwaad's personal deliverer of justice to assault him, but the huge man motioned with his finger for a pasty-faced man in king's livery to step from the shadows at the back of the chamber.

Aramyss' eyes bulged at the sight of the messenger who had found him on the King's Stagger escorting Reecah toward Draakval. His panic-stricken gaze returned to the prince.

Prince J'kwaad unfolded his fingers and leaned forward. "Aye. Perhaps the messenger's appearance serves to refresh your memory, hmm? If you wish to retain your position as royal blacksmith, I think it's high time you audition as the wizard's rat."

Reecah's Gift

Flight

Tamra Stoneheart's exquisite eyes never left the dragons as she made her way around the dying fire and stopped in front of a stunned Reecah.

Reecah held her bow at her side, not the least bit concerned about the wicked-looking battle-axes clutched in Tamra's fists. "What do you mean? In me lies the magic of the dragon."

Tamra leaned an axe against her leg and extended her hand. Reecah bent back, but Tamra's fingers grabbed hold of her earlobe and rubbed the bloodstone earring; a look of wonder on her face. "It *is* true."

Reecah jerked her head away. "What's true? Who are you?"

"Who I am is not important. I've waited a long time for this day."

Junior walked up beside Tamra; his movement not lost on the strange woman.

Tamra's claim to have been waiting for her, reminded Reecah of her great-aunt—the village witch. "You have mistaken me for someone else."

Tamra picked up her axe. Ignoring Reecah, she spoke to Junior, "*Your* presence confuses me."

Junior's brows furrowed. "Me?"

"You don't possess the gift. How is it you fly these dragons? You don't belong here." Tamra hefted her axes in an aggressive manner.

Reecah's Gift

Reecah wasn't keen on his presence either, but Tamra's words startled her. She hadn't thought about how Junior had arrived with the dragons. He must have flown one!

Part of her hoped Tamra would attack Junior, but Lurker had insisted there was more to him than she knew. Nevertheless, the image of the ageless Grimclaw slain outside the Dragon Temple wouldn't leave her alone.

The lack of sleep from the night before and the rigours of Anvil's lessons, coupled with the excitement of finding Lurker and the other dragonlings safe, left her exhausted. There were so many questions to be answered, and now this strange woman had entered the fray—claiming she knew this day would come. Tamra's assertion that Reecah possessed something called dragon magic had come out of nowhere.

The last thing Reecah wanted was to get between Tamra and Junior. By the look of the woman, Junior didn't stand a chance. She nodded toward the slain trainee. "We're going to have worse things to worry about if Catenya has her way."

Everyone gave Reecah a blank stare.

"Catenya is one of the people you chased off. She'll be at the city gate by now. I suggest we get far away from here as fast as we can." She glanced at the dragonlings. "If the Watch saw you land, they'll be forming a slaying party."

"We were careful," Lurker said.

"Three dragons drop out of the sky, not more than a longbow's shot from a castle full of king's men, and you don't think anyone noticed?"

"We saw an army march south yesterday. The castle must surely be empty."

Reecah rolled her eyes. "It *surely* is not." As she spoke, she remembered the movement of the king's army. "Now that you're here, we need to stop the king's men from wasting another colony!"

Reecah's Gift

"We aren't strong enough. If we die, we lose the only chance we have of saving dragonkind from extinction."

"And what chance is that?" Reecah asked, but already knew the answer Lurker would throw back at her.

"You, Reecah. That's why you're here. To talk to the high king and change his mind."

Shaking her head in frustration, she gritted her teeth. "And a fine job I'm doing. While I fight with the spoiled children of the upper-class, dragons are about to die."

"I *am* right about you," Tamra interrupted, casting Reecah a curious gaze. "You're talking to the dragons, aren't you?"

Reecah had grown used to the voices in her head—something she never thought possible until this very moment. She forgot most people weren't able to hear them. Uncharacteristically, she snapped at Tamra, "Why? What's it to you?"

"I can hear them too!" Junior piped up, but the women ignored him.

Tamra tilted her head, regarding Reecah with a curious stare. "It is as I said. You're a Windwalker."

"People keep telling me that…Wait, how do you know?"

"I am the Maiden of the Wood. It is my duty to know all things."

"Ya, well apparently, my great-grandmother was a Windwalker, but other than possessing the ability to talk to the dragons, I'm afraid I'm not who you think I am."

A distant shout sounded from the direction of South Fort.

"I hate to interrupt this female bonding session but it's time we were away," Junior said, running several steps toward the edge of the forest and squinting into the evening darkness.

Raver squawked twice from high in the treetops as the jingle of tack and thundering hooves reached them on the wind.

Reecah broke eye contact with Tamra. "Horses! We'll never outrun them."

Reecah's Gift

"Do they have dragons?" Lurker asked.

"No. Of course not. Why would you ask such a…?" Reecah trailed off. There were three people and three dragons. "Do you think Swoop and Silence are up to it?"

"Only one way to find out."

Junior's eyes grew wide, looking from Lurker to Reecah. "Wait a minute. Who's flying who?"

Tamra frowned. Not part of the whole conversation, it was obvious she was piecing together Reecah and Junior's words. Her eyes narrowed regarding the dragons.

Reecah approached Lurker and hugged him—something she should have done as soon as she saw him. "Oh, my precious friend. I'm so glad you're safe. I feared some of the king's men had remained at Dragon Home."

"Hey! He's my mount." Junior slid his sword home.

"Swoop will carry you. With your chainmail, you'll weigh more than Tamra," Lurker said, nuzzling Reecah's face with his own.

Junior backed away from Swoop, his hands up. "Uh uh. I've seen her fly. I've no wish to become a human missile."

Swoop stepped up to him and knelt down. *"Either get on or learn to fly on your own."*

Junior gaped, his frightened gaze on Reecah.

She raised her eyebrows and flapped her arms. "Well?"

Junior bit his lower lip. "I have a bad feeling about this."

"Don't worry. I've never dropped anyone," Swoop said. *"Hurry up. They'll be here soon."*

Junior glared at Swoop. "How many people have you flown?"

"You're the first."

Reecah spit out a laugh as a movement in the darkened forest caught her attention. Silence's deep purple colouring made her hard to see away from the flickering light of the campfire. The quiet dragon lowered to the ground behind Tamra.

Tamra regarded Silence the same way Junior had Swoop.

Reecah's Gift

"It's okay," Reecah assured her. "Silence won't hurt you. Mount between her neck and wings. Much like a horse. Watch."

Reecah was by no means a professional dragon rider, but she climbed aboard Lurker like she had flown him her entire life. "Secure your weapons and get on. Wrap your arms around her neck, but don't squeeze too tight. The last thing you want is to choke her unconscious in the air."

Tamra hesitated. "The last thing I want is to fly her."

The sound of horses galloping across the open field rose in crescendo. Bobbing torchlight carried by the riders could be seen through the break in the trees where the roadway exited the King's Wood.

Junior settled onto Swoop with terror in his eyes.

Reecah wrapped her arms around Lurker's neck. "Suit yourself. I don't know who you are, but if they catch you, it won't go well."

She patted Lurker's neck, anticipating the rush of feeling the wind in her hair. "To the air, Lurker. Let's fly!"

Lurker leaned back and sprung forward, flapping his wings in rapid succession. Lifting off the ground, he folded his wings to pass through a narrow gap in the treetops before winging his way east, over the broad expanse of the King's Wood.

Behind them, Junior's cry of helplessness made Reecah laugh. Now that they were past the rough part of the take-off, she eased her grip on Lurker's neck and searched for Silence. It took her a moment to locate the dark blot against the treetops far below. It was hard to tell, but she noticed a wisp of long hair behind the quiet dragon's neck.

Reecah's Gift

If You Fall, I Will Carry You

Junior paced around the campfire thankful to be alive. They had flown well into the night until they came across the shores of a lake so large it could have passed for an inland sea. Tamra claimed the body of water was known as the Lake of the Lost—dangerous to anyone sailing its choppy waters. She had mentioned something about krakens.

Lurker and Swoop knelt on either side of Reecah, carrying on what he assumed was a private conversation as the dragons' voices never entered his head although Reecah could be heard whispering to them. Where Silence had flown off to, he didn't know.

Tamra Stoneheart had ridden the purple dragon quite bravely, though when all was said and done, she had dismounted, staggered behind a clump of groundcover and promptly thrown up. She now sat quietly in front of the large campfire she had built—her great axes resting upside down in holders across her back.

Junior shivered, never wishing to be on the receiving end of those weapons.

Standing by himself, he didn't want to interrupt Reecah's reunion with her dragons. He almost laughed out loud—her dragons. Witnessing their bond firsthand, he knew he wasn't far off the mark.

Clad as he was, the temperature had dropped considerably, chilling him to the bone. He puffed out a visible breath, eyeing the fire. Its warmth called to him, but the coldness Tamra exuded deterred him from getting closer.

A shiver passed through him. Sucking up his dread of the fur clad woman, he approached the fire.

Tamra's uninviting glare regarded him from beneath a heavy brow.

He forced a smile for her benefit but she returned her gaze to the stick she used to stir the embers.

Swallowing his discomfort, he held his hands out and rubbed them together. "Gonna be a cold night."

Tamra didn't respond.

"I envy you your furs."

Tamra carried on as if he hadn't spoken.

It was obvious the woman wanted nothing to do with him. She had made it clear from the outset that she didn't approve of his presence. He had no idea why. He hadn't done anything to her. As much as he realized that she wished to ignore him, his nerves got the better of him and he blurted, "Where're you from?"

Tamra's eyes flicked up to meet his though she never moved her head. "What's it matter to you?"

"Um, I, uh…it doesn't, really, I guess."

Tamra held his gaze for a moment before dropping it back to the stick.

He couldn't stop himself. "You just look different. I mean, your ears. They're…" He didn't know how to phrase what he meant.

"Pointed?"

"Yes, pointed."

Tamra lifted her head, squinting her light-blue eyes with contempt. "You want to make something of it?"

Junior gaped. "No! Not at all. I just thought—"

"You should keep your thoughts to yourself," Tamra growled. "They may end up being the death of you."

Reecah's Gift

Junior swallowed, watching her hands—afraid they might pull those damned axes free. Considering her muscular, bare arm, she probably didn't require a weapon to dispatch him.

He glanced at Reecah and the dragons. A strange jealousy seeped into him. He couldn't tell whether he was envious of Reecah's devotion to the scaly beasts—creatures whose company he had shared for over a fortnight—or how the dragons doted on her. It was as if Reecah hardly knew he existed. His family history hadn't done him any favours.

"What are you doing here?" Tamra asked, her intense gaze boring into him.

He flinched, not sure how to answer. "I'm cold. I thought you wouldn't mind if I shared the fire. I'll leave if you want."

"Not *here*," Tamra growled. "Why are you with the dragons and the Windwalker? You don't fit in."

If the woman only knew how prophetic her words were. He didn't fit in anywhere. A nervous chuckle escaped him as he shook his head. "Truth be told, I don't know myself. I was on my way to join the dragon hunt when the dragons dropped out of the sky and demanded I join them."

"You're their hostage then?"

"Not exactly." Thinking back, Lurker *had* threatened to drag him here, but he had never thought twice about accompanying them if there was a chance he might save Reecah. Flying the massive lizards was another issue, but after surviving the flight out of the Draakval Colony, and despite his recent flight aboard the erratic flying Swoop, he found himself looking forward to the otherworldly sensation of being transported through the sky at incredible speed.

"The dragons thought I could save her from the dark heir."

"J'kwaad? Why would the prince wish her harm? Unless he knows about her already."

He didn't think it wise to share their role in the battle for Dragon Home with a stranger. If Tamra proved to be a royal sympathizer, she might kill them while they slept. "It's a long story."

"Then sit. I have all night."

Junior hesitated.

Lurker's voice startled him. *"It's okay. Let's see how she reacts to the whole story."*

He looked at Lurker, barely visible beyond the flames' reach. It was like the green dragon heard everything that went on.

Lurker nodded.

Taking a deep breath, Junior lowered himself to the ground. "Alright. Lurker said it's okay to tell you our story."

"When did he say that?"

"Just now."

"So, you speak with the dragons? Interesting."

"I said so earlier. You weren't listening."

Tamra nodded. "So you did. Perhaps I was wrong to contemplate killing you."

Junior blinked at that. Tamra's one hand held the fire poker while her other remained hidden beside her. He checked to make sure both axe handles protruded over her broad shoulders. They did, but he couldn't help wonder what other weapons she hid within her fur shawls and boiled leather armour.

"Convince me you're worthy of the Windwalker's company."

Junior swallowed. "I never claimed to be worthy of anything. They chose me."

Tamra's piercing stare did little to ease his mounting discomfort but there was nothing to be done about it. He started his tale from the time he and Jaxon stumbled upon Reecah lying beside the slain purple dragonling. He left nothing out, except his observation of Reecah at the base of the waterfall. That was a private memory he would take to his grave.

Reecah's Gift

He explained how he had sent Jaxon away when they found Reecah trying to comfort the dying dragonling. Of how his father had beaten him for his transgression of helping Reecah elude the hunt as they returned home after the adult dragons attacked. Of how he prevented his father's men from catching Reecah in her hut the day she had returned home to find it in shambles. Of how he purposely missed shooting Raver out of the air when the king's men had set up camp outside of her hut to await the rest of their army. Of how Prince J'kwaad and his nasty brother had attacked him and left him for dead in the valley below the Dragon Temple. Of how he had tried to warn Reecah of her danger at the Dragon Temple, not once, but twice, and had taken an arrow in the back for his efforts.

Tamra said nothing during the retelling. He piqued her interest when he spoke of Grimclaw. Lamenting at the tragedy of the noble beast's demise, he worried he had said too much as Tamra's mood darkened at the mention of the elder dragon's death.

He was so caught up in retelling his story from his point of view that he hadn't heard Reecah walk up behind him. He jumped when she dropped to her knees beside him and wrapped her arms around his shoulders, tears streaming from her cheeks.

"I'm so sorry, Junior. I never knew," Reecah whispered into his ear.

He was so dumbstruck that he froze, not knowing what to do. Two larger than life dragons and a female warrior out of his darkest nightmares stared at him while the woman of his dreams cried on his shoulder. He was afraid to wrap her in his arms in case Reecah, or the others, took his actions the wrong way. If it were up to him, he would have hugged her tight and never let go.

Reecah's Gift

Not knowing what to do, he pursed his lips and hung his head. Fighting back his own tears for making Reecah cry, he let her emotions run their course.

Tamra had rebuilt the fire by the time Reecah released Junior and leaned back on her knees to wipe at her smeared face. She looked sheepishly into his eyes. "I'm so sorry. I was wrong about you. I hope someday you can find it within your heart to forgive me."

Junior swallowed at the lump in his throat. He fought to keep his eyes from spilling over.

Reecah hung her head in what looked like shame. "You shouldn't have come. When the prince learns who I am, he'll come for me. I'm not strong enough to stand up to him."

Junior's vibrant green eyes darkened at the thought of anyone harming her. Forgetting his reservations, he cupped her chin, lifting her tear-stained face to look him in the eye. "Reecah. If you fall, I will carry you."

Reecah's Gift

New Recruit

Long before the sun pushed aside the night, two dragons circled south, flying dangerously low across the frigid waters of the Lake of the Lost; one green and the other brown.

Raver and Silence had flown ahead, scouting their flanks to ensure the king's army had passed beyond the eastern foothills of the Altirius Mountains, and to make sure the patrol who had come to investigate the dragon sighting last night hadn't turned their intentions south.

The wind buffeting her unkempt hair, Reecah yawned wide and smiled at Junior clinging to Swoop's neck. She had found it difficult to sleep after fleeing from the riders in the King's Wood. She couldn't quieten the thoughts rampaging through her head. Being reunited with Lurker and the other dragonlings was a wondrous occasion, but the knowledge of the king's army marching south on another dragon campaign assaulted her mind—leaving her feeling helpless. The appearance of the powerful elf woman and her strange mannerisms unsettled her more than she cared to admit, but it was Jonas Junior's revelation that threw her rational thought processes into a whirlwind of raw emotion.

She had fought so hard to lock away her feelings for the Waverunner boy, but once again, his presence had muddled her ability to think straight.

They approached the edge of the great lake with astonishing speed. Her stomach felt like it rose into her throat when Lurker suddenly shot up and over the treetops as the forested slopes of the King's Wood rose up before them.

With Silence flying watch to the south and Raver to the north, they hoped that skimming the ground cover would avoid detection from afar—the shadow of South Fort on the northern horizon was visible in the predawn light.

Passing over a break in the trees marking the south road, Reecah said, "Drop us behind the hill east of the city. Come at it from the far side."

Lurker and Swoop dropped below the western edge of the forest, their passage raising a trail of dust in their wake.

Though their speed had dropped off, flying close to the ground proved disconcerting as clusters of rock and bushes zipped by at an alarming rate.

Reecah was relieved when Lurker thrust out his back legs and reigned in their progress with a subtle back flap of his wings. She slipped from his shoulders and hugged his head—a feat that was getting harder to do. The dragonlings were growing at an astonishing rate.

Lurker rose to his full height. *"We'll be here when the sun goes down. If you need us before then, have Raver circle this spot."*

"Be safe, my friend." Reecah patted his shoulder and stepped away to give him room to take off.

Swoop followed Lurker toward the unseen shoreline of the Unknown Sea. Silence appeared from the south, joining their westward course. It was everyone's hope that someone would observe their flight over the sea and report back to South Fort that the dragons had returned to the Draakval Colony.

Raver dropped from the sky and rolled on the ground in a flurry of feathers and squawks. He righted himself and stared at Reecah, blinking twice.

Junior straightened his gear nearby, running his fingers through his unruly length of blonde hair. "Is he always that graceful?"

Reecah's Gift

Reecah smiled. "Hardly. That was one of his better landings."

Raver bobbed his head.

"It's a wonder he doesn't knock himself senseless."

Reecah laughed. "Done that."

The trek to South Fort allowed Reecah and Junior to get some warmth back into their bodies after their frosty, early morning flight. The sun broke over the eastern treetops across the field separating South Fort from the King's Wood.

Reecah looked over at Junior a couple of times as they walked, admiring his chiselled features. His nose looked slightly different—a faint bump where someone had broken it. When Junior caught her staring, she shyly turned her head away, smiling to herself.

Rounding the city's southeastern corner and approaching the drawbridge, Junior said under his breath, "Are you sure this is a good idea?"

Reecah searched the high battlements for eavesdroppers as she considered his question. There were signs of unusual activity. Perhaps it wasn't as safe as it had been before. She feared for Raver hanging about the castle.

She stopped and whistled for him. He took his time meandering back but when he landed on her vambrace, he did so flawlessly.

"Okay, buddy. I need you to listen. Fly back to where Lurker and Swoop dropped us off and wait for us there. Do you understand?"

Raver blinked.

"I wish I knew what you were thinking. Blinking at me isn't helpful." She leaned her face next to his. "Fly back to Lurker. Begone."

Throwing her arm into the air, Raver took flight, gaining altitude and disappearing beyond the castle to the west.

Reecah's Gift

Junior waited for her to start walking again. "What about me? Do you think they'll welcome a man with a sword and no money?"

"I don't see why not. They're always looking for new recruits to augment the king's standing army. Now that the main army has left on campaign, I would think your sword will be welcomed more than ever."

She paused at the end of the lowered drawbridge and nodded to the guards standing outside their huts. "It's okay. He's with me."

Across the drawbridge, the portcullis was still down. That was good. They had arrived on time.

It wasn't long before the winches creaked into action and the latticed iron gate rose.

Reecah recognized three of the eight watchmen at the wall. The number startled Reecah. They had doubled the Watch.

Four guards separated from the others and approached them halfway across the drawbridge. The tallest guard, Sir Batkin, the man who had first walked her into South Fort to meet Anvil all those days ago, winked at her, his eyes darting to Junior.

"Sir Batkin, allow me to introduce you to my brother, JJ."

Reecah and Junior held their breath as Sir Batkin studied Junior's appearance. His eyes rested on Junior's black and silver sword hilt before they took in Junior's wonderfully crafted, shining chainmail.

Sir Batkin's serious face softened. "GG and JJ. Your parents didn't spare any sweat naming you, did they?"

Reecah forced a nervous laugh. "Ha-ha. That's for sure, isn't it, JJ?"

She cringed as Junior's fake laugh sounded worse than her own.

Sir Batkin turned to Junior. "State your business in South Fort. Or are you just checking up on your sister? From what I hear, there's no need. She can look after herself quite well. Giving old Bone Breaker a run for his coin if the rumours run true."

Junior looked at a loss.

Reecah spoke up, "Ha-ha, you're too kind. Don't let Anvil hear you talk that way. I'll try not to let it slip you said that."

Sir Batkin's look of confidence dropped.

"Not to worry. I wouldn't do that to my favourite guard." Reecah winked. "Actually, JJ is a new recruit. Our father couldn't spare him until the crops were in."

She smiled at the guards blocking their way, hoping her fear wasn't obvious. If they decided to haul Junior in front of the king, there was a good chance he would be noticed by the dark heir—something she wasn't prepared to let happen. Especially after realizing how much Junior had suffered to keep her safe.

Sir Batkin mulled over his decision. "Your brother or not, none of us are aware of JJ's appointment with Anvil. I'm afraid we'll have to ask the weapon master personally." He nodded and the three guards with him drew their swords.

"Wait here while I confirm with the Bone Breaker."

Sir Batkin turned to walk away. Reecah grabbed him by the elbow. "Wait."

Sir Batkin narrowed his eyes, his dark gaze resting on the hand gripping his arm.

"Sorry." Reecah released him. "Do you think it wise to upset Anvil? You know how he gets when someone questions his orders."

That gave Sir Batkin pause. Visibly swallowing, he shook his head and said grimly, "Aye. I ain't looking forward to it but after last night, I have no choice."

Reecah's breath caught. She grasped his arm again, tighter than before. "Why? What happened?"

"You mean you ain't heard?" Sir Batkin pulled his arm free, rubbing the spot she had squeezed. "Not sure where you've been sleeping, but you can consider yourself lucky you weren't eaten."

"Eaten? By what?"

"Dragons! Lots of them. I hate to be the one to inform you, but one of your mates was killed last night."

"Nooo…" Reecah feigned surprise, which wasn't hard since she was shocked by how much activity was going on within the walls and upon the battlements. She hadn't thought of the ramifications of the dragonlings' sighting, but it made sense. South Fort prepared for an imminent attack.

"Aye, lass. Seems you may see action sooner than you thought. Especially with the bulk of the army marching south." Sir Batkin strode under the portcullis and around the corner of the stable toward the training ground with Reecah hard on his heels.

Rounding the far end of the stable, Reecah hoped Anvil wasn't in his usual spot. Her heart sank seeing the bare-chested goliath sitting on the stump, honing the keen edge of his battle-axe with a whetstone. The man kept his weapon so sharp, she wouldn't be surprised if it was capable of severing stone.

"Master Anvil!" Sir Batkin called out from across the training yard, his long strides shortening.

Reecah watched as Sir Batkin's earlier bravado wore thin now that he was in sight of the Bone Breaker.

Anvil looked up from his work with a scowl.

Reecah slowed down beside Sir Batkin—the surly weapon master didn't like surprises.

Anvil's eyes found hers. If she didn't know better, she thought she glimpsed a momentary look of relief on his face.

His gaze lingered but for a moment before boring into Sir Batkin. Rising to his full seven-foot-five height, the bald-headed weapon master snarled, "If yer here to tell me about one of me trainees, save yer spit."

Reecah's Gift

Sir Batkin stopped well short of Anvil. "No, Anvil. Though, I am saddened to hear of his death. Such a waste of—"

"Ain't got time for yer sympathy, Batkin. Spit out what ye came to say and be off with ya."

"Yes, Anvil." Sir Batkin licked his lips. "There's a man at the gate claiming to be a new recruit."

"Ain't expecting no new recruits. Take him before the Inquisitor. Let the serpent will deal with him."

"Aye, Master Anvil. At once." Sir Batkin spun to walk away.

Reecah grabbed his arm with two hands. "Wait! Let me speak to him. He's my brother!"

Sir Batkin glared at her hands, visibly trembling with outrage. He ripped his arm free and snarled under his breath, "If you *ever* grab me like that again, I'll cut your hands off."

He started past her but a massive hand clamped down on his shoulder, stopping him in his tracks. He must've been expecting Reecah because he raised a long dagger—the point barely missing Anvil's rippled stomach muscles.

"M-Master Anvil. I didn't expect you—"

Anvil grasped the wrist bearing Sir Batkin's dagger and turned it over—the guard's face twisting in pain as the dagger fell to the ground. Anvil leaned his massive head against Sir Batkin's terrified face, his voice harsh. "Ye've forgotten me first rule. Never turn yer back."

Sir Batkin said nothing, his body stiff with fear.

"The next time ye threaten me prized pupil, I'll use yer lily-livered neck to test the edge o' me blade. Ya get me, Sir Batshit?"

Reecah detected the slightest nod from Sir Batkin who looked no more than a child in Anvil's grasp.

"Good!" Anvil thrust Sir Batkin backward.

The guard stumbled. Throwing an arm out to catch himself, he kept his feet under him.

Reecah's Gift

"Tell GG's brother I'm waiting. Ye know how kind I take to waiting."

"Yes, Master Anvil. Right away, Anvil." Sir Batkin's eyes flicked to his discarded dagger, but he didn't bother to retrieve it.

Reecah watched Sir Batkin disappear around the stable, feeling sorry for him. He had only been doing his duty. Keeping her back away from Anvil, she eyed the dagger. "Do you mind?"

Anvil kicked the dagger at her and threw up a hand in disgust as he turned and stomped back to the stump. "Bah! Suit yerself. Yer softness will get ya killed one day. Go and help Batkin find his way back here with yer brother."

Reecah nodded and jogged after the guard. The way Anvil had referred to her *brother*, she knew he didn't believe her.

Prince J'kwaad watched on as the bizarre scene in the training ground unfolded. Weapon master, Anvis Chizel, had just tossed a city guard to the ground while a familiar woman watched on. A woman he had seen somewhere recently. He couldn't put a name to her, but he was sure he hadn't seen her around King's Bay. That left Thunderhead or that troll infested, rat hole, fishing village south of Dragonfang Pass.

Whoever she was, she was more than she appeared. His left ring finger told him that. If he wasn't mistaken, she was the ripple in the magic he had detected from Draakhorn.

He turned to Calor, a man almost as large as the weapon master and easily as brash. It would be a good battle if Calor and Anvis ever came to blows. Perhaps that time wasn't far off. Calor would make a better sibling to Anvis than the weapon master's spineless brother, Aramyss.

J'kwaad had great plans for Calor—ascending the Ivory Throne with him as his champion when the time was right. *If* the man didn't meet his death before then, of course. A good possibility given the dangerous assignments the prince sent him on.

Being a wizard's apprentice was a hazardous occupation at the best of times. Who better than Calor to experiment on in order to better understand the efficacy of his spells?

J'kwaad tapped his manicured fingers on the waist-high, stone battlement. He had more pressing concerns to worry about than a stowaway woman his father thought he was looking for. Why the king wanted her so badly, he had no idea. There was no way J'kaar knew of her gift. Or was there?

The dark heir had been summoned to South Fort late last night to investigate a dragon sighting in the King's Wood. The day before he was to leave on campaign. An ill-timed request seeing that his father had more than enough slayers at his disposal—even with the recent departure of the main army. Why J'kaar insisted he look into every petty occurrence irked J'kwaad to distraction.

He sighed. The dire straits of the knight being assaulted by Anvis did little to lift his spirits. "Who's the poor knave on the wrong end of Bone Breaker's wrath?"

"That would be Sir Batkin, my prince."

J'kwaad nodded, drumming his ringed fingers with rhythm. "And the woman?"

"Not sure, my prince. Our informants claim she's new to the bay area. Her skill with a bow is reportedly uncanny."

J'kwaad leaned out over the crenelated wall as the familiar woman turned to watch Sir Batkin scamper away. She wore her hair in a distinct, thin braid that gathered her hair from a point above her left temple. Another indicator that he'd seen her recently, but where?

The woman bent over to retrieve Sir Batkin's discarded dagger—her brown cloak parting around her waist to reveal green pants.

Reecah's Gift

"That's her! The miscreant." J'kwaad snapped his fingers and pointed at the training yard. "The woman the spy from the Thunderhead brig spoke of. I'm sure of it."

Calor leaned out with him. "The timing fits. Shall I have her detained?"

J'kwaad fingered the ruby adorning his left ring finger. It tingled with magic not of his making and was much too strong to be Calor's. If he read the signs correctly, the magic the ring sensed might be stronger than his own. And yet, the woman didn't carry herself like a magic user.

Not many witches were adept with bows and other crude weapons used to kill one person at a time. Why would they be? Blades and bludgeons were such sloppy weapons.

If the woman possessed the gift, she hid it well from anyone not versed in its detection. She deserved further inspection, but with the dragon raid looming over his head, she would have to wait until he returned from Cliff Face.

The appearance of the dragons in the King's Wood went a long way to confirm his earlier fears. The ripple in magic was so profound that it could only have been caused by an all-powerful wizard, or worse—a Windwalker. If he was right about this, the time had come for him to ascend the Ivory Throne. Expedience was required if they were to exterminate the dragon threat before the old line of wizards and witches reared their annoying heads and brandished their troublesome staffs.

"No. Leave her be. I have a better idea." J'kwaad pushed away from the battlement and strode toward a door breaching the side of the wall tower.

The man standing guard snapped to attention and opened the door without a word—his eyes not daring to meet the dark heir's.

Once inside the tower, J'kwaad descended the worn stairs circling the interior wall with Calor close behind.

Reecah's Gift

Calor's deep voice echoed faintly in the enclosed space, "Shall I inform your father?"

J'kwaad considered the question. The obvious answer was yes. Turn her over to the king and be rid of the problem. But the fact that she possessed the gift intrigued him. Perhaps keeping her hidden from J'kaar might mete out as an auspicious ploy when the time came to deal with the king and the golden heir. With proper nurturing, he might have stumbled upon a way to ascend the Ivory Throne sooner than he thought possible. Perhaps the high wizard might even play a role in the grand scheme of things. If nothing else, the girl was in possession of something he wished to get his hands on.

"Not yet. Send for the tracker I brought back from Dragonfang Pass and gather together a couple dozen of our best youth fighters. Make sure one of them looks like the miscreant."

Reecah's Gift

Precious Spawn

Junior looked up from where he sat with his legs hanging over the edge of the drawbridge. He gained his feet, expecting the worst, as the tall guard who had accompanied Reecah into South Fort stomped across the drawbridge looking none too happy.

"You! Come with me."

The three guards watching Junior raised their swords but the tall guard glared at them. "That won't be necessary."

Without explanation, Junior was led into a wide bailey between the outer and inner walls. The size of the place mesmerized him—the height and thickness of the walls were incredible to someone who had only been as far as Thunderhead. South Fort was a sight to behold.

Rounding the stables, he couldn't believe the number of stalls abutting the high outer wall. A movement at the far end of the long building diverted his attention. Reecah strode toward them, a long dagger in her hand.

"Sir Batkin." Reecah handed the blade to the knight. "I'm sorry I caused you trouble."

Sir Batkin snatched the dagger from her and wiped the grit from its blade. He pointed it at her. "I always suspected you would some day." Without another word, he sheathed the dagger and strutted away, turning his shoulder to avoid bumping into Junior on his way past.

Junior watched him go. "What's that all about?"

Reecah's Gift

Reecah shook her head. "Nothing to worry about. He's actually a nice man."

Junior raised his eyebrows. "Seems like it."

"Ya, well, come on. Wait until you meet Anvil. You're in for a real treat."

Reecah offered nothing further, so he followed her beyond the far end of the stable into an open area of hard-packed dirt that lay between the inner wall moat, and the outer wall.

His eyes fell on a behemoth pacing in front of a knee-high stump. A battle-axe leaned against the wall behind a dented bucket, the items barely registering. Junior stared at the bald-headed beast whose expression was anything but inviting.

Reecah walked straight up to the brute and turned to include Junior. "Anvil, my brother, Junior. Junior, meet Anvil."

Junior nodded, inwardly nervous about Reecah referring to him as her brother—something they had contrived last night. He thought about stepping forward to shake Anvil's hand, but the weapon master's glare held him back.

"Yer brother, eh?" Anvil spat on the ground. "I don't see the resemblance."

"Well, he's not *exactly* my brother. He's more like someone who watches over me."

Anvil stepped up to Junior. "Judging by yer fancy clothing, I'm thinking ye need no lessons from me." He gave Junior a thorough once over. "So, yer GG's protector, then?"

Reecah answered for him. "Yes. Something like that. I misled Sir Batkin so Junior wouldn't have to waste time seeing whoever this Inquisitor person is."

Junior caught Reecah's mischievous gaze. She lied so smoothly he almost believed her himself.

"Humph." Anvil returned to the stump and sat down. Grabbing his axe, he ran a whetstone along its edge and muttered, "Seems to me, yer the one protecting him."

Reecah cast Junior an anxious smile.

Reecah's Gift

Junior said quietly, "What now?"

"Now we wait. The rest of the trainees will be eating breakfast. When they get here, we train until the sun goes down." Anvil smirked. "Or until GG wears ye out."

Anvil's words startled him. He didn't think they were talking loud enough for the man to hear. Glancing at the hulk, Anvil's eyes were trained on his axe as he ran the whetstone along its edge.

Reecah leaned in and whispered, "Let's go sit against the wall. Make sure your back isn't exposed or he'll attack you."

Junior frowned.

"He's funny that way." Reecah grabbed his wrist and impelled him to a spot on the wall away from Anvil.

They no sooner sat on the cold dirt when a broad-shouldered young man with brown hair past his shoulders rounded the corner of the stable and searched the training ground. His gaze found Reecah and a broad smile erased the worry etched on his face.

"GG! You're safe." The man jogged over to where they sat. Junior noticed the newcomer made a conscious effort to keep the weapon master in sight.

Reecah jumped to her feet and embraced him. "Of course, I am. Why wouldn't I be?"

Returning her embrace, the newcomer watched Junior from over Reecah's shoulder, his green eyes full of suspicion.

"Didn't you hear about the dragon sighting?"

Reecah stepped away, feigning innocence. "No. Where?"

The man's gaze darted from Reecah to Junior.

"It's okay." Reecah smiled. "Flavian Silvertongue, I want you to meet a good friend of mine, Junior Waverunner."

It wasn't lost on Junior that Reecah had omitted his first name. He gave Flavian a once over, not caring for the way his face lit up in Reecah's presence. Silvertongue, indeed. Already, Junior didn't like him.

249

Reecah's Gift

Flavian stepped forward with an extended hand.

Like it or not, Junior needed to be pleasant with Flavian. At least in Reecah's company. His mood darkened as he studied how her face beamed while speaking to Flavian.

Rising to accept Flavian's handshake, Junior forced a smile. "Nice to meet you."

Flavian crushed his hand. Letting go, Flavian turned to Reecah, grabbing her hands. "The Watch were dispatched last night to the King's Wood. Three dragons were reported to have landed just inside the treeline. When I heard that, I thought of your campsite. I tried to accompany the Watch, but the gatemen wouldn't let me leave the city."

The concern on Flavian's face soured Junior's stomach. An unusual rage burned beneath his skin. Making an effort to steady an onset of rapid breathing, he struggled to concentrate on the conversation.

"Three dragons? Yes, actually, I did hear the rumours at the gate. Dragons, huh? That's scary," Reecah said, flicking a nervous glance at Junior, but keeping her attention on Flavian.

"You're not kidding. On top of that, Catenya and her groupies were attacked by a woman in the King's Wood."

Reecah touched her shoulders with her fingertips. "You thought I was the woman who had accompanied the dragons and killed Wirt?"

Flavian was about to respond but something Reecah said gave him pause.

Junior noticed Anvil had stopped honing his axe.

Worried she had revealed too much, Junior couldn't help himself from dwelling on what had been bothering him about Reecah since finding her again. Her amicable relationship with Flavian topped the list, but there was more. The frightening Tamra Stoneheart's unexplained appearance in the King's Wood and her claim that she knew Reecah would come was unsettling. As were her vehement assertions that Reecah possessed magic.

Perhaps his father had been right about the hill witch all along. Aligning with dragons and consorting with Grimelda—a witch who had instilled fear into the populace of Fishmonger Bay for as long as he could remember should have been his first clue that something was different about Reecah.

He shook his head, not knowing why his thoughts had become so dark concerning the woman he couldn't stop thinking about. Had she placed him under a spell? He blinked a few times at the absurdity of that and forced himself to listen to Reecah and Flavian.

Flavian took a step back. "I never said anything about *who* was killed."

Reecah's face paled. "Huh? Oh. One of the guards knew him. I overheard him talking to his friend."

Her explanation wasn't convincing. Junior feared Flavian would question her more, but Reecah kept talking.

"I can see how you would think it was me. I promise you, I had nothing to do with his death."

"I must admit, it crossed my mind, but when Catenya burst into the bunkhouse in the middle of the night looking like she'd been," he lowered his voice, and nodded toward Anvil, "beaten for hours by him, I overheard her describe a woman built like you know who, wearing furs, and wielding axes a normal man would have difficulty using. I knew then that it wasn't you." He finished, out of breath.

Their attention was drawn by the weapon master as he pulled a pale, suede leather shirt from behind the stump and pulled it over his head—the fabric barely able to contain his physique. Grabbing a black leather shoulder harness that crossed over his shoulder blades, he attached its ends to his belt. He rose to his feet and expertly snapped his battle-axe into the hardened leather clasps embedded into the cross-piece. How he managed to twist his massive arms behind his back to complete the procedure amazed Junior. Anvil was a physical specimen like no other.

As the first rays of sun gleamed off the heights of the inner wall, the rest of the trainees began entering the training ground—their eyes immediately falling on Junior.

Junior offered them a shy smile. It wasn't lost on him that the young men and women kept together, talking amongst themselves; nobody acknowledging Reecah or Flavian.

The hushed conversation of the new group was curtailed by the arrival of a blonde-haired, fit woman carrying on an animated conversation with a powerfully built, scruffy youth who appeared younger than the rest. Two more males and a female followed on their heels. As one, they looked at Junior with interest, but their glares settled on Reecah.

"About time little miss high britches decided to grace us with her presence," Anvil's gravely voice boomed.

Junior thought the weapon master was talking to Reecah, but the brute's attention lay on the blonde-haired woman who glared death back at him.

Reecah leaned in. "That's the Cat. The one I told you about last night."

Junior nodded. Reecah claimed Catenya was the daughter of the Viscount of Draakhall and had it in for her.

Anvil ignored Catenya's contemptuous glare. "I hope ye've got yer marching boots on. Today's the day we take yer training to a new level."

For a reason unknown to Junior, everyone shot Reecah a disgusted look.

"It's time to separate the jetsam from the flotsam."

Junior frowned, thinking that an odd analogy, but dared not say anything.

Reecah's Gift

"You're about to undergo your first, forced march. We leave immediately for Headwater with whatever you have on your back."

Stricken faces stared at the weapon master.

"Don't look so surprised. If ya ever make it into the king's service, yer petty issues will be of no concern. When His Majesty gives the signal to march, ya either get yer arse moving or get trampled in the process. To add realism to this lesson, I intend to reach Headwater Castle by full moon."

Junior could tell that most of the trainees had no concept of how much time that gave them, but Catenya's face transformed from irate to incredulous.

"That's four days from now," Catenya said with disgust. "Headwater is a two-day ride from Sea Hold on horseback along the bay road. We'll have to run the whole way."

Anvil hooked his thumbs in his suspender-like leather harness and rocked back and forth in his boots. "We ain't taking the bay road."

Everyone looked at each other, but it was Catenya who said, "You can't be serious? It'd take a seasoned warrior a week to reach Headwater along the south shore. Much of that route is impassable. Besides, we have no food."

Anvil returned Catenya's stare with a smug grin. "Aye. Won't the viscount be pleased to hear what a good little hiker and hunter his precious spawn has become."

"What happens to anyone who can't keep up?"

"They'll be kicked out of me training and can fend for themselves. Shouldn't take 'em too long to find their way home." Anvil raised his eyebrows. "Not with dragons about."

Reecah's Gift

Tracker

Jaxon nodded to the guard and stepped through the lower door of the Draakhorn. Heights had never bothered him, but looking up, following the imperfect, triangular steps spiralling the inside walls of the lofty tower, he experienced a moment of panic.

The door banged shut behind him and latched, dropping the steps into murky shadows. Odd, slotted holes were spaced along the tower's lofty walls, spilling faint light into the silent spire.

Since he was summoned by the dark heir, he decided it best to swallow his misgivings and get on with the long ascent. A cold wind assaulted him whenever he passed one of the open-air windows. He wondered how treacherous the climb would be in the dead of winter. Blowing snow would render the stairwell impassable.

So preoccupied with the exhausting climb, he almost forgot about his earlier apprehensions. While breaking his fast in the royal dining hall, he had overheard Princess J'kyra discuss with Prince J'kye about J'kwaad's imminent departure on the next leg of the dragon campaign. Hearing the dark heir had decided to leave his new lackey behind, piqued his curiosity. He wanted to know more, but he caught the princess looking at him from across the room.

It wasn't long after that a pasty-faced messenger delivered Prince J'kwaad's summons. The dark heir requested Jaxon's presence without delay.

Reecah's Gift

As fearful of the high king as he was, nobody instilled a deeper dread than Prince J'kwaad. Magic came with a price. Usually to those on the receiving end of it.

Jaxon's thighs burned, screaming at him to rest before he was halfway up the tower. *You would think someone might install a few handholds in the blasted place,* Jaxon thought as he willed his thighs to recover. Looking up deflated him, but casting his gaze downward left him reeling. He vowed to never do that to himself again. He wasn't looking forward to the descent.

In several places, the edges of the steps were darker, as if stained by blood. He couldn't imagine anyone fighting inside the tower. One misstep would be their last. On one step, about three-quarters of the way to the top, one of the dark stains appeared to contain a clump of scraggly hair. Too nervous to bend down and inspect the blemish, he shuddered and kept climbing.

The top step, narrower than the rest, slipped under a wooden door. Swallowing his apprehension, he raised a fist to knock, but his knuckles found only air. The heavy door swung open, buffeting him with a blast of warm air.

Prince J'kwaad's personal aide ushered him inside—closing the door behind them.

Jaxon swallowed and nodded to Calor before scurrying to kneel before Prince J'kwaad, bowing his forehead to the flagstone at the dark heir's boots. "My prince."

The prince didn't respond at first, leaving him prostrated uncomfortably, awaiting whatever fate J'kwaad had in mind. Sweat dampened his armpits more than it had during the climb.

"Arise, my faithful tracker."

Jaxon did as he was bidden but didn't dare meet the prince's gaze.

"Calor and I are about to set off for Cliff Face. As soon as my business with you is complete, in fact."

Reecah's Gift

Jaxon couldn't help himself from swallowing—the act reminding him of the necessity to breathe. "Yes, my prince."

"I won't require your services on the campaign."

The ominous bent of the prince's words raised beads of sweat on Jaxon's forehead. Not trusting himself to speak, he nodded, his eyes staring at Prince J'kwaad's boots.

"Take a deep breath. You have nothing to fear."

Jaxon met J'kwaad's shrewd stare. There wasn't any warmth reflected in those brown eyes, but nor did he detect any malice.

"You have heard me go on about a rather lowly task the king wishes me to see to, I assume?"

Unwilling to say anything that might upset the prince, especially since he had no idea what the dark heir was on about, Jaxon lied, "Yes, my prince."

"Good. Good. It has come to my attention that the miscreant my father so desperately searches for has been sighted in South Fort."

Relief flooded Jaxon as he realized what task the prince had been talking about. Some stowaway out of Thunderhead. Out of respect, he said nothing; allowing the prince to continue at his leisure.

"Her name is GG. She's wanted for assaulting the baron of Thunderhead. Baron Carroch desperately seeks her capture and return so she can atone for her behaviour. For some reason, known only to the king, we are compelled to oblige."

The prince stopped worrying at his many rings and leaned forward. "There is another person who has come to my attention. A man no one has seen before. You can't miss him. He's dressed in black with a full suit of chain mail. He apparently knows GG. They're being trained by a nasty piece of work known as Anvil, the Bone Breaker. What I require from you is to keep an eye on them, her especially, until I return. Track her movements and make a note of anyone else she comes into contact with."

Reecah's Gift

"Yes, my prince."

The prince held a multi-ringed pointer finger between them and leaned forward. "Heed my warning. Nothing is to happen to her until my return. Is that clear?"

"Yes, my prince."

"Good. I shall be displeased should you lose sight of her."

Jaxon hoped his knees weren't knocking together. Failure meant observing the road leading to Draakhall from the end of a pike. "I understand, my prince."

"Very well, Jaxon Waverunner. Don't fail me in this. There is more to GG than the king comprehends. Do your job well and perhaps you may find yourself attaining rank and privileges unknown to commoners."

The prince produced a thin scroll that Jaxon hadn't seen until this moment.

"This will grant you the title and all the permission you need to carry on however you feel best. Don't disappoint me."

Jaxon dipped his head. "No, my prince."

The tower door creaked open.

"Leave us."

"Yes, my prince." Jaxon offered Prince J'kwaad a deep bow and hurried away. Not daring to look Calor in the eye, he stepped onto the top step of the spiralling stairwell and nearly fell into the yawning abyss at its centre as the door whapped him in the backside.

Unable to prevent himself from looking down, he wavered. With two hands against the rough stone wall, he slowly descended the Draakhorn.

Calor approached Prince J'kwaad, a crooked smirk lifting his mustache. "I wouldn't doubt the boy wet himself. You honestly think he's up to the task?"

Reecah's Gift

The prince studied his rings. After thinking on it, he nodded. "He's green around the ears, but I sense great ambition in him. He reminds me of you when I found you grovelling in the streets."

"I would hardly call fighting for money, grovelling. I made a rather decent living if I do say so myself."

J'kwaad flicked a hand out and kept his little finger extended. "Pfft. This ring is worth more than you'd make in a lifetime in that boorish pit. Good thing for you I happened by when I did."

"Yes, my prince. I am forever grateful. What of the tracker? If GG, or whatever her name is, is the one who caused the ripple in the magic, she might prove too much for him to handle."

J'kwaad looked thoughtful. "Perhaps."

"What if he falls for the deception planned to lure the dragons to Sea Reach?"

J'kwaad raised his eyebrows and shrugged, nodding toward the stairwell door. "Not to worry, my faithful friend. Devius will keep an eye on her. You gave Anvis his orders?"

"Yes, my prince."

"And you found a man and woman to match?"

"Yes, my prince."

J'kwaad leaned back in his chair. A satisfied smile lifted the corners of his thin lips as he nodded at the stairwell door. "If Jaxon fails me in this, his next visit will see him exit via the accelerated route."

Reecah's Gift

Sensations

Reecah purposely kept to the back of the pack as Anvil followed his charges along the King's Wood Road—the route heading due east toward the arcane town of Arcanium—a nine-day hike away. The pace the lead runners set was an easy trot for her, but she dared not take the lead lest she receive further grief from her peers.

Staying at the back had the added advantage of allowing her to keep an eye on Catenya and her clique. An unfortunate accident was the last thing she needed in the wilderness. Knowing Anvil, he wouldn't lose any sleep leaving someone to die.

Flavian jogged on her right, a light sheen of sweat covering his exposed skin despite the cool temperature. Junior ran on her left. The fact that Junior kept pace in his chainmail hauberk bore testament to his conditioning, though he wore a pained expression. There was no wonder. She doubted she could have run this far, this long, burdened by the weight of the shiny armour.

Engaging the two in casual conversation throughout the morning helped take her mind away from her dragon friends. Come sundown, Lurker, Swoop, Silence and Raver would be left waiting for her and Junior, wondering what had happened to them. There was no way to get word to them.

She regretted sending Raver away, but with any luck, tonight's campfire would alert them to their new location.

Reecah's Gift

Though Flavian and Junior maintained a civil air, she sensed hostility between them. She couldn't understand where the dislike for each other had come from. They had only just met. Shaking her head, she muttered, "Men."

"What's that?" Anvil had dropped back to allow the group free reign of its progress—with the underlying threat that if they didn't reach Headwater in the time he had allotted, there would be trouble.

Startled, Reecah realized she had spoken her thoughts. "Oh, nothing, Anvil. Just talking to myself."

"It's a shame ya can speak at all. I'm thinking the leaders need to pick up the pace if yer to reach Headwater on time."

Those within earshot grumbled at the exchange. Reecah could only imagine the negative things being said about her as a result. Rather than engage Anvil in further conversation, she decided it best to keep her thoughts to herself.

Anvil allowed them a brief respite at high noon as they crossed a small bridge constructed of natural rocks pieced together. A babbling brook cut a lazy swath through the thick woods, flowing beneath the span—a pretty sight as beams of sunlight filtered through the deep shadows, illuminating the arch.

Anvil spent his time examining the bridge; adjusting a few of the looser stones to solidify it. Reecah watched him as she bent to refill her waterskin.

He returned her stare. "Wouldn't do to have a horse turn a hoof way out here."

The afternoon's pace picked up at first, the strain noticeable on Junior and several others, but it didn't last. With Catenya and her crew forming the lead pack, Reecah didn't think they cared whether they met Anvil's deadline. Catenya probably didn't. As much as Anvil harped on her, Reecah knew that at

Reecah's Gift

the end of the day, he wouldn't allow anything to happen to the viscount's daughter.

Seeing Junior struggling to keep up, she nudged him with her elbow and said quietly, "Let me carry your sword belt."

Junior searched those around them and shook his head.

Typical pig-headed male pride, Reecah thought, but she empathized with him nonetheless. No one else bore half the weight he did. She didn't know how much training Junior had undertaken over the last few weeks, but she guessed it was nowhere near the amount the rest of them had undergone. If only there was a way to alleviate his burden.

An aching pang fired through her earlobes. She reached up, afraid her earrings had fallen out, but they remained firmly attached. Without severing the lobes, there was no way they would ever fall out. Great-aunt Grimelda had seen to that.

She rubbed at the dark crimson stones, and frowned. Was that heat coming from them or was she imagining things. The heat was likely due to them being affixed to her ears.

The afternoon wore into lengthening evening shadows; the lingering ache from her ears had lessened but it wasn't forgotten. Daylight hours were getting less and less with each passing day—coinciding with the dropping temperatures. The winter solstice wasn't far off if she recalled the time of year correctly. If not for the dragon cycle every three years, she would have lost track of her age.

The group happened upon a flock of wild turkeys as the setting sun lost its hold on the land. Two well-placed arrows— one from Flavian and another by one of Catenya's groupies— dropped two of the birds before the flock dispersed into the underbrush and were gone.

Catenya's decision to run well into the night surprised her. The turkeys were passed around as they ran lest to burden one person. It turned into a fun game of pass the turkey.

Reecah's Gift

Keeping an eye on Junior, he appeared to have gained a second wind earlier in the day. Reecah marvelled it had lasted this long.

It wasn't until they stopped for the night and began gathering fallen brush to act as lean-tos that Reecah realized her ears no longer ached.

Junior observed her playing with her earrings. "Do they hurt?"

"Huh? These? No. Not really."

He reached out. "Do you mind?"

She shook her head.

Junior grabbed an earring, rubbing it between his thumb and forefinger. "Grimelda put these in?"

"Yes. Without my knowledge."

He released her. "How'd she do that?"

"It's a long story. I'll tell you about it someday..." She lowered her voice and indicated the others with a nod. "When we're not with them."

"I'd love to hear it."

Several people gathered wood and rolled stones into a large circle.

Anvil stormed up to the fire ring. "What're ye doing?"

The strapping youth, Edo, was poised to apply his dagger to a sliver of flint. He looked up from his crouched position. "Starting a fire, Anvil."

"No fires!" Anvil boomed. "Fires give away your position."

Reecah gaped at the weapon master, echoing the grumbling of the others. How were they going to cook the wild turkeys? Worse, without a fire, Lurker and the others would never find her and Junior.

Lying beneath a well-built lean-to she had erected, Flavian and Junior on either side of her, she lay awake, staring at the dark, forest canopy. Sporadic gusts revealed dark clouds roiling across the sky between gaps in the treetops. It promised to be an ugly night.

Braving the rain in the early morning twilight, Jaxon glared at the tall guard manning South Fort's outer gate, aware of the other guards keeping an eye on him. No one looked happy standing out in the persistent drizzle. "What do you mean they left yesterday morning? I've been assigned by Prince J'kwaad to keep a close watch on two of them. What's your name?" He thrust the scroll the prince had given him into the guard's hands.

He had spent the previous day searching South Fort for the stowaway girl and her long-haired companion dressed in black, with no success. Several times he had visited the open area beyond the first stable on the advice of multiple people. Everyone that knew of her, also knew that she was one of Anvil's charges.

His spirits had ebbed as the sun tracked across the sky. If Prince J'kwaad became aware of his inability to locate the miscreant, he dreaded the repercussions—regardless of whether he had anything to do with her disappearance.

A rational thinking person would surmise that there was no way he could carry out his task if the person he was sent to keep an eye on had disappeared before he came on duty. Unfortunately, no one ever accused J'kwaad of being rational.

Jaxon had spent the entire night searching the nooks and crannies all over South Fort, braving the onset of rain. He unearthed interesting people and witnessed many strange goings on, but there was no sign of the Bone Breaker or his trainees.

Returning to the training ground at first light, he attempted to employ his tracking skill. The well-trodden ground covered in puddles left him little to go on, but it was obvious a group of people had gathered around the stump and an old bucket lying on its side.

Where they had gone from there was a mystery. Toward the first stable was the best he could determine, but from there, their tracks were obscured by the passage of the rest of the city.

The guard he questioned let the damp scroll roll back on itself and returned it; the perturbed look on his face softened into one of newfound, if not forced, respect. "Forgive me, Lord Jaxon. I had no idea."

Lord Jaxon. That was an honorific he could get used to. He stuffed the scroll beneath his belt and decided it was time to exploit his new title. He peered down the end of his nose in haughty arrogance. "See you don't forget it."

"No, m'lord. I'm Sir Batkin, captain of the South Fort Watch. I had no idea you were in South Fort. The group you seek left at sunrise, yesterday. Down the King's Wood Road."

Jaxon had no idea where that was. He fought to subdue his mounting frustration. "When are they expected back?"

"The Bone Breaker didn't say."

"Didn't say?" Anger slipped into Jaxon's tone. "As captain of the guard, is it not your responsibility to know the comings and goings of the people?"

"Yes, m'lord, but not when it involves those of higher station."

"So, this Bone Breaker outranks you?"

"Oh aye, m'lord," Sir Batkin answered, a puzzled look crossing his face. "Begging your pardon, but you're not from around here are you?"

Not caring to explain himself, Jaxon ignored the question. "Was there a girl with brown hair and a tight braid in the group?"

"Do you mean GG, m'lord?"

"Yes! That's her. And a man with long, blonde hair, wearing black livery and chain?"

Reecah's Gift

"Aye, m'lord. The newcomer. GG claimed he was her brother."

Jaxon mulled that over. There was something peculiar about this GG person. Something that resonated with him at a deeper level, but the mention of her having a brother threw him off. He almost laughed out loud as to who he had thought GG might be.

"Is there something funny, m'lord?"

Jaxon wiped the smile from his face. "Certainly not, you twit. Point me in the direction of the King's Wood Road, and be quick about it."

Sir Batkin bowed slightly and started onto the drawbridge. Halfway across, he stopped and raised a hand. "Keep on that road. Follow the left fork as it passes beyond the city wall. That's the King's Wood Road. There's nothing along the route for over a week's travel on foot. It leads to Arcanium."

Jaxon had heard of the fabled wizard conclave of Arcanium. He wasn't keen on visiting a den full of magic users, but Prince J'kwaad's insistence that he not fail in his surveillance of this GG woman overrode his fear of wizards and their ilk.

"Were they on horseback?"

"No, m'lord. All on foot."

Jaxon nodded, more to himself than for Sir Batkin's benefit. A smirk twisted his lips. If the group was headed for Arcanium, he had no doubt he could catch them long before they reached their destination.

"Very well, Captain Batkin. I'll inform the prince how helpful you've been."

Sir Batkin bowed deeply. "Thank you, m'lord. Safe travels."

Jaxon nodded and started away. He stopped at the end of the drawbridge, sheltering his eyes from the rain with a hand. "Sir Batkin?"

The guard hadn't moved. "Yes, m'lord."

Reecah's Gift

Stomping back across the wooden span, Jaxon offered the man the kindest smile he could muster. "There's one other thing you can help me with."

The rising sun, hidden by the interminable wood and incessant downpour, provided little warmth as Anvil roused the group.

Choking back a strip of hardened beef Flavian provided her and Junior, Reecah rung out her cloak and slipped into its cold material; goosebumps riddling her skin. She located the Dragon's Eye safely tucked within its inner pocket with a grim sense of satisfaction. Its presence a constant reminder of a promise unkept.

She had protected her useless diary as she slept by stashing it within her shift, close to her waist. When the rain came, she stuffed it into a leather pouch hanging off her belt—stretching the holder's seams.

Using her fingers, she brushed wet strands of hair from her face and mentally prepared for what promised to be a challenging day. According to Anvil, if they improved on the distance travelled yesterday, they would leave the comfort of the King's Wood Road sometime in the afternoon and begin their arduous trek northward through the untamed stretches of the King's Wood. The easy part of the trek would be behind them.

Catenya set a slow pace as they set out in the rain, which suited most of the group just fine.

At one point in the middle of the dreary morning, Anvil growled from behind Reecah, "Bilge rat. Why don't ye get up there and get us moving? At this rate, we'll be lucky to reach the cursed pile of rock afore the snow flies."

Reecah's Gift

Reecah smiled at his endearment, but didn't honour him with a response. Her mind was far away. Along the shores of the Lake of the Lost worrying about her friends taking unnecessary chances to find out what had happened to her and Junior. The king's men's response would be harsh if they were ever to discover their location.

The sound of a stick breaking preceded Flavian's cry of pain. He fell to the wet roadway in a heap.

Reecah watched him hit the ground hard. She searched the immediate area but couldn't see the offending stick until it dawned on her the snap had been his ankle.

"Hey!" Anvil barely missed tripping on him.

Reecah, Junior and Anvil stopped but the rest of the group kept on trudging through the mire—soon lost beyond a bend in the road.

Flavian held his right ankle, his face scrunched up in agony.

"Let's see the damage, boy." Anvil stepped over him and took a hold of his boot.

Flavian screamed, but if Anvil cared, he didn't let on. Yanking the boot free, the weapon master shook his head. Flavian's ankle had already swollen and turned a convoluted mixture of purplish-black.

"Not good. Ye ain't travellin' on that fer a while."

Flavian grabbed his bare ankle, fear in his pained eyes.

Anvil straightened to his full height. "Pity. I had high hopes for ye."

Reecah gaped. "You can't just leave him here."

"Ain't much else to do with him. Unless ye plan on carrying him all the way to Headwater. Given the weather, we'll be lucky to get there on time as it is."

"You can't be serious. Who cares about Headwater? Flavian needs a healer."

Anvil scanned the thick undergrowth. "Ain't to be seeing one."

Reecah's Gift

Reecah searched for a way to help her friend. The image of Grog being hauled out of Dragonfang Pass came to mind. "We can make a litter and carry him back to South Fort."

"And ruin a valuable lesson. I think not. Ye'd best be followin' after yer mates afore they get too far ahead. I'll see to him."

Reecah didn't like the sound of that. She refused to leave Flavian in Anvil's company. "A valuable lesson? Flavian's life depends on us getting him out of here."

Anvil's face darkened. "Ye think the king will halt his march every time someone twists an ankle? This is a real time exercise with real time consequences. Ain't no exceptions on Flavian's account. High King J'kaar depends on me to weed out the weak."

Reecah put her hands on her hips. Rain dripped off her face, running freely beneath her cloak, but she didn't care. "Flavian isn't weak. He slipped in the muck because of the rain. It's not like he was careless."

Anvil shrugged. "Ain't me problem. Ye need to choose. Catch up to yer mates and continue yer training, or stay with him and throw away the chance to better yerself." He turned to leave. "I'd really hate to lose my two best archers, but rules ain't to be broken."

Reecah's temper flared. "Rules be damned, you unfeeling brute. Go join your precious trainees. See how proud you are when the best your class has to offer the king is that malicious bitch Catenya and her group of spineless followers. A fine lot of good they'll be when the king needs them to protect his royal hide."

Anvil's face turned purple.

Reecah braced to defend herself, expecting to eat his fist. From the corner of her eye, Junior's hand wrapped around the hilt of his sword. She placed a staying hand over his, fearing it would go badly for everyone if Junior bared steel.

Reecah's Gift

Anvil's heavy brow came together. "Suit yerself. If ye weren't a woman, I'd throw ye to the ground and beat ya senseless."

Reecah stepped up to him, throwing her shoulders back and puffing out her chest. She had to crane her head back to stare him in the face. "If you weren't a man, I'd take you up on that threat. Know well, it'd be the last thing you did."

Anvil's laboured breaths were visible in the cold air. He clenched his hands tight, his bronzed knuckles turning white, but he didn't rise to the bait. With the meanest glower Reecah had ever witnessed, Anvil grunted and pushed by her, knocking her to the ground.

Junior slid his sword halfway out of its sheath but one look from the angry beast as he stomped by, stopped him from making a fatal mistake.

Anvil broke into a swaggering jog and disappeared around the bend.

"That was a stupid thing to do," Junior said, offering Reecah a hand up. "Brave, but stupid. He might have eaten you."

"Ya, brave is but one mistake removed from stupidity." Reecah grunted, wiping the worst of the muck from her rump. "Good thing it's raining. I think I wet myself."

Ignoring Junior's gaping stare, as if he wasn't sure whether to laugh or not, she knelt at Flavian's side. "Can I? How's it feeling?"

The pain behind Flavian's eyes told her all she needed to know. She gently probed the ankle with her fingertips, subconsciously noting an aching sensation in her earlobes.

"Ow!" Flavian regrasped his ankle, brushing her touch away.

She stood. Her expression grim, she whispered to Junior, "It's broken."

Junior ran a hand through his rain-soaked hair. "Oh, for sure. I can see it from here. Now what?"

"We carry him back to South Fort."

Reecah's Gift

She could tell Junior wanted to protest, but to his credit, he held his tongue. Taking a deep breath, he positioned himself on Flavian's far side.

The rain ceased and the clouds parted, bathing them in the welcome heat of early afternoon sunshine whenever they hobbled beneath a gap in the forest canopy.

At first, it was all they could do to help Flavian keep his weight off the ankle but with the departure of the rain, their progress had quickened.

Reecah attributed their pace to the break in the weather and the three of them getting used to walking as one, but watching Flavian step gingerly on his affected foot she brought them to a halt.

She slipped his arm from her shoulder and faced him. "You're walking on it. Doesn't that hurt?"

Flavian glanced at his feet, both firmly planted on the ground. A look of wonder crossed his face as he cautiously stepped back and forth. "I can't believe it. I thought it was broken."

Though not an expert on injuries and healing, Reecah agreed with Flavian's assessment. It had certainly appeared broken when Anvil pulled his boot off.

"Remove your boot. I want to see something."

Reluctantly, Flavian lowered himself to the ground with Junior's assistance. Experiencing a great deal of discomfort, he wiggled his boot free and stared at his ankle. The swelling had gone down considerably, though the bruising didn't appear any better.

Reecah inspected the ankle. "How's it feel?"

As soon as her fingers touched his skin, her earlobes ached. She pulled her hands away and the sensation subsided.

Reecah's Gift

Flavian rotated his foot. "It's a miracle. It's still sore, but it doesn't feel anything like before. I must've just twisted it after all."

Reecah stood and exchanged glances with Junior. There was no way Flavian had only twisted it. She had felt the broken bone beneath the skin.

Junior shrugged, shaking his head. "Beats me."

Reecah swallowed, unwilling to accept what her premonitions were telling her. There was more to the sensations she had been experiencing lately than she knew.

Reecah's Gift

Witch Hunt

Muted sunshine drove the chill from the King's Wood, but did little to remove the dampness from their clothing as they stopped to take advantage of the last rays beaming through a wide gap in the trees.

Flavian's sore ankle kept them from sustaining a steady pace for long—having to stop frequently to let him rest, but that didn't prevent him from asserting they chase after Anvil and the trainees.

Each time they rested, Reecah insisted on wrapping her hands around his ankle. With every application of her gentle touch, she experienced the peculiar sensation in her ears.

As the last rays of light lingered, they sat Flavian on a large tree that had fallen recently along the edge of the roadway. Reecah asked to see the injury, but Junior held up a hand for silence.

Junior peered up the roadway toward South Fort. His gaze wandered into the dense forest on either side of the trail before he cocked his head in thought and strolled back to where she stood with Flavian.

Reecah shrugged her bow free. "What is it?"

Junior shook his head. "Thought I heard something."

She took a few steps and stared down the barren roadway but didn't see or hear anything out of the ordinary. The low-lying sun cast bright rays into the gloom making it difficult to see anything to the west. Birds sang various choruses all around them, while a gentle breeze blew the remaining leaves from

272

their branches—covering the forest floor with a multi-coloured carpet.

She returned to Flavian. "Let's see how it's doing."

Slipping the boot from his injured foot, Flavian's face lit up in wonder. The swelling had all but disappeared and the ugly bruising had faded to pink.

"I don't understand. That's impossible. How did it…?" His eyes widened. "You did this."

Reecah knelt on one knee in the wet loam. She reached out to inspect the injured area but he jerked his foot away.

"You're a witch."

Not knowing what to say, Reecah couldn't dispute the claim. It appeared Jonas Waverunner had been right all along. The truth of it stunned her as much as it did Flavian.

Like it or not, she had inherited her great-aunt's penchant for magic. She didn't know if it was residual power lingering in her earrings from whatever rite Grimelda had performed, or whether she possessed an arcane ability she had no comprehension of.

She couldn't recall when the sensations had first started. It must have recently surfaced. Thinking hard, she thought beyond Flavian's injury and recalled Junior's struggle during yesterday's hike. She had worried about him maintaining the pace set by the group and offered to relieve him of his sword belt. The more she thought about it, that was around the time Junior had found his second wind. One that had lasted the remainder of the day. Had she facilitated Junior's recovery as well?

Not wanting to divulge too much for fear of alienating Flavian for good, she said, "I don't know if I had anything to do with it. I think it might be my earrings."

Flavian's Adam's apple convulsed. "Your earrings?"

"It's a long story. They were given to me by someone versed in the magical arts." She reached for Flavian's ankle. "May I?"

Reecah's Gift

Reluctantly, Flavian extended his leg.

Reecah probed what remained of the injury. The dull ache immediately settled into her earlobes—more of a faint twinge than uncomfortable. Concentrating on her hands, she could almost feel something flowing from her fingers into his ankle. She withdrew her touch and looked at her hands, but nothing about them appeared out of the ordinary.

Pulling his boot on, Flavian got to his feet and tested his ankle. "That's incredible. You healed me. It feels so good I bet I could run on it."

To prove his point, he started up the forest path without Junior or Reecah's aid—a pronounced stiffness in his gait, but he ran nonetheless.

"Looks like we're not needed anymore." Reecah raised her eyebrows at Junior and started after Flavian.

Hidden behind a tree, unable to believe his eyes, Jaxon stared hard at the vision of a broad-shouldered man in chainmail and black surcoat. What was his brother doing here?

His eyes widened. Could Junior be the blonde-haired man the prince sought?

He was about to step clear of his hiding spot and confront Junior when his breath caught in his throat. A tall, slender woman draped in a brown cloak stepped onto the path, gazing his way.

The hill witch!

Jaxon's knees felt weak. Prince J'kwaad wanted him to keep an eye on Reecah Draakvriend! His brother was bad enough, but Reecah? Judging by the way Junior and Reecah passed each other on the road, they were comfortable in each other's company.

He thought of his father. He could only imagine what Jonas would say if he learned that the dark heir had sent his favourite

274

Reecah's Gift

son on a witch hunt only to discover his oldest son in league with Grimelda's great-niece.

He searched the thinning treetops, half expecting to witness a motley raven watching him.

Battling to still his whirling emotions, the dragon sighting a couple of days ago began to make sense. They were Reecah's dragons.

He glanced behind him, his horse not visible beyond a bend in the road, and wondered whether he should return to South Fort with as much haste as possible to report what he had discovered. From his brief interaction with Prince J'kwaad, it was obvious the prince hadn't put it together that the woman he sought was the same one they had encountered during the raid on Dragon Home. The same one who had, according to what he overheard the prince say to Calor, stolen a priceless artifact the prince so desperately sought.

He ducked behind the tree as Reecah's head turned his way—a great smile splitting his face. When the prince found out the true identity of who he tracked, J'kwaad was sure to knight him on the spot.

Reecah retreated to where a third person sat on a log.

With the greatest of skill, as only a tracker of Jaxon's quality possessed, he darted amongst the trees and undergrowth without a sound until he was within earshot.

He expected to recognize the third person as well, but whoever the young man was, he wasn't from Fishmonger Bay. Reecah appeared to massage the man's bare ankle.

Stranger still—she released his ankle and stared at her hands.

The young man pulled on his boot and got to his feet, staring at Reecah with awe. "That's incredible. You healed me. It feels so good I bet I could run on it."

The man didn't wait for a reply. He started up the trail toward Arcanium.

Reecah's Gift

"Looks like we're not needed anymore," Reecah said and chased after the man with Junior on her heels.

The young man's words echoed through Jaxon's mind. *'You healed me.'* How had she done that? With her touch? She *was* a witch.

Trying to come to terms with the affirmation of the rumour that had been part of Reecah's life, Jaxon watched them get smaller and smaller up the trail.

Another thing bothered him. What would possess his brother to wear their family armour and surcoat? Those were specifically meant to be worn when the duke of Zephyr called his banners—something that hadn't occurred during his or their father's lifetime. Not since the wizard war.

He swallowed. Could they be on the verge of another? Prince J'kwaad was on his way to engage a dragon colony. Perhaps Reecah knew something they didn't. Something that might affect the outcome of the dark heir's campaign.

He glanced back toward South Fort—toward where his tethered horse awaited his return. He thought about riding hard to catch up to the prince to inform him of his findings but if he did that, he would lose track of Reecah and Junior. If their destination wasn't Arcanium, the dark heir would stick his head on a pike.

Looking back, his quarry had disappeared in the deepening twilight. He exhaled heavily. The hill witch had a knack of haunting him in the strangest of places. It would be best to abandon his horse to the creatures of the wood. Junior wasn't a tracker like himself, but his brother would likely catch wind of a horse following them.

Stepping free of the thick underbrush, Jaxon started up the trail toward Arcanium.

Reecah's Gift

Elven Intervention

Flying a dragon above the clouds left Tamra breathless. Up until now, nothing in life unnerved her. She feared no man or beast, not even a full-sized dragon. That was the reason she had been selected above all others by the leader of South March, Ouderling Wys. Her mission: journey north into the Great Kingdom's vast wilderness to keep track of the comings and goings of High King J'kaar and his heirs.

Ouderling Wys had been concerned about the upstart king's malicious intentions ever since his father's unfortunate accident at sea. J'kaar had ascended the Ivory Throne under a pall of dark accusations from those close to the old king. Rumour had it, High King J'kneaj's flagship had been lost in the kraken feeding grounds of the southern Unknown Sea, but Ouderling Wys had her suspicions. Tales of deception and betrayal spread like dragon fire throughout the Great Kingdom and beyond—High King J'kaar had orchestrated a coup to murder his father and everyone aboard his ill-fated ship. No doubt the scuttling of J'kneaj's boat led to a feeding frenzy of the underwater leviathans, but the *real* serpent had lived on to assume the rule of the largest kingdom in the known world.

The elves of South March were keen to keep to themselves, not wishing to partake in the petty strife inherent in their close relatives, the humans. Rather, the elves believed themselves superior. As such, if the world around them was bent on its own destruction, South March deemed it prudent to remain a neutral force in the affairs of other races.

277

Reecah's Gift

To this end, they were successful, except when it came to dragons. As with every relationship involving sentient beings, the elves believed that the relationship between mankind and dragonkind needed to be nurtured to ensure the survival of both species; of which the elves begrudgingly belonged.

To facilitate this, they went against their creed and appointed a group of elves to maintain peace between the two species. The Windwalkers. As with all sentient creatures, there were those who would stray from the path.

Over the centuries, the Windwalker lineage became diluted through cross marriages and wanton greed until the dragon riders had become so weak, they lost touch with their elven heritage and their inherent magic. Thus began the beginning of the end of the magical race of flying serpents.

Tamra shook her head, as much to clear the tears caused by the rushing wind as to rid her mind of the senseless abandonment of the elven cause. Had she been around during the time of the Great Upheaval, she would have eradicated every known half-elf to ensure the purity of the Windwalker line.

The weakness of her people shocked her. If someone had had the fortitude to do what needed to be done, their kingdom, and the lives of the larger world, wouldn't be in the desperate straits they found themselves in.

"You're a hard one, Tamra Stoneheart."

If not for her iron grip on Silence's neck, Tamra would have fallen through the wispy cloud cover to her death along the northwestern coast of the Great Kingdom.

She searched the skies around her, expecting to see a second dragon rider, but other than Lurker and Swoop, only the raven was visible.

"You're choking me," a strangled voice sounded.

Tamra's eyes opened wide, despite the icy winds buffeting her face. "Did you just speak to me?"

278

Reecah's Gift

"If you don't relax your hold, we'll be meeting the ground much faster than either of us would like."

Tamra unclenched her muscles and almost slipped from Silence's back. She regripped the purple dragon's neck, taking care not to hold on as tightly as before. "How is this possible? I don't possess dragon magic."

"You possess elven magic. The two are closely related. I have permitted you into my circle of trust."

Tamra let Silence's words sink in. She still had a lot to learn about the world.

"Your thoughts, though dark, prove you're worthy of my trust. Your elven heritage runs deep with dragonkind. Forgive our initial distrust. We are overly defensive when someone lifts a blade in Reecah Windwalker's presence."

Goosebumps riddled her skin beneath her furs. "I was right about the Windwalker," she half said, half asked.

"According to our recently deceased leader, Reecah is the last. Born to a human mother who possessed the gift. A Windwalker who had died trying to make a difference."

"Was killed, you mean," a second voice sounded, this one male. "Lurker?"

"Aye."

"I can hear every dragon?"

A third voice sounded in her head—a female voice much throatier than Silence's, *"Only those who grant you permission. Unless you're a Windwalker, you'll never hear a dragon speak without their consent."*

"And even that only happens if the Windwalker has been properly trained," Silence added.

Tamra thought about her meeting with Reecah two days ago. The young woman had shrugged off Tamra's claim that she possessed dragon magic, even though, to a trained eye like her own, Reecah exuded the lost magic like a heady odour.

Reecah's Gift

"Reecah claims she's unaware of her heritage. Did she say this to deceive me?"

Lurker answered, *"We wish it were that simple."* He went on to give Tamra a brief history of Reecah's life, including her attempt to impede the dragon hunt and her role at the Dragon Temple. He included Junior's role as of late and their visit to the Draakval Colony to speak with Demonic.

Tamra didn't know what to say. Not one to mince words, she was never without a strong opinion. As a result, most of her kindred had avoided her while growing up.

She smiled at the recollection. They had good reason to. She viewed the world in black and white—never allowing hues or shades to mar her ideology. From the time she could walk, Tamra either agreed with someone or pummelled them. Long before reaching puberty, she had battled countless elves— most of them older than her. On more than one occasion, she had beaten them to within a heartbeat of their lives before someone else had intervened.

Once puberty filled out her physique with muscles most men coveted, there wasn't an elf crazy enough to go against her. As a result, she was shunned by most of her people. All except Ouderling Wys—a clear-headed thinker who didn't allow the weakness of emotion to muddle her decision making. Ouderling Wys had lived through the Great Upheaval and witnessed first hand the rise of the Great Kingdom.

"So, your survival depends on someone who has no idea who she really is? One who has never tapped into her gift? That doesn't sound like a promising future. With Dragon Home fallen and Draakval soon to follow, that leaves only the Draakvuur Colony."

"Not necessarily. The Wyrm Colony might intervene," Lurker said, not sounding like he believed what he said.

"The wyvern colony? There's no way wyverns will support them. Not after the way Demonic and his horde have treated them over the years. If I were a wyvern, I would help the dark heir and clean up the spoils after he moves on."

"You know a lot about dragons," Lurker said.

"I was entrusted to keep an eye on the outside world. My life has been devoted to knowledge."

Nobody spoke for a while. The dragons tried to keep hidden above the cloud cover as best they could, counting on Raver to alert them if Reecah's group deviated from the northerly ocean road between Serpent's Kiss and the Sect.

After fretting the first night over why Reecah and Junior hadn't shown up, the dragons and Raver had returned to the Lake of the Lost and consulted with her. Though she knew the ways of man better than her scaly companions, she couldn't shed any light on what might have happened to them. In the end, they all flew back to the rendezvous spot and waited—hoping Reecah and Junior had been detained for some reason.

Tamra had offered to visit South Fort, but Lurker wouldn't have it. The king's men would be looking for her as well.

When night fell and still there was no sign, they took to the skies, risking detection.

Using the blotchy cloud cover to their advantage the next morning, they soon discovered a large group of people on horseback galloping north along the coastal road.

Raver had dropped to take a closer look and reported seeing Reecah and Junior amongst the riders. The group followed a bald-headed man who Tamra identified as Anvis Chizel. Raver tried to get closer to the group, cawing a warning to Reecah, but the people fired arrows to keep him away.

Tamra sensed Lurker's unease at Raver's concern. There was no way Reecah would permit someone to indiscriminately shoot at him. "Drop me up ahead. There's only a score of them. It's high time for an elven intervention."

"I don't want to endanger Reecah or Junior. If they discover they're with us, we may not get to them in time."

Reecah's Gift

"Can't you speak to her?"

"Our range is limited, especially with humankind."

Tamra bristled at the term. Humankind included elves.

Passing over a small break in the clouds, Swoop asked, *"Where's Raver?"*

Lurker's flight pattern wavered. *"What do you mean?"* He dropped dangerously low, the bottom edges of the cloud swirling off his pointed wingtips. *"He's gone!"*

Raver's faint voice reached them. "I'm here. I'm here."

The dragons drifted dangerously low, threatening to give away their position, but they couldn't see their little friend. The damp wisps of cloud prevented Tamra from keeping her eyes open long enough to concentrate on anything but maintaining her grip on Silence

Lurker asked, *"Where are you?"*

"The tree. The…ack!"

Swoop's somber remark stunned Tamra.

"They've caught him."

Reecah's Gift

Parting Ways

Trekking through the underbrush, following the unmistakable path taken by Anvil and his group, proved tougher than Reecah would have thought. Back home, she had often strayed off the beaten path to discover newer, faster ways to a destination, but the overgrown groundcover, even hacked apart and trampled by Anvil and his group, was thicker than most places she had hiked through.

It was fortunate that Flavian's ankle had healed as well as it had as the path veered off the roadway into virtually impassable underbrush. There was no way she and Junior could have hauled him over the uneven forest floor.

The freshly hewn swath tracked north for the most part, veering east around unclimbable rock formations and sudden crevices. Judging by the unforgiving terrain, it seemed a miracle they hadn't caught up with the group already.

Three days out of South Fort left them sweating profusely on the coldest day yet. Sitting on a flat boulder, taking a much-needed rest, they chewed on the last of Flavian's beef strips—the oversaturated salt content made Reecah pucker.

Sweat poured from Junior's face, making it appear like he had just breached the surface of a lake. "How much farther?"

Flavian spoke around a chunk of the chewy meat, "No idea. I've only been to Headwater once in my life and we sure didn't come this way." He took a healthy swallow from his waterskin. "It'll depend on whether Anvil points them in the right direction or lets them determine their own course."

Reecah's Gift

Junior frowned. "Surely he wouldn't do that?"

Reecah rolled her eyes. "With that man, anything's possible." She studied Flavian. "How's the ankle?"

"Never better, thanks to you. You're amazing." He stared longingly into her eyes, a great smile on his face.

Junior shook his head and grumbled something unintelligible before starting off again.

Reecah smiled, patting Flavian's thigh as she slid off the rock. "Come on. I'm thinking we have a long day ahead."

The absolute darkness after the sun went down made travel impossible; heavy cloud cover obscured the moon. Before they had a fire going, light snowflakes drifted to the ground.

Flavian constructed a makeshift spit to hold a wild turkey Reecah had taken down with an arrow shortly before sunset.

Junior shivered in the flickering light—unconcerned about Anvil's warning not to build a fire. If the bull-headed man wanted to freeze, that was his problem.

Reecah sat next to Flavian, plucking the bird with wild abandon—more than once playfully throwing a handful of feathers at the South Fort trainee.

Junior bit his tongue, his mood darkening. He was tired and sore—the weight of his armour had chafed his neck and armpits. He laid his sword belt and leather shoulder harness beside him, and wriggled free of the hauberk.

Thankful to be free of the pressing weight, the difference in temperature shocked him—his sweat-soaked undergarments cold against his skin. He absently noted the injuries he had sustained at the Dragon Temple no longer bothered him. Grunting, he wrapped himself in his long cape and huddled across the fire from his companions to stare into the flames.

He had wanted to express his feelings to Reecah that first night on the shores of the Lake of the Lost, but in the end, he had ironically, *lost* his nerve. He felt foolish now. Although he knew she was grateful for what he had gone through on her behalf, expecting her to forgive him his family's atrocities toward her family was an unreal expectation.

Watching her laugh with Flavian left a bitter taste in his mouth. He bit his lips, angry. At what, he wasn't sure. Life in general? Himself? Flavian? Reecah?

He swallowed. Never Reecah. Who was he to tell her who to like, and who not to? Well aware of her struggles in life, if she had finally found comfort in Flavian, he should be happy for her. And, that's what irritated him most. He wasn't. Whether it be unfair, selfish, or self-serving, he couldn't help the way he felt. He detested how the two of them carried on.

He had secretly hoped that when Flavian realized she was a witch, he would back off. At first, he had, but as the day went on, the young man's cynical view softened. By the time they made camp, he had shown an interest in discovering what being a magic user actually involved.

Junior had debated taking her aside to pour out his aching heart, but somewhere through the course of the night's conversation, he had lost his nerve.

Brooding over what might have been, he considered slipping into his chainmail and returning to South Fort. If not for his fear of losing her altogether he would have done so already.

Nodding to himself, he made up his mind. Flavian would look after her. Once Reecah was safely back in the company of Anvil, he would quietly bow out and return to...?

He looked up, puzzled. Where would he go? Definitely not Fishmonger Bay. Swallowing the lump in his throat he chewed on his lips. He had nowhere *to* go.

"I hear something," Junior said shortly after high sun the next day.

Reecah's Gift

They had stumbled across the trainees' campsite halfway through the morning but Anvil and his crew were long gone.

Reecah and Flavian stopped behind him to listen. The distant sound of snapping foliage and the whacking of blades against stalks came from somewhere ahead.

"We should go around them," Flavian suggested. "I'd love to see the look on Catenya's face if she found out we beat them to Headwater."

"Or Anvil's." Reecah liked his idea but worried they weren't up to it. "Do you think you can guide us there without the aid of the trail they are laying down?"

"Can't be that hard. Just follow a straight line from here on in."

The plan seemed obvious but Reecah knew better. Nature was never straight forward. They would be forced around impassable landmarks and bodies of water. Their direction would become disjointed. Without a distinct landmark to find their bearings, they would soon become hopelessly lost.

She had caught a glimpse of how expansive the King's Wood was while riding Lurker. She had no desire to spend the rest of her days finding a way out of them again. "I think it's best for us to catch up to them and go on together."

She waited for Junior to start moving but he remained stationary. "What's wrong?"

The look on Junior's face scared her. Fearing he saw something she and Flavian hadn't, she scanned the woods. When she returned a worried glance Junior's way, he wouldn't meet her eyes.

"It's time I left."

Junior's words couldn't have hit her harder had they been delivered on the edge of Anvil's battle-axe.

"What are you talking about? You can't leave. We're almost there."

"You'll be safe now. Flavian will watch out for you."

Reecah's Gift

Reecah didn't know what to say.

Junior hung his head and turned to leave.

"So that's it? You're just going to up and leave when we need you most?"

Flavian joined Reecah and searched their faces. "What's going on?"

"None of your business," Junior snarled. He started walking but Reecah reached out and grabbed him by the elbow.

"Whoa. Wait a minute. You came here with…" She glanced at Flavian and swallowed—almost saying too much. "You came here to help me and now you're leaving? Why?"

"I was asked to help find you and I did. They thought you were in trouble. It seems you can look after yourself just fine." Junior yanked his arm free and started down the visible swath of destruction toward the King's Wood Road.

Reecah stared after him. After everything he claimed to have undergone for her, he had suddenly decided it was time to leave? It made no sense. If Flavian hadn't been there, she might have opened her heart to him, but the trainee's presence silenced her.

An odd sense of rage gripped her. One that had no place being there and yet, it was all she could do not to lash out at Junior's receding back.

Flavian put a hand on her shoulder. "Let him go. He's not right in the head if you ask me."

Reecah shot Flavian a look of contempt, shrugged free of his grasp, and stomped through the desecrated undergrowth, following Anvil's trail. She had been right about Junior all along. He was just another self-serving Waverunner. When would she ever learn?

Reecah's Gift

If not for the fact that Junior had his head down, he would have seen Jaxon navigating the swath of hacked and mangled underbrush.

Jaxon ducked behind a clump of evergreen bushes, his hand on the hilt of his dagger. He no longer feared his brother. Junior might be taller and stronger, but Jaxon had learned a lot in his short time with Prince J'kwaad's men.

Junior stumbled by, oblivious to everything around him.

Searching the forest, Jaxon wondered where Reecah and the other guy had gotten to.

Junior mumbled incoherently on his way toward the King's Wood Road. Were those tears on his face?

Jaxon resisted the urge to rush out and confront him. The last thing he wanted to do was get into a confrontation with his brother—one that might prevent him from keeping up with the hill witch.

He shuffled around the bush, keeping out of sight. The prince asked him to keep an eye on Reecah *and* his brother. If they were parting ways, he was left with little choice. As much as he wanted to keep tabs on his wayward brother, the prince had made it clear that Reecah was his priority.

For some reason, Reecah's group had left the main road and cut through the wilderness. Relieved they weren't headed to Arcanium, he grew concerned as to where their final destination lay. If he lost them out here, they would be hard to find again.

He waited long after the sound of Junior's passing had left the deep woods before stepping clear of his hiding spot. Taking one last look after his brother, Jaxon hurried up the trail in pursuit of Reecah.

Tears fell freely from Junior's cheeks. He didn't care. Who was going to see him in the middle of nowhere?

288

Reecah's Gift

What an oaf he had become. He had had a great future set in front of him less than four years ago. Now, his family had disowned him, the dragons weren't keen on him, the elf beast had professed her desire to kill him, and Reecah didn't know he existed. He had half a mind to fall on his sword. He might have if he thought his death would bring grief to someone, but no one cared. He was just another soul who had lost his way. If anyone discovered his lifeless body, they would strip him of anything useful and kick his corpse off the path.

Feeling sorry for himself made him angry. He detested the trait in others—it drove him crazy. He firmly believed if your life wasn't going the way you wanted, it was no one else's fault but your own. Until you faced that sobering thought, you were powerless to change. But, tough as things might become, he had learned that a positive thought was all someone needed to build upon—provided they kept it alive.

He wiped his cheeks—his chain and fingerless, leather gloves rough on his skin. It was time he took control.

The King's Wood Road loomed in the distance ahead. Heaving a heavy breath, still more than a little frightened at the prospect of facing his inner demons, he spun around and stared at the roughly hewn pathway with renewed purpose.

Vigour powering his determined steps, he was damned if he would let her go that easily.

Reecah's Gift

Headwater

Anvil's face was priceless when Edo cried out, "GG!"

Catenya's evil-eyed glare was worth all the hardship they had gone through.

Reecah cast the vile woman a smug look and purposely shouldered her way past her nemesis.

"Ow! Watch it, bitch!"

Ignoring her, Reecah walked up to Anvil. "GG and Flavian reporting for duty, Anvil."

Before Anvil had a chance to inquire about Flavian's miraculous recovery, she pulled her sword free.

A collective gasp escaped everyone present, but she turned to the uncut undergrowth; speaking loud enough for Catenya to hear as she hacked at the vines and dead scrub with reckless abandon, "If it's all the same to you, allow me to get us back on track."

Anvil's roar made her jump. Thinking he was about to cleave her in two, she looked over her shoulder to see him doubled over, laughing hysterically.

He shouted, "You show 'em, bilge rat. About time someone with a spine took charge!"

Anvil stopped laughing long enough to sneer at the others. "Well? What're ye waiting on? Or are ye expecting GG to carry yer sorry arses all the way to Headwater?"

Flavian stepped in beside Reecah, placing himself between her and Catenya. Through the corner of his mouth, he whispered, "Good going, GG. Better watch you don't eat an errant sword."

The chatter after nightfall occurred in three distinct camps. Catenya held court with her half dozen lackeys on one side of a hastily cut clearing; separated from Reecah, Flavian and Anvil by the rest of the trainees.

Reecah didn't miss the fact that everyone cast glances her way—mumbling beneath their breath. Snatches of, "Anvil's pet," and, "Just wait, her time's coming," amongst other things she didn't wish to entertain. She pushed it out of her mind, not caring what they thought. She wasn't doing this for them.

To her surprise, Anvil produced a heel of bread and a wedge of cheese and handed her a generous portion. "Here. Ye've earned it."

Reecah looked at Flavian, unsure what to do.

He shrugged.

Swallowing her misgivings, she forced a smile. "Thank you, Anvil."

Her eyes unconsciously searched the angry glares of those around her.

"Bah," Anvil said around a mouthful, spitting crumbs between them. "Don't ye be worryin' about them, bilge rat. They's jealous is all. Ain't appreciatin' being humiliated. They ain't worth yer time. If ya manage to get them to Headwater afore the full moon tomorrow, yer to be moving on to the king's guard when we return to South Fort, and that's sure."

Flavian frowned, exchanging glances with her.

Reecah washed a mouthful down with a swig from her waterskin. "What of the rest of them?"

Anvil looked pointedly at Flavian. "They'll have to earn their own way in. Ye can't be expected to carry the lot."

Reecah raised her eyebrows, nodding at Flavian.

Reecah's Gift

Anvil bit into a chunk of bread, tearing off a large piece. With half of it hanging from his mouth, he grunted, "As long as he keeps up with ye, I reckon he's ready to join ya." He chewed his bread and swallowed. "Be cruel to leave him with this lot. The Cat'll tear him to shreds."

As much as the group grumbled and cast dirty looks Reecah's way, they were a whirlwind of motion in the morning—striving to outdo one another.

At one point during the day, Anvil stood atop a large boulder they had revealed and nodded. "That's more like it. I might make knights of yer sorry hides yet."

Reecah smiled through the sweat dripping from her face, but cringed when Anvil added, "Of course, that's only if ya can keep up with the bilge rat."

Like the comment or not, it fueled the rate at which they progressed. Thankfully, Anvil guided their direction. At one point, the distant waters of King's Bay were visible through the trees on their right.

They stopped briefly to eat and rest as the sun dropped into the western sky. Their progress slowed considerably after that as most of them had given up trying to reach Headwater before the moon rose.

With the last rays of sunlight basking them in its faint warmth through a break in the forest, Edo cried out, "Look! Headwater!"

Reecah stepped back from where she hacked and caught a glimpse of a yellow-stoned fortress nestled on the top of a natural rock formation towering above the forest.

A brief cry of joy went up but their spirits were crushed by Anvil.

Reecah's Gift

"Hah! Ye can see it, sure, but do ya think ya can reach it afore high moon? I dare say, it's a deceptive piece away. The way ye lot carry on, we'll not reach it afore morn."

Reecah wiped the sweat from her brow. She cast a furtive glance at Catenya—the malicious woman locking eyes with her. Reecah broke contact and turned her attention to the task at hand. Raising her eyebrows at Flavian, she took a deep breath, adjusted her grip on her sword, and began hacking a path wide enough for the rest of the group to follow.

Anvil's laugh from somewhere behind, drove her forward; irate the big fool didn't realize the difficulties he caused her and Flavian. Or did he?

The night dragged on—their progress slowed by the darkness. Someone suggested they light a few torches to assist them and had his ears boxed by an incredulous weapon master.

"Are ye daft? The Watch'll see ya coming for leagues."

Reecah feared they weren't going to make their deadline but as the forest floor crested a ridge and fell away, the full moon glinted off a wide river emptying into King's Bay.

Anvil crossed his arms over his lightly clad chest. "Ah, the mouth of the Dragon. Just a wee swim to Headwater Sanctum."

Reecah looked questioningly at Flavian.

"He means we're looking at the end of the river, Dragon Rush. If you look up and to the left, you can see the flickering torchlight from Headwater Sanctum."

Reecah let her sword tip hit the ground—her jaw falling in disbelief.

"You mean we have to swim across the channel?"

Flavian shrugged.

"That's crazy. Look at us. We'll drown before we reach the other side." She pulled her cloak tight, staving off the biting

293

wind blowing off the bay. "The water will be freezing. What about our weapons?"

"Hey! Where's he going?" Catenya shouted, her focus on Anvil's receding backside as he picked his way down the steep embankment.

Reecah stepped in line behind Flavian, following the weapon master down a faint animal trail. Carefully watching where she stepped as she reached the brink of the drop-off, she noticed a large fortress nestled at the bottom of the embankment, its parapets illuminated by torches and sconces placed at regular intervals along their heights.

She wanted to ask Flavian about it, but it was all she could do to keep up with the group as they ran after a maniacally laughing weapon master. The man must have gone mad.

They came to an abrupt halt at the bottom of the hill as the shoreline jutted into the bay—a massive keep blotting out the starry skyline ahead.

Anvil faced them, holding his hands high and wide, a great smile splitting his pointed goatee. "Against everything I believed, ye've proven me wrong. The moon is still far from its peak and here we are."

"You mean we don't have to swim the channel?" Reecah asked confused.

Anvil frowned. "Ye can if ya like. Ain't to be stoppin' ya."

Reecah's gaze took in the castle across the channel, its flickering lights making it appear like it hovered in midair over the bay in the darkness. "I'm confused. You said we must reach Headwater by the full moon."

Anvil started walking toward the fortress walls on the near shoreline. "Aye, ya silly rodent. The castle, not the high wizard's sanctum."

Reecah's Gift

Devius

The wooden portcullis creaked into the air on the end of massive, rattling chains, rousing Reecah from a restless sleep. She had dreamt of standing tongue-tied in front of the high king before a hall packed tight with red-faced nobles laughing at her. Thankful for the timely interruption, she fought to calm her rapid breathing.

The full moon shone into the bailey separating the fortress walls from the keep proper. The celestial body didn't appear to have moved any farther across the sky than when she had closed her eyes.

On their approach to Headwater, they had been met by the point of two dozen halberds until someone in the Watch realized it was the Bone Breaker who led their party. The heavy gate had lifted long enough to allow them passage inside the outer wall. A meagre meal had been scrounged together for them from the servants' stores.

The Watch commander claimed the lord of the keep, Baron Fangbottom, wasn't to be disturbed until morning.

Reecah had gaped at the baron's name and asked Flavian whether it was a nickname. Flavian shook his head, not seeing the humour in it.

The gentle snoring of her companions informed her she might be the only one that the raising of the gate had disturbed. She propped herself on her elbows and looked around. Several men conversed with Anvil near the gatehouse. The weapon master pointed a finger her way. Noticing she was awake, he motioned for her to join them.

Flavian lay beside her, oblivious to the world as she soft-stepped amongst the sleeping bodies and joined Anvil—the chilly night air more noticeable now that she moved around. Shivering uncontrollably, she raised her eyebrows in question.

Anvil gave her a once over as if seeing her for the first time. "Seems ye've drawn the attention of the high wizard. He requests an audience with ya forthwith."

Reecah frowned.

"That means right away."

She knew what forthwith meant. It was the wizard's interest that bothered her. First Grimelda and Grimclaw, then Tamra, and now someone she hadn't met before. It seemed as if everyone knew when and where she would turn up before she did. She staggered as a dark thought crossed her mind.

Anvil's reflexes grabbed her by the arm. "What is it, rat?"

"The wizard. Is he the prince?"

Anvil's chiselled features scrunched together. "That's an odd question. Of course not. High Wizard Devius ain't related to the king." His face transformed into contemplation. "Least, I don't think he is."

He looked at the Watch. They shrugged, shaking their heads. Blinking several times he said, "Yer to accompany the Watch to High Wizard Devius' sanctum."

"Now?"

Anvil's face darkened. "No. We're gonna stand here all night and hope the dawn will bring us news as to when. Of course, now, ya silly rodent."

He folded his arms. "Get yerself movin' afore I shove me boot up yer arse."

One of the Watchmen held out an arm, indicating she precede him toward the raised gate. "This way, m'lady."

Reecah's Gift

She bristled at the term, *lady*, but now wasn't a good time to take offense. She slipped back to where Flavian slept and collected her gear. Following the lead men beneath the spiked edge of the raised gate, she espied the river and balked.

"M'lady?" The first guard asked.

"I'm not swimming across the river."

The guard frowned, looking questioningly at the others. "Nor should you. A launch awaits us at the pier."

She followed his extended arm to a large jetty jutting into the bay at the base of the outer wall—the moon glistening off the rolling water around it. Looking closer, the masts of several ships stood out, dark against the water.

Glad the shadow of the gatehouse masked her humiliation, she threw her head back and said with a touch of arrogance as she strode boldly past him, "Of course, it does. What're you waiting for?"

The wind whistled around the stone monolith supporting the high wizard's sanctum, battering the hillside with such force that it threatened to blow Reecah and her escort from the spiralling ledge rounding its way to Devius' imposing lair.

In the darkness, the circular towers of the fortress above appeared larger than Headwater Castle.

Storm clouds roiled across the bay, blotting out the moon as the small group passed beneath a gaping entrance tunnel in the outer wall and confronted an intricately carved section of stone lining the towering keep. Reecah reached out to run her fingers along the stone but jumped back as the section swung outward without a sound.

The guards looked around; their nerves reflected in the way they shuffled their feet. The head Watchman who had spoken with Reecah in Anvil's company muttered, "I hate it when he does that."

Reecah's Gift

Reecah looked at him but the guard merely gestured for her to enter.

Stepping across the threshold, runes engraved all around the inside edges of the stone doorway piqued her curiosity—symbols that appeared more like the words Grimclaw had inscribed in the back of her journal than regular runes.

She hesitated on a small landing at the base of a flight of stone steps. None of the guards made a move to follow. "Are you not coming?"

"Heh. In there? Not on your life."

She went to step back out but the door swung shut, faster than she would have thought possible for something of its size—especially since none of the guards stood anywhere near it.

She gasped as the door grated into the wall. Unable to see the nose on her face, muted silence blanketed the air around her. It was like she stood in the middle of nothingness. She probed with her fingers and found the wall—the cold stone providing her a small sense of security. Other than the runes, there was nothing discernible to indicate the edges of the doorway.

A muted growl chilled the blood in her veins. She spun around and threw her back against where the door should have been, staring into the absolute darkness.

The growl sounded again. Closer. Something was coming for her. Unsheathing her sword and waggling it in front of her, she noticed a faint glow within her cloak.

The journal!

Pulling her diary free, the crimson gemstone illuminated the landing in a bloodred glow. At the edge of her vision, on the lip of a small landing up a short flight of steps, the glowing eyes of a white lioness stared back at her.

The lion emitted a guttural growl.

Reecah's Gift

She jumped, pressing harder against the wall. With paws bigger than her hands, the cat appeared to weigh more than she did. Fearing it was about to launch itself at her, she searched the confined stairwell but nothing stood between them.

She flinched as the lion moved, but it turned to pad up a continuation of the stairwell into the darkness above. Before it rose out of sight, it stopped to look over its shoulder. Swishing its tail back and forth, it growled and disappeared from view.

The last thing she wanted was to follow the creature. The light from her journal cast the runes behind her in an eerie, crimson relief. Had she not entered, she would never have known a door existed.

Recalling how the runes of Grimclaw's passage in her journal closely matched those before her, she wondered whether the high wizard and the dragons were somehow connected. Considering the king's crusade, that didn't seem likely.

Not knowing what else to do, she took a few hesitant steps across the landing and climbed to the spot she had first seen the cat. Shining her gemstone up the stairwell, she was confronted by countless steps spiralling through the close walls of the yellowed stone tower.

From somewhere above, the muted growl of the cat reached her. Swallowing her reservations, she started up the next flight.

Her thighs burned by the time she rounded a bend in the endless passageway and confronted a dead end. Searching the walls and the steps below, she was positive she hadn't passed any openings in the walls. She couldn't help but fret over the cat's location.

The wall blocking the head of the stairway instilled her with a memory of her journey into the bowels of the Dragon Temple. The gemstone in her journal had triggered a reaction while she sat helpless on the brink of the schism. She shone the gem's light all around but nothing happened.

Reecah's Gift

Digging out the Dragon's Eye Aunt Grimelda had made her promise to retrieve, she wondered if this was why the old crone had been so insistent on her attaining it? She held it in the palm of her hand, but the stone lay dead to her touch—its facets catching the light from her journal and surrounding her with glittering spots that danced along the walls.

She held her breath and touched one of the spots, expecting to feel something. Nothing met her probing finger but cold stone. She shook her head at her foolishness. Worried about where the lion had gotten to, she half expected it to materialize behind her. Leaning back to look past the bend in the stairwell, she nearly fell to her death as a low growl sounded from the dead end.

The cat stood beneath a round topped doorway that opened onto a polished, white marble-floored chamber lined by tall windows. It hadn't been there a moment before.

"Do come in, Marinah's child." A deep voice beckoned.

She thought the cat had spoken, but the voice sounded from within the chamber.

"Don't worry about the walking furball. Useless as a mute wizard, that one. Even the mice chase it around. Come on, Fleabag, move aside. We haven't had a Windwalker in…" His voice trailed off.

Not reassured by the disembodied voice, Reecah remained on the stairs, stunned by his knowledge of her heritage. "Who're you? I'm supposed to seek the high wizard."

"Then you're in luck. I seem to be home." The voice sounded closer. "Come on, Fleabag. You brought her here, now go lie down."

Fleabag stretched and yawned, taking her time, before sauntering into the chamber.

Reecah climbed the last few steps and paused on the threshold of an octagonal room. Tables and benches of all shapes and sizes were illuminated with candles that flickered

Reecah's Gift

light upon tomes and scrolls held open with ornate stones. The faint light from the moon hidden behind roiling storm clouds filtered through the southeastern window pane; each section of glass comprising an eighth of the chamber's perimeter—stretching from floor to ceiling to provide a bird's eye view of the glassy waters of King's Bay far below.

Large, gawdy coloured cushions lay at the base of each window. Fleabag settled onto a red pillow set before the east-facing window.

"It'll be a long while before the sun rises, fang face," Devius chuckled, a wrinkled complexion visible through his white-bearded face.

A genuine warmth exuded from his pale, blue eyes as he studied Reecah. "Ah, incredible. It's really true. I was beginning to doubt your existence until recently."

Reecah maintained a distance between them.

Devius' long, white hair hung around his shoulders as he hobbled toward her with the aid of a gnarled staff, but he stopped when she banged into a table.

"If I didn't know better, I would swear to my ethereal gods that you are Marinah. A more perfect portrait of your mother could not be painted."

Reecah let her guard down, mesmerized by the pleasant-faced old man draped in dark blue robes that were festooned with celestial bodies. "You knew my mother?"

Devius sputtered a short laugh. "Knew her? Not exactly."

Reecah frowned.

He held up a crooked, bony finger. "*But,* I knew of her, and that's what's important."

"Then how do you know I look like her?"

"I saw her on two occasions. Once at High King J'kaar's coronation, and…" His face lost its cheerfulness. He looked away, as if ashamed. "And at her funeral."

Reecah's Gift

Goosebumps shot up Reecah's neck. "Her funeral? You were in Fishmonger Bay?"

Devius bit his thin lips, his eyes glassing over. He cleared his throat and shuffled to the far side of the chamber to stand beside Fleabag.

Reecah stared at him in disbelief, waiting for him to elaborate, but he looked out the window—its surface marked with light rain.

When he spoke, his voice was barely audible. "I arrived too late to save her."

Reecah walked up behind him, wary of the ever-vigilant cat. "I never knew my parents. My father died before I was born. If you were at her funeral, you must know how she died."

Devius' shoulders tensed.

"You do! Tell me. Please. I need to know."

Devius kept staring out the window, the rain splattering the surface as gusts of wind threw it around. Lightning flashed in the distance—disconcerting while standing in the wizard's chamber high above the bay.

"My grandmother claimed the dragons killed my parents but I have since been told differently."

She could tell by the way he held himself, Devius listened to every word.

Not sure of the sanity of divulging the information, she had to know. "I spoke with an ancient dragon. Before he was slaughtered by the king's men. He told me High King J'kaar—Dragonscourge, he referred to him—is responsible for my parents' death. And that of my uncle, Davit."

Devius' head perked up. "Grimclaw."

"Yes. The guardian of the Dragon Temple. He was slain by Prince J'kwaad and his death squad."

Devius turned slowly, eyes lowered. He appeared to be fighting back tears.

Reecah's Gift

"Grimclaw's loss has shaken the world's foundation. He will be greatly missed." He lifted his gaze to stare at her. "It's up to you to avenge his death."

Goosebumps riddled her body. "Me? What can I do against the king and his wizard son? I can't even get an audience to speak with those responsible for the dragon war." She shook her head, afraid Devius was deceptively trying to discern her true intentions. "Why would you say that? You're the high wizard of the realm, so I guess I'll soon get my audience with His Majesty...In shackles, no doubt."

Devius shook his head, his voice taking on a dangerous timbre. "I'm not J'kaar's lackey. There's a reason I was sent here to Headwater all those years ago. My stance on the dragon campaign was the last straw."

"But..." She didn't know what to say.

He lifted his bushy eyebrows. "Why does the king still suffer my existence?"

"Well, no. Um, actually, yes."

"I'm the high wizard for a reason. Let's just say there would be considerable collateral damage if J'kaar or the upstart, dark heir, were to make a move on me."

"That doesn't make sense. Why do you remain here?"

"The best way to keep an eye on my enemy is to keep him close. Alas, even my magic has limitations." His thin lips turned up at the corners, a glint of mischievousness in his eyes. "But, with a Windwalker at my side, who knows what greatness we can achieve?"

Reecah stepped back, not confident her legs would support her. What was the old conjurer getting at?

Devius nodded, as if affirming all of the questions whirling through her head. "Besides, who better to train you in the ways of your gift and help you undermine the king?"

Reecah's Gift

Familial Fracture

Junior pulled back, hugging the trunk of an ancient willow; its bare branches hanging like skeletal fingers reaching for the ground. The creaking of the lowering portcullis told him he was too late to catch up with Reecah, Flavian, and the others.

He searched the grounds around the massive fortress for a sheltered spot to shiver away the night. A furtive movement in the deep shadows by the city gate caught his attention.

Jaxon!

What was his brother doing skulking around the walls of a fortress on the edge of King's Bay? As soon as the question formed in his mind, he knew the answer. On more than one occasion he had suspected someone of following their group through the King's Wood.

He shook his head. The little bastard was in the employ of Prince J'kwaad. That he knew, but to be caught sneaking around, spying on Anvil's group didn't make sense, unless…

He swallowed. The dark heir was aware of Reecah. If Tamra had sensed the special traits that made her a Windwalker, there was a good chance the wizard prince had also.

Junior's teeth rattled as the deepening cold chilled him to the bone. He needed to move, but he dared not lose sight of Jaxon.

The night darkened; the air cooling off even more as the moon moved across the sky. Searching the grounds for signs of others who might have accompanied Jaxon, the ratcheting of the great chains hoisting the portcullis drew his attention to the gatehouse.

304

Reecah's Gift

Jaxon was difficult to see in the shadows, but he hadn't moved. He had his back pressed against the wall. Curious that he deemed it necessary to remain hidden if he were in the employ of Prince J'kwaad.

Several armed men strode after a tall woman in a dark cloak, her back burdened with a bow, quiver, and quarterstaff. Her identity wasn't readily apparent from where Junior sheltered behind the willow, but there was no doubt in his mind it was Reecah.

The Watch had no sooner left the gatehouse than the portcullis lowered and thumped into place; its spikes meshing with the ground. Jaxon's shadow slipped across the face of the gate, following the procession down a steep hill to the piers.

Making sure no one else was around, Junior scurried to the base of the wall and followed his brother down the embankment.

With Reecah in their midst, the Watch clomped along the length of the second pier to where a large rowboat waited. Junior lost sight of Jaxon, but movement beneath a gangplank halfway up the dock gave his brother away.

In the muted moonlight, the rowboat slipped across the mouth of the Dragon Rush toward the far shoreline.

Jaxon stepped free of the gangplank and ran to the end of the dock, swerving from one side to the other, peering over the edge. He stared after the receding boat before making a beeline to a small skiff tied off behind a large brig.

Chainmail chinking as he ran, Junior sprinted down the dock, his boots announcing his passage.

Fumbling with the rope securing the small launch, Jaxon froze.

"Going somewhere, Jaxon?"

Clad in the prince's livery, Jaxon rose to meet him. Shock crossed his face but for a moment before it was replaced by that despicable sneer of his. "From this time forth, you will address me as Lord Jaxon."

Junior laughed, eyeing the kink in Jaxon's nose—a result of Reecah's boot. "Father isn't dead yet. As long as I'm alive, you'll never be the lord of anything except arrogance."

"Prince J'kwaad would disagree. I no longer require our familial background. I'm a Lord by J'kwaad's decree. Now, if you'll excuse me, I've royal business to attend."

The sound of Junior's sword sliding free of its sheath surprised him almost as much as it did Jaxon.

"You dare draw steel on your brother?"

"Brother by virtue of birth. The bond ends there."

"I'll have you in irons."

Junior motioned with his sword for Jaxon to start walking toward the fortress. "By all means. As long as you leave that launch alone, I care little what you do."

Jaxon's gaze fell on the recently departed boat as it tied off on the far side of the river. He turned a dark glare on Junior. "You know what your problem is?"

Junior wouldn't dignify him with an answer.

"You're a witch lover. Always have been. Ever since Reeky inquired about joining the hunt. I saw it in your eyes. I thought you were infatuated with her body. Who could blame you? A young man would be foolish not to be, but I never thought her capable of bewitching you."

Junior swallowed. Jaxon knew him well.

"Turning your back on your kin for the sake of a witch. Disgraceful."

"You know what's disgraceful?" Junior blurted, not waiting for Jaxon to respond. "You working for the dark heir. Spying on a helpless woman. Accusing her of things you know nothing about. You're just like your father."

Reecah's Gift

Jaxon's eyes narrowed, his hand resting on the hilt of his sword. "My father? So, you've disowned your family now, have you? Thrown your lot in with…with the dragons!"

Junior raised his sword, daring Jaxon to draw his.

Jaxon let his hand fall away from his waist and stepped forward, an accusatory finger in the air. "What're you going to do? Slay me? Go ahead and try. I might teach you a few things. You don't deserve to be a Waverunner. Father was right about you."

Fully aware of their father's feelings, it still hurt to be slapped in the face with it.

"You're an embarrassment to everything our family stands for."

"And what's that? Tyrannical lechers who slaughter babies because they're too afraid to take a stand against the real monsters threatening the realm."

Jaxon's sword jumped into his hand. "Treasonous words. They sound like the words of the hill witch. I'd love to—"

Junior swung his sword, meeting Jaxon's. Locking blades, they glared at each other. As much as Junior despised his brother, the fact that he was family took the edge off his fury. He didn't think he had it in him to physically harm Jaxon.

Considering the evil look he received, he wasn't sure his brother shared his empathy.

"I'll not warn you again. Leave Reecah alone."

"Or what?" Jaxon disengaged and struck low and then high—both times defended by Junior's counter swings.

Jaxon barraged him with a series of feints and strikes. The power behind his attacks surprised Junior. His brother had learned a lot since the last time they had locked swords on the training grounds. His newfound skills no doubt attributed to time spent amongst the prince's men.

He lamented his inability to come up with smart retorts on the spot; not knowing how to respond to his brother's taunts with words that had bite. He hated getting involved in a battle of wits, whereas Jaxon excelled at it.

The creaking of the portcullis sounded from the hilltop.

Jaxon stepped back, avoiding a ferocious swing from Junior's longer blade. "Ha! Your strength is no longer sufficient to best me. Come on. Let's see what you got. When I finish with you, I plan on laying my hands on Reeky. When I do…" He lifted his eyebrows twice with a suggestive smirk and ran his tongue over his upper lip.

Junior's inhibitions fell away. He hammered Jaxon's blade repeatedly with everything he had. Although he forced his brother backward, his frenzied attack never came near to scoring a hit. Feeling his arms tiring, he disengaged, gasping for breath. "You ever…lay a hand on her…I'll kill you."

Several members of the Watch gathered where the dock met the shore but made no move to intervene.

Matching Junior's heavy breathing, Jaxon flashed his irritating smirk. "Not unless you learn to fight like the prince's elite." He nodded at the Watch. "Once these fine gentlemen learn who sent me, they'll hand little miss dragon lover to me to do as I please."

Junior moved on instinct, so fast he had no idea what he did. His sword took Jaxon's out wide as he stepped into the space between them and smashed his forehead between Jaxon's eyes.

White light exploded in his skull, sending him staggering to his knees. Hitting the dock hard, he put his hands over his head expecting to feel the bite of Jaxon's sword.

A dull thud shook the dock in front of him.

Jaxon was sprawled motionless on his back, an expanding pool of blood radiating from beneath his head and dripping between the dock planks.

Footsteps approached from behind, accompanied by a deep voice. "Bind him! He's killed one of Prince J'kwaad's men."

Reecah's Gift

The Maiden of the Wood

Tamra shook out her wavy locks, thankful she had adopted shaving the left side of her head. Flying dragons was torture on hair that had a penchant for tangling itself in the slightest breeze.

Lurker and Swoop had flown ahead in an effort to keep hidden from the group of humans travelling up the coastal road while Silence settled behind a steep hill to let her dismount.

Not one for words, the purple dragon asked, *"You sure you'll be okay?"*

A rare smile crossed Tamra's scarred complexion. "One can never be sure how life will deal with us from one moment to the next. Am I scared? Hardly. Concerned? Yes, but that's only common sense. I'll be as okay as the moment allows."

"If they can treat Reecah's friend that way in front of her, I can't imagine what they might do to someone who demands they explain themselves. I should come with you."

"And throw away any chance of me speaking rationally to them? No. Your presence will make matters worse. For Raver *and* Reecah and Junior."

"I don't like it. How can you be certain he's still alive?"

"I'm not, but there's only one way to find out. From what you told me, his death will crush Reecah, and yet, she doesn't appear too upset by his capture. That concerns me."

Checking her weapons, Tamra hiked up the hill. Nearing the summit, she crawled the rest of the way and waited.

309

Reecah's Gift

Swoop reported seeing Raver suddenly drop to the ground—
the victim of an expertly tossed slingshot. The man responsible
had retrieved his body and stuffed him into a burlap sack.

Tamra bided her time, running a whetstone along the edges
of her axes. She smiled at the sentiment many elves expressed
as she lovingly tended her weapons. More than once someone
had said to her, "You spend so much time cleaning and
sharpening them, perhaps you should marry them."

Each time she had forgiven their impertinent remark and
replied, "Take care of your equipment and it will take care of
you."

Movement from down the road forced her to her stomach.
Reecah's group came into view—the bald man with a massive
battle-axe strapped to his back in the lead. From the way
Reecah had spoken of the weapon master, Tamra relished the
chance to have a go at him. It had been a long time since
anyone had given her any *real* trouble.

Staring through the grass, she spotted Reecah and Junior
walking together in the middle of the group. A man carrying a
burlap sack, presumably bearing Raver, walked behind them.

Tamra clenched her axe handles tighter. Something wasn't
right. The way Reecah carried herself made it appear that she
wasn't the slightest bit concerned about her friend stuffed in
the sack.

Though still a long way off, the absence of Reecah's dragon
magic jarred Tamra's sensibilities. It was like Reecah
Windwalker's heritage had abandoned her.

"What is it?" Silence's voice sounded far away and broken.
The distance between them made it difficult to communicate.

"Something's not right with Reecah."

"I'm coming!"

Tamra held up an axe to stay Silence as the dragon prepared
to take flight at the bottom of the hill. "No. I sense a trap."

𝕽𝖊𝖊𝖈𝖆𝖍'𝖘 𝕲𝖎𝖋𝖙

Not caring about remaining hidden any longer, Tamra stood. Straightening her furs and leather armour, she strutted down the front of the grassy knoll to confront the group. It was time to find out what was going on.

Swords were drawn and arrows were held at the ready as the group from South Fort laid eyes on her.

Tamra stopped in the middle of the road, axes in hand. The bald-headed man held up his hands for the group to stop and walked forward to meet her—a tough-looking fighter on each side of him. She had heard of the weapon master's reputation, but had never met him before. Rumour had it he was the child of a dwarf-giant coupling. A strange arrangement for sure, Tamra thought as she scanned the three men's hands and eyes, taking note of their subtle mannerisms as they considered her calm demeanour.

The leader pulled his battle-axe over his shoulder and held it across his waist; eyes locked on her axes held beside her thighs. "M'lady. Who do we have the pleasure of meeting out here in the middle of nowhere?"

Tamra walked toward the man, conscious of his tensing muscles. "I'm here to speak to GG." She made to go around the trio but the leader stepped sideways, hoisting his axe.

"I'm sorry. I don't think you understand—" He raised his axe in defense, his face agog at the speed at which Tamra attacked.

The man deflected her right axe with the head of his own—sending Tamra's axe head bouncing out and down, but he couldn't prevent her left axe from splitting the haft of his weapon between his hands. He barely pulled his stomach back in time.

Before he had a chance to comprehend his difficulty, Tamra's first axe carried its momentum down and around in a blurred windmill, its blade cleaving his head in two.

Reecah's Gift

Gore splattered his shocked companions as they stepped away from the confrontation in disbelief.

Tamra's fluidity of motion never faltered. She swung her axes out sideways in unison, burying their spiked counterbalance into the helpless men's chests.

An arrow zipped past her head.

She pulled her axes free and turned her attention on the group of men and women running at her.

She leaned sideways as a second arrow flew past her chest. Lowering her chin and narrowing her eyes, she prepared to meet the man leading the charge. Raising his sword high, he hollered an incoherent battle cry and chopped down, throwing his body weight behind the attack.

Tamra's left axe deflected his sword, sending it out wide. She spun with his forward momentum and severed his spine with her right axe—the blade cleanly exiting his crumpling body before it became entangled.

She kept spinning, delivering a backhanded axe chop to the next attacker's cheek, taking the bottom half of the female's face off.

The group surrounded her, obviously nervous about getting too close to her deadly axes. Several bows and a couple of spears penned her in—the spears suspiciously like the heavy shafted ones used to penetrate dragon scales.

Tamra kept her axe heads in front of her, observing the men and women from between their raised edges. She located the woman with the tight braid, brown tunic and green pants. Though pretty in her own right, she wasn't Reecah. Nor was the blonde-haired man beside her, Junior. They had been duped into following the wrong group; Reecah and Junior had presumably gone somewhere else.

Stepping toward Reecah's imitator, Tamra wasn't the least bit distracted by the sight of tightening bowstrings. "Where's the one you call GG?"

Reecah's Gift

Comprehension registered on the man pretending to be Junior. His chainmail lacked the luster of Junior's and his surcoat wasn't exact, but she had to admit, he looked convincing enough from a distance.

"You're the Maiden of the Wood," Junior's lookalike gasped.

"And unless someone answers me, you're all about to die," Tamra snarled, searching the group for the man carrying the burlap sack.

An arrow loosed from behind her, the close-range shot burying itself in her furs and piercing her boiled leather jerkin. She staggered under the hit, her glare latching onto the red-bearded man responsible.

Without a word, she strode toward him as he frantically strung a second arrow.

A man with a sword and a woman with a single axe similar to Tamra's, but smaller, stepped out from either side of the bowman.

The woman swung first.

The swordsman followed suit, expecting Tamra to sidestep the axe chop. Tamra's forearms recoiled and unleashed their burden so fast neither man nor woman made a move to stop the whirling axes from biting into their faces. Before they hit the ground, Tamra grasped the handles—wrenching them free in time to smack away the point of the bowman's arrow as he raised it to shoot her.

The archer watched in horror as his arrow flipped away. By the time he looked back, his head left his neck.

An arrow thwapped Tamra in the back, below her left shoulder blade, followed closely by a heavy spear tearing into her furs—its tip deflected by her armour but the weight of the dragon-slaying projectile made her stagger.

Another arrow took her in the back of the thigh, dropping her to one knee.

Reecah's Gift

Two men charged in to attack her exposed backside. The first man's chest met the spiked end of her left axe as she released it into the air behind her.

The second man sidestepped to avoid his companion's collapse.

Tamra spun on her knee and severed his planted leg, mid-shin, dropping him screaming to the ground.

A curved dagger appeared in Tamra's left hand so fast the injured man didn't see it coming as she plunged it into his chest.

Another spear churned up the ground at Tamra's side but no else made a move to close in on her.

She estimated there were still over a dozen adversaries to be dispatched if she hoped to survive. Judging by the increasing immobility of her left leg and the searing pain in her shoulder, she doubted she had the fortitude to survive them all. The archers and spear throwers concerned her the most, but for the moment, they appeared content to contain her, allowing their melee weapon brethren to finish her off.

A large smile crossed her pain-laced face, her apparent madness giving her attackers pause.

Three shadows fell over the circle. Before anyone but Tamra knew what was happening, Lurker, Swoop, and Silence dropped out of the sky like an avalanche—each dragon pummeling an archer beneath them as they hit the ground hard.

Silence charged forward and stood over her. Those who were brave enough to close in on Tamra, backed away in alarm.

A hastily thrown spear deflected off Silence's scales behind her wings.

Lurker roared so loudly that Tamra feared the din would rupture her eardrums—his angered gaze on Reecah's imposter. The sound instilled terror in everyone, slowing their response.

Reecah's Gift

Through pain-laced eyes, Tamra searched the remaining assailants for the one holding the burlap sack. It wouldn't be long before they realized the dragons weren't old enough to breathe fire.

Swoop jumped and landed in front of an archer fumbling to nock an arrow to his bowstring. A wobbling burlap sack sat at his feet. Raver's muted squawking rose above the commotion.

Seeing Swoop's interest in the sack, the archer raised his heavy boot and stomped down hard—silencing its contents.

Swoop roared. Mouth open wide, she clamped her jaws around the archer's midsection and shook hard before releasing his lifeless body in a bloody heap at her feet.

Silence extended her wings and flapped twice, lifting off the ground.

Sharp talons wrapped around Tamra's arms and hoisted her into the air—Silence's grip excruciating but she cared not. Seeing the death of Reecah's pet bird had affected her profoundly. It struck her as silly. It was only a bird. Silly wasn't a condition she liked to associate with herself.

Fighting hard to retain her hold on her axe, she spied her second axe embedded in the chest of a man who struggled to remove it while lying on his back—his leather armour dark with blood.

She reached out and missed. "My axe!"

"Take her!" Lurker commanded.

The battle scene rapidly diminished. Dangling from Silence's claws, the wind threw her hair into her face. Fraught with concern over Lurker and Swoop, she was helpless to render them aid.

Her body spasmed in excruciating pain and her vision blurred. Sensing she was losing consciousness, she screamed to vent her frustration. Her friends needed her.

At least she thought she screamed. As the ground dropped away, so did her grasp on reality.

Reecah's Gift

Her last vision was of Lurker and Swoop roaring together at those who remained alive. The men and women who had been dispatched to draw them away from South Fort.

The group appeared to have recovered from their initial shock of having three dragons fall into their midst.

Her last image was of the group closing in on Swoop and Lurker.

Reecah's Gift

Ancient Magic

Devius stood in the middle of his wizard's chamber, pouring over the contents of an ancient tome; the leather cover cracked and faded. The book lay at the base of an eight-sided brass bowl inscribed with runes similar to the ones Reecah had seen in *Grimelda's Clutch*.

She studied the bowl, at first believing it to be the same one, but its edges were unblemished. Grimelda's had suffered damage to the pointed vertex between the south and southwest edge. "Where'd you get that?"

Devius touched a fingernail to the viscous liquid within. A series of ripples radiated to the centre, narrowing to a point and disappearing as they reached the midsection. "This is a powerful artifact. Handed down from one high wizard to the next for as long as history recalls."

"I've seen one just like it."

"Aye. I wouldn't be surprised." Devius nodded, her statement interrupting whatever he was doing. "Your great-grandmother showed it to you?"

"No. My great-aunt."

Devius' shaggy brows knit together. He cast her an odd look. "Your...?" Comprehension softened his wrinkled features. "Ahh, Kat's other daughter. Yes, that makes sense. Where is this bowl now, hmm?"

The name, 'Kat,' threw Reecah, reminding her of Catenya. She swallowed her dislike for the noblewoman. "It was destroyed in a great fire."

317

Reecah's Gift

Devius stiffened.

"The people of Fishmonger Bay murdered my great-aunt. They burned her house to the ground with her in it." Just speaking the words made her tremble.

Devius cupped his bearded mouth, pinching his lower lip. "Only two of these scrying bowls were ever created. Forged centuries ago, deep within the bowels of Dragon's Tooth."

Reecah had heard the name, Dragon's Tooth, before. It was the name given to a solitary mountain somewhere in the northeast of the Great Kingdom, if she wasn't mistaken. A mountain higher than any in the land.

"The first wizard and the first Windwalker formed an alliance. A mutual pact to oversee the alliance between dragons and people with the hope that they might coexist in peaceful harmony. The future generations of wizards were to represent mankind, while the Windwalkers—predominantly elves from South March, were entrusted by the dragons to act on their behalf."

Devius arched his back as if to stretch out the kinks. "Anyway, the scrying bowls are identical in every way. They were forged by lava fire. Not even dragon fire burns that hot. If the twin to this bowl was involved in a fire, I assure you, it survived."

Reecah's eyes grew wide. If that were true, her aunt's bowl lay somewhere beneath the rubble. Recalling a night before her great-aunt's demise, Grimelda had her immerse a dragon scale into the bowl. She looked abashedly at the ground. "They may not be identical anymore."

"What do you mean, child? They cannot be tampered with. I would know if something catastrophic happened to this one's mate."

"Maybe not catastrophic, but I dented it."

Devius shook his head as if to rid it of a cobweb. "You did what?"

Reecah's Gift

"I dented it. Grimelda was testing me. Seeing if…" She drifted off. Her aunt had suspected what Grimclaw later claimed to be true.

Without thinking, she grasped the sleeves of Devius' robes. "Do you really think I possess dragon magic?"

Devius smiled patiently at her grasp. When she let go, he said, "Of course. Why do you think I brought you here?"

"Brought me here?" She frowned. "You mean, to your chamber?"

"To Headwater, child. Anvis Chizel brought you on Aramyss' counsel."

"Aramyss Chizel? The royal blacksmith?"

"Yes. That is his present role at the castle."

"Why would…? I mean, how would…? It doesn't make sense. I barely know him."

"Aye, but he knows *of* you. Or do you believe your meeting in Sea Hold was a coincidence?"

"I don't understand."

"In good time, my child. What's important at the moment is you found your way here."

Reecah swallowed. She hadn't done anything of the sort. She had been led here. A muddled sense of understanding flitted about the periphery of her mind but she found it impossible to rein it in.

"Think hard. The answer has been fighting to find you. Struggling to surface ever since you were a wee lass."

Reecah's short temper threatened to overcome her, but she kept it at bay. Having a fit in front of the highest wizard in the land didn't bode for a good outcome.

"But…What about the woman I met in the King's Wood? And Anvil? And, and…the dragons?"

Devius grabbed her soft hands with his skeletal fingers, enwrapping long fingernails around her palms. A warm smile parted his lips. "Child. Whether you choose to believe it or not, you *are* the world's last Windwalker. We have waited many years for you to show yourself. Tamra Stoneheart claims she was sent by her people many years ago to keep an eye on the king. I know better. Ouderling Wys, the ancient leader of the elves, foresaw the day you would attempt to confront the king. Tamra was sent to assist you."

"Tamra was sent to help me convince the high king of the madness of his ways?"

Devius' laugh made her wince.

"No, child. Tamra was sent to stop you, or at least save you when you did."

"Save me? From What?"

"Not what. Whom?"

Reecah blinked several times. "High King J'kaar wouldn't harm me just because I spoke my mind, would he?"

"You have much to learn, child." Devius squeezed her hands and let them fall. "The king has ordered the extinction of dragonkind. Don't you think he would take the life of an orphan girl opposing his mandate? *Especially* when it becomes apparent who you really are? The last in the line of dragon protectors." He raised an eyebrow and dipped his chin. "Think about it."

The horror of his words sent cold tendrils of doubt surging through her. "If what you say is true, I've wasted all this time training when I should've flown to the next colony to help them organize a defense. Perhaps I could've convinced them to leave before the king's men attack them. Now another colony is going to be slaughtered. How many are left?"

Devius held up his hands. "Before we go any further, I need you to tell me your real name."

Absorbed with how much time she had wasted, Devius' question caught her off guard. "Huh?"

"As cute as GG sounds, I'm confident it's not your real name. From what I know, you would be a…" He looked to the stone ceiling as if for an answer. He lowered his gaze, with a knowing smirk. "A Draakvriend. Correct?"

"How do you know that?"

"I'm the high wizard, remember. I've spent my whole life sympathizing with the downfall of the Windwalker line. Until recently, I mourned over the fact that the dragon magic had died with your mother. You cannot know how profoundly my foundations were shaken when you appeared on my doorstep."

"But *you* summoned me."

"On the recommendation of a dwarf." He winked. "What do they *really* know, immersed in a tankard of ale for the entirety of their waken lives?"

Reecah didn't know what to say to that because she didn't understand.

"Correct me if I'm wrong. You said you should have *flown* to the next colony?"

Reecah found herself nodding before she had a chance to consider how wise it was to reveal her secret.

Devius' jaw dropped. "You've flown a dragon?"

A flippant reply filled Reecah's head. What other creature with wings was big enough to carry a person? She bit her tongue and nodded.

"Incredible. There hasn't been a dragon rider since Kat's great-grandfather flew Grimclaw."

Reecah almost fell backward. She reached out for Devius—the wizard's reactions faster than she would have believed.

"What is it?"

"Someone actually flew Grimclaw?"

"Aye, child. The last of the true, elven Windwalkers."

"What happened to him? Katti's great-grandfather, that is."

"Viliyam Windwalker died of old age, if I'm not mistaken. He became a recluse for his last hundred and fifty years if the tales of him are true. We lost track of him."

Reecah's knees felt weak. "Viliyam?"

Reecah's Gift

"Aye. Truly a great elf to have flown Grimclaw."

Reecah could only imagine. If her brief interaction with the cantankerous curmudgeon were any indicator of how the ancient dragon behaved, flying Grimclaw would have proven an interesting prospect.

She smiled at Grimclaw's memory. She couldn't imagine flying a beast that big. Though, Lurker was growing up fast. It wouldn't be long before his size became intimidating.

Her anxiety rose—thoughts of Lurker triggering a question in her mind. "I can't begin to understand what you're saying, but you said you can detect dragon magic. Tamra mentioned sensing it in me when I met her."

"Oh yes, child. You possess the gift. Of that there is no doubt. For some reason, it has been hidden from you. I need to find out how."

"Grammy hid my heritage to protect me."

"I'm afraid she's done more harm than good. She's blocked your gift. Was she a magic user?"

Reecah couldn't help laughing. "Grammy? She detested magic."

Devius nodded. "Well, whoever's responsible knew what they were doing. Dragon magic is no small thing to trifle with. For someone to contain it, they must be able to wield it."

Of all the stunning information Devius had related, that last bit shocked her the most. "I need to sit down."

"Of course." He grabbed her by the arm, the strength in his grasp surprising. He led her to the pillow beside the sleeping Fleabag.

Her wariness of the monstrous cat was overshadowed by the weakness in her legs and her whirling emotions. There was only one person who wanted to keep the knowledge of her dragon magic from her, and that certainly wasn't Grimelda.

Her vague memories of Poppa ruled him out. He had been adamant that she never give up on her dreams. Even at an early

322

age. Looking back, his insistence made sense. It was as if he had tried to coax her into discovering her inner gift. The one that Grammy had locked away.

She wanted to be angry at the woman who had devoted her life to raising her in the shadow of her heritage—keeping the truth from her while the forces around them gathered strength and perpetrated a terrible tragedy. But she couldn't. Grammy may have been misguided, but Reecah truly believed her guardian had done what she had to in the name of love. To protect the only person she and Poppa had left of their family. Poppa's death would have solidified Grammy's resolve.

Fleabag's eyes opened, watching her.

Reecah flinched when the lioness placed a massive front paw on her thigh.

Devius smiled. "Fleabag senses your mood. She wants to comfort you."

The weight of Fleabag's paw surprised Reecah. "Why do you call her Fleabag? Does she have…" She raised her eyebrows, not wanting to upset the cat. She almost laughed at the notion, but considering her relationship with the dragons and Raver, perhaps it wasn't such a preposterous presumption.

Devius shrugged. "I've always called her that."

She reached out a hand. "May I pat her?"

"You'll have to ask her."

Reecah stopped and stared.

"I assume you speak to your dragon friends."

"Yes, but—"

"But nothing. There is no difference. It is the dragon magic in you that allows you to cross a threshold most people cannot."

Reecah fingered her earrings. "I thought it was because of these." As soon as she said it, her thoughts drifted to Junior. "Are you saying that unless someone possesses dragon magic, they're unable to communicate with dragons?"

Reecah's Gift

"As far as I know."

Reecah was thankful to be sitting down. The thought of Jonas Waverunner possessing dragon magic was staggering. She wondered if he knew.

"Either that or they have elven blood."

Reecah swallowed, nodding. Junior's fair appearance and long, blonde hair would support that theory.

She tentatively rubbed Fleabag behind the ear. "There now, big girl. Reecah won't hurt you. You're a pretty kitty, aren't you?"

Fleabag closed her eyes. Leaning into Reecah's touch, she emitted a soft moan.

Reecah listened, hoping to bear witness to an incredible experience, but if Fleabag were communicating with her, she couldn't hear her.

"Is she talking to you?"

Reecah shook her head, disappointed.

"Give it time. She will. First, we need to begin your training."

"My training?"

"Of course, my child. You think I dragged you up here to pat my cat?"

"But…" She searched for what she wanted to say. "But, what about Anvil and the others? I need to get back to them. Anvil promised to submit my name for inclusion with the king's guard. It's the chance I've been waiting for."

"A chance you won't be taking. Not as long as I draw breath."

Reecah's temper darkened her mood.

"Easy, now. Remember what I said about meeting the king? If he doesn't know who you really are, he may not kill you, but I can't say the same for J'kwaad. My sources tell me he's suspicious of your presence. He's no fool. I should know. He was taught the use of his gift by the best in the land."

Reecah stared hard at him.

Reecah's Gift

"I taught him everything he knows. Someday, he'll try to use that knowledge to take my place."

"Can he do that?"

A mischievous smile lifted Devius' complexion. "On his own? No. I made sure I never taught him everything. While he attacked Dragon Home on his father's order, J'kwaad had an ulterior motive for leading the campaign. He sought a talisman concealed deep within the sacred Dragon Temple. If he has it, it'll only be a matter of time before he comes for me."

Reecah got to her feet and reached into her hidden pocket. Holding a closed fist between them, palm up, she slowly opened her fingers.

Devius gasped. "Is that what I think it is? Where did you get it?"

"From the dragon, where else?"

Devius covered her hand in his and looked around with wild eyes, as if trying to hide the gem from would-be thieves.

Reecah followed his gaze. Even though she knew no one else was in the chamber, she couldn't help checking the shadows. "What is it?"

"You're holding one half of an ancient magic. One so powerful that if it's ever reunited with its mate, it will give its bearer the strength to summon a dragon. If I'm not mistaken, the dark heir is suspicious of your presence."

Reecah searched the shadows again.

"We need to get you as far away from here as possible. I wish we had more time. There's so much I need to teach you, but first, I must figure out a way to unravel the binding preventing you from your gift."

He paused, concern on his face. "What's wrong, child? You've turned pale."

Reecah grasped his forearm for support. Staring into his eyes, she pulled forth her journal and handed it to him.

325

Reecah's Gift

Devius read the inscription, *Reecah's Diary*, a vague sense of understanding transforming his ghastly features into one of awe. He turned the journal over and staggered. Glittering of its own accord, imbedded in the leather cover, lay the other half of the ancient magic.

Reecah's Gift

The Unbinding

Strapped to a sacrificial table, Reecah worried that she had been foolish allowing Devius to restrain her to the marble slab. He had assured her it was necessary, but lying there, vulnerable to his every whim, she wasn't so sure. She didn't even know the man.

Turning her head to one side, she spotted her journal and the Dragon's Eye on a table on the far side of the underground chamber, deep beneath the high wizard's sanctum.

A black marble fount, similar to Aunt Grimelda's, sat at the head of the slab. The viscous liquid in the wide bowl resembled something she dared not contemplate.

Smoldering incense filled the chamber with hazy swaths of smoke; filling the rock hewn room with a pungent scent.

Devius stood over her dragon talismans, softly incanting words she had never heard before. She wanted to ask what he was doing, but knew from her experience with Grimelda that once a magic spell had begun, it was unwise to interrupt the caster. She had to be content with his explanation that the unbinding process necessitated the restraints.

The high wizard stopped chanting and offered her a calming smile. The placating gesture heightened her anxiety.

Pulling at the thongs around her wrists and ankles, she tried to push her hips and shoulders off of the marble slab, but thick leather straps across her thighs and stomach kept her firmly in place.

"Are you uncomfortable?"

Reecah's Gift

The closeness of Devius' voice startled her. She hadn't heard him approach carrying a deep, white marble bowl cradled in his hands.

She shook her head in a lie.

"Good. It shan't be long now. It is good that we have both Dragon Eyes. I don't think I could do this without them. Just a few minor…" He trailed off, absorbed in carefully setting the bowl beside her head.

She tried to catch a glimpse of its contents, but could only see a dark crimson rivulet dripping down its exterior. "What's that?"

"Hmm?" Devius ignored her question. "Careful you don't knock it off."

His eyes met hers. He held up a finger. "Oh yes! I almost forgot."

He shuffled across the room, shaking his head and mumbling, "That wouldn't have been good. A mistake like that would bring the tower down."

Reach's eyes grew wide.

Devius retuned with her talismans. "With your permission, I'm going to attempt to remove the Eye from the back of your diary."

Reecah didn't know what to say. She had no knowledge of the use of the Dragon Eyes. If the high wizard of the realm determined it was something he needed to do, she had no right to object. Still, the idea terrified her. She associated the gemstone with Lurker's life.

"Will it hurt Lurker?"

Devius cast her a quizzical stare. "Lurker?"

"My dragon."

"You own a dragon, do you?"

She felt silly. "Well no. Of course not. I mean, he's my friend. I think that gemstone is bonded to him somehow."

Reecah's Gift

Devius raised his eyebrows and nodded. "Aye. You would be correct to assume that. The Dragon Eyes form a direct link between the Windwalkers and dragonkind. Had I known that one of them was taken from the Dragon Temple, I would've searched it out long ago. Perhaps the realm wouldn't be in such a catastrophic dilemma."

"The dragons you mean?"

"No, child. The realm. Everything. Everyone. What do you suppose the dragon queen will do when she learns that two of her three colonies have been destroyed?"

Reecah shrugged; the intensity in his eyes, frightening.

"They'll raze the land and torch the skies. There'll be nothing but ruin. In the end, they will fail. It's a war they can't win."

"What can I do?"

"Nothing. Yet." Devius' smile was oddly warm. "Anyway, to answer your question, I don't believe it'll bother Lurker."

Turning his back on her, Devius intoned a few words, her journal clasped in his hands. Telling her he didn't *believe* removing the gemstone would have any ramifications on her friend did little to alleviate her fear.

She winced as a crimson light flashed within the chamber.

Devius turned to her; two gemstones in one hand and the journal in the other. He laid the diary on her stomach and repositioned the marble bowl on the sacrificial altar. Her head lay between it and the black marble fount on the floor.

"What're you doing?" Her voice was little more than a squeak.

"Nothing you need worry about, my child."

She forced a smile, more for her own benefit. "You keep referring to me as, your *child*. Why is that?"

He paused what he was doing and tilted his head.

"Not that I mind. I actually think it's cute."

"Cute, eh?" He nodded. "Hmm."

Reecah's Gift

He turned his attention back to the Dragon Eyes, holding one in each palm as if weighing them. His eyes glossed over until he yelped and jerked his left hand back; dropping the stone to the floor.

If not for the strapping, Reecah would have leapt from the slab in horror. A wisp of black smoke emanated from a sooty patch in the centre of Devius' left palm. "What happened? Are you alright?"

"Bah. Just a flesh wound." He bent to recover the gemstone and held it to the candlelight between his thumb and forefinger. "So, you're the evil one."

"Excuse me."

"I'm surprised I was able to differentiate the two. That's a good thing, no?"

Reecah had no idea what he was talking about. "Sure, I guess."

"Yes. Yes. I agree," Devius mumbled, paying her no attention.

Lying on the altar, she half expected to see Raver come flying into the chamber. The memory of Grimelda severing his toes assaulted her. She was glad he was safe with the dragons.

Her friends would be worried about her and Junior. With any luck, they wouldn't get into trouble searching for them.

Carrying an open book in one hand, the high wizard dipped his unburdened pointer finger into the black fount. Pulling his hand free, the long fingernail dripped with what Reecah suspected was blood. "Look straight up and stay still."

His strange actions petrified her, but she did as he asked. It was all she could do not to jerk her head away when his fingernail touched her cheek.

"Steady."

She swallowed, unsure if she trembled as hard as she thought.

Reecah's Gift

Referencing the book, he traced a peculiar pattern on her face, pausing a few times to acquire more blood.

She thought better of asking why—afraid she wouldn't like the answer.

Devius walked around the head of the altar and stood in front of the white marble bowl. "Keep your eyes on the ceiling."

Her eyes tracked his progress as he switched the book to his other hand. Dipping his opposite pointer finger into the white bowl, he meticulously traced what felt like a different pattern on her other cheek.

He stepped back, admiring his handiwork. "Okay, I think I'm as ready as I'll ever be."

Reecah kept her head in place, swallowing the lump of fear threatening to suffocate her. "You think?"

Devius shrugged. "Magic is a tricky creature at the best of times. Finicky, if you will. Inflecting the wrong emphasis on a syllable is done at the spell weaver's jeopardy. A slip of speech, or a missed word, could prove disastrous. For instance, if I placed the evil Eye in the white vessel and the good Eye in the black fount, there's a real possibility I would lose containment of the dark magic involved in unravelling your binding."

His words made her head spin. She hoped he knew what he was talking about because she hadn't a clue. "Is it dangerous? To me, I mean."

"Honestly?" Devius considered her for a moment as if contemplating his answer. "Let's just say, if this doesn't go as planned, neither of us will be the wiser."

"What's that supposed to mean?"

"You don't want to know." He cleared his throat. "Now, where was I. Oh yes. The Eye of Light."

He raised his right hand, his bony fingers holding the Dragon's Eye above the bowl. His eyes glossed over and foreign phrases passed his lips.

Reecah's Gift

Reecah heard a barely audible plop as he released the gemstone, followed by a vigorous bubbling. Rose-coloured steam hovered above the bowl, mingling with the pall of incense smoke.

"So far, so good." Devius walked around the head of the altar to position himself on Reecah's other side, confronting the black marble fount.

"Provided I haven't misread the signs, this is the Eye of Darkness. Thus, the larger fount to contain its theurgy."

She assumed by his explanation that dark magic required a bigger vat to contain it. Though she didn't understand the words he chanted as he performed the rite, she believed they weren't the same ones he had chanted at the white bowl.

Releasing the second Dragon Eye, the fount hissed and gurgled; a darker crimson vapour escaped the fount, stretching above the altar to comingle with the lighter vapour of the white vessel.

The vapours collided and the chamber lit up with a blinding flash.

Reecah closed her eyes and tried not to cry out as tendrils of vapour stretched down to her. Her skin crawled as the mist traced the lines Devius had drawn on her cheeks.

A tingling sensation crept through her skin and into her skull, triggering an intense headache. The pain grew, consuming her every thought. It felt like a boulder rested on her forehead—its weight threatening to crush her skull.

She rolled her head back and forth to escape the ethereal tendrils and the agony they inflicted, but they moved with her.

The thongs restraining her ankles and wrists stretched, biting into her skin as she bucked and thrashed—moaning in agony.

"Reecah!" Devius' voice sounded leagues away, though she was vaguely aware of him cradling her head in his hands. "Don't fight it. Give in to the pain. Let it consume you."

Reecah's Gift

The high wizard's words struck her as bizarre. She couldn't take much more. A scream of absolute agony ripped from her lips; her throat raw.

The pressure increased. If not for Devius' hands fighting to keep her from bashing her head off the marble altar, she was certain her brains would have squeezed through her ears.

"Reecah! I'm losing you! Let go! Let it consume you!"

She screamed in rage. He was killing her.

"Reecah Windwalker! Remember the dragons. Their magic will free you!"

A vision of the first time she had seen Lurker, *lurking,* on the trunk of a dead tree high above the path she trod, fought its way through the pain. The excruciating hurt of Devius' spell lessened—not much, but enough that she noticed. She resisted the urge to break free of his grip.

"Yes! Let it take you. Your salvation lies down that path."

A blur of memories bombarded her. The night Lurker and Silence rescued her from certain death at the hands of Jaxon and that snake, Viper, took shape. The pain subsided a moment longer before it increased again.

She closed her eyes tight. The boulder pressed harder, dashing her memory. She wanted desperately to bash her head off of the altar to make it stop, but Devius held on.

It seemed as if she had detached herself from the chamber beneath the tower—her deafening scream far removed from her physical body.

"Remember the dragons!"

Wind flew through her hair. The moon sparkled off a river far below. Her inaugural flight. Her escape from the Dragon Temple eased the all-consuming pressure from her mind, soothing her with the indescribable sensation of freedom that flying through the sky on the back of a dragon evoked.

The euphoria was short-lived. Replaced by the vision of Grimclaw lying slaughtered before the threshold of the temple he had protected for as long as there had been mountains. It sickened her.

The pressure moved in to claim her. She doubted she would survive a third wave.

Not knowing how to prevent her inevitable demise, it was as if her cheeks were kissed by a butterfly—a sensation so soft that it was almost non-existent. A feeling like nothing she had ever experienced before. Comforting and safe—not a worry in the world. The feeling of her naked body being wrapped in the loving embrace of a dragon wing.

Time stood still. She didn't dare open her eyes. She was content to lie in Lurker's embrace until the end of her days.

A warmth radiated deep within her mind; from a place she never knew existed. Negligible at first, it grew—its presence pushing aside the crushing pressure threatening to exterminate her existence.

Her eyes fluttered open to stare into the high wizard's—his concern for her plainly evident on his sweaty face.

"You made it." He released her head and leaned forward to rest his forehead on hers, exhaustion in his voice. "I thought I had lost you."

She smiled, her brain tingling with a newfound sensation. Though she had nothing to compare it to, she instinctively knew what it was.

"You released Reecah's Gift," she said dreamily, as her body gave into the mental fatigue of the unbinding—vaguely aware that she spoke of herself the way Grimelda had many years ago.

Reecah's Gift

The Power of Evil

Prince J'kwaad surveyed the carnage littering the approach to the Draakval Colony's main entrance. Countless bodies of both man and beast lay contorted in their death throes on the platform overlooking a roiling bed of molten rock; the victims scorched black or riddled with heavy war arrows and ballistae bolts.

It had taken the better part of three days to establish a front line that was able to sustain its position while under the voracious assault of the flying nightmares. More than once he believed his attack force was on the verge of being routed as the dragons forced his men from the cliffs to fall to their deaths into the flaming lava lake. If not for his expertly employed tactics and well-drilled army, they wouldn't have survived to witness this day.

It was only a matter of time before his troops coaxed the great Demonic from his lair. Dragons were all but impervious to fire, but they were mortal creatures, dependant on taking breaths. Sealing off the colony's tunnels one by one and lighting bonfires within to deprive the tunnels of their oxygen would force the monstrous lizards into the open where his ballistae crews were finalizing their preparations. Not even dragon fire could stop a well-aimed bolt delivered by these modified crossbow installations.

Looking to the east, the setting sun glinted off a snow-capped mountain peak visible beyond the volcano's lip.

Reecah's Gift

Earth-toned scales reflected the brilliant rays, bearing evidence that many wyverns observed the spectacle unfolding close to their mountain home on the far side of Cliff Face.

Just as J'kwaad suspected, the wyverns hadn't interfered with his campaign. As far as he knew, if anyone were able to converse with the misshapen dragon kin, the wyverns might even be coaxed into lending their support. There was no love lost between the colonies.

A smirk contorted his features. A terrified rider from Cliff Face had recently delivered a message from Headwater. One of his spies had reported the death of the tracker from Fishmonger Bay. The news was bittersweet. The Waverunner boy had apparently lost sight of the miscreant, GG, so his future lay in doubt anyway, but J'kwaad had taken a shine to the insolent youth. Jaxon had shared a kindred spirit with Calor. As such, J'kwaad had had great plans for the boy, but the report claimed that GG's new friend had slain him.

The prince sent word back with the rider that the one responsible for Jaxon's death was to be sent to Sea Keep to await his return. Perhaps through this new player, J'kwaad could finally unlock the mystery of the girl disrupting the pattern of magic.

The sighting of dragons in the King's Wood had unnerved his sensibilities, but their appearance supported his theory that this miscreant represented a danger to their plans of eradicating the dragons. Should a Windwalker truly still walk the land, they might yet make a difference.

Staring at the line of armaments honed in on the main entrance, finishing this battle couldn't happen soon enough. He needed to get back to the castle and deal with her.

He sighed his impatience. The report mentioned that GG had been summoned by Devius; a fact he already knew. What troubled him was she hadn't been seen since. Why the high wizard hadn't discovered her true identity and returned her to the king disturbed him more than he cared to admit. Devius was no fool.

Ever since his days under the high wizard's tutelage, J'kwaad never fully trusted the old codger. He had sensed an underlying purpose in Devius' agenda. Considering the newest complication, the old wizard's plans likely had nothing to do with those of the high king.

It was a good thing J'kwaad had the presence of mind to send a group of impersonators north, upon the open road. A previous report informed him that the dragons had taken the bait and followed the group northward—away from GG. He needed to keep GG separated from the dragons at all costs.

"My prince." A knight watching his back pointed to the platform. "There."

J'kwaad's gaze followed the man's arm to a spot along the far wall close to the colony entrance. Even from high above, J'kwaad knew the figure moving through the shadows was none other than Calor. Who else would be brave enough—or crazy enough—to enter a dragon colony on his own to flush out the fiercest dragon in the land? He doubted Grimclaw would have been a match for the leader of the Draakval Colony. Perhaps in centuries gone by, but by the time they had confronted the ancient guardian at the Dragon Temple, Grimclaw had been exceptionally old—even in dragon years.

"It's time to flush Demonic into the open and finish this." The prince absently looked to the east to ensure the wyverns weren't circling to ambush his depleted ranks. If ever they were vulnerable, now would be the time. Satisfied that his instincts served him well, he dismissed the wyvern threat. "Signal the flanks to light the fires."

"Aye, my prince." The knight motioned to men in key vantage points along the crags. Those spotters in turn disappeared; reappearing amongst a squad of slayers as they ran into cleverly concealed side tunnels and were gone from sight.

J'kwaad's aide awaited his nod before starting along a thin ridge that took them directly above the main entrance.

The ground beneath their feet shook long before they heard the deep rumble. Demonic was being forced from his lair. Even through his boots, J'kwaad sensed the terrific heat exuded by the creature's flaming breath. Demonic would test his men to their limits.

J'kwaad remained back from the edge, leaving the knight in the open to draw Demonic's attention should the dragon turn their way.

Insignificant in the mouth of the entranceway, Calor held a palm out—a small flame appearing between his fingers. The apprentice wizard did well to cast a spell under extreme duress. The flame signalled Demonic's approach.

Movement from the corner of his eye informed him that his three main ballistae crews were ready to discharge their killing bolts.

A flame-red dragon charged into the open, spewing fire at anything that moved. Calor ducked behind a tower shield, the state of his wellbeing undiscernible from where J'kwaad stood.

The dragon's crimson eyes locked on the ballistae battery and its mighty roar reverberated off the cliff faces surrounding the entranceway.

Something wasn't right. J'kwaad prided himself in his extensive knowledge of his enemies. Though red in colour, there were subtle differences in this dragon's detail. The dragon wasn't Demonic.

He stepped to the edge of the brink and shouted, "Hold your fire!" but his voice was lost to the roar of the dragon.

J'kwaad winced as the ballistae recoiled simultaneously. Two of the tree-sized bolts ripped into the red dragon and knocked it from its feet, while the third exploded against the cliff face beside it, showering the entranceway with splintered wood.

The dragon fire ceased.

Calor threw his shield aside and leapt into the open; a glowing stave in his hands—the heavy spear magically enchanted to stop the heart of whatever creature it impaled.

J'kwaad bent at the knees and cupped his hands to his mouth, trying to shout over the agonized roar of the writhing dragon. "Calor, no!"

Faithful Calor never missed a step. Hoisting the lance high, he jumped into the air. With all of his considerable weight behind the thrust, he drove its point into the dragon's unprotected chest.

The stave pierced the dragon's hide with ease. The concussion of the ensuing explosion within its body threw Calor across the entranceway. He flailed his arms and legs, landing in a heap of clanging armour and lay still.

The sound of a deeper growl made J'kwaad's skin crawl. The ballistae were busy reloading and the magic of Calor's stave was spent.

A dark red behemoth charged from the entryway, dousing the dozen men and women around the ballistae with deadly fire.

Agonized screams rent the mountainside as the operators dropped to their knees and fell face first to the ledge, burning alive.

Demonic grabbed the nearest ballista as if it were a child's toy and threw it off the ledge. His spike tailed whisked around, smashing the furthest machine against the far wall. Rearing his head, he emitted a horrendous shriek and doused the last ballista in withering flames.

Arrows rained down on the enraged beast, but they had no effect on his thick hide.

Reecah's Gift

Demonic grasped the burning ballista in his mouth and bit down hard, snapping the heavy wood with ease. He whipped his head around until his eyes located J'kwaad above the entry. With a flick of his neck, Demonic threw the burning remnants of the ballista at the prince.

J'kwaad barely escaped being crushed by the wreckage. His aide wasn't so lucky.

Demonic screeched. His bloodred eyes squinted, tracking J'kwaad's retreat across the ledge.

Sensing he was about to meet his fate, J'kwaad stopped to face the dragon. Taking a deep breath, Devius' extensive training took over. He cleared his mind of everything but the confrontation; cracking his neck muscles and throwing his shoulders back in preparation for what must be done.

As calmly as possible, he incanted the words to his most powerful spell—speaking them faster than ever before. If the spell went awry, the outcome mattered little—he would be dead.

A blue fog coalesced between his palms; the magic augmented by the various trinkets twinkling on his fingers. A white vapour wisped into the mix from a teardrop shaped, opal amulet dangling from his neck.

Demonic hunched down and sprung into the air—his immense, black-tipped wings spreading wide.

J'kwaad thrust his palms forward, shouting the last words of his spell. Releasing the pent-up energy, he crumpled and rolled sideways to evade the dragon's leap.

An ice-blue ball of magic hammered into Demonic's open mouth, visibly freezing his head and neck down to where his wings extended from his muscular shoulders.

Demonic crunched into the edge of the shelf and fell back to the platform below, taking a good part of the rock's face with him.

J'kwaad crawled to the lip of the damaged ledge.

Reecah's Gift

Demonic dragged his frozen head across the platform, banging it off the entrance walls. Chips of ice and chunks of scales and horn shattered with each earth trembling hit, but the berserk dragon didn't appear to feel any pain.

J'kwaad searched his immediate surroundings. His escape route had fallen to the platform below with the flailing dragon. His only way off the ledge was down the trail of debris to the feet of the rampaging beast.

Getting shakily to his feet, he cleared his head, summoning the strength he required to hurl another ice blast. He wished he had taken Devius' advice about employing a staff when performing magic, but being young and headstrong at the time, he had believed he didn't need to rely on a crutch.

The effect of his first spell faded from Demonic's shoulders—a visible line from the freezing spell receded up the dragon's neck.

Not waiting for the beast to get its senses back, J'kwaad chanted again; drawing deeper from his gift and augmenting that power with his trinkets.

The colour of Demonic's eyes returned as the freezing lost its hold. Shaking his head, ridding himself of the last remnants of the spell, he located J'kwaad. A mighty roar rumbled the area as he prepared to leap again.

J'kwaad released his ice ball—the brunt of the spell taking Demonic between the eyes.

The dragon stumbled backward and fell to his side. His legs kicked and scrabbled but they lacked any sense of coordination.

J'kwaad searched for the best way to scale down the landslide without dying in the process. His attention was drawn to the shadows beneath the entranceway where Calor had fallen.

Much to his surprise, Calor limped over to stand beside Demonic's head. He struggled to pull his serrated scimitar free of the thong binding it to his belt. Hoisting the curved blade over his head, he drove it into Demonic's unblinking eye.

The dragon's frozen head deflected the blow, showering Calor with ice chips and knocking him onto his backside. Demonic's body convulsed, but no apparent damage had been done.

J'kwaad contemplated hitting the dragon with another ice blast, but the expenditure of releasing a spell big enough to stun such a large dragon left him reeling.

Shouts echoed up and down the valley as more of the dragon hunt encroached upon the scene. There were no more screeches from overhead, nor did there seem to be any life left within the colony itself, but they had their hands full with the colony leader.

A mobile ballista team approached the platform from the far side. They constructed their smaller machine and loaded a bolt capped with a barbed, metal tip—pushing the contraption as close to the writhing dragon as they dared.

Conjuring three, smaller ice-balls, J'kwaad launched them at the struggling beast, hoping to keep it off balance.

The ballista throws ratcheted back and the mechanism was triggered without delay.

The heavy bolt hammered into the top of Demonic's head, shattering his frozen skull into dozens of gory chunks. His wings collapsed upon themselves and the mighty dragon lay still.

J'kwaad silently gave thanks to his well-drilled troops. Without their total devotion, the king's campaign would never have survived Dragon Home, let alone their subsequent encounter with the Draakval Colony. It had been obvious right from the start of their offensive three days ago that someone had tipped off Demonic's colony.

Reecah's Gift

Picking his way down the rockfall, slipping many times until he reached the entrance platform, the prince nodded his thanks to the mobile ballista crew and made his way to Calor's side.

He offered him a hand up, and without taking the time to ask if he was okay, looked to the line of wyverns staring at them from the eastern ridge of the crater. "See to it they're destroyed before you lead the army home."

Calor nodded, pain evident on his face. "Aye my prince. Are you not accompanying us?"

J'kwaad stared at Calor, but his mind was elsewhere. Back in the wizard's sanctum, high above Headwater Castle. Devius Misenthorpe was up to something. He sensed it. There was no doubting the old wizard had identified the ripple in the magic—had probably done so long ago.

"Dispatch our best runner to fetch me three of our best horses. Have them ready by the time I reach Cliff Face. I plan on being home before the sun rises three days hence."

Calor nodded, the slightest surprise reflected on his face. "You'll kill them, my prince."

The prince smiled. Something he wasn't prone to doing. "That's exactly my intention."

Reecah's Gift

Dragon Breath

Tamra had learned all about dragon magic under the watchful eye of Ouderling Wys, but that knowledge did little to prepare her for what unfolded before her pain-laced eyes.

Fleeing the group that had purposely led them astray, the dragons had landed on a small sprit of sandy beach uncovered by the receding tide, far from the mainland.

She had no idea how long she had lost consciousness, but the cold sea water washing over her legs revived her to a dull sense of awareness. It couldn't have been too long as the sun hadn't changed position in the sky.

A coldness that had nothing to do with the water seeped into her back and shoulders, numbing the excruciating pain of her wounds. Shock was setting in. If her wounds weren't dealt with soon, they would turn mortal, but she lacked the wherewithal to deal with them.

Silence had left her in the sand and stood with Swoop and Lurker around a lump of black feathers. One of the dragons had taken it upon themselves to bring the raven's body along.

Raver lay dead at their feet, the poor bird's mangled toes the least of his worries now. Judging from what Lurker and Swoop had told her, Reecah would be devasted if she were to find out. Had Swoop not dispatched the one responsible, Tamra would have dragged herself off the sandy shoal and gone after him, even though she would have drowned in the choppy surf. Once someone became her friend, she valued their life over her own.

Reecah's Gift

A darkness took hold of her. She wasn't prone to tears but seeing the lump of feathers lying on the sand between the dragons bothered her. A lot of good her friendship had done Raver. She had stood within reach of his captor but hadn't been strong enough to rescue him. Worse, had she not confronted the group, Raver might still be alive.

She wiped at the unwanted tears threatening to escape her bloodshot eyes. Never show weakness.

"You really think you can do it?" Swoop's voice sounded far away; her words not directed at Tamra.

"I don't know," Lurker answered. *"What harm can it do?"*

"Have you ever tried it before?"

"No, but something inside me tells me I know what to do."

"What if you're wrong? What if it hurts you, instead?" Genuine concern reflected in Swoop's voice.

Lurker didn't respond at first, but when he did, compassion filled his voice. *"I have to try. He was our friend too. I don't think my heart could bear Reecah's hurt. I'd rather die myself."*

Blinking to clear her vision, she held her breath as Lurker dipped his head and held his nostrils a hair's breadth from Raver's beak.

It was difficult to see from where she lay, but she thought she saw a translucent, green vapour drift from Lurker's nostrils. It swirled around Raver's head momentarily before slipping into the slits on his beak.

Lurker pulled his head back to where Swoop and Silence hovered over the raven.

"Nothing's happening."

Lurker's sadness choked Tamra further. She wiped at her eyes again, angry she couldn't control the tears spilling down her face.

A strong wind buffeted the thin sprit of reclaimed sand, blowing her tangled locks around her face. Raver's feathers ruffled. She thought nothing of his wings curling up and dropping back to the sand, but her heart almost stopped when Silence burst out with excitement.

"Raver! You're alive!"

Raver flapped his wings and craned his neck to climb to his feet. His beady black eyes searched the scaly faces leaning over him. "Alive! Alive!"

The dragons laughed; one of the strangest noises Tamra had ever heard. She likened it to tree boughs rubbing together in the breeze.

Tamra's senses heightened. Voices carried above the surf. With difficulty, she turned her head toward the shore. A dozen or so blurred forms shouted and pointed in their direction. The imposters.

"Dragon friends," she croaked, her throat dry. "We need to find out where they took Reecah. Fly me to them. I'll make them tell us where Reecah and Junior are. Trust me, I can make people talk."

She wasn't sure she had spoken at all, but as one, the dragons turned their heads her way.

"Do you think you can heal her, or must we wait until she dies?" Swoop asked.

"Hard to say." Lurker started toward Tamra. *"Worst thing that will happen is I expedite her death."*

The dragons spoke as if she wasn't there.

"Bringing back a human might prove different. They're complicated creatures."

Lurker nodded. *"She won't last much longer. Look at her blood loss. Be doing her a favour to put her out of her misery before her people figure out a way to reach us."*

Tamra wanted to scream they weren't her people, but lacked the strength. She turned her sand-covered head to observe Lurker's approach. Something about the way the dragon looked at her filled her with a dread she hadn't known in a long time.

Reecah's Gift

She swallowed at the lump in her throat—one not formed of compassion. She lay vulnerable, helpless to prevent herself from becoming the experiment of a dragon.

The wooden shafts protruding from her body prevented her from dragging herself away.

Reecah's Gift

Revelation

Reecah groggily realized it was early morning. Filled with exhaustion from the previous day's training, she was vaguely aware of a soft warmth snuggled into her.

Not wanting to open her eyes just yet, she knew instinctively what the softness was. Fleabag had flopped down beside her on the giant pillow at the base of the window like she had done everyday since returning to the chamber after Devius' unbinding ritual. How she had gotten from the sacrificial table to the top of the tower that day was a mystery. Judging by Devius' appearance, it was all the old wizard could do to bear his own weight.

Opening her eyes, the lioness' thick neck lay right in front of her. She smiled and scratched Fleabag behind the ears.

The cat groaned in satisfaction, craning her head back to snuggle into her.

Over a fortnight had passed since the unbinding and it still unnerved her to be this close to a four hundred pound killing machine. The notion seemed silly after flying a dragon, but she had never felt in danger while in Lurker's company. Quite the opposite. Lurker's presence filled her with a sense of safety she hadn't experienced since before Grammy had died.

Careful not to startle Fleabag, she got to her feet and looked around. The chamber basked in early morning twilight—the period of enlightening between darkness and the appearance of the sun on the eastern horizon.

Reecah's Gift

A gentle snore filled the octagonal room. She didn't have to search out the cause. Devius always slept beneath the northern window, claiming it was the direction of purity. She hadn't bothered to ask him why. He had filled her head with so much information over the last couple of weeks that she had more important questions to concern herself with.

She approached the scrying bowl—the one artifact in the magical room that intrigued her more than anything else. It reminded her of her great-aunt. How different her life might have been had she been afforded the opportunity to learn from Grimelda.

She fingered her diary beneath her cloak to ensure it was secure. Devius had enacted a spell to fuse the gemstone Poppa had given her back into the cover of her journal.

The second Dragon's Eye—the dark eye according to the high wizard, lay at the base of the scrying bowl beneath the northern edge of the eight-sided, brass bowl.

To his credit, Devius had asked permission before he performed further experiments with the stone. Who was she to tell a wizard of his standing what he could and could not do? Besides, unlocking her link to her dragon magic had indebted her to him.

Her gift's presence had come as a shock to her after recovering from the ritual—a gentle pressure inside her head that never went away. Not quite a headache, but an annoyance nonetheless.

Devius had assured her the unpleasantness would dissipate over time. Her body and soul would learn to adapt. Being a natural part of who she was, the gift was a sensation she had been deprived of feeling since before her earliest memories, so naturally, it would take time to adjust.

Already, the gift had slipped into the background of her consciousness. She detected it easily enough when Devius asked her to perform the simplest of magical spells. It was an extension of herself. Magic tricks like lighting candles and the fire in the hearth were performed with little more than a thought. Awed by her newfound ability, she quickly learned to welcome the comforting warmth it instilled in her.

Standing before the scrying bowl, she studied her hands and contemplated what she was about to do. Devius had warned her not to on more than one occasion, but she couldn't see the harm.

Her fingernails were nowhere near as long as the wizard's— nor Aunt Grimelda's if memory served her. Being an outdoorsy person, she had never been able to grow nails to match those of the ladies in Fishmonger Bay. That made her smile. Perhaps they were all witches.

Holding her pointer finger over the opaque liquid in the scrying bowl, she considered the runes written along its surface. She had already known most of the symbols, but over the last few days, Devius had expanded her knowledge to include the magical runes that had eluded her.

Spell casting by chanting in the ancient language still tripped her up more often than not, but with each passing day, her confidence grew.

Devius had intoned a simple vision spell on several occasions while she had watched on—the spell showing them various places around King's Bay. The shorelines. The harbour. The Sea Gate Bridge.

To take the vision spell to the next level had sat in the back of her mind for days. If she could see into Sea Keep, she would be able to track High King J'kaar's movements. It would also enable her to keep an eye on the dark heir. She had offhandedly mentioned this to Devius but his angry response that they weren't to meddle in the affairs of individual people on pain of serious repercussion had put an end to the conversation.

She looked to the north window. Devius lay crunched up in the fetal position, snoring softly. The only time since they had met that he ever left her alone was when she needed to relieve herself. She would have to speak softly if she wished to utilize the scrying bowl to serve her ultimate purpose.

The words flowed past her lips like she had spoken them from childhood. At the appropriate time, she dipped her fingernail in the viscous liquid inside the western lip. Ripples formed a wedge shape, radiating from her fingertip and moving slowly into a point at the centre of the bowl where they disappeared.

She turned her mind to envision Prince J'kwaad. His angular nose. His well-trimmed, black goatee. His thin lips. His shining black plate armour inlaid with golden piping that denoted him as a member of the royal family.

At first, nothing happened, but as she stared, the reflection of the ceiling transformed into a scene of trees speeding by on both sides of a black-clad man. Hunched over the neck of a profusely sweating horse, his shrewd eyes were focused on the trail ahead. A second, riderless horse galloped along behind him—man and beasts charging up a well-trodden roadway. One that looked unnervingly familiar.

Prince J'kwaad suddenly slowed his horse to a canter in front of a crude path that appeared to have been roughly hewn from the thick undergrowth. He looked up with a questioning scowl, searching for something.

J'kwaad's head jerked—his eyes appearing to lock onto her own.

"What have you done, child?"

Devius' voice sent sparks of terror coursing through her veins. She hadn't heard the old wizard approach.

The scene in the bowl turned opaque, but she knew Devius had seen what she had.

His face turned purple beneath his white beard and bushy eyebrows. "Do you realize what you've done?"

She shook her head, afraid to speak.

Reecah's Gift

"You've alerted the dark heir to your presence as surely as if you stood in front of him and proclaimed yourself a Windwalker."

"I-I-I didn't think—"

"You're damned right you didn't think! Have you not learned anything I've been teaching you?"

"Why, yes, but—"

"But nothing! He'll be coming for you. He'll have sensed you spying on him. J'kwaad is no ordinary wizard." Devius trembled with rage. "What do you think he'll do when he discovers I'm the one who is instructing the last Windwalker on her gift?"

"But you're the high wizard. Surely you—"

"I'm not immortal! How long do you think the king will back me when he hears of this? Let me tell you! As long as it takes to stick my head on a pig pole."

Reecah bowed her head in shame. "I'm sorry."

Devius' chest falls came fast and heavy. He tilted his head and pointed a bony finger at her face, but bit back whatever he had planned on saying. He stormed over to the western facing window as if expecting to see the prince riding along King's Bay Road.

Even Fleabag sensed she had done something terrible. She looked at the cat on the cushion, beseeching a friendly face, but Fleabag grunted and turned her head away.

Reecah remained beside the scrying bowl until the sun rose high enough to gleam off the brass surface. She grasped the dark Eye and made her way to Devius' side.

"So, what now?"

Devius tensed. When he finally spoke, she had to lean in to hear him.

"We need to get you far away from here. I'm talking *really* far, or else he'll track your magical presence."

"How can he do that?"

Reecah's Gift

Devius spun on her, anger in his light blue eyes, but he kept his tone in check. "What does it matter how? It's too late for such questions. You've seen to that. What matters now is preserving the dragons' last chance at salvation."

He obviously spoke of her. She shook her head. "I can't go. I came to talk reason into the high king. To explain to him that what they're doing is wrong. If I leave, everything I've done will be for nothing."

"Ya? Well, you only have yourself to blame for that. I told you not to misuse your gift." Devius appeared on the verge of exploding. "You've been training with me for what? Ten days?"

"A fortnight."

"Great! A fortnight. It took you two weeks to break one of my steadfast rules." He threw his hands in the air and looked away. He turned back just as quickly; a bent finger held in front of her face. "It took J'kwaad months before he was brazen enough to employ his magic to suit his own ends."

"I'm sorry."

"Little late for that."

The atmosphere in the sunny chamber was anything but cheery. Devius left her by the window and searched through the large pages of a dusty tome sitting on its own table near the southeast facing window.

Fleabag got up from her bed and stretched, padding to a metal bowl on the floor to lap at the water within.

Reecah remained by the western window, absently watching the tall ships come and go in the distant harbour at Sea Hold. Even from this distance, the Sea Gate Bridge stood out on the horizon.

"Come here, girl."

Reecah blinked a few times, afraid to move. She glanced at Devius.

Reecah's Gift

The darkness had left his face. His kind eyes and forced smile served to set her nerves at ease.

Joining the wizard before the tome's pedestal, she glanced at the colourful map displayed across the open double-page and tried to appreciate what Devius pointed at.

"This is where you must go. Into the desert. Search for the Draakvuur Colony. The home of the dragon queen. There you will learn the way your gift was intended to be used."

Reecah swallowed. The thought of visiting a dragon colony, especially the home of the queen, scared her more than she cared to admit.

"If dragonkind has any chance of surviving J'kaar's purge, it will happen in the Wilds."

"The Wilds?"

"Aye child. The name of the desert along the remote eastern border of the Great Kingdom. Nothing survives out there but hardened souls and magical creatures."

Reecah swallowed. "And you want *me* to go out there?"

"Now that you've exposed your true identity, nowhere else is safe. You must make haste, and do not stray. It's vital you go straight there. Do you hear me?"

Reecah nodded, a million questions swirling around her head. "How will I know when I have truly harnessed my dragon magic?"

He sighed, offering her a patient smile. "That isn't easily answered. You'll recognize it when the time comes. When it does, you'll be surprised at how much you inherently know."

"I wish I had found you earlier. I wasted so much time in South Fort training with Anvil."

"Tsk, tsk." Devius raised his eyebrows. "A true Windwalker must be trained in all forms of combat. There will be times when magic cannot save you. The skills the giant dwarf has instilled in you are as important as your gift. Your time with

Reecah's Gift

Anvil will serve you well, never doubt that for a moment. If you die, so will the dragons."

Reecah tried hard to appreciate his words.

"I wish we had more time."

Reecah bowed her head. The shame of what she had done weighed heavily upon her.

"We need to find you a mate."

Reecah's head jerked up. "What?"

"A mate. You know? Somebody to breed with."

The wizard's matter-of-fact way of stating what was on his mind shocked her.

"We need to get you an heir."

"An heir?" Did the old man think she was royalty?

"Absolutely. Should you die before then, the dragon cause will follow you to your grave."

Devius pursed his lips, and placed a crooked finger on his chin, changing the subject again. "Too bad I didn't have a staff for you to use."

Reecah frowned. She was still trying to get over his last comment. She couldn't imagine who in the world that mate might be. She had never in her life seriously considered that type of relationship with someone else. Let alone having a baby. Just the thought jarred her senses to the core. The only person she would even consider *might* be—

Devius' voice interrupted her thoughts.

"A staff is a wizard's best friend, next to their mind of course. A proper staff, enhanced by the right talisman," his gaze drifted to the dark Eye she held in her hand, "would make you a force to be reckoned with."

"Why? What can it do?"

"A staff, in and of itself, is only as strong as its bearer. It's used to amplify the magic of the user. Sure, it can provide those without the gift a small arsenal of magic that is enchanted into its fibre, but a staff's real use is to enhance the power of the truly gifted."

"Where can I find such a thing?"

Devius shrugged. "The last staff of import was lost when Viliyam went into hiding."

Reecah grasped Devius' forearm. Hearing Poppa's name sent gooseflesh over her skin. She knew Devius meant her great-grandmother's great-grandfather, but the coincidence that Poppa bore the same name wasn't lost on her. Someday she meant to discover the connection.

"Who makes them?"

Devius frowned. "Who makes them? Why no one, child. They're the result of an ancient spell being cast during a momentous event." He looked to the ceiling as if beseeching its help to describe something so intrinsically basic that its explanation was beyond him. "Other factors have to be taken into consideration. Suffice it to say, a true staff of import is more than just a talisman. It is an extension of someone's spirit."

Devius stopped. His hopeful smile fell. "I see you have no idea what I'm talking about."

She shook her head.

"Bah! It's not important. Perhaps, when this is all over, I'll assist you in discovering your own staff, hmm?"

"Um, yes. That would be wonderful."

"Good. Good. Now all you have to do is survive long enough to escape from here."

Reecah's Gift

Dwarf, Giant Dwarf

Fleabag padded to the base of the tower steps and awaited Reecah and Devius, the former assisting the latter down the long flight. Staring at the wall where Reecah was certain a door had been, Fleabag's upper lip lifted in a snarl.

Devius descended the bottom step. "Easy girl. It won't do to warn the guards."

Reecah's gaze flicked between the lioness, the wall, and Devius. She hadn't noted anyone else in the Wizard's Sanctum all the while she was here. "You have guards?"

"They aren't mine, child. But they are there. Waiting."

"Waiting for what? Me?"

"You. Me. Makes little difference. If we're taken, all will be lost."

"What do we do?"

"Why, we fight. Use our dragon magic."

Reecah stared at him in awe.

"Aye. How did you think I knew all about you?"

"But…I thought *I* was the last Windwalker."

He graced her with a patient smile. "Don't become too cocky with your newfound gift. Windwalkers aren't the only ones capable of coexisting with dragons and their ilk. Remember your roots."

'*The elves*,' Reecah formed the words with her lips without speaking.

"Precisely. Don't be thrown by my human ears. People say I look like my father."

Reecah's Gift

There was so much Reecah still had to learn about the world. Important facts she believed would prove instrumental if she were to stave off the dragons' extinction.

"Are you ready?"

Other than lighting candles and employing the magic of the scrying bowl, most of her training with Devius had been devoted to learning the magical runes and their various intonations, paying particular attention to how their enunciation affected the casting of the spell. Devius had been quite succinct about exact cadences, pitches, inflections and timbres. Placing the emphasis on the wrong syllable invited disaster.

The old wizard patted her sword hilt. "How about I use magic and you stick to what you know best. It's time you made Anvis proud."

Reecah swallowed. It was like the wizard had read her thoughts. She pulled her bow free and strung it. Satisfied, she nodded.

Devius bowed his head in return, his face losing all expression. A strange word escaped his lips. One that Reecah had learned while in his care.

"*Patefacio.*"

The large stones comprising the wall shimmered, revealing the door.

Fleabag growled, the hair on her back standing straight up— her muscles tensed in anticipation.

Devius nodded and the door swung open, blinding them with morning sunlight.

Reecah held her forearm to her brow, squinting. Though she couldn't see much, she was aware of Fleabag vaulting through the doorway with a feral growl.

The sound of a man's surprise turned into a cry of despair as Fleabag snarled and snapped, rending flesh.

Reecah's Gift

More shouts went up. The sound of swords being freed of their scabbards rang through the air.

"Reecah! Down!"

She shouldered her bow, took a step forward, and squatted on the threshold, her sword in hand.

A crackling 'whoosh' zipped past her head.

Her vision adjusted in time to see a burly man clad in boiled leather and shoulder plate take a fist-sized fireball in the face.

The man dropped his sword and fell to his knees, screaming in agony; frantically wiping at the flames devouring his head.

An arrow cracked against the doorjamb by her shoulder, showering her with splinters.

A second arrow thudded behind her, the sickening wet sound all too familiar.

Devius staggered backward, the flights of a war arrow protruding below his right collarbone.

Ducking back into the narrow entranceway, Reecah noted at least two archers on a ridge, fronting the base of the tower.

"The wizard's down!" A husky voice announced from outside.

Reecah put her sword on the ground and pulled her bow free. An arrow appeared in her hand as if by magic; the movement so natural, she didn't have to think about it.

Rising to her feet, nocking the arrow as she did, she pulled back on the string, stepped into the open doorway long enough to sight one of the archers and let fly. Before the arrow had taken the man in the cheek, she slipped behind the opposite doorjamb—narrowly avoiding two arrows that deflected off the interior wall and ricocheted against the steps.

On her way across the gap, she identified at least half a dozen men running toward them as well as two more archers. The blurred form of Fleabag streaking up the hillside toward the line of archers made her smile and wince at the same time. The

Reecah's Gift

cat couldn't slay them all before the guards cut her down and converged on the tower.

She turned to Devius, wincing at the end of the arrow clutched in a blood-covered hand. "Close the door!"

The wizard lay on the stone floor, his teeth clenched in pain. "We can't stay here."

Reecah barely heard his clipped words. "You're hurt. We can't leave yet. What's the word?"

Devius grunted something indecipherable.

Another arrow notched, she dropped to a knee and leaned out. The guards bearing down on them were only steps away. Her arrow pierced the closest man's stomach. The arrow passed straight through and took the man behind him in the ribs.

The remaining guards stumbled over their falling brethren.

Reecah ducked back. An arrow bounced off the edge of the doorway she had vacated and rattled around the confined space.

Her mind spun with different spell words, desperately searching for the word she should know. Devius had taught her so much in such a short time. She tried to make sense of what he had grunted. It obviously had something to do with shutting a door. Seal? Close?

That was it! Enclose! Now, if she could only recall the word for enclose. What had Devius said?

His ashen face stared back at her.

"What's the word for enclose?"

A roar from outside reminded her of two slabs of rock grating together. A cold wave of fear washed over her. Anvil!

She placed her back against the wall and slid to sit on the cold stone, dejected. She couldn't hope to defeat four swordsmen, an archer *and* Anvil.

A second growl, similar to Anvil's, disturbed the courtyard outside the tower entrance.

Reecah's Gift

Screams of pain accompanied metal clanging off metal. Someone had joined the fight.

Afraid to poke her head around the doorway lest she have it chopped off or skewered, she stared at Devius. Why was the old man smiling?

Chainmail chinked directly overhead. Her blood ran cold.

"Well I'll be a horned owl. What're ye doing hangin' around an old dodderer like him?"

Reecah craned her neck, gazing past a large stomach and a set of powerful arms leaning on the doorjamb, and stared into the eyes of a man she never expected to see again—one eye brown, the other green—framed by an open-faced, flat-topped helm plumed down its middle with what looked like a thin strip of black fur.

She jumped to her feet, her voice high-pitched with disbelief, "Aramyss? What are you doing here?"

"Saving me brother from certain harm."

Reecah hugged him, her troubled mind reeling. "You mean...?"

"Aye, lass." He winked, his blood-splattered, pudgy face sporting bruises that appeared to predate this attack. "His bark be worse 'n his bite, of that I assure ye."

A loud slap announced the arrival of Anvis Chizel, his heavy hand impelling Aramyss into the tower entrance. "I'll be bitin' hard if ya don't be watchin' yer mouth, runt."

Aramyss staggered to the steps beside Devius, a great laugh echoing up the stairwell. Clad in chainmail, with pieces of plate at his shoulders and elbows, his gaze fell on Devius. "Whatcha ya doing lyin' there?"

"What do you think I'm doing, you bow-legged ingrate? Having a nap?" Devius grunted through gritted teeth.

"Always the ungrateful one, eh wizard?" Aramyss squatted at Devius' side to inspect the arrow. He shook his head.

361

Reecah's Gift

Fleabag pushed her way past Anvil and bumped Aramyss to his backside. She nudged Devius with her head and licked his face.

"Still hangin' around this useless spellcaster, eh Fleabag?" Aramyss patted the lioness like they were old friends.

Anvil held a meaty hand out, assisting Reecah to her feet. "That was a nice shot you made."

She dusted herself off and looked outside, expecting to see guards surrounding the doorway. She gaped at the gory scene of broken bodies strewn from the entrance to the outer wall, her gaze settling on the archer with an arrow protruding from his cheek.

A man near the doorway groaned, bleeding profusely from a nasty axe wound. He reached out a blood-covered hand, begging for help.

Anvil hefted his axe and split the man's chest, silencing him. Pulling his axe free, he hocked and spat on the man's corpse. "Worthless lackey. Trained that one meself."

"I don't understand." Reecah walked into the yard, taking stock of ten dead guards in king's livery.

Anvil ignored her and entered the tower to stand over Devius.

Aramyss scrambled to allow him access to Devius and joined Reecah outside. He searched the grounds and the outer wall. "Walk with me lass. I'll explain it to ye."

Reecah lingered by the doorway, afraid to leave Devius alone with Anvil.

"Don't ya be frettin' o'er mister magic britches. He's in good hands. Anvis is better than most healers." He flashed a crooked-toothed smile. "Surely he's tended to yer training mates afore?"

She had to admit Anvil had proven himself knowledgeable whenever anyone suffered a serious injury during their rough training sessions.

Reecah's Gift

Aramyss pulled the pieces of a long-stemmed pipe from a leather satchel hanging from his belt and put them together. He gave her a sideways look, making sure to keep the pipe away from her as he stuffed the bowl and sparked its contents with a cleverly crafted flintstone.

Had she not been so overwhelmed, she would have smiled remembering their first encounter. "I still owe you a pipe."

"Och lass. Ye can't be replacing me ma'am's heirloom."

Though fairly certain he was joking, she couldn't be sure.

He winked and waddled toward the gaping outer gate. "Come on. Ye and I need to make sure we ain't got company."

"Take the damned cat with ye!" Anvil's muted voice bellowed from inside the tower.

Aramyss removed the pipe from his thick lips and whistled. "Come on, Fleabag. Walk with uncle Aram."

"Uncle?"

"Hah!" Aramyss spat as he slapped his leather leggings and stared at the entranceway. "Come on, kitty."

Fleabag bounded from the tower, running headlong for the dwarf.

Aramyss held out his palms. "Whoa. Whoa! Whoa girl!" He caught her in his embrace, her momentum knocking him backward, but he kept his feet as the cat licked at his scruffy cheeks bulging from the edges of his helm.

"Alright, alright, alright." Aramyss separated himself and started toward the yawning gateway.

Reecah kept pace, careful not to tread on Fleabag sauntering between them.

"I don't understand any of this. Anvil is the king's weapon master." Her eyes strayed to the dead archers as they passed them. "And you're the royal blacksmith."

"Tis a long story, I'm afraid. One we ain't got time for at the moment. Perhaps if we live long enough to get away from here, I'll explain it to ye."

Reecah's Gift

"But—"

Aramyss held up a silencing hand and waited until they reached the shadows of the thick, tunnel gate. Taking care not to expose himself to anyone who might be waiting outside, he spent a long time studying the steep roadway spiralling to the dock at the bottom of the hill. He lifted his head to gaze at Headwater Castle on the far side of the estuary. Withdrawing into the tunnel, he flashed her a smile. "Okay, GG."

"Reecah."

"Of course. Reecah." He puffed on his pipe. "Anyway, me brother and I've been awaitin' this day. We may be in the employ of the king, but we're Devius' men."

He puffed again, noting her expression. "Aye. Believe it or not, the mangy spellcaster has foreseen this day. Least, that's what he told me and me brother." He gazed at her, raising his thick eyebrows as if expecting a reaction.

"I know all about your relationship with Anvil. He told me."

"He did, did he? What else did he say, if I may be so bold as to be asking?"

"Not much, really. He spoke briefly of your parents. Of your father's transgressions."

Aramyss' face darkened. He spat with force against the wall. Reecah feared she had said too much.

"Don't speak of that man," Aramyss grumbled. Knocking the bowl of his pipe against the wall, he pulled another pinch from a separate pouch and stuffed the pipe.

"How did Devius know I was coming?"

Aramyss shrugged as he set the pipe bowl alight, puffing rhythmically until he was satisfied. "All I know is that when I found out the prince suspected who you are, I rushed here as soon as I could convince the king to let me attend Headwater to gather supplies." He winked.

"I find all of this upsetting." Reecah threw her hands up, pacing the short tunnel. "Everyone knows about me but me!"

Reecah's Gift

Aramyss stared after her but said nothing. He peeked around the outer edge of the tunnel.

"Do you know what I found out this morning?"

Aramyss shook his head.

"The dark heir is coming for me."

The pipe slipped from Aramyss' lips. He barely caught it in time. "Aye. I suspect he will. I'm the one who originally informed Devius of your arrival in Sea Hold. That's why you were summoned here. Unfortunately, the prince took notice of your arrival as well."

"How did he know?"

Aramyss stared at her. "Look at my face. Ain't much to be seeing, but J'kwaad's hired dog did a number on it. Made me answer questions I weren't easily divulgin'."

Reecah lifted his bearded chin to study his bruises. Recently inflicted hurts were evident beneath his thick facial growth.

"He did this to you? To find out about me? Why? How did he know I was here?"

"Don't rightly know. From what I pieced together, someone from the ship that brought you to King's Bay informed him."

Reecah's mind spun. Who would have told Prince J'kwaad? Cahira? Certainly not. Cookie. Maybe. Perhaps Captain Dreyger K'tric. Of the three, the captain made the most sense. His last name was spelled with an apostrophe.

She traced an ugly looking weal hidden beneath his beard.

He flinched.

"Oh, Aramyss. I'm so sorry. Everywhere I go, I bring pain to those around me."

Aramyss' nod, though well deserved, shocked her by his directness.

"It appears yer blonde friend has been captured."

"My blonde friend?" She didn't know who he was talking about. She didn't have any friends other than Raver and the dragons. Flavian came to mind, but he wasn't blonde. There was also Tamra, but she doubted Aramyss knew about her. Who had she come into contact with recently? Cahira's hair was red.

"Catenya?"

Drawing on his pipe, Aramyss choked on the smoke as sparks flew from the bowl. "That highbrow slag? Not likely." He studied the pipe's contents. "I'm talkin' about the new man in Anvil's group. The one with long hair and fancy chainmail."

Reecah grasped Aramyss by his wide shoulders. "Junior? That's impossible. He went back to South Fort weeks ago."

"I ain't sure who Junior is, but I knows who they got locked up in the hole. I see'd him meself. Wears a long, black surcoat. Dark purply, actually, and fancy as ya like. Gots himself flowing locks akin the finest maiden. Apparently has a date with dark ol' Mighty Britches himself."

Reecah bent low, her nose touching his. "J'kwaad?"

Aramyss' barely perceptible nod rubbed his tough forehead against hers.

"We need to get him out of there! The prince will kill him. Junior was at Dragon Home. He tried to save me."

Aramyss wrapped her wrists in his callused hands and gently pulled her off him, his serious stare never losing contact. "Simmer yerself, lass. I arrived with those who are to escort him to Sea Keep. They have business in Headwater first. We're not to leave until day after next. I'll spring him afore then."

Reecah ripped her hands from his grasp and ran to the edge of the tunnel to gaze upon Headwater Castle. "You don't understand. The prince knows I'm here."

Aramyss joined her on the threshold beneath the rusted portcullis that had been stuck in the open position for years. "Bah. Mighty Britches is a long way from here. Battling dragons in the south. We'll have you long gone afore J'kwaad can sink his fangs into ye. If the campaign goes well..." He

Reecah's Gift

trailed off, apparently struck by the panic in her eyes and her shaking head. "What do ye know that ye ain't tellin' me?"

"I saw him in a vision this morning. Riding hard along King's Wood Road."

Aramyss' eyebrows knit together, his large Adam's apple convulsing.

"He'll be here before nightfall."

Reecah's Gift

No Mercy

Leaving Devius behind was one of the hardest things Reecah, Aramyss, or Anvil had ever done. Anvil had expertly removed the arrow without inflicting more damage, but Devius had lost a lot of blood. If infection set in, he would be dead in short order.

Reecah couldn't imagine how hard the climb must have been, but Anvil carried Devius up to the octagonal chamber where the wizard assured them he would be fine. Reecah had her doubts, but the imminent arrival of the dark heir had forced their hand.

Fleabag could only protect him so long before the king's men slew her to get at the wizard. Devius had been adamant they heed his order—charging the dwarf brothers with escorting Reecah to the Draakvuur Colony in the eastern Wilds. A task that must be seen to at any cost. The wizard had emphasized their lives were of little consequence should she come to harm before they presented her to the queen.

Before they left him, Reecah placed her hands on Devius' injured shoulder. The sensation in her earrings no longer surfaced now that her dragon magic had been released. She no longer required Grimelda's gift.

The old man's order echoed through Reecah's mind as she kept her back against a section of stone wall marking the older part of Headwater Castle on the opposite side of the river.

Aramyss and Anvil checked each other's armour and equipment. Satisfied they were ready to go, Aramyss checked hers. "Okay, lass. Yer to stay here until we get back with Junior."

Reecah nodded, not happy they were excluding her from their foray into the castle but she understood. There would be those inside who were aware of her attendance with the high wizard. If they saw her wandering around without advance warning from the men guarding the wizard's tower, they would be compromised.

"What if somebody finds me here?"

Anvil said matter-of-factly, "Kill them."

Aramyss glared at his brother. Offering her a calming smile, he said, "Ye have little to fear. This section is no longer considered safe for human habitation. The only ones wandering the old fortress are the spirits of the dead."

Reecah gaped. "That doesn't make me feel any better."

Aramyss and Anvil, the dwarf and giant dwarf, slipped past a break in the wall and were gone.

Reecah listened for their passing but only the gentle lapping of the bay on the rocks below, and the random squawk of water fowl, disturbed the hillside.

A bird chirruped from a tree growing inside the old wall, filling her with thoughts of Raver. How she missed the mischievous imp.

Her attention was drawn to the mountain spire housing Devius' fortress at its peak. She hoped she hadn't left him to die. Once the dark heir discovered the bodies around the base of the Wizard's Sanctum, Devius' life would be in jeopardy.

She pulled her quarterstaff, bow, and quiver from her shoulders and laid them on the ground so she could sit against the wall and wait.

Aramyss and Anvil were putting their lives in peril to rescue Junior, a man she had doubted time and time again. The eldest Waverunner boy had apparently changed his mind and

Reecah's Gift

followed her to Headwater. Now he lay in a cell awaiting the dark heir. A visit that would mark Junior's death.

Gazing across the expanse of King's Bay, she felt insignificant. Dangerous forces were in play all around her. High Wizard Devius Misenthorpe and the Maiden of the Wood were better suited to deal with the threat than her. Just because people she had never met labelled her as a Windwalker didn't mean anything in the grand scheme of things. She had recently learned to perform carnival tricks, nothing more.

The image of Prince J'kwaad in the scrying bowl wouldn't leave her. It was like the dark heir had looked into her soul.

A corner of her diary dug into her ribs. Pulling it free, she flipped through the first few pages and smiled ruefully. Her first conversations with Lurker's mother and Lurker himself were written there.

How she missed him and the others. She should never have left them after they had found her in the King's Wood. She should have insisted they take her to the Draakval Colony to offer the doomed dragons assistance.

It was too late now. If J'kwaad were on his way back, that could only mean that their foray had been successful. Another dragon settlement lay in ruin. She bit her lips, trying to steel herself. How many dragons had died this time?

A breeze blew up the grassy slope from the bay, snatching the pages from beneath her thumb. Gripping the book, she glanced down at the last page and absently read the ancient runes.

She concentrated harder, not believing what stared back at her. The lines, though no different than when Grimclaw had etched them, made sense. She understood every word. Leafing back to where Grimclaw's words began, she read in earnest.

He had left her the means to a spell. A very powerful spell, if she appreciated the runes' context. Without ever having performed anything remotely this complex, she instinctively

Reecah's Gift

knew she could cast Grimclaw's summoning spell. But, what could she summon? A fireball like Devius? The ice-balls J'kwaad liked to employ?

As clear as the words were, she didn't understand their usage. From observing Devius and J'kwaad, their spellcasting had never struck her as remotely complicated as this spell. She needed to return to Devius. He would know.

She stood up, her limbs trembling from the revelation, and froze.

Birds called from over the lapping water. Tall grass on the hillside swayed in the sporadic breeze as buzzing insects flitted about the weeds. Nothing seemed out of the ordinary, but the hairs on the nape of her neck told her differently.

She walked to the break in the wall and peered into the grassy ruins. Nothing moved aside from the rustling vegetation that had overgrown the interior. Not taking the time to consider the foolishness of her actions, she decided to investigate what her senses were telling her. Something, or someone, was close by.

Her sword slid from its scabbard without a sound. Stepping quietly through the gap in the wall, she searched the shadows within what appeared to have been a great hall in years gone by. Though weeds choked the ancient stone and wooden benches, she imagined the high king's ancestors might have ruled the realm from this very spot.

With as much stealth as she could employ, she stepped deeper into the gloom; her keen eyes searching everywhere at once.

A screech echoed across the bay, sending shivers up her spine. Forgetting her desire to remain quiet, she returned to the break in the wall.

Peering across the water, the distant form of a dragon rounded the eastern battlements of the Wizard's Sanctum. The sight of the brown dragon left her breathless.

Reecah's Gift

"Swoop?" she uttered as an evil laugh whipped her attention back to the shadows—her dagger appearing in her left hand.

If she had the breath, she would have screamed. Stepping through an open doorway at the back of the ruined chamber, a man in black armour inlaid with golden piping regarded her with a smirk—his well-trimmed black goatee lifting slightly on one side.

"Well met, GG." He chuckled, but there was no mirth in his voice. "Or should I say, Reecah, the nettle in my side from the Dragon Temple? Reecah Draakvriend, the miscreant who almost slew the baron of Thunderhead with her own hands." He nodded, his wicked grin growing wide. "A shame you never finished the job."

Reecah tried to speak, to say anything, but her throat and mouth had gone dry.

Prince J'kwaad stepped from the shadows, his black cloak billowing behind him. "Or perhaps, I should call you, Reecah *Windwalker*."

The emphasis he placed on her last name told her he knew exactly who she was. She backstepped through the gap, stumbling on a rock half-buried in the ground. Catching her balance, she searched the grounds.

"Looking for that pair of traitorous dwarfs? You needn't fear their return. The Watch will soon be placing them with the Waverunner boy. I daresay, Father will be quite unhinged by their treachery."

Reecah forced herself to swallow. "They had nothing to do with it. I don't really know them."

"Sure, you don't. I suspected Aramyss was up to something when he suggested you train with his brother. Odd that someone fresh off a trading scow—a stowaway I might add, would be recommended by a member of the royal smithery to train with the king's weapon master. A man who just happens to be his brother."

"All I want is an audience with the king. I want him to reconsider the dragon hunt."

"Hah! You haven't met my father. He'll have your head off in the grievance hall. You'd have a better chance converting Baron Carroch to a life of celibacy."

Reecah frowned, taking a moment to grasp his reference to the baron of Thunderhead. Not knowing what else to do, she turned to sprint down the outside of the old wall but stopped. A squad of men in king's livery rounded a collapsed wall tower, cutting off her escape.

She poised to run down the hill and stopped again. Four skiffs scraped into the shoals bearing king's men. They were pinning her in.

She thought about sprinting past the gap, but J'kwaad appeared on the slope.

"It takes this many guardsmen to capture a skinny girl like me?" Her gaze darted to her bow and arrows at J'kwaad's feet. Even if she hadn't left them on the ground, they would have been of little use against so many.

Reecah's Gift

J'kwaad started toward her. "There's nothing ordinary about a Windwalker. We haven't seen your likes in what, twenty…, twenty-one years? Ever since my father ordered the death of your parents. And your meddling uncle."

Reecah had fought hard over recent years to curb her short temper. It had gotten her into trouble more times than she cared to remember. J'kwaad's biting remark brought Grimclaw's words home. *J'kaar Dragonscourge is the bane of my kin. Because of his intervention two decades ago, your uncle and your parents were lost to us. The high king is responsible for their deaths.'*

She charged J'kwaad.

The prince crossed his arms, watching her come.

Her dagger leading the charge, she trailed her sword behind her to deliver the prince a fatal blow. Screaming in rage, she swung her sword with all her strength.

The wildly swung sword struck a hastily raised tower shield held by one of two knights who emerged from the gap on either side of the prince.

Her shoulder screamed at the jarring impact—the strike vibrating up her arm. Her hand went numb. She had put everything into the killing blow, not expecting to meet resistance. Two more knights emerged from behind the wall and stripped her of her blades; pinning her arms behind her.

She growled and spat, struggling to break free of their grasp, but their iron grip held her fast. She kicked out at Prince J'kwaad and missed; one of the knights yanked hard on her hair and threw her off balance. The man's foul breath reeked as he held his black-bearded face next to hers from behind. "Try that again and I'll slit your throat."

She hadn't seen it come, but a dagger's keen edge rested against her windpipe.

The prince cast her a smug look. "Now that that's out of our system, I shall leave you in capable hands. I look forward to our next meeting high atop Draakhorn." He ran his tongue

Reecah's Gift

along the inside of his upper lip. "I welcome the challenge of extracting the dragon magic from your soul without killing you. When I'm done, perhaps we'll see how well you fly. Now, if you'll excuse me, I have an appointment with a pair of dwarfs."

The prince spun, his black cape swirling in his wake, and disappeared beyond the gap.

"Coward!" Reecah called after him. "Fight me with your bare hands. Just you and me. Get back here!"

Not caring about her safety, she stomped on the dagger bearing knight's toe. He howled and released his grip.

She shrugged free of the second knight's grasp but before she could do anything further, another knight drove his shoulder into her ribs, taking her to the ground and forcing the wind from her lungs.

The knight kept his weight on her, making it impossible to breathe. Excruciating pain wracked her core. Gasping and pointing at her throat, she tried to throw the man but he refused to let her up.

The guard whose toe she had stamped, kicked her in the ribs. "Ain't so tough now, are you? Can't see what the prince finds so dangerous about you. You're nothing but a tart."

She thought for sure he would hoof her again, but he limped out of her line of sight.

"Let her up, you imbecile," a gruff voice snarled. "Kill her and we all face his wrath."

The man on top of her didn't comply at first but as his weight lifted, an agonizing breath slipped into her lungs. She sucked in great, heavy breaths.

The man who had taken her down spat on the top of her head and walked away. "Witches should be burned."

"Burned! Burned!"

Reecah's head snapped around. A welcome sight stared at her with beady, black eyes, from the branch of the tree inside the gap.

Reecah's Gift

The relative serenity on the slope outside the wall turned into pandemonium as three dragons, larger than she remembered, dropped from the sky.

Massive claws latched onto archers by the head and shoulders, their talons puncturing armour.

King's men ran in all directions. Some screaming in terror, while others formed makeshift lines to offer a weak defense.

Reecah's lungs hurt so bad she couldn't lend a hand, but the relief at seeing her friends put a smile on her face.

Her grin grew wider. The faces of the guardsmen turned from bewilderment and fright to absolute panic as Tamra Stoneheart slid from Silence's neck—her axes whirling before her feet hit the ground.

The dragons chased down the bulk of the fighters who had abandoned the fight and were attempting to reach the boats, while Tamra took up a position over Reecah, daring those caught in between to come at her.

Three men rushed Tamra from different directions.

Reecah had never seen anyone thrust, jab and chop as fast as Tamra's weapons cleaved the air—her weapons extensions of her arms; a graceful fluidity of motion as she met their charge with footwork so deft, she appeared to float. Reecah wasn't sure she didn't. Within moments, the chaos was replaced by the pathetic moans of the men who were unfortunate enough not to die immediately.

The Maiden of the Wood wandered from one man to the next, systematically chopping their necks—offering no mercy. A couple of heads rolled down the hill to splash into the water before she finished the grisly task.

Tamra strode back to Reecah, holding an axe handle out to assist her to her feet. "Where's Junior?"

"Taken." Reecah's voice was harsh and faint.

"Where?"

Reecah's Gift

Reecah pointed to the gap where J'kwaad had disappeared. "They locked him in some place they call the hole."

Gathering herself, Reecah recovered her sword and dagger and fetched her discarded weapons from against the wall. "I think it's this way. Follow me."

"Reecah, wait," Lurker's voice stopped her at the gap. *"Can we fly you there?"*

Reecah gave Tamra a questioning look. She had never been here before.

The tough woman nodded. "I know of this *hole*. It lies outside the main castle. I can take us there."

Reecah approached Lurker and hugged his head, ashamed she hadn't thanked the dragons for their intervention. "I'm sorry. It's good to see you."

"No apology necessary. Luckily Raver spotted you in time."

"In time! In time!"

She laughed and released him. Kissing his nose, she greeted Silence and Swoop the same way.

"So, can we fly you to Junior?" Lurker asked.

Tamra nodded.

Reecah climbed onto Lurker's shoulders, a broad smile on her face, despite the dire circumstances. "I hope they get to him before the prince."

Before anyone could ask what she meant, Reecah added, "How many people can you carry?"

"Why?"

"Because, there will be five of us."

Reecah's Gift

Reecah's Gift

The flight above Headwater Castle, though quick, filled Reecah with a surreal euphoria; the indescribable, heady sensation she experienced every time she soared through the sky on Lurker's shoulders.

The castle grounds were immense. Flying beyond the main keep, an ice-ball zipped past Silence. Tamra ducked to the side, nearly losing her tentative purchase to avoid the magical blast.

Far below, the running form of Prince J'kwaad led countless knights and city guardsmen toward the eastern ramparts.

"There!" Tamra's melodic voice rang out as she repositioned herself on Silence's shoulders and pointed.

A large crater, walled in on all sides against the outside of the main battlement, sat between two wall towers in the centre of the courtyard. A metal-lattice grate lay discarded to one side.

A furious battle raged around the crater. Two remarkably different sized dwarfs faced down a score of attackers—the guardsmen backing Anvil and Aramyss against the edge of the pit.

Reecah gaped at the number of lifeless bodies sprawled on the ground, stretching from a small door in the outer wall of the main battlement, to where Anvil and Aramyss held the Watch at axe-swinging length.

Reecah searched the grounds. "Where's Junior?"

The dragons banked over the pit.

Tamra pointed with an axe. "There! In the hole!"

378

Reecah's Gift

Reecah marvelled at the keenness of Tamra's elven eyes. Looking hard, she made out the form of someone at the pit's bottom.

The Watch looked up in alarm; their disciplined ranks failing.

Before Reecah and Tamra slid from their mounts, Anvil and Aramyss made quick work of the distracted guards.

Reecah ran to the edge of the hole, but jumped back to avoid Swoop as she dropped hind feet first into the deep pit—its diameter too narrow to allow her to spread her wings.

"Swoop! You'll get stuck!"

Anvil and Aramyss backstepped away from the dragons— their axes held defensively before them.

"It's okay. They're my friends." Reecah placed herself between the dragons and the dwarfs. "We need to move fast. He's here."

Anvil and Aramyss exchanged looks.

"The prince! He'll be here any moment. He knows about you two. We have to leave."

Anvil smacked his palm with his axe handle. "Stay with her. I'll secure the door."

Anvil lumbered to the iron door and looked into the bailey beyond. A crossbow bolt and the remnants of an ice-ball shattering against the swinging door resounded in the small courtyard as he slammed the portal shut. He dropped an iron restraining bar into the brackets on either side of the door. "That won't hold J'kwaad long."

The weapon master ducked into a small wooden guard shack and reappeared bearing Junior's equipment. He ran back, his thick arms cradling his battle-axe, Junior's chainmail hauberk and sword belt. Reecah estimated the load weighed more than she did.

"Reecah?"

Lurker's inquiring voice drew her attention.

"There are only three of us and five of you."

Reecah's Gift

"You need to carry two."

Unable to hear Lurker, Aramyss and Anvil frowned at her odd statement.

"We can barely get off the ground with one. There's no way."

Flustered, Reecah scanned the unscalable walls and walked over to the edge of the pit. "Swoop. How're you going to get out of there?"

As if in response, the brown dragons' front claws dug into the rock wall and pulled her bulk upward.

"What about Junior?"

"I have him."

"Just don't drop me!" Junior's muted voice was a joy to Reecah's heart.

"Look to the walls!" Tamra shouted and ducked as several arrows whistled into the courtyard, bouncing off Lurker and Silence's scales; impaling the ground around her.

"Send for the ballista crews!" The ominous words echoed off the courtyard walls.

Reecah shrugged her bow free and dropped to a knee to make herself a smaller target. Sighting the closest threat, she dispatched a rapidly strung arrow, the missile shattering against a crenellation.

The archer on the wall focused on her, raising his bow.

Reecah's second arrow took him between his nose and upper lip.

Lurker and Silence manoeuvred themselves between the wall and Reecah; arrows ricocheting and splintering off their scales.

It was only a matter of time before they took an arrow to the eye or their more vulnerable undersides. "Swoop! Hurry!"

Brown claws crunched the stone lining the rim of the hole. *"Almost there."*

Lurker drew her attention back to the courtyard. *"Reecah, we have to leave the dwarfs behind."*

Reecah's Gift

Shaking her head, Reecah strung an arrow and stepped free of Lurker's protective cover. "We're not leaving anyone!"

The arrow took an archer in the neck. He dropped his bow off the wall—his body hanging between two crenellations.

"Unless they learn to fly, there's no way. You're our priority. My father's spirit will never forgive me if I let you die. If only Scarletclaws had come with us."

She nodded. She had never known what had happened to the red dragonling from Dragon Home. Scarletclaws' presence would have gone a long way to solving their predicament. "We have to try. Look at you. You're bigger than before. You take Anvil and Aramyss. I'll fly with Junior and Swoop."

"Whoa, bilge rat!" Anvil took refuge beside her. "If I didn't know any better, I'd say yer conversing with the beast." He gave Lurker a wary look. "An' I ain't to be liking what I'm hearing. Dwarfs don't fly dragons."

Swoop's unfurling wings drew her attention as she emerged from the hole with Junior clutched in a back foot.

Lurker's voice pulled her back to their dilemma. *"I know my strength, Reecah. I won't risk you."*

His words grated at her. "I *order* you! You're honour-bound to obey a Windwalker!" As the words left her lips, they hurt her as much as she was sure they affronted her friend.

Lurker's head swung to look her in the eye. Such was his dark look, she fleetingly thought he might eat her.

She hung her head. "Forgive me. I'm panicking."

Anvil must've thought she was talking to him. He winced and ducked as an arrow zipped past his head. "It's okay. You get aboard yer dragons and be gone. Me brother and I'll hold off the prince."

A loud bang resounded throughout the courtyard. Dust sifted down the wall over the small guard hut. Something had impacted the metal door.

Reecah's Gift

Reecah strung an arrow but her attention fell on the small door. Once it gave in, the fight would be over. "The prince will kill you. You have no choice. Fly or die."

Anvil glared. "Ye ain't listening, rat. I'm not to be flying a lizard. I choose me own path."

The courtyard shook as another detonation hammered the door. The rusted metal bulged inward, straining the metal bar.

Swoop's voice barely registered as the brown dragon spoke to Lurker. *"We should have convinced Scarletclaws to fly east with us."*

"I agree, but she's a stubborn one. She won't leave until she's certain no one else is coming back. If we survive this, we should go get her."

Angry at the stubborn dwarf giant, and distracted by the odd dragon talk, Reecah's next shot missed her target. She leaned back against Lurker, beseeching herself to think. They needed more...dragons!

A cold chill made her shudder. She gaped, craning her head to see Lurker's face. "Scarletclaws is alive?"

"She was the last time we saw her."

"Why didn't you tell me?"

Lurker sounded sheepish. *"I never thought."*

Shouldering her bow, she wrestled her journal from her inner pocket, the action harder than it should have been because of the stress she was under.

She flipped to the back of the book. Grimclaw's spell stared her in the face. Had he meant for her to summon a dragon? Was such a thing even possible?

Misgivings about her ability to enact such a complicated spell feathered her skin with tingles of doubt. If she wasn't up to it, Scarletclaws' life might be the consequence.

Arrows thwapped against the dragons standing over their human charges. Reecah could tell from the way they flinched that the missiles were hurting them.

"We better fly soon!" Junior shouted from where he cowered behind Swoop. "Ballista crews are setting up."

Reecah's Gift

Anvil grabbed Reecah's bow and pulled a handful of arrows from her quiver. He sighted and killed one of the nearest ballista crew members but two more took the man's place.

Silence took to the air, flying at the first ballista. As soon as she crested the wall, an ice-ball smote her backside.

Careening into the battlements, she dropped to the earth on the *hole* side of the wall.

"Silence!" Lurker and Swoop called out.

Dragging her frozen hind quarter across the courtyard, she said, *"I'm okay."*

The courtyard shook. One of the massive stone blocks lining the doorway and holding an end of the crossbar bracket sat askew of its natural resting place.

Aramyss peered from beneath Lurker's chin. "They're coming through!"

Reecah forced the distractions from her mind, remembering Devius' teachings. It wasn't proving quite as simple as when they trained in the tower. Taking two deep breaths, it had to be done now.

The words of Grimclaw's spell flowed from her lips. Slowly at first, but as her confidence grew that she knew every rune, her cadence increased in pace and strength. Pausing to flip the page, she sensed the presence of her gift behind her temples pressing against her skull as if it was trying to escape. Oddly, the sensation was neither painful nor frightening.

Arrows twanged into the earth. Men screamed from the battlements as Anvil's marksmanship took out one guard after another.

Without thinking what she was doing, Reecah stood up and stepped onto Lurker's foreleg to hoist herself onto his shoulders. Her instincts urged her to get clear of the surrounding walls. There was something about the proximity of the Wizard's Sanctum that called to her.

Reecah's Gift

Distantly, Aramyss pleaded with her to get down before she got herself killed.

Oblivious to the distractions but conscious of Lurker lifting a wing to shield her, she kicked her heels into his shoulders much like she would direct a horse.

In tune with his Windwalker rider, Lurker hunched down and sprung into the air, quickly rising above the chaotic scene below. His flight took him over the outer wall, avoiding J'kwaad's line of sight. As if in a dream, the vision of Silence winging after them flitted at the edge of her mind and was gone.

Using her heels, Reecah directed Lurker to the far edge of King's Bay and hovered below Devius' fortress on the rocks, the vantage point allowing her to visualize the bay area and Headwater Castle. Had she realized she did this without hanging on to Lurker with anything but her thighs, she would have been mortified.

Flipping the last page of her diary, she stared across the bay to the Sea Gate Bridge and beyond.

Unnatural clouds coalesced above, roiling with a sinister blackness. She struggled to complete the spell. A nagging dread made her hesitate. Fearing she was losing her grasp on the magical forces involved, she sensed a dragon fighting her summons—its presence flitting in and out of the boundaries of her gift.

A sudden, violent storm boomed overhead—the black clouds unleashed a torrential rainfall; driven by a wind that should have blown her from Lurker's shoulders, but the faithful dragon turned and dipped, keeping her firmly in place.

Reality flooded her senses as she spoke the last word. Gasping in fright, she clung to Lurker's neck, only now, fully aware she had taken to the sky. She clutched her journal against Lurker's hide to keep it from falling and looked around.

Reecah's Gift

The sun broke through rapidly dissipating clouds over the Wizard Sanctum; glinting off the middle of the bay. A strange mist had formed around the rocks beneath her, obscuring the water.

Reecah's Gift

A shriek pierced the calm. The mist dissolved to reveal Silence flying above the rocks—the purple dragon giving chase to a stunned red dragon who was struggling to remain airborne.

"Scarletclaws?"

Scarletclaws flapped vigorously to gain altitude and tilted her wings to bank around Devius' tower. *Who said that?*

Reecah urged Lurker to her altitude and fell in beside the confused dragon, taking a moment to secure her diary.

You? The woman who ran through Dragon Home and brought the king's men down on us? Smoke billowed from Scarletclaws nostrils. Her eyes narrowed.

Lurker recognized the danger and plummeted toward the bay.

"What the—" Reecah's stomach rose into her throat. She craned her neck to see Silence drop in beside Scarletclaws, the purple dragon's voice barely audible.

Scarlet! Reecah is a Windwalker. She didn't bring about our colony's destruction. She tried to save us.

How did I get here?

Lurker's wings beat several times to match their altitude. *You're here because of Reecah's Gift. She used Grimclaw's spell to summon you.*

Lurker tilted his wings to veer back to Headwater Castle. *There's no time to explain. We need you to transport two humans away from the castle.*

Scarletclaws coughed, emitting a small burst of flame.

You got your fire!

Of course. I'm a red dragon. What did you expect? We mature faster than you.

Lurker beat his wings faster than Reecah would have liked—the old part of Headwater castle, littered with the fallen bodies of king's men, rushed by in a blur. She couldn't help but choke him, fearing he was unable to avert a crash landing as the

Reecah's Gift

crenellated, eastern wall, lined with archers both alive and dead, zipped by.

Wings turned out to beat rapidly, Lurker caught enormous amounts of wind. Reecah was sure her body would push through his shoulders. They hit the ground hard, his back legs absorbing the worst of the shock.

Recovering her wits, she surveyed the situation.

Swoop stood close to the pit, her body barely large enough to protect Tamra, the dwarfs, and Junior who had donned his gear. Dozens of arrows littered the ground around them, accompanied by several heavy spears, but everyone appeared unharmed.

Silence raked the battlements until another ice-ball whooshed by her hastily pulled back head.

Following close behind, Scarletclaws dropped from the sky, her body twice that of Lurker. She doused the ramparts with dragon fire before hitting the ground hard beside the other dragons.

Two ballistae that had been close to becoming operational were devoured by flame.

Men and women fell screaming to the ground on both sides of the wall.

"That's our chance!" Reecah shouted over the chaos. "Junior! Tamra! Ride Swoop and Silence. Aramyss and Anvil, meet Scarletclaws. She'll fly you out of here."

She wasn't sure who was more shocked—the dwarfs or the red dragon.

"Leave me here, rat. I'll take me chances with the prince afore I get anywhere near that thing!" Anvil stepped away from Scarletclaws.

"Suits me fine," Scarletclaws replied, though Reecah didn't think either dwarf could hear her.

The ground shook. The metal door bulged. How it hadn't collapsed was a wonder. It wouldn't withstand another blast.

Reecah's Gift

"Come on, Anvis. Ye ain't wanting yer wee brother to upstage ya now. Watch this." Aramyss slapped his axe into its holders across his back and timidly approached Scarletclaws.

The red dragon growled, spewing puffs of smoke as she sidestepped away from the three-and-a-half-foot dwarf.

"Scarlet!" Lurker admonished.

Scarletclaws stopped moving and dropped her chest to the ground. *"If I must, but I'm not responsible when they fall off."*

A thunderous detonation rocked the courtyard. Hinges and chunks of rock exploded inward—the mangled iron door that Reecah estimated weighed as much as Silence, cartwheeled across the dirt-packed compound, coming to a rest close to where Scarletclaws had shuffled to.

"Come on, Anvil! Don't you turn your back on me!" Reecah screamed, her eyes riveted on the settling dust cloud that marked where the entrance door had stood. "Lurker, away!"

The brilliance of a conjured ice-ball shone through the haze long before the black form of Prince J'kwaad materialized within the cloud.

Reecah urged Lurker to slow his ascent, wanting to ensure the others got away. Swoop winged past them with Junior hanging on tight, followed closely by Silence and Tamra, but Scarletclaws remained on the ground.

Anvil appeared to be gripped by indecision.

"Get up here, ya bonehead!" Aramyss shouted. He held out a hand.

Anvil looked like he would refuse, but he clasped his brother's hand and climbed in behind—the difference in their size laughably apparent.

Reecah held her breath. This would be Scarletclaws' maiden flight with riders.

Scarletclaws flapped once and then twice, but her body didn't rise off the ground.

Reecah's Gift

"Even straddling a dragon, you aren't big enough to defeat me, Anvis. Magic beats brawn every time." A growing sphere of sparkling ice-blue pulsed in J'kwaad's hands. "It's time to rid the king's household of your inferior race."

The prince thrust his hand away from his body, releasing the crippling ice-ball. It soared in a straight line, beneath Scarletclaws extended hind legs, and detonated against the exterior wall, freezing a section of the wall. Scarletclaws had leapt into the air, furiously beating her enormous wings.

Dust rose up beneath her but she struggled to gain altitude.

"Come on Scarletclaws! You can do it!" Reecah's gaze darted between the dragon and the prince—her heart sinking as another ice-ball formed between J'kwaad's hands.

She wished she had her bow. She could see it slung over Anvil's back. "Lurker. We have to do something. Take me to them."

Lurker's sad voice infuriated her. *"I can't. You're the last Windwalker."*

She pounded his neck with a fist. "What good is being a Windwalker if I can't save anyone?"

Scarletclaws started to gain altitude, but it wasn't quick enough. She hovered in the air, struggling to fly higher. There was no way J'kwaad would miss a second time.

"I shall enjoy watching you fall from the sky, Anvis." J'kwaad thrust his hands to the sky.

"Oi!" Anvil pushed off Aramyss' shoulders and stood shaking upon Scarletclaw's unsteady neck. Reecah's bow in hand and an arrow notched, Anvis Chizel drew back on the string and let himself fall.

The giant dwarf weapon master released his arrow a moment before his body bore the brunt of the ice-ball and shattered into grizzly pieces.

Reecah looked away, closing her eyes tight, not believing what she had just witnessed. The whoosh of Scarletclaws rising

Reecah's Gift

past her, and Aramyss' anguished cry, confirmed her worst fear. Anvil, the Bone Breaker, had given his life to save his brother and the dragon who had terrified him.

Lurker's wings beat faster, his flight following the others over the northern stretches of the King's Wood.

Reecah's last, tear-filled sight of the killing ground was of the dark heir lying on the ground with an arrow protruding from the top of his shoulder—his long, black hair splayed around his head.

Reecah's Gift

Wooden Treasure

Sitting around a crackling fire Scarletclaws had lit on the north shore of the Lake of the Lost should have been a happy occasion. Anvil's sudden death and Aramyss' unbridled grief left the others in a state of shock.

The weapon master's passing had affected Reecah more profoundly than she would have thought. She took comfort in the fact that the man had died the way he had lived. Confronting his fears head-on regardless of the consequences. He had overcome his dread of flying a dragon and sacrificed his life to save his brother.

Reecah held Aramyss in her arms deep into the night, rocking him back and forth and cooing to him. There was nothing to say that would ease his pain, but holding him helped him through the worst of his grief.

The others solemnly went about their business, leaving them alone.

As she comforted him, she absently thought about the loss of her bow and the odd feeling of emptiness its absence instilled in her. Of course, she would have gladly traded the bow for Anvil's life, but they were both lost to her.

When she finally left Aramyss' side, his gentle snores carried across the campsite. Stretching her back, she wiped at the smeared mess her face had become with the edge of her cloak.

The dragons lay around the clearing with their eyes closed. Tamra had gone off earlier, stating she would keep watch for the night.

Reecah's Gift

Still awake, Junior rose from the far side of the fire and smiled for her benefit.

Seeing the man filled her with emotions she wasn't sure she was prepared to acknowledge.

Junior approached her. "A long night."

Reecah fought her tears, but was unsuccessful.

Gently wrapping his arms around her, Junior led her to the log he had been sitting on; patiently allowing her to vent her own sorrow.

She thought she had cried herself out with Aramyss, but apparently, she had her own demons to exorcise.

Releasing her as her breathing settled, Junior wiped her cheeks with the edge of his dirty cloak, further streaking her skin. "Oops. Now look what I've done. I guess that wasn't a great idea."

She spit out a moisture-laden laugh.

Junior's cheeks lifted. "What do you plan on doing now? Is it true you're going to seek out the dragon queen?"

Reecah hung her head and shrugged. "I don't know. Every time I set out to do something, I bring sadness to those around me."

"Wasn't that what Devius said you were to do?"

She raised her weary eyes to meet his. "I guess."

"But?"

"There's something I need to do first. Something I promised someone special, a long time ago."

Junior respected her silence when she didn't elaborate.

He jumped when she suddenly grabbed his nearest hand in hers. "Do you believe in fate?"

He frowned, scrunching up his face in thought. "Ya. I guess. I'd like to believe there's more to life than just bumping around until we die."

Reecah's Gift

Reecah nodded, considering whether or not to tell him what was on her mind. Swallowing her inhibition, she raised his hand and softly kissed it. "Me too." Was all she said.

Embarrassed, she released his hand and looked away.

She heard him rustling around, digging through a pouch he carried beneath his cloak.

He pulled something out, but kept it hidden. "I have something for you."

It was Reecah's turn to look bewildered. She gazed into his tired, green eyes, lifting her eyebrows for him to continue.

He handed her a small, sloppily wrapped, cloth bundle. "It's not perfect. Woodworking isn't exactly my strength. I hope you like it."

She tilted her head and accepted the package. Unrolling it in her lap, her breath caught in her throat. She thought her heart would burst.

Tears blinded her, falling from her cheeks onto the wooden dragon Poppa had made for her mother. The one Jonas' men had shattered to pieces. Junior had found a way to put it back together.

Unable to speak, she clutched the crudely pieced together dragon to her chest and wept into his shoulder.

The End

...is near.

Available now!

<u>Sadyra, Larina, and Pollard—3 books, 1 amazing story</u>

At the request of the fans of the Soul Forge Saga, The Banebridge Companion Novels. The backstory of everyone's favourite archers and the man who recruited them to join the Splendoor Catacombs Guard.

Coming early 2021, the much-anticipated series that gave rise to the Windwalkers

<u>Keeper of the Jewel, book 1 in the Highcliff Guardians</u>

Something dark is creeping across the elven kingdom of South March. Something so sinister, that if it is allowed to thrive unchecked, will lead to the end of dragonkind and quite possibly the termination of life as a whole.

The only thing standing in the way of the pervasive evil is a privileged young woman who wants nothing to do with her high standing in life, nor the oppressive responsibilities that accompany the title: Heir to the Willow Throne.

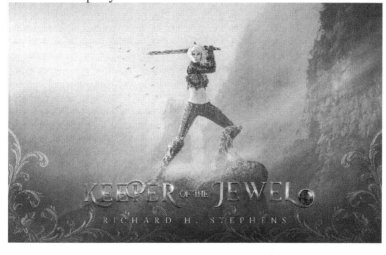

Reecah's journey concludes in book three in the
Legends of the Lurker Series.
Enjoy the first chapter.

Reecah's Legacy

Promise to a Dead Witch

Breathtaking. There was no other word to explain the wonder gripping Reecah Windwalker as she gazed through a gap in the clouds at the edge of a great lake. Nestled amongst a circular chain of mountains, the lake funneled between two of the taller peaks to plummet thousands of feet to the mainland below—a great bank of mist shrouding its bottom.

The silent serenity of the moment warmed her heart despite the frigid winds blowing off of windswept snow ridges above. Escaping the chaotic scene at Headwater Castle, she relished the brief luxury of peace, surrounded by her eclectic group of friends.

Junior Waverunner's hand at her waist filled a spot in her soul she had no idea existed until recently. His chiseled profile caught the setting sun, illuminating scant facial hair in golden relief as his blonde locks whipped around in unison with the bitter gusts swirling the snow beneath their feet.

A stone-faced elf, clad in thick fur and boiled leather, and a melancholy dwarf beneath an open-faced, flat-topped helm, followed her gaze to the grandeur of Splendoor Falls. A more calming place in the world, Reecah couldn't imagine.

If not for the pressing need of dragonkind, she envisioned living out her life in a place like this. Raising a family and enjoying the simple pleasures that comprise life's greatest treasures. Thinking about what was to happen if she wished to have a child, she hoped the others attributed her red cheeks to the cold.

Devius Misenthorpe, the high king's wizard, had planted in her mind the need to produce an heir if the dragons were to survive the rapidly changing world. A world where mankind's whims manifested an unbalance in nature to suit their desires.

Bearing a child meant coupling with another person—allowing someone else access to her most intimate self, both physically and mentally. Being a loner, Reecah wasn't sure she was able to give that to another human being in return. She shivered.

Reaching up, she patted the scaly cheek of the one creature she *did* feel comfortable enough with to share her inner self.

Lurker, the green dragonling, nuzzled her palm. She couldn't believe how much he had grown since she first met him several months ago. Nor could she get over how much her life had changed as a result.

A shriek echoed off the peaks of the Muse. Far over the lake, Scarletclaws and Silence winged across the rolling waves, close to the far shore, in search of food.

A distant speck materialized out of the clouds, dropping like a stone in front of them to skim the treetops that clung to the steep mountainside. Swoop, the brown dragon, turned her wings at the last moment and brushed the lake's surface—creating a plume of moisture in her wake.

Reecah's cheeks lifted in a broad smile as Junior regarded her with concern in his vibrant green eyes.

"It's only a matter of time before that crazy dragon does that with me on her back."

Reecah laughed. "You'd best be hanging on tight."

"That's what scares me. With my luck, I'll choke her unconscious and she won't be able to make the adjustment in time."

"Aren't you a good swimmer?"

The appalled look on Junior's face made her laugh louder. She put her arm around his waist and pulled him in close, snuggling into his shoulder—his chainmail cold against her skin. "I'm sure she wouldn't do that with you on board."

Junior returned her squeeze but didn't comment further; his gaze following the flight of his dragon mount.

Lurker's head appeared over Junior's far shoulder. *"I suggest we get you humans off the mountain before you freeze to death."*

Tamra and Aramyss shot Lurker a contemptuous scowl. Neither elf, nor dwarf, appreciated being lumped in with mankind.

Aramyss waddled around Tamra, his unlit pipe in hand, and stopped beside Reecah, staring at her from his three-and-a-half-foot frame clad in chainmail and plate. "Have ye decided yer course? Remember the high wizard's words."

Reecah sighed. She knew in her heart what she wanted to do, but Devius had been adamant. She was to journey to the Wilds and seek out the dragon queen. His deep voice permeated her thoughts, warning her not to do otherwise. *'Now that you've exposed your true identity, nowhere else is safe. You must make haste, and do not stray. It's vital you go straight there. Do you hear me?'*

The old conjurer had scared her more than anything else she had experienced in life when he performed the unbinding rite. She thought her life had come to an end. Surviving the ritual had awakened a new consciousness, providing her with an entirely fresh perspective. Not only on the plight of the dragons, but on life in general. If Devius claimed she must report to the Draakvuur Colony, she would be foolish not to.

She smiled at her new friend. "Do you know where the queen's colony is? The world's a big place. I'm afraid we might wander forever and never find it."

Raver appeared from the steep drop in front of them and stumbled to a stop in the snow at their feet. "Find it! Find it!"

Giving the maimed raven a shake of his head, Aramyss shrugged, his thick lips pursed amongst the unruly growth of his long, brown beard.

They hadn't been speaking loudly, despite the whistling wind, but Tamra's keen ears must've picked up on their conversation. She turned her half-shaved head in their direction and indicated with a subtle shake that she didn't either.

Appreciating the captivating beauty of Lurker's emerald eyes, Reecah asked, "I don't suppose any of you happen to know where the queen's colony lies?"

Lurker hung his head. *"Unfortunately, we don't."*

"Right. You said as much on the flight here." Reecah broke eye contact, staring at the brink of the majestic cataract, marvelling at Swoop's ability to adjust her flight so quickly. The brown dragon skimmed the lake at tremendous speed, approaching the point where the water fell from sight. She disappeared below the brink just as abruptly.

Junior tensed. He had seen it too.

Though she had no problem deciding what she thought was best for herself, she struggled to make a decision that would affect the rest of her party. Being a Windwalker apparently came with heady responsibility. One she didn't care to acknowledge.

Following Devius' instructions made the most sense—the only sense—and yet, she wrestled with a demon she had needed to exorcize since the day *Grimelda's Clutch* burned to the ground.

Grimelda's memory warmed her cheeks and left her feeling empty at the same time. She had feared the witch and everything she represented for most of her life, but in the end, her last living relative had opened her mind to a new reality. One she wished she had been privy to while growing up.

The old crone's words came back to her, as if she and Grimelda were still standing beside the counter along the back wall in her aunt's bizarre shop, *'Locate the earth's schism to claim your heritage. Remove the Dragon's Eye from the Watcher and bring it back here... Promise Grimelda that no matter what happens tonight, you will return with the Dragon's Eye.'*

'...no matter what happens tonight...'

Smiling despite her misgivings, she shook her head at Aramyss. She had a promise to keep with a dead witch.

• • •

Books by Richard H. Stephens

Soul Forge - The Epic Fantasy Trilogy

<u>Soul Forge – Book 1</u>

Haunted by the murder of his family, a forgotten hero embarks upon a perilous quest fraught with demons both real and imagined.

Silurian Mintaka only wants another drink, but when the people of Zephyr need someone to save them from an evil sorcerer, he agrees to put aside his bitterness and wreak his revenge.

Deception, betrayal, and fantastic beasts stand in his way. With the fate of the kingdom in the hands of a homicidal lunatic, the only thing left to do is pray.

Wizard of the North –Book 2

What do you get when you disturb a 500-year-old spirit who is in charge of protecting an ancient magic? A death-defying flight to the heart of a serpent's nest.

If pulling a man through the flames wasn't enough, the highest wizard in the land detonates a thousand years of magical lore.

Not sure whether the king survived the firestorm, the people are left with little choice but to place their trust in a corrupt bishop.

A beast is unleashed and the kingdom's future lies in the hands of an eclectic band of companions who have lost their way.
Can an upstart mage, who isn't what they appear, stand against the evil sweeping the realm?

Into the Madness −Book 3

The epic conclusion of the Soul Forge Saga.

How do you survive a confrontation with a wyrm bent on destroying the world? Walk into its gaping maw and fight it from within.

A ragtag group of assassins set out to end the land's suffering only to discover death awaiting them with open arms.

A carefully hidden truth is revealed—the key to the kingdom's salvation if the Wizard of the North and her unstable companion can live long enough to unlock its secret.

Waylaid by an eccentric necromancer, and suffering a tragic loss that threatens to ruin their poorly laid plan, the companions stagger toward a fate no one ever envisioned.

An obsidian nightmare is summoned and Zephyr will never be the same.

Legends of the Lurker Series

Reecah's Flight –Book 1

Everyone knows dragons are dangerous, but to hunt them is insane. There is something strange about the woman living on top of the hill and the people of Fishmonger Bay leave her alone. At least until the day she visits the village witch.

One magic user is bad enough; the emergence of another—intolerable.

Spinning out of control, Reecah must decide whether to slay the dragon or risk becoming a victim of her people.

Can Reecah find the key to unlock her family heritage or will she fall prey to the secret so many have died to protect?

Reecah's Gift – Book 2

The appalling mannerisms of those entrusted to protect the kingdom are shocking.

Braving the perils of a cutthroat city isn't what Reecah envisioned when she sought out a better place.

Can a ruthless giant equip her with the skills she needs to confront the king, or will his unorthodox ways end up being the death of her dreams?

Is an alliance with a murderous elf and a sly dwarf the best way to avert the plight of the dragons? And what is this *Gift* everyone seems to know about? Everyone, except Reecah.

Find out how the machinations of the evil prince and a traitorous wizard turn Reecah's quest on its head in this epic, second installment of the Legends of the Lurker.

Reecah's Legacy – Book 3

The culmination of the Legends of the Lurker trilogy.

Reecah Windwalker comes into her own as she finds peace with her past and bravely sets out to fulfill her legacy.

Keeping a promise to a dead witch, Reecah seeks those who can help her learn the ways of her dragon magic as she embarks on a desperate journey to save the last of the dragons from the dark heir.

The races come together, but their combined strength may not be enough to prevent the high king's dragon slayers from eradicating the beauty from the land.

Larina –Book 1

Growing up on the streets of Storms End, Larina knows the only way to survive is to take matters into her own hands.

Skulking about the seedy alleyways and taverns of a once great city that has fallen from grace, survival has become a game of steal and lie, or die.

Larina uses her ill-begotten abilities to help the vulnerable, less fortunate souls abandoned by life. An act that fills her with a sense of purpose and pride.

That all changes when the man with the black warhammer comes to town. Now the Storms End Lightning Bolt must decide whether those she has fought so hard to protect will be better off if she ends up dead.

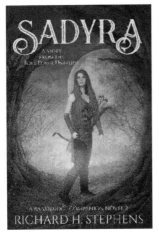

Sadyra –Book 2

Living in the shadows to avoid the brutality of parents harbouring a dark secret, Sadyra must force a violent confrontation if she is to keep her younger sisters from harm's way.

Begrudgingly accepted to work alongside a hardened group of sailors, Sadyra learns how to survive in a ruthless world.

To save her sisters from a fate worse than death, Sadyra goes against everything she feels is right, and life as she knows it will never be the same.

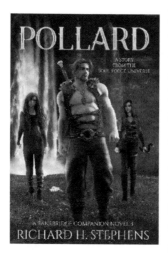

Pollard –Book 3

Called together to prepare for the defense of the kingdom's most sacred resource, the son of Thoril Half-Hand sets out to train the realm's most promising fighters.

To keep the recruits performing as a cohesive unit, Pollard is unprepared to deal with the eclectic personalities of those entrusted to oversee the future defence of Zephyr.

A dark secret assails the band of warriors and their very existence is threatened by creatures they are sworn to protect.

The Royal Tournament

(A story from the Soul Forge Universe)
The Royal Tournament has at long last come to the village of Millsford. For Javen Milford, a local farm boy, the news couldn't be better.

Finally, Javen can perform his chores on the homestead and partake in the biggest military games in the Kingdom, hoping beyond hope that just maybe, he might catch the eye of the king.

Javen enters the kingdom's flagship tournament only to discover that in order to win, one must be prepared to die.

Of Trolls and Evil Things

The (standalone) prequel to the Soul Forge Saga series!

Travel down an ever-darkening path where two orphans battle to survive upon a perilous mountainside, evading the predators and prowlers preying upon its slopes, and within its catacombs.

When the dangers they face force them from their mountain home, they end up in the cutthroat streets of Cliff Face plying their hands as beggars to survive.

Strange circumstances spin their lives out of control, forcing them onto the nefarious slopes of Mt. Gloom in a desperate effort to escape the unpleasant reality looming over them; only to discover their worst nightmare awaits them with open arms

.

Born in Simcoe, Ontario, in 1965, I began writing circa 1974; a bored child looking for something to while away the long, summertime days. My penchant for reading The Hardy Boys led to an inspiration one sweltering summer afternoon when my best friend and I thought, 'We could write one of those.' And so, I did.

As my reading horizons broadened, so did my writing. Star Wars inspired a 600-page novel about outer space that caught the attention of a special teacher who encouraged me to keep writing.

A trip to a local bookstore saw the proprietor introduce me to Stephen R. Donaldson and Terry Brooks. My writing life was forever changed.

At 17, I left high school to join the working world to support my first son. For the next twenty-two years I worked as a shipper at a local bakery. At the age of 36, I went back to high school to complete my education. After graduating with honours at the age of thirty-nine, I became a member of our local Police Service, and worked for 12 years in the provincial court system.

In early 2017, I retired from the Police Service to pursue my love of writing full-time. With the help and support of my lovely wife Caroline and our five children, I have now realized my boyhood dream.

If you wish to keep up to date on new releases, promotions and giveaways, please subscribe to my newsletter by checking out the contact tab on my website.

www.richardhstephens.com

Facebook:	@richardhughstephens
Twitter:	@RHStephens1
Instagram:	@richard_h_stephens
YouTube:	https://bit.ly/2NKpOhn

www.amazon.com/author/richardhstephens

Made in the USA
Las Vegas, NV
08 March 2022

45242977R00238